Boon Island

Including Contemporary Accounts of the Wreck of the *Nottingham Galley*

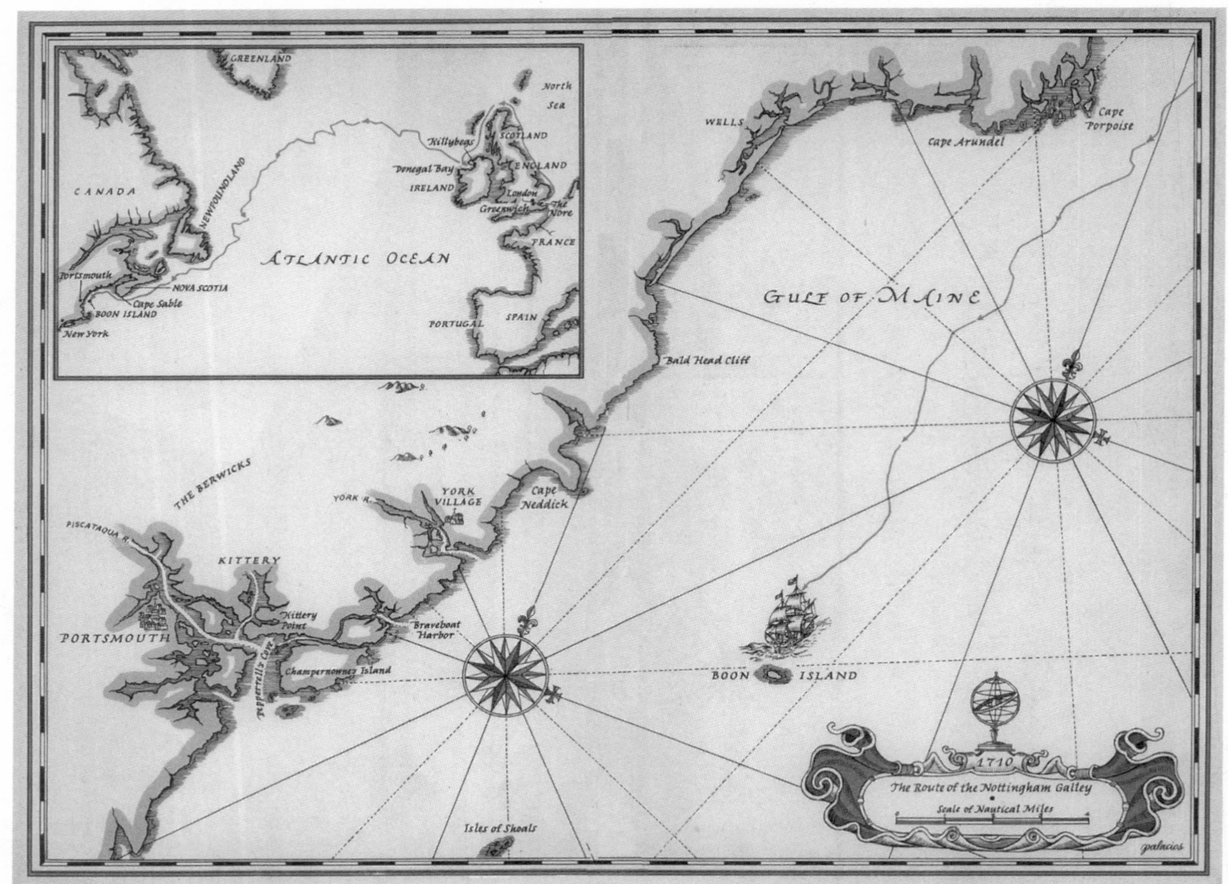

1710
The Route of the Nottingham Galley
Scale of Nautical Miles
GULF OF MAINE
WELLS
Cape Arundel
Cape Porpoise
Bald Head Cliff
Cape Neddick
YORK VILLAGE
YORK R.
THE BERWICKS
PISCATAQUA R.
KITTERY
Kittery Point
Braveboat Harbor
PORTSMOUTH
Pepperrell's Cove
Champernowney Island
BOON ISLAND
Isles of Shoals
GREENLAND
North Sea
CANADA
NEWFOUNDLAND
ATLANTIC OCEAN
Killybegs
SCOTLAND
Donegal Bay
ENGLAND
IRELAND
London
Greenwich
The Nore
FRANCE
Portsmouth
NOVA SCOTIA
Cape Sable
BOON ISLAND
New York
PORTUGAL
SPAIN
palacios

Kenneth Roberts

Boon Island

Including Contemporary

Accounts of the Wreck of the

Nottingham Galley

Edited by

Jack Bales and Richard Warner

University Press of New England

Hanover and London

University Press of New England, Hanover, NH 03755

Published by arrangement with Doubleday, a division of
Bantam Doubleday Dell Publishing Group, Inc.
The novel, *Boon Island*, originally published by Doubleday &
Company, Inc., January 2, 1956

Printed in the United States of America 5 4 3 2 1
CIP data appear at the end of the book

Contents

Preface

In 1710 the trading vessel *Nottingham Galley* set out from London bound for Boston on a perilous, late season voyage. Before making port, it encountered severe storms and struck Boon Island, a desolate rock off the Maine coast. All hands got ashore but the ship and cargo were lost. Devoid of food, shelter, and fire, the crew suffered terribly and was obliged to cannibalize a dead man before being rescued.

Captain John Deane, the master of the ill-starred ship, wrote his account of the disaster, which was rushed to publication by his brother, Jasper, to refute a conflicting account by the first mate, Christopher Langman. His reputation ruined, Captain Deane disappeared into Russian naval service for eleven years. He afterward returned to England, where he entered a new career as a spy and diplomat and cultivated his unavoidable celebrity with frequent reprints of his narrative.

The wreck of the *Nottingham Galley* thus became as well known in the first half of the eighteenth century as the mutiny on the *Bounty* did in the second half. Though its notoriety has since faded, modern readers still know the sea disaster as the subject of *Boon Island*, the gripping novel written by Kenneth Roberts in 1956.

In 1992, a colleague and I had a most curious scholarly intersection when, unbeknownst to each other, our research brought us both to Captain Deane's shipwreck at Boon Island. In the late summer, reference librarian Jack Bales was completing the final chapter of his biography of the novelist Kenneth Roberts, dealing with the author's last book, *Boon Island.* At the same time, I was searching archives in London and St. Petersburg to reconstruct the career of Captain John Deane, a British officer who served in the Russian fleet in the era of Peter the Great. Though I had found Deane's service records and materials about his later activities, I was perplexed about his early life until I discovered the Captain's account of his shipwreck at Boon Island, Maine, in 1710.

I had read Roberts's novel and knew Bales's work. In the fall I brought up the intersection of our research. We immediately realized the value of a collaboration and embarked upon the project that has resulted in the production of this unique collection of the original narratives, scholarly essays, and historical fiction.

Fredericksburg, Virginia Richard Warner
September 1995

Going to the Sources for Historical and Literary Explanation

Philip N. Cronenwett

The line between historical events, historical fact, and historical fiction never has been clear. Often it has been seen as a Maginot Line—an impregnable wall that clearly defines and separates truth from fancy. As we all know, the Maginot Line was not impermeable. Defining historical fiction and setting it off from "history" presents some interesting problems. Charles T. Wood, in a provocative essay on the beginnings of historical fiction, has suggested that "neither historians nor literary critics have ever precisely defined the boundary separating history from historical fiction."[1] He further suggests that, from the seventeenth century to the present, the genre of historical fiction grew to uphold larger historical truths, that the lessons and the nature of the human condition remain the province of writers of fiction.[2] Finally, Wood suggests that new critical theories, borrowed from literary studies, are offering new interpretive tools. "If such theories prevail, the distinction between history and historical fiction will again become one less of kind than of degree."[3]

Definition is paramount. One recent student of the genre has used the terms nonfiction novel, factual fiction, documentary novel, pseudofactual novel, and historical novel[4] to attempt to define, or perhaps confine, the novel that uses fact as a basis for its plot, characterization, and background. The question is not a new one. Henry James, W. D. Howells, Nathaniel Hawthorne, Theodore Dreiser, Mark Twain, Stephen Crane, Willa Cather, and John Dos Passos, novelists firmly rooted in the canon of American literature, all wrote historical fiction. But, are they considered historical novelists?

What makes an historical novel? What makes it valuable? Is it believable? Do we accept the story as true? Or do we accept it simply as fiction? Thinking back to Herodotus and Thucydides, both blurred the lines between fact and fiction simply to make the story more complete and more readable. And, writers of historical fiction often provide great insight into historical events. Both James Fenimore Cooper and William Gilmore Simms understood the importance of the frontier and wrote about it at length long before Frederick Jackson Turner enunciated his thesis. Thus, the fiction presaged the theory.

There are, I think, two kinds of historical fiction in the broadest sense. The first takes a generalized event or a series of events and places characters and stories within them. C. S. Forester's "Hornblower" series, a vastly popular set of novels, has taught a generation more about the naval history of the Napoleonic era and the psychology of command than we, as historians, could ever hope to do.

The second kind of historical fiction is that practiced by Kenneth Roberts. A very specific event, with known characters, plot, and outcome, is fictionalized, often with a reason. In *Boon Island* Roberts wanted to write an allegory of good and evil, with Americanism triumphant in the end. On the title page of his own copy of the novel, Roberts wrote: "the result of six years of contemplation, two years of struggle, and the most agonized summer I ever spent." It is interesting to note that, for the first time in his career, Roberts felt it necessary to use what is now a standard disclaimer on the verso of a title page: "With the exception of actual historical personages identified as such, the characters and incidents are entirely the product of the author's imagination and have no relation to any person or event in real life."

Roberts is one of the few historical novelists, if not the only one, who published revised editions of his novels, not to smooth out text, but to correct factual information. For this alone, he ought to be recognized. His research was as exacting as that of most historians. In his papers at Dartmouth, there are, for example, heavily marked charts of Greenwich, the Thames, and the Maine and New Hampshire coastline, all used to ensure accuracy. In a note in his copy of Jasper Deane's account of the *Nottingham Galley*, Roberts questioned the source of drinking water on Boon Island and, typically, wrote to the lighthouse keeper at Boon Island and received a reply. The result is a completely accurate picture of the need for fresh water in the novel.

Roberts received a special Pulitzer Prize citation for his historical novels in 1957. Although *Boon Island* is certainly not the best of his historical fiction, it is one of the more exciting adventures, with a shipwreck, great deprivation, and interesting menus. It did not receive the critical acclaim of his other novels. There were a number of reviews of the book, in such venues as the *Times Literary Supplement*, the *New Yorker*, the *Wall Street Journal*, and the *New York Times Book Review*. Of these, only Carlos Baker's review in the latter is uniformly positive. Baker greeted the nine-year lapse in publication with great pleasure. After a series of comments about the historicity of the book, he concluded that "the truth makes better reading than trumped-up romance."[5]

Faced with three variant eighteenth-century narratives of a single event, Kenneth Roberts carefully studied them, reworked them, added more historical detail, and then supplied a fictive veneer. His account of the wreck of the *Nottingham Galley* may be, in the end, more accurate than any of the narratives published by the participants in the event. Thus a question that must always be asked of an historical novel—Does it help the reader to better understand the historical event without distorting the truth?—is answered in *Boon Island*, most assuredly.

In Part I of this volume, the reader is offered the unique opportunity of examining the original source materials Roberts used to create his story, introduced by an essay on John Deane, commander of the ill-fated ship. Part II includes a critical essay on Roberts and *Boon Island* and a reprint of the novel, which has been out of print for many years.

Daniel Aaron, in an issue of *American Heritage* devoted to the historical novel, claimed that "the charm of acquiring historical information painlessly can't be entirely discounted. . . . Good writers write the kind of history good historians can't or don't write. Historical fiction isn't history in the conventional sense and shouldn't be judged as such. The best historical novels are loyal to history, but it is a history absorbed and set to music."[6]

NOTES

1. Charles T. Wood, "Richard III and the Beginnings of Historical Fiction," *The Historian* 54:2 (Winter 1992): 305.
2. Ibid., 313.
3. Ibid., 314.
4. Barbara Foley, *Telling the Truth: The Theory and Practice of Documentary Fiction* (Ithaca: Cornell University Press, 1986).
5. Carlos Baker, "To Courage Belonged the Victory," *New York Times Book Review* 61:1 (January 1, 1956): 3.
6. Daniel Aaron, "What Can You Learn From a Historical Novel?" *American Heritage* 43:6 (October 1992). The quotations are from pp. 57 and 62 respectively. The entire issue of this journal is subtitled "Truth and Fiction: The Power of the Historical Novel."

I

THE WRECK OF THE *NOTTINGHAM GALLEY*

Captain John Deane and the Wreck of the *Nottingham Galley*

Richard Warner

In late August 1731 the Duke of Lorraine briefly visited the port of Ostend, one of many cities on his tour of the Austrian Netherlands.[1] It was an official affair, the first time that the future husband of Maria Theresa had met with local dignitaries. They must have been disturbed when, during a banquet in his honor, the duke engaged the British consul, Captain John Deane, in a lengthy personal conversation that had nothing to do with commercial relations or any other serious matter of state. Indeed, the captain later reported, "the Duke knew . . . of my having been shipwrecked [and] he desired me to give him one of my printed narratives, which I accordingly did the next day."[2] As a commercial representative, Deane hardly merited the attention of the future emperor, but he had become something of a celebrity himself, for his shipwreck was as notorious in the first half of the eighteenth century as the mutiny on the *Bounty* was in the second half.[3] Like so many others who read about the ill-starred voyage, the duke undoubtedly was fascinated by the chilling account of the disaster and by the crew's decision to cannibalize one of their members. Though the notoriety of the wreck of the *Nottingham Galley* has faded, it has earned a place in the literature

This essay appeared in *The New England Quarterly* 48, no. 1 (March 1995).

and lore of seafaring, most prominently in *Boon Island*, the last novel written by Kenneth Roberts.[4] Still, little is known about the mysterious Captain Deane and how he used his account of the wreck to enhance his reputation in his own time and for posterity.[5]

In 1710 the *Nottingham Galley*, laden with cordage, set out from London bound for Boston. After taking on an additional cargo of butter and cheese at Killybegs, Ireland, it set sail again for its Atlantic crossing. Arriving off the Newfoundland coast dangerously late in the season, the small vessel encountered severe storms. Just before making port, the *Nottingham* struck Boon Island, a barren and desolate rock off Portsmouth, New Hampshire.

Miraculously, all hands got ashore, but the ship and its entire cargo were lost. There was no food and little left with which the men could build a shelter from the bitter cold. They suffered terribly. The cook died in the first days and was buried at sea; two seamen were lost in a heroic but futile attempt to escape the island on a raft; and the fourth, the carpenter, died and then was cannibalized to sustain the fourteen crew members, who were eventually rescued twenty-four days after losing their ship.

Just a few days before their deliverance, the crew reached the necessary but dreadful decision. The captain later wrote, "We were now reduced to the most deplorable and melancholy circumstances imaginable . . . no fire, and the weather extreme cold, our small, stock of cheese spent, and nothing to support our feeble bodies . . . [with] the prospect of starving, without any appearance of relief." They had reached what he described as "the last extremity . . . to eat the dead for support." After discussing "the lawfulness and sinfulness of their situation," the captain recalled, "[we] were obliged to submit to the more prevailing arguments of our craving appetites." In his memoir Deane was candid about the moral dilemma, and he graphically described how he himself dressed the body, disposing of those parts which distinguished it as human and renaming the rest beef. The enterprise was made the more unpleasant because the survivors had no means of making a fire and were obliged to eat the flesh raw.[6]

Before returning to England, the mate, Christopher Langman, made deposition before a justice of the peace in Portsmouth, New Hampshire, arguing that "this Depondent believeth that the said John Dean, according to his Working of the said Ship in the said Voyage, design'd to lose her." He was seconded by the testimony of the boatswain, Nicholas Mellen, and a seaman, George White. Both claimed that Deane had left the security of a naval convoy on the cruise from London to Ireland with the intent of turning his ship over to privateers so that the owners might collect insurance money. They argued that the captain "was prevented by the Depondent, Christopher Langman, by whose Assistance the said Ship arrived at her Port." They also claimed that Deane endeavored to hand the ship over a second time during the Atlantic passage, that he physically assaulted Langman on the night of the disaster while attempting intentionally to wreck the ship, and that the mate was responsible for getting the crew safely from the sinking ship to Boon Island.[7]

Though the original has not survived, Captain Deane wrote a manuscript account of the voyage and shipwreck soon after his return to England. Jasper Deane, the captain's older brother, owned the vessel and, with Charles Whitworth, the cargo. He immediately moved to protect his interest by rushing the captain's account to publication. In the introduction Jasper wrote that he hoped to preempt "the Design of others, to publish the Account without us." In the postscript he refutes what he calls the "barbarous and scandalous Reflection, industriously spread abroad and level'd at our ruine, by some unworthy, malicious

Persons (*viz.*) That we having ensur'd more than our Interest in the Ship *Nottingham*, agreed and willfully lost her, first designing it in Ireland, and afterwards effecting it at Boon Island." He argues that the vessel was seriously underinsured and the charges "preposterous" that the captain would endeavor intentionally to wreck his ship in midwinter at such a forbidding place. "One wou'd wonder [if] Malice itself cou'd invent or suggest anything so ridiculous," he notes disdainfully.[8]

Langman, Mellen, and White published a response to the captain's account, condemning him for incompetence and renewing their charge against him. Their *True Account of the Voyage of the Nottingham Galley* was published immediately after Deane's *Narrative* and describes the ship as "cast away . . . by the Captain's Obstinacy, who endeavour'd to betray her to the French, or run her ashore." Taking issue with the "Falsehoods in the Captain's Narrative," it depicts the crew as "Sufferers in this unfortunate Voyage . . . from the Temper of our Captain, who treated us barbarously both by Sea and Land." Disputing Deane's *Narrative* point by point, it concludes with the argument that if "the said Master had taken the Mate's Advice, the ship, with God's Assistance, might have been in Boston Harbour several Days before she was lost." Langman warns others "not to trust their Lives or Estates in the Hands of so wicked and brutish a Man."[9]

A third account was published in 1711, an abridged and sensationalized version taken from Deane's *Narrative* and published by J. Dutton near Fleet Street, apparently issued after both Deane's *Narrative* and Langman's *True Account*. Describing itself as *A Sad and Deplorable, but True Account*, it announces that the shipwreck was "very well known by most Merchants upon the Royal Exchange." The last page contains the printed signatures of "Jasper Dean," "John Dean, Captain," and "Miles Whitworth, lately dead," but it does not append Jasper Deane's introduction or afterword. On the cover it sensationally asserts that "having no food, [the survivors] were fain to Feed upon the dead Bodies, which being all Consum'd, they were going to Cast lots which shou'd be the next Devor'd. . . ." It enlarges upon the cannibalism on Boon Island by adding that "the dismal Prospect of future Want obliged the Captain to keep a strict watch over the rest of the Body, lest any of them shou'd get to it, and then being spent, [we would] be forced to feed upon the living. Which we must certainly have done, had we stayed a few days longer." Unlike the *Narrative*, which was written in the first person, the *Sad and Deplorable . . . Account* is a mixture of first- and third-person description and does not seem to have been authorized.[10] A second abbreviated version, taken from the account introduced by Jasper Deane, was published in Boston in 1711, prefaced with a sermon on the subject by Cotton Mather.[11]

Though the Deane *Narrative* has prevailed as the accepted version of the disaster, the sensational story of shipwreck and cannibalism nearly destroyed the captain's reputation. It is not surprising, therefore, that he seized an opportunity to secure a commission as a lieutenant in the Russian naval service, where he disappeared for eleven years. In a new career in a new country, Deane escaped public notoriety as well as his brother's private fury for having lost the *Nottingham Galley*.[12]

In the winter of 1714–15, Deane received his first command, a newly constructed, fifty-gun man-of-war, the *Yagudil*, which he was ordered to transport from Archangel to the Baltic. It was another harrowing, late-season voyage, this time around Murmansk and the North Cape. The experience must have brought back memories of the *Nottingham Galley*, for nearly half of the crew perished before the ship docked in Trondheim, Norway. Deane was then reassigned to the thirty-two gun frigate *Samson*, operating out of Reval. He took over twenty prizes in the next several years and earned a reputation as a daring commerce raider. At the end of 1719, Deane was court-martialed for an incident that had taken place two years earlier, when he had been obliged to give up two prizes at sea. In actuality, he had fallen victim to the jealousy of junior Russian officers who coveted his command. He was reduced to lieutenant and exiled to Kazan. A year later, during the celebration of the victory over Sweden, the Tsar granted a general amnesty to disgraced officers, and Deane was one of many mercenaries expelled from Russia.[13]

Deane departed in the spring of 1722. His former patron, the High Admiral Apraksin, curiously provided him with a document indicating that he had left Russian service with the rank of captain, the title he wore for the rest of his life. Penniless, but rich in knowledge of the Tsar's naval affairs, Deane produced "A History of the Russian Fleet during the Reign of Peter the Great," a secret, detailed account of the rise of Russian naval power in the Baltic, which he used to promote himself as an expert on Russian affairs in the highest circles of the government. Though the original manuscripts have disappeared, two published versions of the history have survived. The original, anonymous manuscript was purchased by Count E. Putiatin from a London bookseller in 1892 and was then translated into Russian and published in St. Petersburg in 1895. Four years later it was issued in London by the Navy Records Society.[14] In 1934 a second version of the manuscript came into the possession of another maritime collector, Captain Bruce Ingram. It was similar in all respects to the Putiatin manuscript except that it contained a final chapter entitled "The History Continued to the Commencement of 1725" and a dedication to George I identifying Deane as the author.[15] In the same year that he circulated his manuscript on the Russian fleet, Deane also reissued his account of the wreck of the *Nottingham Galley*, now stripped of Jasper Deane's introductory and closing remarks.[16]

Deane's self-promotion paid off handsomely, for it brought him to the attention of Robert Walpole and of Lord Townshend, secretary of state for the northern department. Both were haunted by the specter of a European-wide Jacobite conspiracy and, after their ambassador was recalled in 1722, felt particularly deficient in intelligence from Russia.[17] According to Townshend's deputy, George Tilson, "Captain Deane undertook to be useful to us and showed a letter from Admiral Apraksin, who seemed to be of power in that country, which persuaded us he might render service."[18] Deane was appointed commercial consul at St. Petersburg, which Townshend described as a "colour, but his true business is to transmit hither what intelligence he may be able to get for his Majesty's service."[19] The captain had entered a new career as a spy, an occupation for which he was well suited by background and temperament. He returned to the Russian capital in the spring of 1725 but was refused accreditation and was forced to leave after just sixteen days.[20]

After his departure, Deane wrote two illuminating reports. The first, entitled "An Account of Affairs in Russia, June–July, 1725," was a detailed analysis of the political situation after the death of Peter I. The second, "The Present State of the Maritime Power of Russia," was an intelligence report on the standing Russian Baltic fleet.[21] Deane was convinced that he had failed in his mission, however, for what his superiors wanted was an account of the activities of Jacobite emigrés and sympathizers in Russia. In despair, he wrote Townshend that enemies were gathering "to blacken my name . . . and that you will think me a monster."[22]

Before he left St. Petersburg, Deane made contact with a Jacobite courier, a young Irish military officer named Edmund O'Conner. With an offer of monetary reward and promise of a king's pardon, Deane convinced O'Conner to betray the cause. The captain made contact with O'Conner again in Holland and delighted his superiors by penetrating the communications network of the nefarious Jacobite agent John Archdeacon. During the winter of 1725–26 Deane and O'Conner gained the confidence of Archdeacon, gathered new correspondence, forged documents, and manufactured seals.[23]

The following spring Deane was assigned to the squadron dispatched to the Baltic to threaten the Russians in the Gulf of Finland. He was able to acquire current intelligence about the Russian fleet, and he set about recruiting a network of agents to supply future information. He issued a number of dispatches and seems to have influenced or written the report signed by Admiral Charles Wager entitled "The Present State of the Danes, Swedes, and Russians in Respect to One Another and to the English Fleet in the Baltic in the Year 1726."[24]

Back in London in the fall of 1726, Deane released a new edition of the *Narrative*, which was then reprinted the following year.[25] In these new editions, the captain was less actor or subject than author, and the shift from first-person to third-person narration was intended to portray a man ultimately in control of his fate. Again, Deane's goal was to keep his name current, for he now sought continued employment in the Foreign Office as commercial consul for the Ports of Flanders at Ostend. He won the post in 1728, for Walpole, Townshend, and Wager were powerful patrons who admired his service and loyalty. Most of all, they wished to place someone in Flanders capable of assisting the enterprise of suppressing Austria's attempt to enter the East India trade. A perfect choice for the assignment, Deane played a significant role in eliminating the Ostend East India Company.[26]

Deane remained consul in Ostend until 1738, when he retired to his home in Wilford, Nottinghamshire. He continued to recognize the value of his celebrity, and in 1730 and 1738 he reissued the 1727 *Revis'd Narrative* to redefine himself within the context first of Ostend and then of Wilford.[27] In 1735 he arranged for a memorial to the deliverance of the crew of the *Nottingham Galley* and commissioned the Reverend Samuel Wilson to publish "An Abstract Of Consul Deane's Narrative," which described the captain as "a pious Gentleman . . . who wished the great Salvation . . . should be commemorated . . . [and] that the Mercy should not be forgotten, but from year to Year be acknowledged with suitable Gratitude and Praise."[28]

Captain Deane died at his home in Wilford in 1761 at the age of eighty-three. In his will he made provision for a commemoration of the wreck of the *Nottingham Galley* in New England, a generous sum for that purpose to be granted to Doctor Miles Whitworth of Boston, whose father had died as a consequence of the disaster.[29] The following year the younger Whitworth chose to reprint the original 1711 edition, the version Captain Deane had tried to suppress all of his life.[30] Since then it has been reprinted twice more, once by William Abbatt for the *Magazine of History and Biography* in 1917 and again by Mason Smith in 1968.[31] Smith's is a modern photo-offset edition published in just two hundred and fifty copies for book collectors. It contains an interesting physical description of Boon Island.

Because it was the first edition printed in modern type, the Abbatt version has become a favorite for reprint in more recent anthologies of shipwrecks and sea disasters, for example, R. Thomas's *Remarkable Shipwrecks, Fires, Famines, Calamities, Providential Deliverances, and Lamentable Disasters on the Seas*, first printed in 1835 and reprinted as *Interesting and Authentic Wrecks* in 1970, and G. W. Barrington's *Remarkable Voyages and Shipwrecks.*[32] The most recent popularization directed to shipwreck enthusiasts is Keith Huntress's 1975 volume, *Narratives of Shipwrecks & Disasters, 1586–1860*. According to the editor, "the genesis of this anthology was the chance purchase . . . of a battered copy of R. Thomas's *Remarkable Shipwrecks*."[33]

There are no analytic or scholarly accounts of the wreck of the *Nottingham Galley* except for the highly regarded legal history by A. W. Brian Simpson, *Cannibalism and the Common Law*. Surprisingly inaccurate, Simpson claims that the Deane and Langman versions "in general are not in conflict," and although seemingly judicious, he relies upon the Langman account to explain the sequence of events. He also badly miscalculates the length of the crew's stay on Boon Island, dating the rescue in September rather than early January, ten months rather than twenty-four days after the wreck.[34]

Two notable works of fiction deal with Captain Deane and the wreck of the *Nottingham Galley*. In 1870 author of juvenile literature W. H. G. Kingston wrote *John Deane of Nottingham*, a work that confounds fact and fiction.[35] It is a fanciful tale that spins for Deane a Robinhood-like youth as a butcher's apprentice and deer poacher who joins the navy when forced to flee Nottingham. Kingston uses actual ships and commanders of the period to construct a career leading to Deane's promotion to captain by Admiral Rooke after the battle of Gibraltar. Though he may well have served in the navy in the ratings, the admiralty papers show no evidence that Deane ever served as an officer, and it is unlikely that such an attainment would have gone unrecorded in this period. Moreover, had the captain been promoted for bravery in battle, he certainly would have used it to his advantage later in life. Even the most casual reader would find it hard to recognize the wreck of the *Nottingham Galley* in Kingston's book, for it bears little resemblance to the original accounts. Nonetheless, Kingston has had a lasting impact on Deane's biography, for local historians have passed on "knowledge" gained from his book.

Kenneth Roberts's work is quite different. A native of Maine familiar with Boon Island and accounts of the wreck of the *Nottingham Galley*, Roberts is true to his sources. He was an uncommonly principled borrower of historical material who was careful not to make central historical figures leading characters in his novels. The fictional aspects of *Boon Island* are largely devoted to creating a milieu for the development of the characters, among them Miles Whitworth, who is used as the narrator. The captain remains a shadowy, though honorable and strong, figure, not unlike the person he actually seems to have been.

During his lifetime, Captain Deane's account of the *Nottingham* disaster prevailed, for he had outlived his opponents and possessed the resources and desire to promote his own version of events. Indeed, he even attempted to maintain control after his death by making a provision in his will for posthumous publication by Whitworth. Interestingly, Deane's tombstone in the Wilford churchyard records only that the captain "commanded a Ship of War in the Czar of Moscovy's service," that he "was appointed by His Britannick Majesty, Consul for the Ports of Flanders and Ostend," and that he "retired to this village in the year 1738."[36] But the captain could not manage publication from the grave, and it is ironic that all accounts since his death have been based on the narrative published originally by his brother Jasper in 1711, the account the captain had labored so diligently to suppress. Though attached to the old captain, Miles Whitworth apparently preferred Jasper's version because of the way it depicted his father. Others have found the first-person narrative of that account more authentic, dramatic, and compelling, which may explain why it has endured since Deane's death in every collection and anthology. It is perplexing that such a literate man, so protective of his reputation, wrote nothing about himself for posterity and that he did not have the foresight to consider that he might be remembered best in works of fiction. Yet, this too adds to the mystery of Captain John Deane.

NOTES

1. Duke Francis Stephen married Maria Theresa in 1731. Though he lost the throne of Lorraine in 1736, he was compensated with the Grand Duchy of Tuscany. In 1745 he was elected Holy Roman Emperor.

2. John Deane to George Tilson, 26 August 1731, PRO SP 77 / 78 (Public Record Office, State Papers). Deane had just republished the account of the disaster: *A Narrative of the Shipwreck of the Nottingham Galley & Co., first Publish'd in 1711, Revis'd and Reprint'd with additions in 1727, and now Re-publish'd in 1730. By John Deane, Commander* (London, 1730).

3. J. B. Firth wrote that "the adventures and sufferings of the crew of the *Nottingham Galley* were as well known in the days of Queen Anne as the story of the sufferings of the crew of the *Bounty* were later in the century" (*Highways and Byways in Nottinghamshire* [London: Macmillan, 1916], p. 31).

4. Kenneth Roberts, *Boon Island*, reprinted herein; first published by Doubleday in 1956.

5. See my "Captain John Deane: Mercenary, Diplomat, and Spy," in *People of the Sea*, ed. Lewis Fischer and Walter Minchinton (St. Johns, Newfoundland: International Maritime Economic History Association, 1992), pp. 157–73.

6. Captain John Dean(e), *A Narrative of the Sufferings, Preservation, and Deliverance of Capt. John Dean and Company; in the Nottingham Galley of London, cast away on Boon-Island, near New England, December 11, 1710.* Published with an introductory note by Jasper Dean, dated August 2, 1711, Horsly-Down (London: R. Tookey, 1711). Reprinted herein.

7. Information about the deposition is included in *A True Account of the Voyage of the Nottingham-Galley of London, John Dean Commander, from the River Thames to New England, near which Place she was cast away on Boon-Island, December 11, 1710, by the Captain's Obstinacy, who endeavored to betray her to the French, or run her ashore with an account of the Falsehoods in the Captain's Narrative, and a Faithful Relation of the Extremities the Company was Reduc'd to for Twenty-four Days on that Desolate Rock, where they were forced to eat their Companions who had died, but at last were wonderfully deliver'd. The whole attested upon Oath by Christopher Langman, Mate, Nicholas Mellen, Boatswain, and George White, sailor in the said Ship* (London: S. Popping, 1711). Reprinted herein.

8. Captain John Deane, *A Narrative of the Sufferings*, pp. 22, 39 herein.

9. Langman, Mellen, and White, *A True Account*, pp. 42–43, 60–61, 58 herein. Langman even argued that Deane "barbarously told the children in his lodging, he would have made a frigasy of them, if he had had 'em in Boon Island."

10. *A Sad and Deplorable, but True Account of the Terrible Hardships and Suffering of Capt. John Deane, & Company on Board the Nottingham Galley* (London: J. Dutton, 1711), pp. 1, 7.

11. Cotton Mather, *Compassions Called for. An Essay of Profitable Reflections on Miserable Spectacles. To which is added, a faithful relation of Some Late, but Strange Occurrences that call'd for an awful and unusual Consideration. Especially the Surprising Distresses and Deliverance of a Company lately Shipwreck'd on a Desolate Rock on the Coast of New England* (Boston, 1711), pp. 50–60.

12. According to local legend, Jasper was very distressed by his losses and died after an altercation with the captain, which caused him to rupture a blood vessel. See M. N. Barker, *Walks Around Nottingham by a Wanderer* (London, 1835), pp. 50–51; William H. Wylie, *Old and New Nottingham* (London: E. Stock, 1853), pp. 146–47; Cornelius Brown, *History of Nottinghamshire* (London: Longmans, 1891), p. 35.

13. For this period of Deane's biography, see my "Deane: Mercenary, Diplomat, Spy," pp. 23–35. This is based heavily on material located in the Tsentralnyi gosudarstvennyi arkhiv voenno-morskogo flota (TGAVMF), the Central State Archive of the Navy in St. Petersburg. Deane's record of service is in *Obshchii morskoi spisok* (St. Petersburg: Morskoe ministerstvo, 1885), vol. 1, pp. 131–32. There is also much material scattered throughout the magnificent collection *Materialy dlia istorii Russkago flota*, ed. E. L. Elagin, vols. 1–4 (St. Petersburg: Morskoe ministerstvo, 1887).

14. *A History of the Russian Fleet during the Reign of Peter the Great by a Contemporary Englishman, 1724*, ed. Adm. Cyprian A. G. Bridge, vol. 15 of Navy Records Society Publications (London: Navy Records Society, 1899). The original manuscript copy has disappeared from the collection of the London School of Slavonic Studies.

15. "The Authorship of the 'History of the Russian Fleet under Peter the Great,'" *Mariner's Mirror* 20 (July 1934): 373–76. Ingram's manuscript was sold at auction in 1966 and has disappeared. It was signed "Your Majesty's Most Dutiful, Most Sincerely Devoted Subject and Servant, John Deane."

16. *A Narrative of the Sufferings, Preservation, and Deliverance of Capt. John Deane and Company; in the Nottingham Galley of London, cast away on Boon Island, Near New England, December 11, 1710, as it was printed in 1711 and now reprinted in 1722* (London, 1722).

17. See my "Deane: Mercenary, Diplomat, Spy," p. 28, and Paul S. Fritz, *The English Ministers and Jacobitism between the Rebellions of 1715 and 1745* (Toronto: University of Toronto Press, 1975), pp. 130–31.

18. Tilson to Lord Townshend, 17 July 1725, PRO SP 43 / 9 / 239–40.

19. Lord Townshend to Robert Points, 7 July 1725, PRO SP 95 / 37 / 211–12.

20. Deane's dispatches are located in PRO SP 91 / 9 / 387–98.

21. Map Collection: King's Maritime II.51.1, 3–5. "The Present State of the Maritime Power of Russia" (accompanying maps: Ladoga Sea, Retusari [Cronstadt], St. Petersburg), British Library.

22. Deane to Tilson, 5 July 1725, PRO SP 91 / 9 / 398. In August he wrote of "implacable enemies who seek my ruin" and of his fear that he "would be rendered odious to that government whose cause [he] served" (Deane to Tilson, 24 August 1725, PRO SP 84 / 574).

23. Fritz, *English Ministers*, pp. 132–34, and J. F. Chance, *The Alliance of Hanover* (London: J. Murray, 1923), p. 348. These are the only works that deal with the fascinating adventures of Deane and O'Conner in Holland.

24. The seven dispatches Deane wrote while on the cruise are filed with those of Sir Charles Wager in PRO SP 42 / 77. When the voyage was over, Wager wrote Tilson from Spithead on 30 December 1726, "I fear [Deane's] money is all out. I wish my Lord would remedy this. I think him a very honest Man." See also, "The Present State of the Danes, Swedes, and Russians in Respect to One Another and to the English Fleet in the Baltic in the Year 1726," PRO SP 43 / 77.

25. *A Narrative of the Shipwreck of the Nottingham Galley, &c. Publish'd in 1711, Revis'd, and Re-printed with Additions in 1726 by John Deane, Commander* (n.p., 1726), reprinted herein; and Captain John Deane, *A Narrative . . . with Additions in 1727* (London, 1727). Only minor changes were made in 1727, but that edition became the version that Deane used for all later editions during his lifetime.

26. Deane's role in this enterprise awaits historical investigation and is contained in his numerous dispatches from Ostend located in PRO SP 77 / 75–86.

27. See n. 2 for the 1730 account; *A Narrative of the Shipwreck of the Nottingham Galley & Co., First publish'd in 1711, Revis'd, and Reprint'd with additions in 1727, republish'd in 1730, and now propos'd for the last Edition during the Author's Life-time. By John Deane, then Commander, of the Nottingham Galley: but now, and for many Years past, His Majesty's Consul for the Ports of Flanders, Residing at Ostend* (London, 1738).

28. "An Abstract of Consul Deane's Narrative," in Samuel Wilson, *Sermons*. Published at the Request of the Church under his Care, Printed by Aaron Ward, at the King's Arms in Little Britain; and Joseph Fisher, against Tom's Coffee-house in Cornhill (London, 1735).

29. Last Will and Testament of John Deane of Wilford, PRO PROB II.8282: 362–67.

30. Captain John Deane, *A Narrative of the Shipwreck of the Nottingham Galley, in her Voyage from England to Boston, with an account of the miraculous escape of the captain and the crew, on a rock, called Boon-Island, the hardships they endured there, and their happy deliverance. By Captain John Deane, then commander of the said galley and for many years after His Majesty's Consul for the ports of Flanders, residing at Ostend.* Published by Mr. Miles Whitworth, son of Mr. Whitworth (Boston, 1762). Whitworth not only

memorialized Deane with the posthumous republication of the account of the shipwreck of the *Nottingham Galley* but also named his son John Deane Whitworth. This namesake was among the first loyalists brought to trial during the American Revolution. He was described in November of 1776 as "a prisoner taken in arms against the forces of the United States (and) brought before the Committee of Public Safety." "Record of the Boston Committee of Correspondence, Inspection, and Safety, May to November 1776," *New England Historical and Genealogical Register* 63 (1909): 252.

31. William Abbatt reprinted the 1711 account as an extra number of *The Magazine of History and Biography with Notes and Queries* 59 (1917): 199–217. Smith's edition is titled *A Narrative of the Shipwreck of the Nottingham Galley, in her Voyage from England to Boston, with an Account of the Miraculous Escape of the Captain and his Crew, on a Rock called Boon-Island, the Hardships they endured there, and their happy Deliverance. By Captain John Deane, then Commander of the said Galley; but for many years after His Majesty's Consul for the Ports of Flanders, residing at Ostend.* Introduction by Mason Philip Smith (Portland: Provincial Press, 1968).

32. R. Thomas, *Remarkable Shipwrecks, Fires, Famines, Calamities, Providential Deliverances, and Lamentable Disasters on the Seas* (Hartford: Andrus, 1835), and George W. Barrington, *Remarkable Voyages and Shipwrecks, being a Popular Collection of Extraordinary and Authentic Sea Narratives relating to all Parts of the Globe* (London: Simpkin, Marshall, Hamilton & Kent, 1881). An abridged version entitled "Cannibalism in Maine" forms a chapter in the widely read *Great Storms and Famous Shipwrecks of the New England Coast*, ed. Edward Rowe Snow (Boston: Yankee, 1943). Also of interest is "The Grim Tale of the Nottingham Galley," in *Lost Ships and Lonely Seas*, ed. Ralph D. Paine (New York: Century, 1921), pp. 309–30.

33. Keith Huntress, *Narratives of Shipwrecks & Disasters, 1586–1860* (Ames: Iowa State University, 1974).

34. A. W. Brian Simpson, *Cannibalism and the Common Law* (Chicago: University of Chicago Press, 1980), pp. 114–15.

35. W. H. G. Kingston, *John Deane of Nottingham* (London: Griffith and Farran, 1870).

36. M. N. Barker, *Walks Around Nottingham*, p. 49. Deane left no issue and his epitaph records that his wife, Sarah, died just one day before he did.

Appendix

Chronology and Stemma of Accounts of the Wreck of the Nottingham Galley

Jasper Dean(e) Edition, 1711

Dean(e), Captain John, *A Narrative of the Sufferings, Preservation, and Deliverance of Capt. John Dean and Company; in the Nottingham Galley of London, cast away on Boon-Island, Near New England, December 11, 1710.* Published with an introductory note by Jasper Dean(e), dated August 2, 1711, Horsly-Down. Printed by R. Tookey, London and folded by S. Popping at the Raven in Paternoster-Row, and at the Printing Press under the Royal-Exchange, Cornhill, 1711. Conveniently, reprinted by William Abbatt, Tarrytown, New York, 1917, being an extra number of the *Magazine of History with Notes and Queries*. 59:2 (1917): 199–215.

The Langman Account, 1711

Langman, Christopher, Nicholas Mellen, and George White, *A True Account of the Voyage the Nottingham-Galley of London, John Dean commander, from the River Thames to New-England, near which Place she was cast away on Boon-Island, December 11, 1710, by the Captain's Obstinacy, who endeavored to betray her to the French, or run her ashore; with an Account of the Falsehoods in the Captain's Narrative. And a faithful Relation of the Extremities the Company was Reduc'd to for Twenty-four Days on that Desolate Rock, where they were forced to eat one of their Companions who died, but were at last wonderfully deliver'd. The whole attested upon Oath, by Christopher Langman, Mate; Nicholas Mellon, Boatswain; and George White, Sailor in the Said Ship*. Printed for S. Popping at the Raven in Paternoster-Row, London, 1711.

The Sad and Deplorable Account, 1711 (Abridged & Sensationalized)

A Sad and Deplorable Account of the Sufferings, Preservation, and Deliverance of Captain John Deane, & c. London; printed by J. Dutton, near Fleet Street, 1711.

Cotton Mather, 1711 (Abridged)

Cotton Mather, *Compassions Called for. An Essay of Profitable Reflections on Miserable Spectacles. To which is added, a faithful relation of Some Late, but Strange Occurrences that called for an awful and unusual Consideration. Especially the Surprising Deliverance of a Company lately Shipwreck'd on a Desolate Rock on the Coast of New-England.* Boston, 1711, 50–60.

John Deane Edition #1, 1722

Deane, Captain John, *A Narrative of the Sufferings, Preservation, and Deliverance of Capt. John Deane and Company; in the Nottingham Galley of London, cast away on Boon-Island, Near New England, December 11, 1710, as it was printed in 1711 and now reprinted in 1722*, London, 1722.

John Deane Edition (revised #2), 1726

Deane, Captain John, *A Narrative of the Shipwreck of the Nottingham Galley, &c. publish'd in 1711, Revis'd, and Re-printed with Additions in 1726 by John Deane, Commander.* N.p., 1726.

John Deane Edition (revised #3), 1727

Deane, Captain John, *A Narrative of the Shipwreck of the Nottingham Galley & c. Publish'd in 1711. Revis'd, and re-printed with additions in 1727*, by John Deane, commander. London, 1727.

John Deane Edition (revised #3), 1730

Deane, Captain John, *A Narrative of the Shipwreck of the Nottingham Galley, and c. First Publish'd in 1711. Revis'd and reprinted with additions in 1727, and now re-published in 1720. By John Deane, commander.* London, 1730.

Samuel Wilson Edition (abstract), 1735

"An Abstract of Consul Dean's Narrative," in Samuel Wilson, *Sermons.* Published at the Request of the Church under His Care. Printed by

Aaron Ward, at the King's Arms in Little Britain; and Joseph Fisher, against Tom's Coffee-house in Cornhill, London, 1735, 197–203.

John Deane Edition (revised #3), 1738

Deane, Captain John, *A Narrative of the Shipwreck of the Nottingham Galley & Co, first publish'd in 1711, Revis'd, and Reprint'd with additions in 1727, republish'd in 1730, and now propos'd for the last Edition during the Author's Life-time. By John Deane, then Commander, of the Nottingham Galley: but now, and for many Years past, His Majesty's Consul for the Ports of Flanders, Residing at Ostend.* London, 1738.

Miles Whitworth Edition, 1762

Deane, Captain John, *A Narrative of the Shipwreck of the Nottingham Galley, in her Voyage from England to Boston, with an account of the miraculous escape of the captain and the crew, on a rock, called Boon-Island, the hardships they endured there, and their happy deliverance. By Captain John Deane, then commander of the said galley and for many years after His Majesty's Consul for the ports of Flanders, residing at Ostend.* Published by Mr. Miles Whitworth, son of Mr. Whitworth. Boston, 1762.

William Abbatt, Edition, 1917

Dean(e), Captain John, *A Narrative of the Sufferings, Preservation, and Deliverance of Capt. John Dean and Company, in the Nottingham Galley of London, cast away on Boon-Island, Near New England, December 11, 1710.* Published with an introductory note by Jasper Dean(e), dated August 2, 1711, Horsly-Down. Printed by R. Tookey, London and folded by S. Popping at the Raven in Paternoster-Row, and at the Printing Press under the Royal Exchange, Cornhill, 1711. Reprinted by William Abbatt as an extra number of *The Magazine of History and Biography with Notes and Queries* 59:2 (1917): 199–215.

Mason Smith Edition, 1968

Deane, John, *A Narrative of the Shipwreck of the Nottingham Galley, in her Voyage from England to Boston with an Account of the Miraculous Escape of the Captain and his Crew, on a Rock called Boon-Island, the Hardships they endured there, and their happy Deliverance. By Captain John Deane, then Commander of the said Galley; but for many years after His Majesty's Consul for the Ports of Flanders, residing at Ostend.* Introduction by Mason Philip Smith. Portland, 1968.

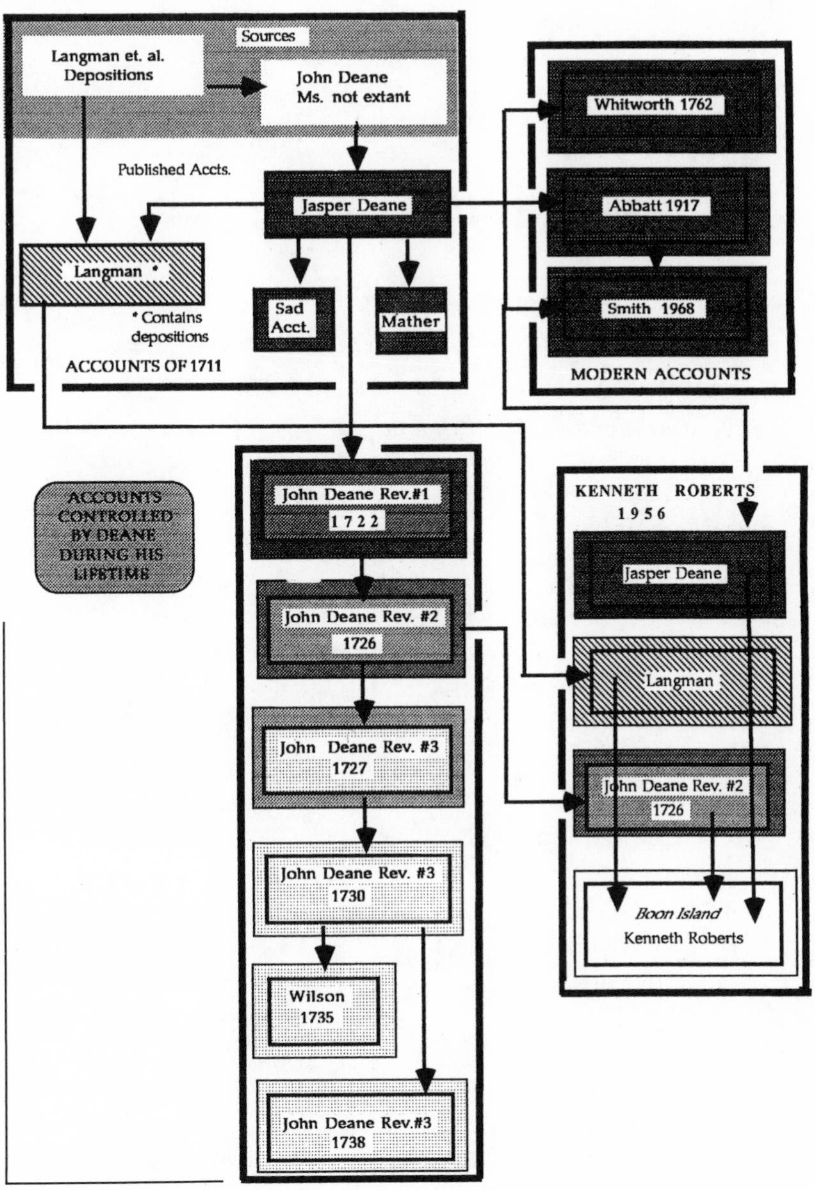

The Wreck of the *Nottingham Galley*. Stemma of Accounts by R. H. Warner

The Jasper Deane Account

A Narrative of the Sufferings, Preservation and Deliverance of Capt. John Dean and Company: in the Nottingham Galley *of London, cast away on Boon-Island, Near New England, December 11, 1710.*

THE PUBLISHER TO THE READER

A few months past, I little expected to appear in Print (especially on such Occasion) but the frequent Enquiries of many curious Persons (as also the Design of others, to publish the Account without us) seem to lay me under an absolute Necessity, least others less acquainted, prejudice the Truth with an imperfect Relation. Therefore, finding myself oblig'd to expose this small Treatise to publick View and Censure, I perswade my self, that what's here recorded will be entirely credited, by all

Published with an introductory note by Jasper Dean(e), dated August 2, 1711, Horsly-Down. Printed by R. Tookey, London and folded by S. Popping at the Raven in Paternoster-Row, and at the Printing Press under the Royal-Exchange, Cornhill, 1711. Conveniently, reprinted by William Abbatt, Tarrytown, New York, 1917, being an extra number of the *Magazine of History with Notes and Queries* 59:2 (1917): 199–215.

This is the first published version of Captain John Deane's narrative. It was brought out in 1711 by the Captain's brother, Jasper, who owned the *Nottingham Galley* and, with Charles Whitworth, the cargo. Jasper rushed it to press in order to protect his interests and to counter the first mate, Christopher Langman, who brought out his own version (which follows) later in the year. None of the manuscripts has survived.

candid, ingenious Spirits; for whose kind Opinion I am really sollicitous.

I presume any Person acquainted with my Brother will readily believe the Truth hereof: And for the Satisfaction of others, I would hope need only offer, that both his Character and my own may be easily gain'd by Enquiry. Likewise several of his Fellow Sufferers being now in Town, their Attestations might be procur'd, if saw a real Necessity.

I have in the whole endeavour'd a plain smooth, unaffected stile; suitable to the Occasion, carefully avoiding unnecessary Enlargements, and relating only Matters of Fact.

I must acknowledge to have (in composing from my Brother's Copy) omitted many lesser Circumstances, least shou'd swell this Narrative beyond its first Design, and thereby exceed the Bounds of common Purchase.

It's almost needless to intimate what Approbation the Copy has receiv'd, from many Persons of the most curious and discerning Judgments who have done me the Favour to view it, urging its Publication, and (at least) flattering me with an Expectation of a general Acceptance, considering it both as Novel and Real.

I cannot but also take Encouragement from the Value and Esteem it met with when appearing under much greater Disadvantages, as to Particulars and Dress in New England, North Britain, &c. So that adventure it into the World, to receive its Applause or Censures, according to its Demerrits or the Fancy of the Reader.

The Account I have receiv'd of those worthy New England Gentlemen's Kindness to the poor Men in their Extremities, affected me in the most near and sensible manner, and which to omitt making honourable mention of, wou'd be the highest Ingratitude (an evil I hope, foreign to my Temper.)

How generous, Christian-like, and worthy of Immitation, have these Gentlemen behav'd themselves, to such Objects of Commiseration who must otherwise (in all Probability) have been render'd unable to serve their Families (methinks I am glad such a noble compasionate humane Temper is still found amongst Men) and how happy wou'd it be for us, did this kind and Publick Spirit more prevail among us, as on the contrary, how much to be lamented is that barbarous and savage Custom of murdering fellow Creatures (shipwrackt on our Coasts) in Order to plunder and rifle them with the greater Ease: A Crime so brutish and agravated (and yet so frequently practic'd as to be the common Disgrace of a Christian Nation.)

I might offer Abundance more Thoughts (pertinent enough) on these and other subjects in this Preface, but I am fearfull lest I shou'd make the Porch too large for the House; therefore conclude, subscribing my self (candid Reader) thine in all Friendly Offices,

JASPER DEAN.

Horsly-Down, August the 2d. 1711.

THE NARRATIVE

The *Nottingham Galley*, of and from London, 120 Tons, ten Guns, and fourteen Men, John Dean Commander; having taken in Cordage in England, and Butter and Cheese, &c. in Ireland, sail'd for Boston in New England, the 25th of September, 1710. But meeting with contrary Winds and bad Weather 'twas the Beginning of December when first made Land to the Eastward of Piscataqua, and haling Southerly for the Massachuset's-Bay, under a hard gale of Wind at North-East, accompanied with Rain, Hail and Snow, having no observation for ten or twelve Days we on the Eleventh handed all our Sails, except our Fore-

Sail and Main-top Sail double reeft, ordering one Hand forward to look out. Between 8 and 9 going forward myself, I saw the breakers ahead, whereupon I call'd out to put the Helm hard a Starboard, but ere the Ship cou'd wear, we struck upon the East End of the Rock called Boon-Island, four Leagues to the Eastward of Piscataqua.

The second or third Sea heav'd the Ship along Side of it, running likewise so very high, and the Ship labouring so excessively that we were not able to stand upon Deck, and notwithstanding it was not above thirty or forty Yards, yet the Weather was so thick and dark we cou'd not see the Rock, so that we were justly thrown into a Consternation at the sad Prospect of immediately perishing in the Sea. I presently call'd down all Hands to the Cabin, where we continu'd a few Minutes earnestly supplicating Mercy; but knowing Prayers without Endeavours are vain, I order'd all up again, to cut the Masts by the board, but several sunck so under Racks of Conscience that they were not able to stir. However, we upon deck cut the Weather-most shrouds, and the Ship heeling towards the Rock, the force of the Sea soon broke the Masts, so that they fell right towards the Shore.

One of the men went out on the Boltspright, and returning, told me he saw something black ahead, and wou'd adventure to get on shore, accompanied with any other Person; upon which I desir'd some of the best swimmers (my Mate and one more) to go with him, and if they recover'd the Rock, to give notice by their Calls, and direct us to the most secure Place; and remembring some money and papers that might be of use, also Ammunition, Brandy, &c. I went down and open'd the Place in which they were but the Ship bulging, her decks opening, her back broke, and beams giving way, so that the Stern sunk almost under water, I was oblig'd to hasten forward to prevent immediate perishing. And having heard nothing of the men gone before, concluded them lost; yet notwithstanding, I was under a necessity to make the same Adventure upon the Fore Mast, moving gradually forward betwixt every sea, 'till at last quitting it, I cast myself with all the strength I had toward the Rock, and it being dead low water and the Rock exceeding slippery I cou'd get no Hold, but tore my Fingers, Hands and Arms in a most lamentable Manner; every wash of the sea fetching me off again, so that it was with the utmost peril and difficulty that I got safe on shore at last. The rest of the men running the same hazard yet thro' mercy we all escap'd with our lives.

After endeavouring to discharge the salt-water, and creeping a little way up the Rock, I heard the three men mentioned before and by ten all met together; where with joyfull hearts we return'd humble thanks to Providence for our Deliverance from so eminent a Danger; we then endeavour'd to gain shelter to the Leeward of the Rock, but found it so small and inconsiderable that it wou'd afford none (being but about one hundred Yards long, and Fifty broad) and so very craggy, that we cou'd not walk to keep our selves warm, the weather still continuing extream cold, with Snow and Rain.

As soon as day-light appear'd, I went towards the place where we came on shoar, not questioning but we should meet with Provisions enough from the Wreck for our support, but found only some pieces of the Masts and Yards, amongst some old junk and cables conger'd, together, which the Anchors had prevented from being carried away, and kept moving about the Rock at some distance: Part of the ship's stores with some pieces of Plank and Timber, old Sails and Canvas &c. drove on shoar but nothing to eat, except some small pieces of cheese we pick'd up from among the Rock-Weed (in the whole, to the Quantity of three small Cheeses.)

We used our utmost endeavour to get Fire, (having a Steel and Flint with us, also by a Drill with a very swift motion) but having nothing but what had been long watersoak'd, we could not effect it.

At night we stow'd one upon another (under our Canvas) in the best Manner possible, to keep each other warm; and the next day the weather a little clearing, and inclining to frost, I went out, and seeing the main Land knew where we was, therefore encouraged my men with hopes of being discover'd by fishing Shallops &c. requiring them to go about, and fetch up what planks they could get, (as also Carpenters' Tools and Stores &c.) in order to build a Tent and a Boat: The cook then complaining he was allmost starved, and his Countenance discovering his illness, I ordered him to remain with two or three more the frost had seiz'd. About noon the Men acquainted me that he was dead, so laid him in a convenient Place for the Sea to carry him away; none mentioning eating of him, tho' several with my self afterwards acknowledged, had Tho'ts of it.

After we had been there two or three Days, the frost being very severe, and the Weather extream cold, it seized most of our hands and feet to such a Degree as to take away the Sence of Feeling, and render them almost useless, so benumbing and discolouring them, as gave us just reason to fear mortifications. We pull'd off our shoes, and cut off our boots, but in getting off our stockings, many whose legs were blister'd, pull'd off Skin and all, and some the nails of their toes; we wrap'd up our legs and feet as warm as we could in Oakum and Canvas.

We now began to build our tent in a triangular Form, each angle about eight Foot, covered with what Sails and old Canvas came on shoar, having just room for all to lie down each on one side, so that none cou'd turn except all turn'd which was about every two hours, upon Notice given: We also fix'd a Staff to the top of our Tent, upon which (as often as weather wou'd permit) we hoisted a piece of cloth in the Form of a Flag, in order to discover ourselves to any vessels that might come near.

We began now to build our Boat of plank and timber belonging to the Wreck; our tools the blade of a cutlass (made into a Saw with our knives) a Hammer and a Caulking Mallet: Some nails we found in the clifts of the Rock, others we got from the sheathing; we laid three Planks flat for the bottom, and two up each Side fix'd to stanchings, and let into the bottom timbers, with two short Pieces at each end, also one breadth of new Holland Duck round the sides, to keep out the Spray of the Sea. We cork'd all we could with oakum drawn from the old junk, and in other places, fill'd up the distances with long pieces of Canvas, all which we secured in the best Manner possible; we found also some Sheet Lead and Pump Leather, which proved of use; we fix'd a short Mast and square sail, with seven Padles to row, and another longer to stear; but our Carpenter who now should have been of most use to us, was (by reason of illness) scarce able to affoard us either assistance or advice; and all the Rest so benumb'd and feeble as not able to stir, except my self and two more, also the weather so extream cold, that we could seldom stay out of the Tent above four hours in the day, and some days do nothing at all.

When we had been there about a week without any manner of provisions, except the cheese before mentioned and some beefe bones, which we eat (first beating them to pieces); we saw three boats about five Leagues from us, which may be easily imagined rejoyced us not a little, believing our deliverance was now come: I made all creep out of the Tent, and hollow together (so well as our strength would allow) making also all the signals we could, but alas all in vain; they neither hearing nor otherwise discovering us: however we receiv'd no small encouragement from the sight of 'em, they coming from S. West, and the Wind at N. E. when we were cast away, gave us reason to conclude our distress might be known, by the wreck driving on shoar, and to presume were come out in search of us, and that they would daily do so when weather would permit; thus we flatter'd our selves in hopes of deliverance tho' in vain.

Just before we had finished our boat, Providence so ordered it, that the Carpenter's Ax was cast on the Rock to us, whereby we were enabled to compleat our work; but then we had scarce strength enough to get her into the water.

About the 21st (December) the boat just perfected, a fine day, and the water smoother than I had ever yet seen it since we came there, we consulted who shou'd attempt getting on shore, I offering my self as one to adventure, which they agreed to, because I was the strongest, and therefore fittest to undergoe the extremities we might be reduc'd to. My Mate also offering himself, and desiring to accompany me, I was allow'd him with my brother, and four more, so committing our enterprize to Divine Providence, all that were able came out, and with much difficulty we got our poor patch'd up boat to the water side; and the Surf running very high, was oblig'd to wade very deep to launch her, which being done, and my self and one more got into her, the swell of the Sea heav'd her along shore, and overset her upon us, (whereby we again narrowly escap'd drowning) and stav'd our poor boat all to peices: Totally disappointing our enterprize and destroying all our hopes at once.

And as that which still heighten'd our afflictions, and serv'd to aggravate our miserable prospects, and render our deliverance less practicable: We lost with our boat, both our Ax and Hammer, which wou'd have been of great use to us if we should hereafter attempt to build a Raft, yet had we reason to admire the goodness of God, in over-ruling our disappointment, for our safety; for that afternoon, the wind springing up it blew very hard, so that had we been at Sea in that imitation of a boat, in all probability we must have perish'd, and the rest left behind had no better fare, because unable to help themselves.

We were now reduc'd to the most deplorable and mallancholy

Circumstance imaginable, almost every Man but myself, weak to an extremity, and near starved with Hunger and Cold; their Hands and Feet frozen and mortified, with large and deep ulcers in their legs (the very smell offensive to those of us, who could creep into the air) and nothing to dress them with, but a Piece of linnen that was cast on shoar. No Fire, and the weather extream cold; our small stock of Cheese spent, and nothing to support our feeble Bodies but Rock-weed and a few Muscles, scarce and difficult to get (at most, not above two or three for each man a day). So that we had our miserable bodies perishing, and our poor disconsolate spirits overpowered, with the deplorable Prospect of starving, without any appearance of relief: Besides, to heighten (if possible) the agravation we had reason to apprehend, lest the approaching Spring-Tide (if accompanied with high winds) should totally overflow us. How dismal such a circumstance must be, is imposible to express; the pinching cold and hunger, extremity of weakness and pain, racks and horror of conscience (to many) and foresight of certain and painful (but lingring) death, without any (even the most remote) views of deliverance. How heighten'd! How agravated is such Misery! and yet alas such was our deplorable Case: insomuch that the greater part of our company were ready to die with horror and despair, without the least hopes of escaping.

For my own part, I did my utmost to encourage my self, and exhort the rest to trust in God and patiently wait for his salvation; and Providence, a little to aleviate our distress, and encourage our Faith, directed my Mate to strike down a Sea Gull, which he joyfully brought to me, and I equally divided every one a proportion; and (tho' raw and scarce every one a mouthful) yet we received and eat thankfully.

The last method of safety we could possibly propose, was, the fixing a Raft that might carry two men, which was mightily urged by one of our men, a Sweed, a stout brave fellow, but had since our distress lost both his feet by the Frost; he frequently importun'd me, to attempt our deliverance in that way, offering himself to accompany me, or if I refused him, to go alone. After deliberate thoughts and consideration, we resolved upon a Raft, but found abundance of labour and difficulty in clearing the Fore-Yard (of which it was chiefly to be made) from the junk, by reason our working hands were so few and weak.

That done, we split the Yard, and with the two parts made side pieces, fixing others, and adding some of the lightest Plank we cou'd get, first spiking and afterwards seizing them firm, in breadth four Foot: We likewise fix'd a Mast, and of two hammocks that were drove on shoar we made a Sail, with a Paddle for each Man and a spare one in case of necessity. This difficulty thus surmounted and brought to a period, he wou'd frequently ask me whether I design'd to accompany him, giving me also to understand that if I declin'd, there was another ready to embrace the offer.

About this Time we saw a Sail come out of Piscataqua River, about 7 Leagues to the Westward, we again made all the signal we cou'd, but the Wind being at N. West, and the ship standing to the Eastward, was presently out of sight, without ever coming near us, which prov'd a very great Mortification to our hopes; but the next day being moderate, and in the afternoon a small Breeze right on shoar, also the Raft wholy finished, the two men were very solicitous to have it launch'd, and the Mate as strenuously oppos'd it, on account 'twas so late (being 2 in the afternoon) but they urging the light nights, beg'd of me to have it done, to which at last I agreed, first commiting the enterprize to God's blessing; they both got upon it, and the Swell rowling very high soon overset them as it did our boat; the Sweed not minding it swam on shoar, but the other (being no swimmer) contin'd some Time under Water and as soon as appear'd, I caught hold of him and sav'd him, but was so discourag'd, that he was afraid to make a second attempt.

I desir'd the Sweed to wait a more favourable oportunity, but he continuing resolute, beg'd of me to go with him, or help him to turn the Raft, and would go himself alone.

By this time another man came down and offer'd to adventure, so getting upon the Raft I launch'd 'em off, they desiring us to go to Prayers, also to watch what became of them; I did so, and by Sunset judg'd them half way to the Main, and that they might reach the shoar by 2 in the morning; but I suppose they fell in with some breakers, or the violence of the sea overset them and they perish'd; for two Days after, the Raft was found on shoar, and one man dead about a Mile from it, with a Paddle fastened to his wrist; but the Sweed who was so very forward to adventure, was never heard of more.

We upon the desolate Island not knowing what had befallen them, waited daily for deliverance, and our expectations was the more heightened by a smoak we saw in the woods, two days after (the Signal appointed if arriv'd safe) which continuing every day, and being willing to believe it made on our Account, tho' saw no appearance of any thing towards our relief, yet suppos'd the delay was occasion'd, by their not being able to procure a vessel so soon as we desir'd; and this hope under God, serv'd to bear our spirits and support us much.

But still our great want was Provisions; having nothing to eat but Rockweed and a very few Muscles, and the Spring-Tide being (thank God) safely over we cou'd scarce get any at all. I have gone my self (no other Person being able) several days at low water, and cou'd get no more than two or three at Piece, and have frequently been in danger of losing my hands and arms by putting them so often in the water, which when got, my stomach refus'd, and rather chose Rockweed.

At our first coming we saw several Seals upon the Rock, and supposing they might harbour there in the night, I walked round at midnight, but cou'd never get any thing: We also saw a great many fowls, but they perceiving us daily there, wou'd never come on the Rock to lodge, so that we caught none.

Which disappointment was very greivous and still serv'd to irritate our miseries, but it was more especially afflicting to a brother I had with me, and another young Gentleman, who had never (either of 'em) been at sea, or endur'd any severities before; but were now reduc'd to the last extreamities, having no assistance but what they receiv'd from me.

Part of a green hide being thrown up by the sea, (fasten'd to a peice of the Main-Yard) the men importun'd me to bring it to the Tent, which being done we minc'd it small and swallow'd it down.

About this time, I set the men to open junck, and with the Rope-Yarn (when weather wou'd permit) I thatcht the Tent in the best Manner my strength wou'd allow; that it might the better shelter us from extreamities of weather: And it prov'd of so much service as to turn two or three Hours' rain, and preserve us from the cold pinching winds which were always very severe upon us.

About the latter end of this month (viz. December) our Carpenter (a fat Man, and naturally of a dull, heavy, Phlegmatick Constitution and Disposition, aged about forty-seven) who from our first coming on shore, had been always very ill, and lost the use of his feet, complained of an excessive Pain in his Back, and stiffness in his Neck: being likewise almost choakt with phlegm (for want of strength to discharge it) so that to our aprehension he drew near his End. We prayed over him, and us'd our utmost endeavours to be serviceable to him in his last moments; he shew'd himself sensible tho' speechless, and that night died: We suffered the Body to remain with us 'till morning, when I desir'd them who were best able, to remove it; creeping out my self, to see if Providence had yet sent us any thing, to satisfie our extreamly craving appetites: Before noon returning and not seeing the dead Body without, I ask'd why they had not remov'd it? And receiv'd for answer, they were not all of them able: Whereupon fastening a rope to the Body, I gave the utmost of my assistance, and with some difficulty we got it out of the Tent. But the fategue and consideration of our Misery together, so overcame my spirits, that being ready to faint, I crept into the Tent, and was no sooner got in there, but (as the highest Addition of trouble) the Men began to request of me the dead Body to eat, the better to support their Lives.

This, of all I had met with, was the most greivous and shocking to me, to see my self and Company, who came thither laded with provisions but three weeks before, now reduc'd to such a deplorable circumstance, as to have two of us absolutely starv'd to death, other two we knew not what was become of, and the rest of us at the last Extreamity and (tho' still living, yet) requiring to eat the Dead for support.

After abundance of mature thought and consultation about the lawfullness or sinfullness on the one Hand, and absolute Necessity on the other; Judgment, Conscience, &c. were oblig'd to submit to the more prevailing arguments of our craving appetites; so that at last we determined to satisfie our hunger and support our feeble Bodies with the Carkass in Possession: first ordering his skin, head, hands, Feet and bowels to be buried in the Sea, and the Body to be quarter'd for Conveniency of drying and carriage, to which I again receiv'd for Answer, that they were not all of them able, but entreated I wou'd perform it for them: A task very greivous, and not readily comply'd with, but their incessant Prayers and Intreaties at last prevail'd, and by night I had perform'd my labour.

I then cut part of the flesh in thin Slices, and washing it in saltwater, brought it to the Tent, and oblig'd the men to eat Rockweed along with it, to serve instead of bread.

My Mate and two others, refus'd to eat any that night, but next morning complied, and earnestly desir'd to partake with the rest.

I found they all eat abundance and with the utmost greediness, so that I was constrain'd to carry the quarters farther from the Tent, (quite out of their Reach) least they shou'd prejudice themselves by overmuch eating, as also expend our small stock too soon.

I also limited each Man to an equal Proportion, that none might quarrel, or entertain hard thoughts of my self, or one another, and I was the more oblig'd to this method, because I found (in a few days) their very natural dispositions chang'd, and that affectionate, peacable temper they had all along hitherto discover'd totally lost; their eyes staring and looking wild, their Countenances fierce and barbarous, and instead of obeying my Commands (as they had universally and readily done before) I found all I cou'd say (even prayers and entreaties vain and fruitless) nothing now being to be heard but brutish quarrels, with horrid Oaths and Imprecations, instead of that quiet submissive spirit of Prayer and supplication we had before enjoy'd.

This, together with the dismal prospect of future want, oblig'd me to keep a strict watch over the rest of the Body, least any of 'em shou'd (if able) get to it, and this being spent, we be forc'd to feed upon the living: which we must certainly have done, had we staid a few days longer.

But now the goodness of God began to appear, and make provision for our deliverance, by putting it in the hearts of the good people on Shore, where our Raft drove, to come out in search of us; which they did the 2d of January in the morning.

Just as I was creeping out of the Tent, I saw a shallop half way from shore, standing directly towards us, which may be easily imagin'd was Life from the Dead; how great our Joys and Satisfaction were, at the prospect of so speedy and unexpected deliverance, no tongue is able to express, nor thoughts to conceive.

Our good and welcome friends came to an Anchor to the South West, at about 100 Yards distance, (the Swell not suffering them to come nearer) but their anchor coming home, oblig'd them to stand off 'till about noon, waiting for smoother water upon the Flood: Mean Time our passions were differently mov'd, our Expectations of Deliverance, and fears of miscarriage, hurry'd our weak and disorder'd spirits strangely.

I give them account of our miseries in every respect, except the want of Provisions (which I did not mention, least I shou'd not get them on shore for fear of being constrain'd by the Weather to tarry with us): Earnestly entreating them to attempt our immediate deliverance; or at least (if possible) to furnish us with fire, which with the utmost hazard and difficulty they at last accomplished, by sending a small Cannoe with one Man, who with abundance of labour got on shore.

After helping him up with his Canoe, and seeing nothing to eat, I ask'd him if he cou'd give us Fire, he answer'd in the affirmative, but was so affrighted, (seeing me look so thin and meagre) that could hardly at first return me an answer: But recollecting himself, after several questions asked on both sides, he went with me to the Tent, where was surpriz'd to see so many of us in so deplorable condition.

Our flesh so wasted, and our looks so ghastly and frightful, that it was really a very dismal Prospect.

With some difficulty we made a fire, determined to go my self with the man on board, and after to send for the rest one or two at a time, and accordingly got both into the Canoe, but the Sea immediately drove it with such violence against the Rock, that overset us into the water; and I being very weak, 'twas a great while before cou'd recover my self, so that I had a very narrow excape from drowning.

The good man with very great difficulty, got on board himself without me, designing to return the next day with better conveniences if weather wou'd permit.

'Twas a very uncomfortable sight to see our worthy friends in the Shallop stand away for the shore without us: But God who orders all our affairs (by unseen movements) for the best, had doubtless designs of preservation towards us, in denying us that appearance of present deliverance: For that night the wind coming about to South-East, blowing hard and being dark weather, our good friends lost their Shallop, and with extream difficulty sav'd their lives: But, in all probability, had we been with them, we must have perish'd, not having strength sufficient to help ourselves.

Immediately after their getting on shore, they sent an express to Portsmouth in Piscataqua, where the good people made no delay in hastening to our deliverance, as soon as weather wou'd allow: But to our great sorrow, and for further trial of our Patience, the next day continu'd very stormy, so that, tho' we doubted not but the people on shore knew our condition, and wou'd assist us as soon as possible, yet our flesh near spent, no fresh water, nor any certainty how long the weather might continue thus, render'd our circumstance still miserable, tho' much advantag'd by the fire, for now we cou'd both warm our selves, and broil our meat.

The next day our Men urging me vehemently for flesh, I gave them a little more than usual, but not to their satisfaction, for they wou'd certainly have eat up the whole at once, had I not carefully watch'd 'em, designing to share the rest next morning if the weather continu'd bad: But it pleased God that night the wind abated and early next morning a Shallop came for us, with my much esteemed friends Captain Long and Captain Purver and three more who brought a large Canoe, and in two hours time got us all on Board to their Satisfaction and our great comfort: being forc'd to carry almost all the men on their backs, from the Tent to the Canoe, and fetch us off by two or three at a time.

When we first came on board the Shallop, each of us eat a bit of bread and drank a dram of Rum, and most of us were extreamly Sea Sick; but after we had cleans'd our stomachs, and tasted warm nourishing food, we became so exceeding hungry and ravenous, that had not our worthy friends dieted us (and limited the quantity for about two or three days) we shou'd certainly have destroy'd our selves with eating.

We had also two other vessels came off for our assistance, if there had been any necessity (so generous and charitable were the good People of New England, in our distress) but seeing us all on board the shallop made the best of their way home again.

At eight at night we came on shore, where we were kindly entertain'd, myself and another at a private house (having Credit sufficient to help us) all the rest at the charge of the Government who took such care that the poor men knew not the least want of any thing their necessitys call'd for or the kind and generous gentlemen cou'd furnish them with (the care, industry and generosity of my much honoured Friends John Plaisted, Esq., and Captain John Wentworth, in serving both my self and these poor men being particularly eminent) providing them a good Surgeon and Nurses till well, bearing the charge, and afterwards allowing each man sufficient cloathing; having themselves in the whole with so much Freedom, Generosity and Christian Temper, that was no small addition to their other services, and render'd the whole worthy both of admiration and Imitation; and likewise was of the last consequence to the poor men in their distress.

Two days after we came on shore my apprentice lost a great part of one foot, the rest all recover'd their limbs, but not their perfect use. Very few (beside my self) escaping without losing the benefit of Fingers or Toes, &c. tho' thank God all otherwise in perfect Health; some sailing one way and some another; my Mate and two or three more now in England at the Publication hereof.

POSTSCRIPT

Having two or three spare Pages, we think it our duty to the truth, and our selves, to obviate a barbarous and scandalous Reflection, industriously spread abroad and level'd at our ruine, by some unworthy, malicious Persons (*viz.*) That we having ensur'd more than our Interest in the Ship *Nottingham*, agreed and willfully lost her, first designing it in Ireland, and afterwards effecting it at Boon Island.

Such a base and villainous Reflection scarce merits the Trouble of an Answer, were not Truth and Reputation so much concern'd: Therefore, as to the Business of Ireland, 'tis really preposterous (the Commander not knowing there was one Penny ensur'd) but being chac'd by two large Privateers, in their Passage North-about to Killibegs, and standing in betwixt the Islands of Arran and the Main, to prevent being taken; the Commander and Mr. Whitworth agreed (if it came to the last Extremity) to run the Ship on Shore and burn her (first escaping themselves and Men, with what else they cou'd carry in the Boat) rather than be carry'd into France and lose all. But being near, they recover'd their Port, and proceeded on their Voyage.

And as for the other Part of the Charge, of willfully losing her at Boon Island, one wou'd wonder Malice itself cou'd invent or suggest any thing so ridiculous, and which wou'd certainly be credited by nobody, that considers the extream Hazards and Difficulties suffer'd by the Commander himself, as well as his Men, where 'twas more than Ten Thousand to one, but every

Man had perish'd: And wou'd certainly have chose another Place to have effected it, if we had such a Design: But alas, what will not vain impotent Malice say, when it intends Injury? Were the Persons reflecting, but to suffer the like Extreamities (we can't but think) they'd be feelingly convinc't. But this Matter speaking so plainly for it self, we think it needless to add more, therefore proceed to the last part of the Charge (*viz.*) Ensurance.

We presume Interest only can induce Men to such Villainies, (indeed that pretended in this Case) therefore to let the World see how little we gain (or rather how much we lose) by the Matter in Hand, as also further to expose the malicious and injurious Scandal, we fairly and voluntarily offer: If any Person can make out that Jasper Dean (who own'd ⅞ of the said Ship, besides considerable in Cargoe) or Miles Whitworth (who own'd the other 8th part) or John Dean Commander of the said Ship, they jointly or separatly, or any others for (or on) their Accounts, or for their (or any of their) Use or Advantage, directly or indirectly, or they (or any of them,) for the Use or Benefit of any others, in any Manner whatsoever, have ensur'd or caus'd to be ensur'd, in Britain or elsewhere, any more than £250 to Ireland (which was not paid the Ship arriving safe) and £300 from there to Boston in New England (which paid, and Premium and Office Charges deducted, was no more than 226£ 17s) if any Person can make out more, they are desired to publish it by Way of Advertisement in some common News Paper and we undernam'd do hereby promise to make the utmost Satisfaction, and stand convict to be the greatest Villains in the Universe.

And now, let the World judge whether 'tis reasonable to imagine we shou'd willfully lose a good Ship of 120 Tuns, besides a valuable Interest in Cargoe in such a Place, where the Commander (as well as the Rest) must unavoidably run the utmost Hazard of perishing in the most miserable Manner, and all this to recover £226. 17s. how absurd and ridiculous is such a Supposition, and yet this is the Reproach we at present labour under, so far as to receive daily ignominious Scandals upon our Reputations, and injurious Affronts and Mobbings to our Faces. Yet we solemnly profess, we are not conscious of the least Guilt, nor even in this Account, of the least Errours in Representation.

JASPER DEAN
JOHN DEAN
MILES WHITWORTH
(lately dead)

FINIS

The Langman Account

A True Account of the
Voyage of the Nottingham-Galley *of* London,
John Dean *Commander, from the River*
Thames *to* New-England,

Near which Place she was cast away on *Boon-Island*, December 11, 1710. by the Captain's Obstinacy, who endeavour'd to betray her to the *French*, or run her ashore; with an Account of the Falsehoods in the Captain's *Narrative*.

And a faithful Relation of the Extremities the Company was reduc'd to for Twenty-four Days on that desolate Rock, where they were forc'd to eat one of their Companions who died, but were at last wonderfully deliver'd,

The whole attested upon Oath, by

Christopher Langman, Mate;
Nicholas Mellen, Boatswain; and
George White, Sailor in the said Ship.

THE PREFACE.

We having been Sufferers in this unfortunate Voyage, had reason to believe, from the Temper of our Captain, who

London; Printed for S. Popping at the Raven in Pater-noster-Row, 1711. (Price Six Pence.)

treated us barbarously both by Sea and Land, that he would misrepresent the Matter, as we now find he has done in a late Pamphlet by him publish'd, intituled *A Narrative of the Sufferings, Preservation, and Deliverance of Captain John Dean, and Company, in the Nottingham Galley of London, &c. London, Printed by R. Tooky, and Sold by S. Popping at the Raven in Pater-noster-Row, and at the Printing Press under the Royal-Exchange.*

Our Apprehensions of this made us refuse the Encouragement which was offered us in New England, and resolve to come home that we might have an Opportunity to lay before the World, and before those Gentlemen and others who have lost their Estates and Relations in this unhappy Voyage, the true Causes of our own and their Misfortunes, and how they might, humanely speaking, have been easily avoided, had Captain Dean been either an honest or an able Commander. This we think ourselves oblig'd to do in common Justice, and to prevent others from suffering by him in the like manner.

We cannot but in the first place take notice of a notorious Falshood he asserts in his Preface, *That he might have had the Attestation of several of his Fellow Sufferers now in Town to the Truth of what he has wrote*, since he very well knows that Two of us did positively refuse it in publick Company, after reading a part of it, and told him to his Face, *that it was not true.*

In the next place, as to what he says of the Encouragement his Narrative met with in New England and North Britain, where it appeared under much greater Disadvantages as to the Particulars and Dress, We think fit to reply, That the Acceptance it met with in New England was occasion'd by our being confined from appearing in publick during our Sickness, and that he compell'd us to sign what our Illness made us uncapable to understand; but when it pleas'd God that we recover'd our Health, and made our Affidavits here subjoin'd before Mr. Penhallow, a Justice of Peace, and Member of Council at Portsmouth in the Province of New Hampshire, New England, in the Presence of the said Dean, who had not the Face to deny it, his Character appear'd in a true Light, and he was cover'd with Shame and Confusion.

The Captain has reason indeed to commend the Charity of the Gentlemen of New England, which is no more than their due, both from him and us, tho' we were unhappily deprived of the chief Effects of it by the Captain's Brother; who being the Person that received it, took care not to be wanting to the Captain and himself, whereas we had nothing but what was fit for such miserable Wretches, who were glad of any thing, since we were then uncapable of working for better.

As to what he says in his Postscript about Insurance, we know nothing further of that matter than what we heard on Board, as will appear by our Narrative, viz. *That there were great Sums insured upon the Ship*, the truth of which is more proper for the Inquiry of others than us who are only Sailors.

We come now to the narrative, wherein we shall represent nothing but the Truth, of which we our selves had the Misfortune to be Witnesses, to our great Sorrow, and the manifest Danger of our Lives.

And since what we deliver is upon Oath, we hope it will obtain Credit sooner than the bare Word of Captain Dean, his Brother, and Mr. Whitworth, who were all Three interested Persons, and but One of them, acquainted with all the Matter of Fact, which for his own Reputation and Safety he has been obliged to set off in false Colours. Besides, Mr. Whitworth is since dead, so that the Captain has no Vouchers but himself and his Brother; and how little Credit they deserve, will sufficiently appear by what follows.

THE LANGMAN ACCOUNT

THE NARRATIVE

The *Nottingham-Galley* of 120 Tons, 10 Guns, and 14 Men, John Dean Commander, took in part of her Lading in the River Thames, which was Cordage, and the rest in Butter and Cheese, at Killybags in Ireland. But Captain Dean in his Narrative has omitted to acquaint the World that 4 of the Guns were useless, and that not above 6 of the Men were capable to Serve in the Ship, in case of bad Weather. She Sail'd from Gravesend the 2d Day of August, 1710. to the Nore, and from thence on the 7th, with 2 Men of War, and several Merchant-Men under their Convoy, towards Scotland. When we came off of Whitby, the Fleet brought to, and several of the Ships were a-stern. We having a fine Gale, the Captain said he would Run it, and make the best of his way for Ireland, which we did. And when we were on that Coast, the 12th of August, we saw 2 Ships in a Bay, towards whom the Captain would have bore down, but the Men would not consent to it, because they perceiv'd them to be French Men of War. Upon this we stood off to Sea till 12 at Night when the Captain coming upon Deck, we Sail'd easily in towards the Shore, by the Mate's Advice, till Daylight, and came so near Land that we were forced to stand off. The next Day we saw the two Privateers again, and the Captain propos'd to stand down towards them, or to come to an Anchor; but the Mate and the Men oppos'd it. The Captain was seconded in this by Charles Whitworth the Merchant, who said in the hearing of the Boatswain, and others, *That he had rather be taken than otherwise, tho' he had an Eighth Part of the Ship, because he had Insured 200 £.* And the Captain said, *He had rather run the Ship ashore than perform his Voyage, if he thought he could be safe with the Insurers, because his Brother had insur'd 300 £. upon her.* Accordingly he put in towards the Shore to find out a proper Place for that purpose, and ordered the Boatswain to get the Tackle upon the Boat and hoist her overside, that she might be in readiness to go ashore. At the same time the Captain and Charles Whitworth went to the Cabbin to get out the best of their Goods in order to carry them with them; and putting them up in a Chest, commanded the Men to carry them into the Boat, which they did. The Captain promis'd that we should want for nothing, and resolv'd to go ashore; so that we all plainly saw he was resolv'd to lose the Ship. But he was opposed by the Mate Christopher Langman, who wrought the Vessel through between the Main and an Island, and she arrived safely at Killybags in Ireland that same Night.

We took in the rest of our Lading there the 25th of September, being 30 Tons of Butter, and above 300 Cheeses, and sail'd for Boston in New-England; which we were very uncapable to do, because the Captain, by his barbarous Treatment of our Men, had disabled several of 'em, and particularly two of our best Sailors were so unmercifully beat by him, because they oppos'd his Design above mention'd, that they were not able to work in a Month. This gave us a very melancholy Prospect of an unfortunate Voyage, since we perceiv'd he would either lose the Ship, or betray her to the French, because she was insured for much above the Value. Besides, he put us to short Allowance, so that we had but one Quart of Water per Head in twenty four Hours, and had nothing to eat but salt Beef, which made us so dry that we were forc'd to drink the Rain Water that run off the Deck. And the Captain was so barbarous that he knock'd down one of our Men for dead, because when he found the Hold open, he went and drew a Gallon of Water to quench our Thirst. In the mean time he wanted nothing himself, tho' he pretended to us that he confin'd himself also to short Allowance, yet we knew the contrary.

When we came to the Banks of Newfoundland we saw a Ship which made all the Sail she could towards us, and soon came up with us. The Captain and Mr. Whitworth hoping she was a Frenchman, put on their best Apparel, and gave us as much strong Beer and Brandy as we could drink: But it prov'd to be the *Pompey* Galley of London, Captain Den Commander, at which we rejoic'd, tho' our Captain was melancholy. We continu'd our Course towards New England; and the first Land we made was Cape Sables, which is about 50 Leagues from Boston in that Country.

We made the best of our way for that Port, but the Wind blew hard, so that we were several Days without sight of Land, and were forced to hand all our Sails, and lie under our Mizzen-Ballast till Daylight; when the Boatswain having the Morning Watch discover'd Land to the Leeward, with which he acquainted the Captain and the Mate, who both came upon Deck. The Captain said that was the first Land we had made; wherein he was justly contradicted by the Mate, which caus'd some Words between 'em: For in Truth we made Cape Sables a Week before; and if we had kept our Course then, according to the Opinion of the Mate and Ship's Company, we had, in all Probability, arriv'd safe the next Day at Boston, but the Master laying the Ship by, and the next Day proving moderate Weather, and the Wind coming to the West, we stood away to the North, and so it was a Week before we made Cape Porpus, which was the same Day we were lost; so untrue is it what the Captain says, that the first Land we made was to the East of Piscataqua. After those Words had pass'd with the Mate, the Captain went down to serve us with Water, according to Custom, and in the mean time the Captain's Brother took a Bottle of Water from the Mate, and struck him; upon which the Captain coming out of the Hold, he took up a Perriwig Block, with which he came behind the Mate, and struck him three Blows on the Head, upon which he fell down and lay as dead for several Minutes, all in Blood. This was very discouraging to the Seamen, who durst not speak to him for fear of the like treatment. Soon after this barbarous Action we perceiv'd the Ship in Danger by being so near Land; upon which the Boatswain being on the Watch call'd the Captain, and the Mate, who being scarce recovered came on the Deck all in Gore, and told the Captain he had no Business so near the Land, except he had a Mind to lose the Ship, and therefore desir'd him to hawl further off, or else he would be ashore that Night. The Captain answer'd, That he wou'd not take his Advice though the Ship should go to the Bottom, threatned to shoot the Mate with a Pistol, and told him, he would do what he pleas'd except they confin'd him to his Cabbin. It fell out according as the Mate had said; we run ashoar that Night, being the 11th of December, between 8 and 9 a Clock, when the Ship struck upon Boon Island, a Rock three or four leagues East from Piscataqua. And here the Captain is false again in his Narrative, when he says p. [25] *that he saw the Breakers ahead, upon which he call'd out to put the Helm hard on the Starboard;* for he was then undressing himself to go to Bed, according to his usual Custom. When the Ship struck the Boatswain told the Captain, *he had made his Words good, and lost the Ship on purpose, whereas had he taken the Mate's Advice, he might in all probability have been safe at Boston Ten Days before.* The Captain bid him hold his Peace, *He was sorry for what had happen'd, but we must now all prepare for Death, there being no Probability to escape it.* Upon this several of our Men went on the Deck, but cou'd not stay there, because the Sea broke in all over the Ship. Then the Captain, who had been Cursing and Swearing before, began to cry and howl for Fear of losing his Life. The Boatswain and another went into the Hold to see if there was any Water there, and finding there was, we went all into the Cabbin to Prayers, being in hopes the Ship would lie whole till Daylight. Soon after this the Mate, though hardly able, went with some others above Deck; for this Surprize made him forget his Pain. He spoke to the Captain, and told him, *It was his Business to encourage the Men, and not to disherten them:* Yet still he insisted it was impossible for us to save our Lives. However, the Mate with three others cut down the Main-Mast and Fore-Mast, which by God's Assistance prov'd the Means of our Preservation; for the Fore-Mast fell on the Rock with one End; and the other rested on the Ship. The Mate went afterwards into the Cabbin, and desired the Captain to use his Endeavours to save the Men, for the Ship would immediately sink, and it was not time to think of saving any thing, but to get ashore as light as we cou'd. By this Time the Water came out of the Hold, and the Sea beat over the Deck, so that there was no standing upon it. The Mate got first on the Mast, and with great Difficulty escap'd to the Rock. He was follow'd by two others, who likewise got on Shore, but were scarce able to stand on the Rock, from whence they hallow'd to us to follow them, and we not hearing them any more than once, were afraid they were wash'd off by the Waves. This put us into a mighty consternation, so that we knew not whether it were best to follow them, or to stay on board till it was Day. The Captain was for the latter; but it being dead low Water, the Tide of Flood coming on, and the Wind beginning to blow hard, the Sea beat into the Cabbin while we were at Prayers, which forced us to go upon Deck: Some more of our Men escap'd to the Shore by help of the Mast, as the others had done, and call'd us to make haste and follow them, which we did, and by the Blessing of God got safe to the Rock, though not without much Danger, being forced to crawl upon our Hands and Knees we were so heavy with water, and the Rock so slippery.

Here again the Captain is false in the second Page of his Narrative; for he neither call'd us down to Prayers, nor order'd us up again, nor did he either command or assist at cutting down the Mast. We know not whom he points at, where he says, several of the Company did so sink under Racks of Conscience, that they were not able to stir; for he himself had as great Reason to be under Terror of Conscience as any Man, since he was the Cause of all our Misfortunes. Accordingly he cryed heartily, and begg'd the Mate to do what he cou'd to save us, for he himself cou'd do nothing. Nor was the Captain ever upon the Deck but once, when he held by the Long Boat, cryed out, and presently went down again, which greatly discouraged us, so that had it not been for the Mate, &c. who cut down the Shrowds, &c., as above-mention'd, we had all perish'd. He is also unjust to the Mate in his third Page, where he says, *That one of the Men went out on the Boltsprit, and returning, told the Captain he saw something black ahead, and would adventure to get on Shore, accompanied with any other Person;* upon which the Captain pretends he desired some of his best Swimmers, the Mate and one more, go with him, and if they recover'd the Rock, to give Notice by their Calls, and direct the rest to the most secure Place; for it was the Mate who went on the Boltsprit and discover'd the Land. After which he desired the Captain and the rest to go ashore before he attempted it himself; but finding them all dead-hearted, the Mate, who cou'd not swim, as the Captain alledges, got on Shore by the Mast as above-mention'd. The Captain is also false in asserting that he attempted to save his Money, Brandy, Ammunition &c. for our Relief, since he had not the Value of one Guinea aboard in Money. It is equally false that he tore his Arms and Fingers in such a lamentable manner in climbing up the Rock; for not one Man was hurt in getting ashore. Nor was the Captain in danger of being wash'd off from the Yard, the Water there being no deeper than our Middle.

When we got ashore we found it to be a desolate small island, without any Shelter; and being wet, and having but few Clothes, some began to despair of being able to live there till the Morning; and besides, we were not certain but it might be over flow'd at high Tide. We comforted our selves however, the best we cou'd, and though we expected to perish there, return'd God Thanks for giving us some more Time to repent. In this dismal Condition we continued till next Morning, without any thing to refresh us: But being in hopes that the Wreck would remain till Daylight, and that we might recover some of our Provisions, we sent a Man down to see what was become of her, but he brought us Word that he cou'd see nothing of her. When Daylight came we went to look for the Wreck in a cold and hungry Condition; but found nothing except one half Cheese, entangled in a Piece of a Rope, and this we equally distributed among us. Soon after we found a Piece of fine Linen and Canvas, of which we endeavour'd to make a Tent, and effected it at last by the help of the Boatswain the second Day, and this preserv'd us from being all frozen to Death, as our Cook was in a little Time to our very great Grief, since we look'd upon it as a certain Presage that we should all have the same Fate. We carried the Corpse to the Seaside, from whence it was soon wash'd off by the Flood. Here the Captain publishes another Falshood in his fifth Page, when he says he knew where he was; for he declared to us that he knew not: Nor is there any more Truth in the Compassion he there alledges that he shew'd to the Cook when he was a dying.

When the Weather clear'd we discover'd the main Land, which we suppos'd to be about a League from us. This fill'd us with Hopes that by the Providence of God we should soon be deliver'd, for which we returned him Thanks, and immediately set about building a Boat out of part of the Wreck which was drove ashore, and heartily pray'd, that God would give us Success. We were so cold, hungry and feeble, that it was scarce possible for us to do any thing, nor could we walk on the Rock in order to keep us warm, it was so craggy, uneven and slippery. We made shift however to finish our Boat, the bottom of which was made of Three Planks, and the Side was Half a Plank High.

We cork'd and lin'd it with Canvas the best we could, and made it about Twelve Foot Long and Four Foot Wide, thinking it sufficient to hold Six of us.

After this some Controversie happen'd who the Six should be. The Carpenter pleaded his Right to be one, because he built it; the Captain pleaded to be another, which was agreed to; and the Boatswain was thought fit to be one, because he spoke the Indian Language; but at last it was concluded that the Mate, the Captain's Brother, Charles Whitworth, and George White, should be the Men; and we carried the Boat to the Shore, where we launch'd her, putting on Board such of the Carpenter's Tools as we had sav'd from the Wreck, in order to build a better when we came on Shore. We begg'd the Assistance and Direction of God, and Some of our Company went into the Boat, taking leave of the rest, and promising to bring them Relief as soon as possible. But the Boat overset, by which our Men were almost drown'd, and narrowly escaped again to the Rock. The Boatswain held the Boat almost an Hour with a Rope in hopes to save her till the Weather grew more calm, and the Gunner came to his Assistance, but soon after she was stav'd to pieces, which was a great Mortification to us. We thank'd God however that he was pleas'd again to preserve so many of us, tho' the Time for our Relief was not yet come. The Captain is out in his Account, pag. [28] when he says, our Boat had a Mast and a Sail, for she had neither.

The Wind blowing hard, and there being a great Snow, we betook our selves to Prayer, and earnestly begg'd that God would have mercy on us, and consider our deplorable Condition. Being wet with our Endeavours to launch the Boat, our Cloaths freezed to our Backs, which proved fatal to our Carpenter, who died a few Days after. The next Day prov'd fair Weather, so that we could see the Houses on the main Land, and several Boats rowing to and fro, which rejoyc'd us very much; and after praying that God might direct some of them to us, we shew'd our selves on several Places of the Rock, and hallow'd to them, but they could not hear us. This quite discourag'd us again, for we had no Provisions but some small pieces of Cheese, four or five pieces of Beef, and one Neats Tongue that we recover'd out of the Wreck, and a small quantity of this was distributed among us every Morning when we went round the Rock to see if it would please God to send us any further Provisions. At last George White, one of our Number, found some Muscles at Low Water, for which we return'd God Thanks, and we found about as many for two or three days as six or seven came to each Man's share; but the Weather was so cold, and the Tides fell out so late in the Night that we could get no more. The Captain then told us, *We must shift for our selves, there being nothing now for us to trust to but the Mercies of God.* There being a piece of a Cows Hide on the Fore Yard of the Wreck, we cut it into small pieces and swallow'd it down, which reviv'd us a little. Some of our Company got Sea Weed, which was also shar'd among us, and this was all the Entertainment we had for several Days; but still we liv'd in hopes of being deliver'd from the dismal Place; and the Captain told us, *If we were, he would sell the Cables, Anchors and Guns that were cast ashore, for our Maintenance.* In this Distress our Mate perceiving a large Sea Gull in a Hole of the Rock, he knock'd it down with the Handle of a Sawce Pan, brought her into the Tent, and shar'd her among us, to our great Relief.

Perceiving no hopes of any Boats coming to us, a stout Dutchman, one of our Company, propos'd the making of a Raft, and proffer'd to endeavour to get ashore with it himself, if no body else would. This Proposal being well relish'd, such of us as were able clear'd the Fore Yard of the Rigging with a great deal of Trouble, for want of sufficient Strength and necessary Instruments; and having split it in two to make the Sides of the Raft, and fastning the End pieces with Nails, we put a Plank in the Middle, with a Mast, and a Sail made of two Hammocks, and accordingly launch'd her, with George White and the Dutchman upon it, giving them Orders, if they got ashore, to acquaint the People with our Distress, and to beg their hastening to our Assistance. But the Raft overset, by which the Men were almost drown'd, so that none would venture upon it again except the Dutchman and another. We pray'd heartily for their Success, and saw them paddle along till the Sun was down, and they appear'd to us to be so near the Shore, that we hoped they might Land safely.

That Night it blew very hard, and the next Day our Carpenter died as above-mention'd, and in the Morning we hawl'd him out of the Tent. That same Day the Captain and George White went out to see what they could find, but return'd empty handed. Upon this the Captain propos'd the sleying and eating of the Carpenter's dead Body, and told us, *It was no Sin, since God was pleas'd to take him out of the World, and that we had not laid violent Hands upon him.* He ask'd the Boatswain to help to skin and cut him up, which he refus'd because of his Weakness, whereupon one Charles Gray help'd the Captain to do it, and brought in several pieces of the Corps into the Tent, where some of our Men eat of it; but the Mate, the Boatswain, and George White wou'd not touch any of it till next Day that they were forced to it by Extremity of Hunger.

Here the Captain is guilty of several Heads, and particularly pag. [29], &c. for he was so far from offering to go ashore on the Raft, that he said, *Let who will go 'twas all one to him.* Nor did the Dutchman or Swede ever desire the Captain to go with him or help him to turn the Raft; nor did the Captain assist George White to get ashore when he was overset in the Raft. It is likewise false, that the other Man who went off in the Raft was found dead with a Paddle fastned to his Wrist, for his Corps was found about 300 Yards from the Shore, and no Paddles to his Wrist. 'Tis likewise false, that the Captain went several times out alone to look for Provisions, for George White was always with him. Nor is it true, that the piece of Cow's Hide before mention'd was brought into the Tent by the Captain's Order, for George White brought it without his Knowledge. It is likewise false, that the Men first requested the Carpenter's dead Body of the Captain to eat, for he himself was the first that propos'd it, and the Three Deponents refus'd to eat any of it until the next Morning that the Captain brought in some of his Liver and intreated 'em to eat of it; so that the Captain's Pretensions of being moved with Horror at the Thoughts of it, are false, for there was no Man that eat more of the Corps than himself. It is likewise false, that any of the Men removed the dead Body from the Place where they laid it at first. It is also untrue, that the Captain order'd his Skin, Head, Hands, &c. to be buried in the Sea, for these we left on the Island when we came off. Nor is there any more Truth in the Care which the Captain ascribes to himself, in hindring us to eat too much of the Corps lest it should prejudice our Health; for we all agreed, the Night before we come off; to limit our selves, lest our Deliverers should be detain'd from coming to us. And as to our Tempers being alter'd after the eating of humane Flesh, as the Captain charges us, p. [35]. we can safely declare, that tho' he says, *There was nothing to be heard among us but brutish Quarrels, with horrid Oaths and Imprecations,* all the Oaths we heard were between the Captain, his Brother, and Mr. Whitworth, who often quarrel'd about their Lying and Eating. And whereas the Captain often went to Prayers with us before we had the Corps to eat, he never, to our hearing, pray'd afterwards, but behav'd himself so impiously, that he was many times rebuked by the Mate and others for profane Swearing.

Having agreed with the Men we sent off on the Raft, that they should kindle a Fire if they got safe on Shore, we were rejoic'd upon the sight of a Smoke, hoping that had been the Signal they promis'd, but it was not. Soon after that we perceiv'd a Boat coming towards us, which made our Hearts leap for Joy, and we return'd Thanks to God for the Prospect of a speedy Deliverance. The Boat came to an Anchor along the side of the Rock, but could not get ashore; and we call'd to 'em for Fire, which the Master sent us by one of his Men in a small Canoe, but no Provisions. This was the 22nd Day after we had been onto this desolate Rock, so that the Man was frighten'd at the sight of so dismal a Spectacle. We all got about him, and cryed for Joy. He told us, that the Reason of their coming to the Rock to see for us, was the finding a Raft on the Shore, with one Man frozen to Death about Two or Three Hundred Yards from it, but they heard nor saw nothing of the other, from whence 'twas supposed that the Man found dead ashore having landed there in the Night Time, and not knowing where to go, he was frozen to Death under a Tree where they found him. After this Discourse, our Captain went to go off in the Boat, but it overset, so that we were forc'd to take up the Canoe, and carry it all over the Rock, seek for a smooth Place to put her off again, which we did after the Man had staid with us Two or Three Hours. He promised to come with a better Boat to carry us off, but lost his Vessel as he came near the Shore, and narrowly escaped with his own and his Mens Lives; upon which he sent an Express to Piscataqua for Relief to us. This Night we had a prodigious Storm, but kept a great Fire, which was seen on the Shore, and prov'd very comfortable to us, both for its Warmth, and by Broiling Part of the Dead Corps, which made it eat with less Disgust.

The next Day it blowed very fresh, so that no Relief could come to us; but on the 4th of January in the Morning, the Weather being fair, several Sloops came towards us, and one Canoe came ashore with Four Men, Two of which were Captain Long and Captain Forbe, Commanders of Ships, and soon carried us all off on board their Vessel; for several of us had our Legs so frozen, and were so weak that we could not walk. These

Gentlemen took great Care of us, and would not suffer us to eat or drink but a little at a time, lest it should do us hurt. Night we arrived at Piscataqua in New England, where we were all provided for, and had a Doctor appointed to look after us. We were Ten who came ashore, Two of us having died on the Island, and Two being lost that were sent off on the Raft. The Names of those that were sav'd are John Dean, Captain; Christopher Langman, Mate; Christopher Gray, Gunner; Nicholas Mellan, Boatswain; George White, Charles Whitworth, Henry Dean, Charles Graystock, William Saver, and the Captain's Boy, who had Part of his Foot cut off to prevent a Mortification, and several others were lame. Thus we were delivered by the Goodness of God (for which we praise his Name) after we had been Twenty Four Days upon that Desolate Island in the Distress above mentioned, having nothing to shelter us but a sorry Tent that could not keep us from wet, and was once in Danger of being carryed off by the high Tide, which obliged us to remove it to the highest Part of the Rock. We had nothing to lie on but the Stones, and very few Cloathes to cover us; which, together with our Hunger, made our Lives a Burden to us.

Some Days after our Arrival, the Captain drew up a Protest, which was sign'd by the Mate, being then very ill of a Flux and Fever; and also by the Boatswain Geo. White, who was also ill, and declared that he did it for fear of being put out of his Lodgings by the Captain, while he was both sick and lame. But as soon as the Deponents recover'd, they declar'd the Captain's Protest to be false, &c. as may be seen by the Depositions hereunto annex'd.

The Captain falsely ascribes to himself, p. [35], the first Discovery of the Sloop that came to relieve us, whereas it was first discover'd by Christopher Gray, the Gunner, he being sent out on purpose by the Mate, who the Night before had dreamt of the Sloop's Arrival. The Captain likewise falsely magnifies his own Danger of being drowned; when the Canoe was overset, since the Water then was scarce half a Yard deep; and instead of being thankful to God for his own and our Deliverance, he returned with the Dog to his Vomit, and behav'd himself so brutishly, that his Friend Captain Purver was obliged to turn him out of his House. He was so little sensible of the Merciful Deliverance from the Danger he had escaped, that he barbarously told the Children in his Lodging, he would have made a Frigasy of them, if he had had 'em in Boon Island; which frighten'd the People that heard him; and made them esteem him a Brute, as he was. He likewise wrong'd us of what the Good People gave us towards our Relief, and applyed it to his own and his Brother's Use; and particularly when Captain John Wentworth gave several of our Men good Cloaths, Captain Dean came and order'd them the worst that could be had; and was likewise so barbarous as to get us turn'd out of our lodgings, before we were able to shift for our selves.

All this we avouch to be Truth, and have no other End in publishing it, but to testify our Thankfulness to God for his Great Deliverance, and to give others Warning not to trust their Lives or Estates in the Hands of so wicked and brutish a Man.

For the Truth of what we have deliver'd, we refer to the Affidavits subjoined, which we made concerning this Matter both in New England, and since our Arrival at London.

AN ACCOUNT OF OUR INTENDED VOYAGE, AND SOME ACCIDENTS THAT HAPPEN'D THEREIN FROM THE RIVER OF THAMES TO IRELAND, IN THE *NOTTINGHAM GALLEY*, JOHN DEAN MASTER.

August the 7th, 1710. we sail'd from the Nore in company with her Majesty's Ship Sheerness, she then being appointed a Convoy for the North Britain Fleet, which we parted from off of Whitby, and made the best of our Way.

The 21st ditto we saw two Sail, and that they gave chace to us, they being to the Leeward of us about Three Leagues. It being then the Master's Watch on the Deck, he called the Mate, and told him, *That he saw Two Privateers.* As soon as the Mate came on the Deck, he desired the Master to run in Shore to the Windward of the Island of Arran, we then being about Two Leagues to the Windward of it. But the said Master would have gone in to Leeward, which we could not have done without speaking with the aforesaid Ships; and he proposed it several times; but the Mate nor none of the Ship's Company would consent to it, but told him, *That if he did, we could not possibly escape the Enemy*. Charles Whitworth then said in the hearing of the Boatswain and some others of the Ship's Company, *That he had rather be taken than not, for he had Two Hundred Pounds Insured;* he having an Eighth Part of the Ship, as he said.

The Master the next Day would have gone ashore and left the Ship, and put a Chest and several other things in the Boat. The Mate told him, *That he would not consent to any such Thing, for he then saw no Danger of being Taken*, and told the said Master, *That it was early in the Morning, and but Seven Leagues from our Port, and a fair Wind to run along the Shore*. The said Master was then heard to say by the Boatswain and several of the Ship's Company, *That, if he thought the Insurance would be paid, he would immediately run her ashore*. So that we all plainly saw that he was willing to lose the said Ship. The Mate told him, *That if he would, by God's Assistance he might fetch his Port before Night, if he would make Sail; but if he had a Design to give the Ship away, he might*. The said Master found the Mate was not willing to what he proposed, and that he could not obtain his Desire, he made Sail, and about Six or Seven in the Evening we arrived at our desired Port Killybags, where we took in 30 Tons of Butter and 300 and odd Cheeses.

September 25. 1710. we sail'd from this Port, bound for Boston in New England.

December 11. 1710. we being then on the Coast of New England, and close on Board of Cape Porpus, the Mate told him, *That he did not know any business we had so nigh the Shore, and that it was his better way to hawl further to the Southward.* The said Master would not take his Advice if the Ship went to the Bottom.

At or about Eight this Morning the said Master came to the Mate and knock'd him down with a Block, such as Barbers make Wigs on. We all thought that he had kill'd him, for he lay dead some time, and lost a great deal of Blood.

Between Eight and Nine this Night the Ship run ashore, the Wind at E.S.E. and a moderate Gale. The Mate being then in his Cabbin, and hardly done bleeding, got on the Deck, tho' badly able, and ordered the Masts to be cut away, which we did, and by God's Assistance got all ashore, it being a desolate Land, about Three Leagues from the Main. We then steer'd W. and by S. so that if we had miss'd it we should have run ashore on the Main. This Island is called by the Name of Boon Island. We remained on it Twenty-four Days, and suffered a great deal of Hardship; at which time we were fetched off by a Piscataqua Boat, and carried ashore.

Some Days after the Master drew up a Protest, which the Mate and Boatswain signed, the Mate being then very ill with a Flux and Fever, and the Boatswain and George White declares, That the Protest was false, and hardly a Word of Truth in it, but for fear of being put out of his Lodging, he then being very Sick and Lame, sign'd it.

As soon as the Mate recover'd, we all and every of us declare, and give our Oath, That this is the real Truth, and the said Master's Protest to be false; which we now before the Worshipful Justice of the Peace disavow and give our Oaths, That this is the Truth; and that if the said Master had taken the Mate's Advice, the Ship, with God's Assistance, might have been in Boston Harbour several Days before she was lost.

CHRISTOPHER LANGMAN, MATE.
NICHOLAS MELLIN, BOATSWAIN.
GEORGE WHITE, SAILOR.

Christopher Langman, Nicholas Mellin, and George White, personally appeared before me the Subscriber, one of Her Majesty's Justices of the Peace at Portsmouth in the Province of New Hampshire in New England, and Member of Council within the same, this 9th Day of February, 1710–11. and made Oath to the Truth of what is above written, Captain Dean at the time of taking this Oath being present.

SAMUEL PENHALLOW.

Christopher Langman, late Mate of the late Ship called the *Nottingham*, of the Burden of about 120 Tons, whereof John Dean was Master, Nicholas Mellon, Boatswain, and George White Sailor, all belonging to the said Ship, do severally make Oath as followeth, *viz.* And first, the said Christopher Langman for himself saith, The said Ship being designed on a Voyage from London to Killybags, and from thence to New England, she departed from the Nore the 7th of August, 1710. in company with her Majesty's Ship *Sheerness*, which they left off of Whitby. That on the 21st of the same Month they saw Two Sail to the Leeward, which gave chace to the said Ship *Nottingham* for about the space of Three Leagues; in which time, (notwithstanding this Deponent told the said Dean they were Enemies) he often would have bore down upon them; that the Day following they saw the Privateers again, when the said John Dean (contrary to the Will of this Deponent) would have brought the said Ship *Nottingham* to an Anchor, which if done, she would in all probability have been taken. That they then left the said Privateers, and arrived with their said Ship that Night at Killybags aforesaid, where they deliver'd what Goods were thereto consigned. That on the 29th Day of September, in the Year aforesaid, they departed with the said Ship *Nottingham* from the said Port for Boston in New England. In Prosecution of which Voyage, being on the Coast of New England, the said John Dean, without any Provocation, came to this Deponent and knock'd him down after a very barbarous and inhumane manner, and between Eight and Nine of the Clock at Night of the same Day, the said Ship *Nottingham* was run on Shore on the Coast of New England, (contrary to the Advice of this Deponent) where she, with the chiefest Part of her Cargo, was utterly lost. And lastly, This Deponent believeth, that the said John Dean, according to his Working of the said Ship in the said Voyage, design'd to lose her.

CHRISTOPHER LANGMAN

And the said Nicholas Mellen for himself saith, That the several Allegations, Matters and Things contained in the aforegoing Deposition of Christopher Langman, are just and true in every Particular thereof. And this Deponent saith, That at the Time they were chased by the said Privateers he was present, and did hear Mr. Charles Whitworth (then on board the said Ship, and adjudged Part Owner thereof) say, *That he would rather the said Ship should be lost than obtain her design'd Port in Safety, having made 200 £. Insurance.* And this Deponent saith, *That the said John Dean at the same time declared, That his Brother Jasper Dean had made 300 £. Insurance;* and immediately after said, *If he thought he could secure the Insurance, he would run the Ship on Shore;* and upon the same order'd this Deponent to hoist the Boat over the Side of the Ship, which done, the said John Dean put therein all his valuable Effects, with a Design to run the said Ship on Shore, but was prevented by the Deponent Christopher Langman, by whose Assistance the said Ship arrived at her Port of Killybags, and having reloaded departed for Boston in New England, upon which Coast making the Land, the Deponent being on the Watch, call'd up the said John Dean, and told him there was Land just to the Leeward of them, and the Deponent Christopher Langman being call'd up also, desired the said Ship might be put off from the Shore, which the said John Dean refus'd *if she went to the Bottom;* and for the said Langman's Advice threatned to fetch up a Pistol and shoot him, and did go down, and came up behind him and knock'd him down with a Loggerhead, by means whereof he lay dead for several Minutes, and the same Night the said Ship *Nottingham* run ashore upon a desolate Rock, and was stav'd in Pieces: And this Deponent saith, *That if the Ship had missed that Misfortune, she would have run ashore on the Main Land,* which he believes was the Master's Design: And on the said Rock we should have been lost our selves, had not the Mate Langman, who was then bleeding and cutting down the Mast (under God) sav'd our Lives; in which Island the Cook was frozen to Death, and the Carpenter dying next having been reduced to Hunger, the Master skinned him and cut him up, and they eat him, when Two of the Ship's Company went on Shore on a Raft, one of which was never heard of, the other was found dead in the Woods, by which means the Country understanding a Wreck, came off with a Shallop, whereby they had a Fire after the 22d Day, with which they broiled the rest of the Man, until the 24th Day after their being arrived on the Island before they were relieved.

Nicholas Mellen.

And the said George White for himself saith, That on the 7th of August, 1710, they departed with the said Ship *Nottingham* from the Nore, on the Voyage to Killybags and New England, that in Prosecution of the voyage on the 21st Day of August, in the Year aforesaid, there appear'd off the Coast of Ireland two Ships to the Leeward, to which the said John Dean would have bore down, but that the Deponent Langman and the Men believ'd they were Privateers, and advis'd to the contrary, and would not consent to his bearing down. And this Deponent saith, That Mr. Charles Whitworth, then on board the said Ship, and said to be a Part Owner thereof, declared, That he had rather be taken than not; and the next Day the said Master John Dean would have run the said Ship *Nottingham* on Shore, provided he thought the Insurance would be paid, and then declared his Brother had 300 £. assured, and Mr. Whitworth 200 £. assured, and so put out some Goods into the Board (which was then in the Tackle) to save, altho the Deponent Langman and the Men declared the said Ship was within so small a way of her Port, and might escape, which she did accordingly. That after her departure from Killybags, when she came on the Banks of Newfoundland was chased by the *Pompey*, Captain Den, at which the said John Dean and Mr. Whitworth seem'd to rejoice, believing him a Privateer; but proving otherwise, they appeared disappointed. That when they came on the Coast of New England, falling in with Cape Porpus, the Mate and the men declared that it was not convenient to stand in the Shore, but to bear away to the Southward. That upon some Words arising John Dean with a Perriwig Block struck the Mate Christopher Langman Three Blows on the Head, which made him lie bleeding. That the same Day the said Ship *Nottingham* was run ashore upon a most desolate Island, call'd Boon Island, (which had they miss'd they must have run ashore on the main Land in a few Hours, which makes this Deponent believe in his Conscience the said Ship was designed to be lost) where the Men had been lost had not the Mate, who was then bleeding, came on Deck, and the Mast being cut down, under God saved their Lives. In which Island one of their Company, being the Cook, died, and the Carpenter dying next, they being reduced to Hunger, eat him, when Two of the Ship's Company went on Shore with a small Rafter, one was never heard of, the other was found dead in the Woods, by which the Country understanding a Wreck, came off with a Canoe, whereby they had Fire after the 22d Day, by which they broil'd the rest of the Man until the 24th Day after their being on the Island before relieved.

GEORGE WHITE.

Predict. Depon.
Christopher Langman,
Nicholas Mellen, and
Geo. White, Jurat.
fuerunt *1st Die Aug.*
Anno Dom. 1711.
Coram me,
W. WITHERS.

FINIS.

The John Deane Account (Revis'd)

A Narrative of the Shipwreck of the Nottingham Galley, *&c.
Publish'd in 1711.
Revis'd, and re-printed with Additions in 1726, by John Deane, Commander.*

The *Nottingham Galley*, off, and from London, 120 Tons, 10 Guns, and 14 Men, having taken in part of her Loading in England, and part in Ireland, sail'd, on a Trading Voyage, for Boston in New-England the 25th of September, 1710; but meeting with contrary Winds and bad Weather, they discried not the Land of New England, then cover'd with Snow, 'till the 11th of December following; and then, in a Quarter of an Hour, lost sight of it again by the Fogs and hazey Weather, that had prevented their taking an Observation for 10 or 12 Days before; which with the unaccountable Currents here met with, they could not, with certainty, determine what Part of the Coast they had seen: however, the Wind being N.E. and the Land lying N.E. and S.W. they concluded it both Safe and Adviseable to steer S.W. 'till 10 a Clock at Night, and then lie by 'till the Morning, with the Head of their Vessel off from the Land. As it blew hard, accompanied with Rain and Snow, they carried but little sail; and about 8 or 9 at Night, the Mate being slightly indisposed, the Master, upon deck, going forward, saw to his infinite sirprize, the Breakers a-head very near them; and instantly called out to the Steerman, to put the Helm hard a Starboard, was so ill obey'd in the sudden astonishment, as to have the very reverse perform'd' tho', had it been otherwise, they were too near to avoid the impending Danger; so the Ship struck, with great Violence, against a Rock call'd Bonne Island, about 7 Leagues Eastward from the Mouth of Piscataqua River. The Night was so dark that they could discern no Land; and the Sea running very high, soon heav'd the Vessel along side of the Rock, where, still continuing to make a free Pissage over them, and the Ship therewith excessively labouring, they could no longer keep the Decks; and therefore the Master calling down all Hands, spent a few Minutes in the Cabbin in earnestly supplicating Mercy; and then, exhorting one and all to use their utmost Efforts to cut the Masts by the Board, he re-ascended the Deck with such as had Presence of Mind to assist him, and cutting the weather-most Shrouds, the Fury of the Winds and Seas, with the violent Agitation of the Ship, soon broke the Masts, and they fortunately fell right towards the Rock.

As they could only perceive something black a-head, without being certain whether Land or Rock, the Master perswaded the Mate, and two others, all good Swimmers, to quite the Wreck, and make the first Essay to recover Land, in Order to give Intelligence of the best Place of Landing for the rest of the Ship's Company, if Providence should favour their Escape.

At this Juncture, the Master went down into the Cabin to secure some Money and Papers that might be of Service, in Case he sav'd his Life; and having first furnish'd himself with a Flint, Steel, and a little Gun-powder, just as he open'd the Box, wherein the Money and Papers lay, the Ship bulging, her Stern sunk into deeper Water, and with much Difficulty he regain'd the Fore-part of the Vessel, where hearing nothing from the first Adventurers, he concluded them lost; however, being under a Necessity of making the like Attempt, he threw off his Cloaths to his Waistcoat, and without either Wig or Cap, cast himself, with all his might, from the Wreck, seconding the Motion of the Sea towards the Rock; and lighting unexpectedly on the Fore-mast and Rigging that lay in the Water, he mov'd gradually forward betwixt every Sea, 'till he touch'd the Rock with his Foot; and yet the Mast proving too short, and the Rock exeeding slippery, he was obliged once more to commit himself to the Mercy of that Element, which heav'd him with such Violence against the craggy Point of the Rock, as bruised his Body, and tore his Hands miserably; and, upon the Recess of the Wave, he was carried off again into the Sea: By this Time his Strength was near exhausted, and he had taken in much Water, yet preserving the Use of his Reason, and being, upon the next Elevation of the Sea, tost upon a more eminent Part of the Rock, and catching hold thereof with such impetuous Force, as tore off the Flesh and Nails of his Fingers, he prevented his being wash'd off again, and crept up into a Place of Security, before the next Revolution of the Sea. After a little Recovery of himself, and some Discharge of Salt-water; the Master gave Assistance to the rest of the People, who, with much less Difficulty, got safe on Shore at a more commodious Place of the Rock. Ascending a little higher, they heard the three Men that first escaped to Land; and by 10 being assembled together, they, with joyful Hearts, return'd their most humble Thanks to Divine Providence for their miraculous Deliverance from so imminent a Danger.

They then sought Shelter, to the Leeward of the Island, from the extremity of the Cold, Snow, and Rain, but found it a mere Rock, without a Shovel full of Earth, and destitute of the Growth of a single Shrub, besides, so small and inconsiderable, as not to exceed 100 Yards in length, and 50 in Breadth at high water; and withal so craggy, as not to admit of their Walking to keep themselves Warm. In this disconsolate Condition they spent the first miserable Night.

At Appearance of Day-light the Master went to the Place of the Wreck, proposing to find Provisions, either in the Remainder of the Ship, or in the Concavities of the Rock, but was amazed to see only a few odd Things, with some Plank, Timber, and Canvas, drove on Shore, but nothing eatable, except a few Fragments of Cheese, beaten into uncouth Forms by the violent Dashing of the Sea against the Rock; this, being carefully collected, might amount, in the whole, to the Quantity of three small Cheeses, and, at some Distance, lay the broken Pieces of the masts and Yards, with some torn Sails and Cordage, all intangled in the Cables, and restrain'd by the Anchors from being driven away, yet kept moving with the Sea, at present out of their Reach.

Fire becoming their next necessary Care, on Account of the West and cold: They fought to procure this Blessing by a Variety of Means, as Flint, Steel, and Gunpowder, and afterwards by a Drill of very swift Motion, but all the Materials in their Possession naturally susceptible of Fire, being, on this Occasion, throughly Water soak'd, after 8 or 10 Days unsuccessful Labeur, they gave over the fruitless Attempt.

The second Night they stow'd, one upon another, under the Canvas, in the best Manner they could Devise to keep each other warm. And the following Day, the Weather clearing up, and inclining to Frost, the Master, seeing the nearest Part of the Main Land, knew it to be Cape Neddock; and from thence took Occasion of encouraging his People with Hopes of being discover'd by Fishing Shallops, or other Vessels occasionally passing that Way; altho' all the while, he was conscious to himself, that rarely any Thing of this Kind happen'd at that unseasonable Time of the Year; however, he thought it good Policy to put the Best Face on the Matter, and take this Advantage of their Ignorance and Credulity; since he already too plainly observ'd their great Dejection, and frequent Relapses into an utter Distrust of Divine Providence.

As, after a Shipwreck, all Discipline and Command ceases, and all are reduc'd to a State of Equality; so the late Master perceiving some refusing to give Assistance even when required in necessary Matters, he purposely withdrew from the Society, under Pretence of collecting Materials for future Use, in Order to give them a fair Opportunity of freely electing an Head, or Chief Commander; but, returning one Evening, he was inform'd by the People, that they had invested him with the same full Powers of issuing all Orders, and Punishing any in Case of Disobedience, as before on board the Ship; and this they had enforced with the stronger Sanction, in Regard to some Opposition made by the Mate and two others, against the Master's any longer enjoying the Supreme Command. And from this Time forward, the Master exercis'd some Authority; but not 'till he had consulted the Body, if in any Affair of Importance.

It will scarce meet with Credit to report how much the Impression of their Misfortunes had impair'd their Memories in so short a Space of time, so that they divided in Opinion concerning the number of Days they had been on that unfortunate Island; the Consequence whereof was, they kept two Christmas-days that Year, and two Sundays every Week, 'till Providence sent the Vessel for their Relief. About the 3d, or 4th Day, our Cook, unused to the Hardships of a Sea-faring Life, complain'd of a violent Illness, which appear'd but too visibly in his Countenance; he was lodg'd with two or three others, the most infirm, and died about Noon. They placed the Corps near Low-water-mark, and the flowing Tide carried it away; none so much as hinting to reserve it for Sustenance; tho' several afterwards confess'd, they had Thoughts of appropriating it to that Use. They as yet retain'd some Sense of Humanity, being hitherto Strangers to the exquisite Torture of excessive Hunger, they receiving the Cheese divided into equal Shares, about half a Pound a Man each Day, as the casting of Lots decided; so that the Master, who, by working very hard, when the Weather permitted, exhausted his Spirits, and render'd his Appetite more importunate, had not the least Particle more than such as gave no Manner of Assistance; however, he reap'd one Benefit, for maintaining of Warmth by Action, preserv'd a due Circulation of Blood, imparting a benign Influence to his whole System; whereas a severe Frost setting in with Extremity of Cold, so benumb'd and discolour'd the Hands and Feet of the Unactive, as render'd them, in a Manner, Useless and past sense of Feeling, not without Danger of Mortification. And such as had quitted the Wreck with Boots on, had Blisters on their Legs to such a Degree, that the Skin came off, with the Nails of their toes: All this still aggravated the Master's Care and Toil, who daily dress'd their Ulcers, and Washing them in Urine, or Salt-water, bound them up in clean Rags, supplied from two Pieces of Linnen, amongst other Things, driven on Shore; and, every Evening, they all of them wrapp'd up their Legs in large swathing Bands of Oakum, pick'd and dried for that Purpose.

Their first Enterprize of Moment, was the erecting of a Tent, in a triangular Form, about 8 or 9 Foot in Diameter, cover'd with Sails and old Canvas, and strow'd with pick'd Oakum for Bedding; it was only Capacious enough to receive them all, lying down sideways, so that no Man could turn himself without the general Concurrence. This occasioning some Disputes, was referr'd to the Master's Appointment, who, usually, once in two Hours perform'd it, upon publick Notice given. On the Top of the Tent a Staff was fix'd, on which, as the Weather presented, was hoisted up a Piece of white Cloth, in the Form of a Flag, in view of discovering themselves to any Vessel that accidentally should pass that Way.

The next Undertaking, was the Building of a Boat out of Timber and Plank extracted from the Wreck; having for Tools the Blade of a Cutlash, made into a Saw with their Knives, an Hammer, and a Caulking-Mallet: Some Nails they found in the Clefts of the Rock, and others they drew out of the Sheathing: Three Planks were laid flat for the Bottom, and two up each Side, fix'd to Stanchings, and let into the bottom Timbers, with two short Pieces at each End, and one Breadth of new Holland's-Duck round the Vessel, to keep out the Spray of the Sea; they caulk'd her with Oakum, drawn from old Junk; and secur'd the Seames with Canvas, Pump-leather, and Sheet-lead, as far as the extent of their small Stock would allow; a short Mast was fix'd, with a square Sail; seven Paddles provided for Rowing, and an eight, longer than ordinary, for Steering: All this was accomplished whilst their Carpenter, thro' a violent Indisposition, was utterly incapacitated from giving his necessary Assistance, almost his Advice; and the Rest so enfeebled and dispirited, that only the Master and two more, could engage in dispatching the Work; and the Rigour of the Season was so extreme, that they could rarely attend it above four Hours in a Day, and sometimes do nothing at all.

They had now been upwards of a Week without any kind of Sustenance, except the Cheese above mention'd, and the Bones of three Pieces of Beef, render'd eatable by Pounding on the Rock, whose Flesh the Fish and Salt-water had almost intirely consum'd; when, at several Leagues distance, they saw three Boats under sail, to their great Rejoicing in Hopes of Deliverance: All crept out of the Tent, and hollow'd as loud as possible, making every imaginable Signal, but all in vain, for they neither heard, or discover'd them. Notwithstanding, from hence they drew Matter of Encouragement; inferring, that as the Wind was N.E. at the Time they were cast away, so Part of the Wreck being driven on the opposite Shore, might discover their Distress, and induce these Vessels from the S.W. to come out in quest of them, which they might continue to do, as oft as fair Weather presented. Their earnest Desire of Deliverance guil'd them into a Belief of this agreeable Delusion; and, tho' the Event discover'd its Fallacy, yet it serv'd, for a while, to amuse a Despair, that vastly aggravated their lamentable Condition.

When they had almost finish'd their Boat, one Day, at low Water, they found the Carpenter's Ax cast upon the Rock of the Sea, and with it completed the Work. It was then consulted, who should adventure in her to get on Shore. The Master, offering to be one, was universally approv'd of; as being, thro' Health and Strength, best able to go through all Extremities; the Mate, the Master's Brother, and four others agreed to accompany him; and then recommending the Enterprize to the Guidance of Divine Providence, all that were capable, assisting with their joint Endeavours, haul'd their ill-made, patch'd up Boat, with infinite Difficulty, to the Water-side: This was on, or about, the 21st of December, being a fine Day, and the Water smoother than usual, yet the Surf running high, oblig'd them to wade very deep to launch her, and as soon as the Master and one more were got in, the Swell of the Sea, in spight of all their Resistance, heav'd the Boat along Shore, and overset her upon them, whereby she was stav'd to pieces, and they narrowly escap'd Drowning; with her were also lost both Ax and Hammer, Instruments that might have been of singular Use to assist them in their last Expedient of Building a Raft. This Disappointment immensely heighten'd their Afflicions, by intirely ruining all future Prospect and Projects of Deliverance; and yet that very afternoon, they had final Reason to adore the Infinite Goodness of God, graciously ordaining this Event for their Safety; for the Wind springing up, blew a Storm, and had they been at sea in that paltry Resemblance of a Boat, they must, humanly speaking, have unavoidably gone to the Bottom, whilst those left behind, through Inability to provide for themselves, would have run an extreme Risque of sharing in a yet more deplorable Fate.

And now again return'd with redoubled Impetuosity, all the Fears and Despair that had been a while suspended; during the mighty Expectations they had form'd from their Boat; and, in Truth, they were reduced to the most melancholick and miserable Circumstances. No Fire, and the Weather extreme Cold; their Hands and Feet frozen to a Degree of Mortification; several with large deep Ulcers, very offensive to the Smell, without any Plaister, save a Linnen-rag to wrap them into. The small Stock of Cheese spent, and nothing left to support their perishing Bodies, except Kelp, a Rockweed growing under Water, and Muscles so difficult to get, as not to allow, at most, above three a Day for each Man; in the mean Time, it became the Master's unavoidable Province, to cleanse and dress their Wounds, and procure these sorry Viands for their Sustenance; scarce a Man besides being in a Condition so much as to help himself; and, to all this, add but a too well grounded Apprehension of inevitably perishing in the next Spring-tide, if accompanied with high Winds, the Sea, at such a Crisis, overflowing the Rock. This was their State, pinch'd with Cold and Hunger, Groaning under the Extremity of Weakness and Pain, with Torture and Horror of Conscience, under a Foresight of a certain, painful, but dubious, whether sudden, or lingering, Death, without any, even, remote View of Deliverance, so that the Sufferers themselves, at any Distance of Time, cannot possibly revive in their Minds an adequate Idea of this Misery.

As it pleased God to indulge the Master in a greater Share of Health and Strength of Body, and likewise a proportionate Vigour of Mind; so he continually endeavour'd to instill into the

Hearts of the dispirited People a Reliance on that Almighty Being, who is not confin'd to particular Means, nor always acts according to Human Probabilities. At the Time of quitting the Wreck, nothing but immediate Death was in View; but after their escape to the Rock, he grew more Sanguine, and scarce ever was without a secret Perswasion of Deliverance. This buoy'd up his Spirits, and enabled him, amidst so many Discouragements, to provide Rockweed and Muscles, to attend the Sick and Diseased; and, in many laborious Instances, pursue the Good of every Individual. But his frequent Exhortations to wait with Patience the appointed Time of divine Salvation avail'd nothing, since he could not possibly assign any particular Medium of Rescue, that probably might take Place in so short a Space of Time, as they had a Prospect of continuing their Lives in their present Indigence of all Things; and, indeed, when Reason only presided, he was oblig'd to give up the Point in Dispute, and pronounc'd them arriv'd at the highest degree of Calamity.

In this Conflict of Afflictions, as a dawning of Hope to alleviate their Distress, it pleased God that the Mate should strike down a Seagull, which he brought with Joy; and the Master equally dividing, though raw, and scarce every Man a Mouthful, yet was gladly receiv'd, and eaten with great Thankfulness.

And now, as the last Resource of Hope, they began to resolve upon composing a Raft, capable of bearing two Men; a Project all along mightily urged by a Swede, a stout, brave Fellow, that had unhappily lost the Use of both his Feet by the Frost since he came upon the Rock; and here again open'd a new Scene of Labour and Difficulty, to build this without Tools, and, almost, without Hands; however, at length, after abundance of Toil in clearing the Fore-yard from Junk, they split it in the midst, and constituting the two Parts for Side-pieces, twelve Foot long, interfix'd Spars, cover'd with the lightest Plank, four Foot broad, first Spiking, and then Seizing them firm; a short Mast was also fix'd, with a Sail made of two Hammocks driven on Shore, a Paddle was likewise provided for each Man, and a spare one made fast to the Raft in Case of Necessity. During the 5 or 6 Day's Time, wherein this Work was completeing, the Swede frequently importun'd the Master to accompany him in the attempt; yet giving him to understand, that if he refus'd, another was ready to embrace the Offer. The Master, deliberately weighing the Difficulties of the Adventure, judg'd them, rationally speaking, unsurmountable; considering, that Persons already so much reduc'd, must, in so severe a Season, set up to the Waist in Water 10 or 12 Hours at least, with the utmost Favour of Wind, Tide and Weather, and therefore resolv'd to decline it; but, out of Prudence, concel'd his Reasons and Resolutions, 'till Opportunity presented to put the Design in execution.

At this time they saw a Sail coming out of Piscataqua River, about 7 Leagues to the Westward, to whom they endeavour'd to manifest themselves by all possible Devices; but the Wind being N.W. and the Ships standing to the Eastward, was presently out of Sight, to a Renewal of their Mortification.

The next being a moderate Day, and a small Breeze of Wind in the Afternoon fitting right on Shore, and the Raft now intirely finish'd, the Swede, and his Companion, that desir'd to go upon the Master's Refusal; were very sollicitous to have the Raft launch'd, in order to pursue their, Enterprize; the Mate, on the contrary, as strenuously opposing it, in regard to its being so late as two in the Afternoon; but they replying, it was full Moon, and light Nights; and redoubling their Entreaties, extorted the Master's Consent. First, then with earnest Prayers committing them and their Design to the Divine Blessings, afterwards they launch'd the Raft, and both of them being placed upon it, the Swell of the Sea going high, maugre all their Endeavours, overset the Raft, as heretofore the Boat, and away went the Mast and

Sail; the Swede, being an excellent Swimmer, soon recover'd the Shore, and little regarded it; but the other, unskill'd in that Art, continued a while under Water, and upon his Appearance being dragg'd to Land by the Master, was too much discouraged to make a second Essay. The Master then desir'd the Swede to assist in getting the Raft out of the Water, in Order to wait a more favourable Opportunity; but the Swede, persisting in his Resolution, tho' unable to stand upon his Feet, and, as he was kneeling on the Rock, caught hold on the Master's Hand, and, with much Vehemency, beseeching him to accompany him, said, I am sure I must die; however, I have great Hopes of being the Means of preserving your Life, and the rest of the Peoples; if you will not go with me, I beg your Assistance to turn the Raft, and help me upon it, for I am resolutely bent to venture, even, tho' by myself alone. The Master us'd further Dissuasives, representing the Impossibility of reaching the main Land in twice the Time they might have done before they were disarm'd of their Mast and Sail; but the Swede remain'd inflexible, affirming, with Imprecation, I had rather perish in the Sea, than continue one Day more in this miserable Condition. By this Time another, animated by his Example, offering to go with him, the Master consented, and giving them some Money; that accidentally was in his Pocket, fix'd them on the Raft, and help'd to launch them off from the Rock, committing them to the Mercy of the Seas, under the Care of Divine Providence. Their last Words at parting were very Moving, and deliver'd in a Pathetic Accent: Pray Sir oblige all the People to join in Prayers for us as long as you can see us. All to a Man crept out of the Tent at this doleful Separation, and perform'd their request with much Devotion. About Sun-set they judg'd them half Way to Land, and hop'd they might gain the Shore by two in the Morning; but in the Night the Wind blew very hard, and two days after the Raft was found on Shore, about a Mile distant from the other Man, having his Paddle still fast to his Waist, but so much worn, as shew'd he had labour'd hard, but the bold Swede was never seen more.

The Master had appointed these Adventurers to procure a Fire be made in the Woods, on a certain Hill, within Ken of this desolate Island; as a Signal of their getting alive on Shore, and the other expeditious Relief, and two Days after a Smoke arising from that Quarter, and daily continuing, tho' upon a different Occasion, was yet, with Reason, interpreted by them as a Token of speedy Deliverance. This Flush of Hope, under God, subserv'd for a Time to support them, accounting for the Delay by the Difficulty of procuring a Vessel, and the Freezing up of the Rivers, common in such an Inclemency of this Season of the Year; but, at last, Famine, deaf to all Remonstrances, began a new to excite Impatience.

The Spring Tide, so justly dreaded, was now, God be thanked, safely over; however, one Inconvenience follow'd; the Waters, not falling so low as before, depriv'd 'em, in a good Measure, of the Advantage of taking Muscles, a principal Branch of their daily Aliment. This irksome Employment, others refusing, fell to the Master's Lot, who ran a great Hazard of losing both Hands and Arms by so frequently exposing them in the cold Water, altho, when taken, his Stomach rejected them as offensive thro' excessive Coldness, preferring Rockweed, of much easier Digestion, yet, either the Quality of the Herb, or the Effects of Hunger, render'd the Eaters very Costive. At their first Arrival they saw, and even stumbled upon, several Seals on the Rock; the Master thence inferring, it was their nightly Harbour, took frequent Walks at Midnight in View of intercepting them, but they had intirely forsaken the Island. Multitudes of Sea-Fowl also appear'd, but observing Men daily there, refus'd to lodge on the Rock.

Their Necessities, in Regard to fresh Water, were indifferently well supplied all the Time by Rain, and melted Snow, lodging in the concavities of the highest Part of the Rock, though the Taste was something brackish by the Spray of the Sea, at Spring-tides, breaking over it, tho' God, of his infinite Mercy, by restraining the High Winds, prevented a total Inundation. During the Frost they preferr'd the eating of Ice, which is fresh, though congel'd from Salt-water; this the Master brought in great Lumps to the Side of the Tent, and every Man took what he pleased. They drank their Water out of a Powder-horn, and applied another to the Use of the diseased in the Tent.

At this Time the Master set the Infirm, and otherwise useless Hands, to open Junk, and with the Rope Yarn, drawn from thence, thatch'd the Tent, according to the best of his Skill in that science; this serv'd to turn off 2 or 3 Hours Rain, and skreen them, from the Asperities of the cold cutting Winds. Of this Oakum likewise the Master made Swathing Bands, in which he swath'd up himself at Night, when he threw off his wet Cloaths, and obliging his Boy, swath'd in the same Manner, to lie upon him; this Device contributed much to the Conservation of his Health.

About the latter End of December, the Carpenter, a fat Man, naturally of a dull, heavy, phlegmatic Constitution, and aged about 47; always very Ill from his first coming on Shore, and had since lost the Use of his Feet, now, in particular, complain'd of an excessive Pain in his Back, and stiffness in his Neck; and, moreover, was almost suffocated with an Inundation of Phlegm. He soon grew Speech'less tho' retaining his Senses, and drawing near to his End, in all Apprehension, they pray'd over him; and in all Things, to the Best of their Power, were serviceable to him in his last Moments. Dying that Night, his Body remain'd in the Tent 'till the Morning, when the Master, as usual, going out in quest of Provisions, order'd the People to remove the Corps to some distance. Finding Part of a green Hide, fasten'd to a Piece of the Main yard, newly thrown up by the Sea; he first endeavour'd to eat it, but his Teeth made no Impression; at Noon returning, the Men importuned him to bring it into the Tent, and mincing it small, it was soon swallow'd down with a voracious Appetite. The Master, then observing the Carcass not carried off, began to expostulate warmly, demanding the Reason of their Disobedience: They excus'd themselves on the Score of Inability; he, imputing this to their Want of Spirit and Resolution, already the Cause of much Chagrin and Fatigue to him, and Mischief to themselves; he gave them a Rope, bidding them, make it Fast to the Corps, and his Spirits being still in a Ferment, he essay'd to draw it out himself, but was soon convinc'd of the Decay of his Strength, by not being able to stir it: Another however assisting, the dead Body, at length, was haul'd a few Paces from the Tent. The Master, afterwards, returning into the Tent, with his Powers enervated by this violent Exertion of himself, and his Mind oppressed with the most acute Sense of the various Miseries they were involv'd in, occasionally reinforced by the present melancholic Instance, was ready to expire with Faintness and Anguish; and placing himself so as to receive some Refreshment by Sleep, he observ'd an unusual Air of Intentness in the Countenances of all the People, when, after some Pause, Mr. Whitworth, a young Gentleman, his Mother's darling Son, delicately educated, amidst so great an Affluence, as to despite common Food, as he then, with Remorse of Conscience, acknowledg'd, began, in the Name of the Assembly, to court the Master's Concurrence in converting the Humane Carcase into the Matter of their Nourishment; and was immediately seconded by a great Majority, three only opposing, on account of their esteeming it a heinous Sin. This affair had been thus consulted, and concluded upon in the Master's Absence, and the present Method concerted of making it known by a Gentleman reputed to be much in his Favour. The Master remain'd in his former

Posture, observing an invincible Silence, whilst they were urging their Desires with irresistible Vehemence, for nothing that ever befel him from the Day of his Birth, no not the Dread and Distress of his Soul upon quitting the Wreck, when he did not expect to live a Minute, was so amazingly Shocking as this unexpected Proposal; but, after a short Interval, resuming his Reason, and concealing his infirmity for Decency Sake, he maturely weighing all Circumstances, pronounc'd in Favour of the Majority, arguing the Improbability of its being a Sin to eat Humane Flesh in a Case of such necessity, provided they were no ways accessary to the taking away of Life. The Master then acquiesing, on Condition of throwing into the Sea the Skin, and all parts discovering it to be Humane; and receiving from Time to Time their respective Portions, according to his Prescription, the People appear'd in a Transport of Joy; but all to a Man excused themselves from engaging in so odious a Work; alledging their Inability of abiding so long in the Cold, and therefore most humbly implor'd the Continuance of his good Offices, even in this very disagreeable Instance. The Master took this extremely ill, and refus'd a good while to comply; but, at last, their incessant Prayers and Tears prevail'd, and by close of the Day, with another's Assistance, he had dispatch'd this very nauseous and difficult Task. A few thin Slices, wash'd in Salt-water, were brought into the Tent, and given to every one, with a good Quantity of Rockweed to supply the Place of Bread. The First the Master eat, was Part of the Grissels that compose the Breast, having the Flesh scraped clean off, for his Stomach, as yet, abominated the loathsome Diet, though his importunate Appetite had, more than once, led him to survey with a longing Even the Extremities of his fore Fingers, and a Day or two before compell'd him to taste his own Excrements. The Mate, and the two other Opposers, refus'd to partake of the Flesh that Night, but were the first next Morning to beg an equal Share in the common

Allowance. The Mater, to prevent Dispute, distributed it by Lot, with the utmost Impartiality; and to take off any Aversion, enjoin'd them to call it Beef; tho' this last Precaution was needless, since they devour'd it in a rapacious Manner, and crav'd greater Quantities than consisted with health, and the Extent of their small Stock; and, in a few Days, Lame and Infirm as they were, he found himself oblig'd to remove the Pieces and Quarters to a craggy Eminency of difficult Access, as likewise to hold a stricter Hand, and exercise all the Authority he had taken at their Request, over them, which their present Impotence, and his comparative Strength, empower'd him to maintain; for on a sudden, he perceiv'd an Alteration on their Dispositions, infinitely to the worse, from a quiet, peaceable, affectionate Temper, a resign'd, submissive, religious Frame of Mind; the Majority grew fierce, brutish, barbarous, Impatient in their Afflictions, and Refractory to Command, using ill Language, Oaths and Imprecations, so that the Master almost repented he had not turn'd the dead Carcass adrift in the Sea, instead of reserving it for Food, since attended with such detestable Effects; however, this Deportment convinc'd him of the absolute Necessity of keeping a strick Watch over the Remainder of the Body, since he had Reason to apprehend future Want would drive them to sacrifice one another's Lives to their inexorable Hunger, and the Prolongation of their miseries a few Days would infallibly have terminated in this dreadful Event. This Nutriment had also an ill Effect upon their Ulcers and Sores, endangering a Mortification more than ever; and herein the Master incurr'd as great a Risque as any, having the Ends of his Fingers torn, and his Nails dislocated, on his first Recovering the Rock, and they had ever since been constantly employ'd in Building the Tent, Boat, and Raft, and a daily Acquisition of Victuals, without either Ease of Medicine to supple and heal them. To remedy this Inconvenience, the Master tried an Experiment of his own Conception, that sufficiently answer'd the Intention, *viz.* He applied Plaisterwise to the distemper'd Part, first cleansed and wash'd in Salt-water, the Fat taken off from the Kidneys of the Deceased, reduc'd to a proper Consistence, by working it with a Stone on a smooth Place of the Rock; and this proved a cooling, mollifying Medicament, giving much Ease to the Patient, and, peradventure, from something of this kind, improved by the Hands of the Learned, may be prepar'd an excellent Digestive.

The Close of the old Year left them in a most forlorn Condition; the Master's Brother attack'd with Convulsive Fits, and frozen in several Fingers; Mr. Whitworth, his Friend, in both his Feet, so that he oft, express'd himself willing to compound for Life with the Loss of a Limb, the Master, through Sympathy with them, and Concern at the ill Success of every Enterprize for Deliverance, together with the daily Care and Fatigue unavoidably revolving upon him, became diminish'd in his Strength, and dissipated in the Faith and Resolution of his Mind; the rest of the People, half frozen, more than half famish'd, distemper'd, ulcerous, dispairing, unable to help themselves; yet Murmuring, Prophane, and Blasphemous. In a Word, labouring under a Complication of the greatest Evils, Cold, Diseases, Famine, Prospect of Death, and Dread of Damnation.

But the Almighty, whose Mercies endure for ever, was graciously pleas'd to extend his undeserv'd Favour, for on the 2d of January, in the Morning, as the Master was creeping out of the Tent, he saw a Shallop half Way from Shore, standing directly towards the Rock, under a brisk Gale of Wind, and immediately crying out, a Sail, a Sail, unable to utter more thro' an Ecstacy of Joy; not a Soul amoungst them, how Weak and Infirm soever, but instantly thrust out his Head to see so desirable a Sight, and to express the Raptures diffus'd throughout the whole Company, upon the Prospect of so sudden and unexpected a Deliverance, outstrips the Powers of Tongue and Mind; 'twas Life from the

Dead, The Master kept walking on the Rock to direct their Good and Welcome Friends to the properest Anchorage; but they not understanding his Signs, let go in a very indifferent place, about 100 Yards S.W. off the Island, the Swell of the Sea not permitting a nearer Approach, their Anchor coming Home, they were obliged to weigh, and stand off 'till Noon, in Expectation of smoother Weather on the Flood; in the mean Time the weak and disorder'd Minds of the poor Creatures on the Rock were strangely hurry'd with fluctuating Passions, thro' Fears of Miscarriage, and Hopes of Deliverance.

At Flood the Vessel coming nigh, cast Anchor by the Master's Directions in a commodious Place, within Call of the Island; where the Master gave them an Account of their Miseries in every Respect, except the Want of Provisions; concealing this, least an Apprehension of being constrain'd to abide on the Rock, thro' any Extremity of Weather should deter them from coming on Shore to their Assistance: observing also, they were unprovided of a proper Boat to carry them off, he earnestly requested them to furnish him with Fire, if they could not possibly accomplish their immediate Deliverance, Hoisting but a small Canoe, one Man came off, and gaining the Rock with Abundance of Difficulty, the Master assisted to haul the Boat on Shore, and perceiving no Eatables therein, enquir'd of the Man, If he could help him to Fire? He reply'd in the Affirmative, after some Hesitation, occasion'd by his Astonishment at the Master's thin and meagre Aspect. Several other Questions being alternately resolv'd, as, What Day of the Week it was? ie., and, in particular, a Relation made of the Manner of finding the Raft and dead Corps, which mov'd the Government to send them out on the present Design; as they were passing on towards the Tent, the Man casting his Eyes on the Remains of the Flesh, expos'd to the Frost on the Summit of the Rock, express'd his Satisfaction at their not being destitute of Provisions; and the Master acquies'd in the Justice of his Sentiments, without unravelling the Mystery. Arriving at the Tent, he was perfectly affrighted at the ghastly Figure of so many dismal Objects, with long Beards, nothing but Skin and Bone; wild staring Eyes, and Countenances, fierce, barbarous, unwash'd, and infected with Humane Gore. After kindling a Fire, with much Labour, the Master accompany'd the Man to his Boat, intending to go on Board with him, and afterwards fend for the Rest, one or two at a Time, and carry them all off that Night; both getting in, the Sea drove the Canoe with such Force against the Rock, as overset her in the Water, whereby the Master, so greatly reduced in his Strength, was a long while unable to recover himself, and narrowly escap'd Drowning. The good Man, making a second Attempt alone, recover'd the Shallop with Difficulty; having solemnly assur'd them at parting, of coming again the next Day with better Accommodations, if Weather permitted.

Now again, as an Allay to their newly conceiv'd Joy, they beheld their worthy Friends in the Shallop, standing away from the Shore without them; but the infinitely Wise and Good God, whose sole Prerogative it is to appoint the Time, as well as Means, of Man's Deliverance, by frustrating the present Appearance, effectually secur'd the Accomplishment of their Preservation, for the Wind coming about to S.E. blew very hard, and the Night proving exceeding Dark, the Vessel was stranded in returning, and the Men, with much Hazard, escaped to the Main Land; but had these helpless Wretches been there, they must have perish'd in all probability. Immediately upon their Landing, an Express was sent to Portsmouth, on Piscataqua River, and the good People there laid hold on the first fair Weather to hasten to their Relief. In the mean Time, tho' they had Reason to believe their Condition known, and therefore to expect a speedy Assistance; yet their Flesh being near spent, the next Day proving Stormy, and the Uncertainty of such bad

Weather's Continuance, all serv'd to revive their Griefs, and exercise their Patience; however, the Misery of their Circumstances was much allieviated by the Advantage of Fire to keep them warm, and broil their Meat, from thence assuming a much more Savoury Relish.

The Fire was made in the middle of the Tent, and hemm'd in with Stones to prevent its Excursion; the Fewel-Ropes cut into short Lengths, and brought up to the Tent by the Master. At the first making of the Fire, no Vent being contriv'd for the Smoke, the People were almost suffocated, several Fainting away, and others grew extreme Sick; but an opening being made in the Top of the Tent, the ill Effect ceased. A Constant Watch of two at a Time, continually attended the Fire; and were statedly relieved every two Hours, tho' subject to some Inequality, being reckon'd by Computation.

The Men now urg'd the Master, to enlarge their Allowance of Flesh; and he in part comply'd but not to their Satisfaction: in the night, as he lay amongst the People, asleep to all appearance, he overheard the Two that had the Watch, whispering with something of an earnest Accent; and soon after perceiv'd One creep out of the Tent, and e're long returning with a Part of their small Stock, tho' the Flesh lay at a considerable Distance; the Rock was rough and uneven, and this very fellow for some Time past, especially when any thing was commanded to be done, had no other way of moving but on his Hands and Knees; as they were busie in broiling their Purchase, the Master suddenly starting up, seiz'd it, and forthwith acquainting the whole Company, it was proposed to inflict an exemplary Punishment, but as the Case then stood, they came off with a severe Reprimand.

And now when they came to [so] low an Ebb in the Article of Provisions, that the whole Remainder of the Flesh was allotted for the next Repast; as it pleas'd God, the Wind abated in the

Night of the 3d of January, and early on the 4th in the Morning, whilst at their Devotions, they were agreeably surpriz'd at the Report of a Musquet, and looking out, saw a Shallop near the Rock. They came to an Anchor, and having a good Canoe, the Master's much esteemed Friends, William Long of Old-England and Jethro Furber of New-England, both Masters of Ships, with three others, soon came on Shore, the Master standing at the Waterside to receive and welcome them to that desolate island. After first Salutations past, and learning the summary State of their Case, having look'd about as far as Curiosity prompted, they first took the Master on board of the Shallop, and then, being very brisk, strong Men, brought the rest, two or three at a time, most of them on their Backs, from the Tent to the Canoe, tho' none of them were free from Vermin; and in two Hours time they were all on board to their Worthy Friends Satisfaction, and their own inexpressible Joy. The first Sustenance they received, was a bit of Bread and a dram of Rum each, and soon after a Mess of Water-Gruel every one, prepar'd in sufficient Quantity by a charitable Gentlewoman, whose Husband own'd the Shallop, and this was excellently accommodated to their Condition, and prov'd of Singular Benefit; for the Wind being contrary, and blowing a Gale, they were obliged to carry much Sail, which rendered the poor hunger-starved Wretches extremely Sea-sick; and the Water-Gruel promoting a Facilitie in vomiting, serv'd to cleanse their Stomachs, after which they grew excessively hungry and Ravenous.

In the Close of the Evening they got within the Mouth of Piscataqua River; and the Master hir'd a Canoe to carry Mr. Whitworth and himself to their Lodgings at Mr. Furber's with greater Expedition. By eight a-Clock they landed, and the Master being shew'd the House, ran directly in, to the terrible Affrightment of the Gentlewoman and her Children, who took the first Opportunity of making a fair Escape, and left all to his Discretion; and he, tho' emaciated to a Skeleton, yet being in perfect Health, was unmercifully hungry, and therefore taking occasion to rumage the Pot on the First, found the Contents to be Beef and Turnips, resolving thereupon to stand Cook for once; before the Men that row'd them up arriv'd with Mr. Whitworth, whom they were obliged to carry, he had taken up the Turnips and spread on the Table to render them Mouth-meat, and some small Portion he had already secured in his Belly; but the People unacceptably intervening, restrain'd him from eating any more at that time. The Mistress of the Family, learning who they were return'd to the House, and the Master, with his Friend, was put into a Room apart. Soon after, they were visited by Mr. Packer, Practitioner in Physick and Surgery, by especial Order of the Government, whose Administrators, by an Excess of Generosity, had Sent out, that Day, two other Vessels to their Assistance in case of Necessity; and now, in farther Prosecution of the same Pious and Charitable Care, Lodgings, Food, and Nurses were provided for the People, during their infirmity, and Cloaths, Linnen and Woollen, given them upon their Recovery, all at the Publick Expence: and had not their unworthy, intemperate Behavior, plainly evinc'd them to be guilty of In gratitude toward God and Disregard to Man, they were upon the Point of receiving yet farther Instances of their Charity and Christian Compassion. The Gentlemen, most forward in promoting this generous Benevolence towards the Distress'd, were, the ever to be Respected John Plaisied and John Wentworth, Esqrs, to their own considerable private Charge, tho' the Master and Mr. Whitworth, having sufficient Credit, bore their own Expences.

A limited Diet and requisite Purges being Administred, in process of Time all recover'd, tho' every one, excepting the Master, lost the Use of Fingers or Toes, or some other part of his Body; and in particular, the Master's Boy suffer'd the Loss of a Foot. At the first Publication of this Narrative, the Master, the

Mate, and Mr. Whitworth, were all in England; but, in a Course of fifteen Years since, the Master alone survives of all that he particularly knew.

And now, after such an Interval of Time, to do Justice to the Names and Memories of those beneficent Gentlemen, whose admir'd Humanity on this Occasion, deserves Applause and Imitation throughout succeeding Ages; and in order to perpetuate the Remembrance of the Gracious Proceedings of Divine Providence in its admirable Conduct towards them, the Master is making a Provision to have the Annual Commemoration of their Wonderful Deliverance celebrated in New-England, as nearest adjoining to the Principal Scene of Action; and that in such a Manner, as may, with the Divine Blessing, prove of Service to reclaim some of the unthinking Part of his own Fraternity.

FINIS.

II

KENNETH ROBERTS AND *BOON ISLAND*

Kenneth Roberts and *Boon Island*

A Study of Historical and Literary Perception

Jack Bales

Boon Island is located about 14 miles off the coast of Maine, measuring 150 yards by 50 yards. It is so few feet above sea level that every year it is flooded by the spring tides, and in the winter the entire surface is pounded by wind, snow, and freezing rain. The weather and the island's barren desolateness were just two of the conditions that 14 men faced when they were shipwrecked during a snowstorm on December 11, 1710. Ten of them managed to survive and were rescued after living for 24 days on the tiny island. One of the reasons they *did* manage to survive was that on December 28 they decided to eat the ship's carpenter, who had died the day before. The men's struggles, both moral and physical, are the subject of *Boon Island*, Kenneth Roberts's last historical novel, first published by Doubleday in 1956 and reissued in this volume.[1]

Although it is his shortest work and probably the least critically acclaimed, *Boon Island* deserves study for two reasons. (1) As with only a few of his other works, a lack of primary sources on his subject required Roberts to draw from his own imagination many of the events and incidents portrayed, but always within the framework of the existing evidence, and (2) this is the only novel in which Roberts uses symbolism to convey his various themes and ideas.

From the late 1930s to his death in 1957, Kenneth Roberts was one of America's most popular historical novelists, writing such best-sellers as *Northwest Passage*, *Oliver Wiswell*, *Arundel*, and *Rabble in Arms*. A few months before he died, his collective body of work, spanning nearly three decades, earned him a special Pulitzer Prize "for his historical novels which have long contributed to the creation of greater interest in our early American history."

Roberts's novels were not only enjoyable to read but they also had the reputation of being historically accurate. Admittedly, many historians and scholars differ over some of Roberts's conclusions. *Arundel* and *Rabble in Arms* cover the career of Benedict Arnold and his Northern Army, and Roberts steadfastly maintained all his life that Arnold was "the most brilliant soldier of the Revolution," and that all Arnold biographies and studies were "marred by gross unfairness, misplaced patriotism, inexcusable plagiarism, reliance on untrustworthy evidence, a narrow-minded and confused interpretation of facts, slovenly research, loose thinking, atrocious writing and other grave faults."[2]

In August 1937 the headline of a Maine newspaper was emblazoned with the words "Roberts Shocks Portsmouth" after he fervently praised Benedict Arnold during a question-and-answer session, insisting that "you ought to be proud of a country that could produce a fellow like him."[3] According to Roberts, Arnold's so-called treasonous motives stemmed from the commander's conviction that it was better to give the colonies back to England rather than let them, through an incompetent Continental Congress, fall into the hands of France.

Despite Roberts's differences with historians and academicians, however, his works *were* well researched, and he would spend months and often years poring over primary resource material. As he freely admitted, he did this not only to portray events accurately and realistically, but also because he had difficulties working out plot and characterization in his novels. Thus, in his research he was able to obtain story lines from historical events, and his characters from histories and genealogies. With the 1937 *Northwest Passage*, a chronicle of the Colonial Indian fighter Robert Rogers, Roberts succeeded in writing a novel that was an artistic as well as a commercial success, largely because he transcended his usual reliance on printed sources. As he wrote in his notes while planning the book, "I can't do it as straight history (even if I wanted to) because the material is too fragmentary."[4] Consequently, when he found the historical evidence lacking in details, he felt free to elaborate and invent the information he needed, but never in such a way as to contradict the implications of his source materials.

The plot of *Boon Island* can be easily summarized. During a storm on the evening of December 11, 1710, the British ship *Nottingham Galley*, enroute from Greenwich, England, to Portsmouth, New Hampshire, runs aground and is wrecked on Boon Island, a small uninhabited island off the coast of Maine. Although the crew of fourteen manages to scramble safely onto the island, little more than a barren pile of rocks, they have few tools, little food, and no shelter except for a makeshift tent that helps keep out snow and freezing rain. The ship's cook soon dies, and the men set his body adrift in hope that it will wash ashore and draw the attention of would-be rescuers. With their crude tools, they laboriously build a boat, which capsizes soon after they launch it. They then manage to construct a raft, on which two men set out for shore. One of them dies, while the other reaches the mainland but is found frozen to death by two men, who come to Boon Island to investigate. They rescue the remaining ten of the castaways, who have managed to survive for twenty-four days.

As Roberts mentioned during an interview shortly before the book's publication, he had long been familiar with both the island and the famous shipwreck:

> I've thought about that story for a long, long time—thirty years, say. As a boy I used to go fishing out there, so probably it dates back even more. But fooling around with the idea, thirty years.
>
> You'll find the story of Boon Island in footnotes in all Maine histories. They'll keep telling you that you couldn't live twenty-four days on a rock in a Maine winter. These people did. Then I've always wanted to put together a group who had nothing, and see what they'd do.[5]

When Roberts researched his story, the only primary account of the episode he could find was one by *Nottingham Galley* Captain John Dean, which he felt was "a jumbled, garbled, incoherent mass of generalities in which practically no one was named."[6] Seeking corroboration of the details, as well as some sort of focus and "lead" to the story, he asked his cousin in Greenwich, England, the city from which the vessel had sailed, to comb through eighteenth-century records for him. His relative found a narrative written by the ship's mate and two of its sailors that claimed Dean deliberately sank the ship so that he could collect the insurance money on it. This gave Roberts the angle he was looking for:

> Then, by great good fortune, I found a journal of Dean's first mate. The mate was a liar and a coward. He hated Dean with an abysmal hatred; accused Dean of all sorts of impossible things; but both of these two men, hating each other, agreed in their essential details, so that I knew the Nottingham had been wrecked on Boon Island on a certain date, and that the crew had lived under impossible conditions for 24 days.[7]

Roberts, then, wrote *Boon Island* as a morality story of how the essence of a man's character is first tested and then laid bare by the circumstances that befall him. As the men each day cope with isolation, suffering, and hardships, these unremitting conflicts increasingly reveal either each man's inner strengths or his basic character flaws. At one extreme is Captain Dean, who while marooned on Boon Island "had washed our ulcerated legs and feet with urine . . . [and] almost paralyzed his hands to dredge up mussels for us." At the other is first mate Christopher Langman, who accuses Dean of sinking the ship so he can collect the insurance, and who Roberts describes as "malice personified" and "a whoreson, beetle-headed, flap-ear'd knave" (*Boon Island*, 290, 145, 254).

As one reviewer of the book indicated, a trademark of Roberts's novels is that "his heroes, as a rule, are thorough heroes; and his villains are unmitigated villains."[8] Benedict Arnold, for example, is portrayed in *Arundel* and *Rabble in Arms* as not the despicable character of legend, but a fearless military leader and brilliant tactician shamefully victimized by incompetent generals and a small-minded Continental Congress. Thus, Dean's and Langman's narratives, written from two distinct and opposite sides, fit perfectly with Roberts's typical literary style. Numerous details, however, that were essential to his story were omitted from the two journals, details he had to supply from his own imagination. As with the situation he confronted while writing *Northwest Passage*, the material and episodes he added did not contradict what he learned from the two primary resource accounts, and Roberts's solutions to the problems he faced are a tribute to his—and the men's—ingenuity.

For instance, in an interview Roberts commented on the rather undescriptive narratives of Captain Dean and first mate Langman, giving as an example the rather cursory comment in Dean's reminiscences that the men were able to make a saw out of the blade of a cutlass. In the margin opposite this sentence in Dean's account Roberts scrawled "How! Account for it."[9]

This attention to minuscule facts was not unusual for the author, for as he said in his literary autobiography, a historical novelist—unlike a historian who is usually concerned only with facts—must account for even the smallest detail "to the complete satisfaction of the reader. Otherwise his story doesn't, as the saying goes, hold water."[10] Thus, Roberts wrote in *Boon Island*:

The captain and Swede brought sharp-edged rocks into the tent. While Swede held the blade of the cutlass at an angle against the sharp edge of a rock as a man holds the blade of a razor at an angle against his cheek, the captain would smash at the blade with a similar rock. Thus a V-shaped nick would be broken out of the cutlass blade.

They started with a nick at the hilt end, a nick at the point and a nick halfway between each of the three nicks. Then they subdivided each space between the nicks until the blade became a series of jagged saw teeth.

Then Swede took one of those chisel-like rocks and Chips took another, and they rubbed and rubbed at each nick until both sides had beveled edges and the teeth were sharp.

When they started I didn't believe they could do it. Since Boon Island, I believe the right sort of man can do anything. (227–28)

Roberts neatly fit his elaborations into his good vs. evil theme. After the men laboriously build and launch their boat, only to have it capsize, they lose more than their boat, they lose their ax and hammer as well. As Roberts wrote in the margin of the 1726 Dean account that noted the loss of the tools, "Why take ax and hammer?" Langman explained in his report that when the men carried the boat to the shore for launching, they put aboard "such of the Carpenter's Tools as we had sav'd from the Wreck, in order to build a better when we came on Shore."[11] Roberts expertly weaves this fact into a diatribe against Langman's idiocy and selfishness:

I think the loss of the boat had shocked all of us: first into a state of horrified resignation, then into desperate activity. . . . Certainly there was rancor in the mind of everyone able to think—even in the minds of Langman's cronies, White and Mellen. In all their faces I saw sullen fury at Langman's folly in putting the axe and the hammer in the boat, and at his insolent insistence that he did so to let us build a better boat when we got to land.

We knew that wasn't so: knew that his seizure of the tools was unreasoning hoggishness on Langman's part, and there was hot resentment against Langman, and an irritation against everything. (255–56)

Another example of Roberts's incorporation of history into literature, surrounded by his black and white paradigms of moral virtues and vices, is the men's decision to eat the body of Chips Bullock, the carpenter. Although most of the men favor the idea, Langman and his friends refuse, (1) simply because the Captain approves the plan, and (2) so they could later—if they were rescued—testify that eating him was the Captain's suggestion. Dean writes in his revised account: "The Mate, and the two other Opposers, refus'd to partake of the Flesh that Night, but were the first next Morning to beg an equal Share in the common Allowance. The Master, to prevent Dispute, distributed it by Lot, with the utmost Impartiality; and to take off any Aversion, enjoin'd them to call it Beef" (82). Langman merely notes that "the Mate, the Boatswain [Nicholas Mellen], and George White wou'd not touch any of it till next Day that they were forced to it by Extremity of Hunger" (54).

Roberts's dramatization of this decision is one of the most emotional and chilling sections in the book—and one Roberts fortunately does not overdo, for he intended the novel not to be a morality story of cannibalism but one of survival. Because Langman's account is signed by Mellen and White—the same two who refused to eat the meat—Roberts of course portrays them as Langman's henchmen throughout the entire story:

> When we returned exhausted and depressed to the tent to feed those comrades who had lain there, sunk in helplessness because of some frightened quirk of their disgusting brains, Langman, White and Mellen, as able-bodied as any of us, refused to eat.
>
> "An insult," Langman mumbled, "to the spirit of a friend."
>
> "Langman," Captain Dean said, "my duty by you is done. Eat or don't eat, as you please. But my duty to the rest of us is *not* done, and if I hear any more talk out of you about this meat being anybody's spirit, you'll rue the day!"

"Are you threatening me?" Langman asked.

"Yes, I'm threatening you," Captain Dean said. "If you pour out your spleen on these others, I'll protect them by stopping your mouth. This meat I'm offering is nobody's spirit. It's beef. It was animated once by a soul and a spirit, but the soul and the spirit have gone from this island, leaving only beef behind." (298–99)

As Langman explained in his account of the wreck of the *Nottingham Galley*, he, Mellen, and White ate their share of the dead man the next day. Roberts writes in *Boon Island* that Langman tells the captain that the three changed their minds because they realized "it's not a sin to eat beef. When we understood it was beef, we saw we'd made a mistake" (302).

While book reviewers were pleased to see a new Roberts novel in bookstores, many shared the opinion of one of the author's close friends, who regarded the story as "a failure if judged by the magnificent qualities of his earlier books."[12] As a reviewer for the *Chicago Tribune* elaborated: "This novel lacks the range of character, setting, action, and reflection of Roberts' previous books. Instead of that full fare it offers a somber study in merciless hunger and pitiless cold—and in the greed and endurance, the treachery and loyalty that emerge in men under stress."[13]

But *Boon Island* is more than just this "somber study." Because Roberts, throughout his career, was intent on producing works of fiction that were both historically accurate and readable, he seldom used symbolism or allegories. With *Boon Island*, however, his last novel, not only are his characters symbolic of good and evil but his geography is as well. When the men are finally rescued Roberts several times contrasts England with the United States, portraying America as the safe and secure haven where a man can achieve his potential through diligence and hard work, as opposed to a corrupt and amoral eighteenth-century Europe inhabited by scoundrels, thieves, and ne'er-do-wells. When Miles Whitworth tells one of their rescuers, Colonel William

Pepperrell, that he, Captain Dean, and Henry Dean must return to England to defend themselves against Langman's expected attacks, he explains: "'Colonel,' I said, 'we know people like yourselves and these wonderful friends we've made in Portsmouth wouldn't believe Langman; but people in England aren't like that. Those around the docks believe anything they hear about people of property or position. They're too ignorant to investigate—to find out the truth'" (368).

"Telling the truth" is a common theme in virtually all of Roberts's novels. In *Rabble in Arms*, for example, his narrator's purpose is "to tell the truth—the truth as to why wars are fought, and how they are bungled and protracted, while those who fight them lose their lives and fortunes" (577). In *Boon Island*, however, Roberts's "finding the truth" theme refers to an abstract, motivating force as well as to "what actually happened." As Roberts concludes in his book: "How many of us have our Boon Islands? And how many have our Langmans? But doesn't each one of us have an inner America on which in youth his heart is set; and if—because of age, or greed, or weakness of will, or circumstances beyond his poor control—it escapes him, his life, to my way of thinking, has been wasted" (372).

Thus, Roberts, a fervent nationalist all his life, maintains that America allows individuals to accomplish whatever they are capable of attaining. And while America also symbolizes the goals people wish to achieve, for Roberts Boon Island represents the courage and integrity that a person needs to confront and overcome life's inevitable adversities so he can reach these goals. Roberts summed up his feelings in a memo, written a few weeks before his death in July 1957. It read: "Boon Island is us fighting the world. We ain't got a Chinaman's chance—but with guts we can somehow lick the world."[14]

KENNETH ROBERTS AND *BOON ISLAND*

NOTES

1. Page numbers cited in text refer to the present edition.

2. Kenneth Roberts, *Rabble in Arms* (Garden City, N.Y.: Doubleday, 1947), 577, hereafter cited in text; *March to Quebec: Journals of the Members of Arnold's Expedition*, compiled and annotated by Kenneth Roberts (Garden City, N.Y.: Doubleday, 1953), 43.

3. "Roberts Shocks Portsmouth: Famous Author Stirs Warner House Asc.," *Kittery (Maine) Press*, August 13, 1937, 1, 5.

4. Kenneth Roberts, "Notes for a Discussion with Booth," August 24, 1934, Adams Manuscript Collection, Indiana University, Lilly Library.

5. Lewis Nichols, "A Visit with Mr. Roberts," *New York Times Book Review*, 1 January 1956, 3.

6. Alice Dixon Bond, "Kenneth Roberts' New Novel Proves Own View, That Writer Must Have 'Stood Up to Live,'" *Boston Herald*, January 15, 1956, sec. 1, p. 2.

7. Ibid.

8. Lewis Gannett, "Book Review," *New York Herald Tribune*, January 2, 1956, 11.

9. John Deane, *A Narrative of the Shipwreck of the Nottingham Galley, &c.* Publish'd in 1711. Revis'd, and reprinted with additions in 1726, by John Deane, commander. [London, 1726], 28; reprinted herein; page numbers refer to the present edition; hereafter cited in text as Dean, Roberts's spelling of the name throughout *Boon Island*. Roberts's annotated copy is in the Kenneth Roberts Collection of the Dartmouth College Library.

10. Kenneth Roberts, *I Wanted to Write* (Garden City, N.Y.: Doubleday, 1949), 187.

11. Christopher Langman, Nicholas Mellen, and George White, *A True Account of the Voyage of the Nottingham-Galley of London, John Dean Commander, from the River Thames to New-England, Near which Place she was cast away on Boon-Island, December 11, 1710, by the Captain's Obstinacy, who endeavour'd to betray her to the French, or run her ashore; with an Account of the Falsehoods in the Captain's Narrative* (London: Printed for S. Popping, 1711), 52; reprinted herein; page numbers refer to the present edition; hereafter cited in text as Langman.

12. Herbert Faulkner West, "The Work of Kenneth Roberts," *Colby Library Quarterly* 6 (September 1962): 98.

13. Walter Havighurst, "Kenneth Roberts' Somber Tale of Cold, Desperation," *Chicago Sunday Tribune Magazine of Books*, January 1, 1956, 3.

14. Kenneth Roberts, memorandum, July 1957, Dartmouth College Library.

Boon Island

Kenneth Roberts

To Stephen Nason
Vicar of St. Alfege, Greenwich
with the gratitude and admiration of
his American cousin

Chapter 1

Greenwich, for all its faults, was a fascinating place, and I always left it with regret, especially at Trinity Term, to go up to Oxford.

Twice a year I protested to my father that I'd be better off in Greenwich; but he wouldn't have it so. Roughly speaking, our wrangling went around and around, like moles in their devious underground wanderings; but, after the fashion of mole-holes, they seemed to arrive nowhere.

The sum of all my contentions was that an Oxford education, so called because of the strange professors, dons, fellows and tutors to whom we were exposed, was a waste of time, if not downright dangerous.

My father, however, insisted that no matter how much of a drunken sot a don or a tutor might be, education somehow worthy was bound to be achieved by my mere presence within the stone walls of my college, which was Christ Church, by my daily exposure to the portraits in Christ Church Hall, and to the conversations of those drunken dons, those barnacle-like fellows, all waiting for someone to die and provide them with a Living—and I often wondered what idiot first applied the word "Living" to a bare existence in a miserable parsonage at the end of a muddy lane.

"Look here, Miles," my father would say, "you defeat your own arguments against Oxford without realizing what you're doing. You want to study the writing of plays, and you complain that you're not allowed to do it, so Oxford is a bore and a waste of time. But you *do* do it! You belong to that Buskin Club of yours! You know Colley Cibber made a better play out of *Richard III* than Shakespeare did! 'Off with his head!' 'Richard is himself again.' That's Cibber: not Shakespeare!

"You say your tutors are morose, profligate, insipid asses–and you've learned it by yourself! That's a whole lot better than believing some old fool of a professor who tells you that a knowledge of chemistry is an elegant and desirable accomplishment because it was revealed to Adam by Heaven! To Adam, for God's sake! And by Heaven! Pish! Nobody's educated by that sort of teaching! All anybody does in college–if he's fortunate–is to learn how to make a start at educating himself: to change his mind if his mind needs changing."

He was right, of course. If I'd never numbed my feet and fingers and nose in the cubicles of the Bodleian, reading the nice nastiness of Mrs. Aphra Behn and the humorless comedies of a score of imitation Shakespeares, I'd never have struck up a friendship with Neal Butler. Whether that was a good thing or a bad thing, I can't say, because it's possible that something worse than Boon Island might have happened to me.

That's what I hope those who read this book will bear

in mind: no matter what dreadful thing a man may encounter, he might, but for the grace of God, be overwhelmed by something even more awful. I can't endure people who complain about this or that little thing; but I only reached that state of mind by sad experience.

In the beginning, I had small use for Oxford, and its dreary dullness and monotony. I copied Dr. Atterbury's sermons until I was physically ill; I pored over grammar and rhetoric until my eyelids seemed glued together—and I looked forward to nothing but returning to Greenwich at the end of Trinity Term—to its life and its bustle, its palaces and taverns and parks, its endless traffic on the Thames.

One of my reasons for disliking Oxford—and how I laughed, in later years, at such unreasoning folly—was the fact that Trinity Term made it impossible for me to see the great fair held in Greenwich at Whitsuntide. I never reached home until weeks after Whitsuntide, and to me a three-day fair was of more importance than anything—except, naturally, my father and my dinghy.

So at the end of Trinity Term, in that memorable summer of 1710, my father had my dinghy waiting for me at the yard of the Naval Hospital, and within an hour after he had welcomed me home, I had pushed her out on the river and was being foully cursed by a hundred rivermen.

A failing wind and the incoming tide carried me to Deptford Steps, where the river makes its great bend to the south—the bend that holds, as in a bag, the palaces and the Naval Hospital and all the taverns so famous for their whitebait dinners.

Even before the dinghy had touched the stone, a boy reached out for her bow, turned her sideways and drew her to the bottom step with no apparent effort. This takes strength, and it surprised me, for at first sight the boy didn't look overly strong; but when I climbed from the dinghy and we lifted her from the water to set her on the step, so that she'd be out of the way of the innumerable fishermen who were constantly on the move, he made it seem as easy as lifting out a broomstick.

All these fisherfolk were concentrated between Ballast Quay and Billingsgate—the stretch where the incoming tide pushes whitebait by the millions against the abutments of the Naval Hospital.

Seemingly every one of those thousands—sailors, girls, gipsies, old women, dock workers—had some sort of white-bait basket-trap, and was lowering it into the brown waters of the Thames and flipping it out again, so that the whole waterfront was a flurry of splashing spray.

Above this spray hung a sort of medley of sound, caused by the groans, shouts, curses and shrieks of those who were either successful or unsuccessful in the yankings and jerkings of their traps. Their facial contortions, as they thus toiled, were something remarkable; but this particular boy would flip his wire basket from the water: then, whether the basket was empty or whether it held a glimmering flicker of those succulent little spratlings, he would glance at the whitebait fishers on either side with a sort of disarming concentration of amusement, generosity, amiability, apology . . . apology, perhaps, for the smallness of his catch, or for his good fortune, or for his ineptitude, or perhaps for looking so much cleaner and neater than any of the men or boys who were sousing their baskets down and up, down and up, with dour determination and scowling ferocity.

If I seem to talk overmuch of Greenwich whitebait, it's because those insignificant minnows, in season, were Greenwich's most important product. People came from miles around, especially from London, to dine on them, even to have official whitebait banquets, such as were never held elsewhere—and for an excellent reason. No place in the world produced such delectable morsels as the whitebait brought ashore at Greenwich; and whitebait at its finest arouses a sort of frenzy in the breasts of those who know it. Nobody ate mutton in Greenwich during the whitebait season, nor fowl, nor beef—not if he could get whitebait.

When the boy went back to his fishing-station, I saw that he had been fortunate; for on a square of wet sacking close behind him were perhaps two thirds of a bushel of whitebait, a good part of them still flopping and shimmering; so as a reward to him for helping me, as well as a home-coming gift for my father, I thought to buy some of them at a generous price. To that end I put my hand on his arm to get his attention.

To my amazement he shied away from my outstretched hand, as a puppy might shrink from a threatening foot, and the look he darted at me was almost violent in its wariness. Then, in a moment, he was merely a polite boy again, snapping his trap from the river, bringing with it a score of wriggling, glittering minnows which he dumped skillfully on his square of sacking.

"There's already enough for a dozen suppers," I said. "Spare me a few——two shillings worth, perhaps?" Two shillings should have been enough to buy half a bushel, but the boy only concentrated silently on the submerging of his little trap.

Not wishing to embarrass him by too much talk, I told him to bring all he could to my father's house on Church Lane, two streets beyond the Naval Hospital. "If you have difficulty finding the house," I said, "ask for Magistrate Whitworth. I'm Miles Whitworth."

"I can't, sir," he said. "I'm fishing for Mr. Langman."

"Nonsense!" I said. "I'll pay you two shillings for a quart, and I'll bet your Mr. Langman, whoever he is, doesn't do as well for you!"

"No, sir," he said. "Mr. Langman pays a shilling for four quarts, but I made a contract with Mr. Langman. On the days I don't work for Mr. Penkethman, I catch whitebait for Mr. Langman." He twitched his trap from the water, swung it deftly within hand's reach, spilled another shower of whitebait into his burlap container; then looked apologetic as he lowered his trap to the water again.

"Penkethman!" I cried. "Penkethman of the Haymarket? The actor-manager?"

The boy gave me a look of approval. "Comedian, sir," he said. "He moved his players here this month—some from the Haymarket and some from Drury Lane."

I studied him more carefully. There was almost a look of elation about him, such as young girls so often have, but boys almost never. When he stood, he had an air of being about to rise on his toes. In short, he looked happy.

"Don't tell me," I said, "that you're an actor! Not at *your* age."

"Well, sir," the boy said, "I'm not exactly an actor, but Mr. Penkethman prints my name on the bills—Neal Butler.

I'm only the prompter's call boy for Mr. Penkethman; but my father taught me how to write, so I write parts as well, forty-two lines to a length, and a penny for each one. Whatever I write, I remember, so I'm a quick study."

"How old are you, Neal?" I asked.

"Mr. Penkethman said I wasn't to tell my age," the boy said. "When I play female parts, he says it helps him with the rakes if we leave 'em guessing."

"Rakes?" I said. "Female parts? You play female parts?"

"Oh, yes, sir," the boy said. "There was an accident one night, and Mr. Penkethman let me play the page in Mr. Otway's *Orphan*." He proudly repeated, "I'm a quick study," and he had good reason to be proud, as I had learned at Oxford, when I spent long hours struggling to memorize wordy speeches from *The Fair Quaker of Deal.*

He snatched his fish trap from the water, found only two minnows flopping on it, gave me a look of pretended haughtiness that was vastly amusing; then dropped the trap back into the river. "Once he let me recite Mr. Cibber's epilogue about the Italian singers, and when I'm better at Italian, he'll let me do it again."

Female parts! A quick study! They helped him with the rakes! A penny for a length of forty-two lines! Mr. Otway! Mr. Cibber! Better at Italian! This boy, only a little more than half my age, was a real actor, even though his modesty prevented him from saying so.

"You're learning to speak Italian?" I asked.

"Oh, no, sir, just something that sounds like Italian." He placed his free hand on his breast, regarded me with candid wide eyes, and from his lips there gushed a stream of foreign syllables among which English words were dropped disconcertingly. The whole effect was foreign, but falsely foreign: the words seemed to have meaning; yet they meant nothing, and were merely excruciatingly droll, especially when, as if emphasizing his strange flood of nonsense, he hauled up violently on his fish trap to find it brimming with whitebait. As he swung it sideways, to deposit the minnows on his square of burlap, one of the four cords broke: the basket slipped, and all his minnows spilled back into the brown Thames water.

"Stap my vitals" Neal cried, and I knew he was quoting Otway. He dropped his broken trap beside him on the stone steps, and suddenly and surprisingly he held in his hand a long, thin-bladed knife, with which he went at the broken cord, trimming and splicing it as neatly as any bos'n on the river.

"Where'd you get that knife?" I asked. I held out my hand for it, but the boy made a quick movement and the knife vanished.

"It belonged to my father," he said. "My father says even big men'll shy away from a knife."

His reference to big men floored me, but somehow the mention of his father made his possession of that long thin knife seem excusable, if not exactly reasonable; so I forgot the knife and sat there beside him on the steps of Ballast Quay with the cool scent of the sea drifting past us, borne by the swift tide, which held the bows and the riding sails of all the brigs and schooners and frigates and ships-of-the-line, lying off the Naval Hospital, as steady and true as though carved and mathematically placed there by one of the hospital's ancient pensioners.

Neal's father, he said, had once been a strolling player. Then, when Neal's mother died, his father enlisted in the St. George's Light Dragoons. Later his father joined the

Navy because he thought it offered more opportunities for prize money. After he had been wounded in an engagement, he was admitted to the Naval Hospital, where his scanty allowance barely enabled him to buy tobacco for himself and supply Neal with a weekly two shillings on which to live in a room on Fisher's Alley.

Thus, Neal said, he counted himself fortunate to receive seven shillings a week from Mr. Penkethman, even though that pay was three weeks in arrears.

When the tide was wrong, so that the fops and rakes couldn't sail down from London to Greenwich and sail back again to London the same night, the theatre was closed and he was free to fish for Mr. Langman. On theatre days he fished for himself and turned over his catch to Mr. Penkethman's players, who repaid him by teaching him how to walk and enunciate and have stage manners.

There was something about the way he said the words "fops" and "rakes" that made me wonder what he or his father had endured at their hands; but when I asked him that question, he said abruptly that the whitebait had stopped running. Would I, he asked me, take him as far as Watling Stairs? When I said Yes, he neatly slid the dinghy off the step without any help from me. Watling Stairs, Neal said, was where Langman daily went to collect the catches of his fisherboys.

I saw Neal meet Langman—a swarthy tall man with a dubious half-smile on one side of his mouth; and I never dreamed, as I watched him empty Neal's little bag of fish into a larger sack and give him a few coins from a leather wallet, that I'd ever see that troublesome man again.

Chapter 2

Through all my boyhood and youth Greenwich and its waterfront had been my stamping ground.

Everything about the river was familiar and fascinating to me—the merchantmen and ships of war that moved perpetually or lay at anchor all around the tip of the Isle of Dogs and up past Deptford on the one hand and down past Woolwich on the other: the constant movement of watermen bearing gentlemen on an outing to see the beauties of the palaces: the watermen's hoarse crying of "Oars, Sculls! Sculls, Oars!"; the sloops, loaded with brightly dressed men and women, who, screaming like seagulls, waved at me as I passed; the towering three-deckers, with their carved and gilded stern galleries and their bright red sides: their fluttering lines of newly washed sailormen's togs: the never ending passage up and down gangplanks of women and hucksters, wives, trulls, boatmen, visitors: the vessels battered from long voyages beating up to their anchorages; those setting off for unknown ports with new canvas gleaming from their squared yards and noisy with the shouts of angry mates and drunken sailors.

CHAPTER 2

They were sights and sounds to which I looked forward all through each long winter, when I crouched beside my sea-coal fire in Christ Church, reading and forever reading those tiresome books that had been preserved for generations in the Bodleian's underground caverns.

Greenwich being what it was, I never defied my father's orders to stay indoors after dark; for sailors, whether King's men or merchant seamen, were a scurvy lot, and one who ventured on the streets at night too often found himself in the grip of a press gang, beaten black and blue, stripped of his clothes, and thrown into a vermin-ridden cable tier so far below the water line that his cries were as nothing compared with the gurgle of the tide against the bow.

Greenwich, the life of the river and particularly the life of the theatre, concerning which Neal Butler had spoken so familiarly, was heaven to me by comparison with Oxford.

My professors, my tutors, seemed to me like drone bees, living on some invisible college pollen; whereas actors from Drury Lane and the Haymarket, greatest of England's theatres, by contrast were truly alive.

Even at Oxford I suffered with those actors from the influx of Italian opera singers, who squalled so loudly as to threaten the existence of English players whose education in squalling was neglected.

The truth was, I was stage-struck. Aristophanes to me was a long-dead shadow who had written about frogs; but Penkethman, known by reputation to all of us in the Buskin Club, was Pinky, a genius who now was doubly a genius for having conceived the idea of coming to Greenwich for the summer with scenery such as had been first invented at Christ Church by Inigo Jones, and with all the machines, devices and appurtenances necessary to cause sprites to fly through the air and demons to rise from the earth.

When, that night, I guardedly told my father about Neal Butler, I emphasized his association with Penkethman's players more than I did his aptitude as a catcher of whitebait or his association with Langman; for my father said, "Pah!" and immediately used the very words that Neal himself had used, "Fops and rakes!"

"This boy isn't a fop or a rake," I said. "He's no more a fop or a rake than I was at his age—or than I am now."

"He's an actor, isn't he?" my father asked, putting his hands on the table and thrusting his head toward me, as he did when he'd caught a witness in an outrageous evasion of the truth. "That's what actors are forever representing, isn't it?" he demanded. "Pint-sized clowns in tatters and tarnished gold lace, making faces and laughing like hyenas at their damned dull witlessness. Overdressed harridans with breasts half exposed, pretending to be Sir Courtly Nice's mistress, or aping a droopy doll, all prunes and prisms, fainting if a man says, 'Split me'! Players with perukes two feet high and scented with pulvillio and essence, screeching and squalling, 'A harse! A harse! My kingdom for a harse!' Otway had the right word for 'em! Punks, my dear Miles, corrupting the morals and principles of the youth!"

"But, sir," I protested, "this boy isn't that sort. If I had a brother, I'd be proud if he were like Neal Butler: looked like him: behaved like him. He's as uncorrupted as can be!"

I told him how the boy had shied away from me—not

frightened exactly, but wary, as if he'd had occasion to question the motives of someone.

"I liked him the moment I saw him," I said, "and so would you, unless I'm greatly mistaken. There's something about him—something that makes you sure he'd be good at anything to which he turned his hand. Even the whitebait seemed to be attracted to him. He had a little trap with the edges bent up—a sort of wire platter with a cord at each corner. The four cords were lashed to a larger cord, and the large cord was fastened to a short pole. I think it must have been instinct that told him when to pull that trap! He certainly couldn't see the whitebait—at least I couldn't. The water was brown, as it always is when the tide first turns. I think he might become a great actor."

My father snorted. "He'll probably grow up to rewrite Shakespeare, like so many damned fools—Dryden and Tate and D'Urfey, for example!"

"Or like Cibber," I said. "The *Tatler* seems to like Cibber, and the Butler boy mentioned Otway with a good deal of respect. Was Otway a damned fool?"

"No," my father said, "not when he wasn't rewriting *Romeo and Juliet*. He was no Shakespeare, any more than Shakespeare was, but he makes people talk like people instead of gingerbread mannikins. Come to think of it, so does Vanbrugh."

He pulled off his tie-wig to rub his short gray hair with an impatient hand. "I've no objection to buying this boy's whitebait—have 'em every day for a week if you'd like; but don't for God's sake take a child's opinions about the stage and about actors. They're punks, all of 'em, just as Otway said. Punks, my boy!"

He cogitated for a moment. "Well, not all of 'em exactly. I saw Betterton as Falstaff once, and damn near died laughing!"

I left my dinghy at the Hospital Yard the following afternoon with no thought of Neal Butler except that, with the tide flowing an hour earlier, he had probably netted enough whitebait to let me have as much as I wanted.

He hadn't though. When I caught a barge to Deptford Steps, Neal was where I'd seen him the day before, and on the step above him, in the blue-sleeved summer waistcoat and blue yarn socks of a pensioner of the Naval Hospital, was a lopsided man with a long yellow mustache and clumps of yellow fuzz protruding so far below the round, flat-topped black hat that they covered his ears. His look of being overloaded on one side was due to the way he carried his right shoulder somewhat lower than his left, as if he were about to reach down with his right hand and haul up an anchor.

Neal gave me that quick smile of his, but before he could speak, the lopsided man leaned forward, looked almost fiercely at me and spoke my name.

"Yes," I said, "I'm Miles Whitworth, and you must be Mr. Butler."

"Swede, not 'mister,' " the yellow-haired man said. "Swede Butler. Moses was my name; Neal's too; but they called me Swede because of my hair. I never thought much of Moses. There must have been something wrong with him if it took him forty years to get the Children of Israel out of the Wilderness. Neal dropped the Moses because Penkethman told him to."

That name-changing habit of actor-managers had often

touched me on the raw. They never had the brains to understand that the actor makes the name: not the name the actor. Moses Butler–Neal Butler–what's the difference! It's the inner fire that an audience sees and feels: not the label by which a bailiff knows him!

"I wonder what Anne Bracegirdle's real name is?" I asked Swede.

"I won't even try to guess," Swede said. "I only want to know who my boy takes up with."

"I don't wonder," I said. "Your boy has a knack for catching whitebait. He has a way with him, too."

"Aye," Swede said. "He tells me your father's a magistrate. He tells me you're a member of Christ Church, *in statu pupillari.*" He paused, as if surprised at his use of the Latin phrase: then again stared at me almost fiercely. "And he says he thinks you're an actor."

"That's putting it too strongly, Swede," I said. "We have a club at Christ Church–the Buskin Club. We read plays, and once or twice we've staged one in the Hall; but I hope to write 'em rather than recite 'em."

"Good!" Swede said. "You need fish to fry and I need the advice of someone who isn't an actor. I've been an actor myself, and I wouldn't take an actor's advice any more than I'd take a sailor's. Do you suppose your father would trade a bit of advice for some of Neal's whitebait?"

"I'm sure he would," I said. "He'll take to Neal just as quickly as I did."

Swede put a big hand on his son's shoulder. "Pick up your fishes, boy. We'll go see Mr. Whitworth. Perhaps he can work out a future for you–one that won't leave you rolling in a gutter or living like a beggar in a naval hospital."

Chapter 3

John Dean was an old friend of my family, a sea captain from Twickenham, a little upriver from London, but he loaded and unloaded his cargoes at Greenwich, and always came to our house, before starting on a cruise, to have vessel and cargo insured. I know my father thought highly of him, and frequently ventured a moderate sum, which Dean would invest in coffee or tea or spices, thus providing education-money to be used by me at Oxford.

Behind our house on Church Lane was a walled arbor from which we caught glimpses of the river; and my father and Captain Dean were sitting there when I brought Neal and Swede Butler to the garden.

When Captain Dean saw us, he folded a paper and got up to go, but my father stopped him. "Unless I'm mistaken," my father said, "Miles has found us some whitebait, and we'll have it for supper, with pickle sauce. You'll get no dish to touch it on your *Nottingham* Galley nor in any tavern, for that matter. Maybe, after you've let out your belt a fathom or two, you'll stretch that insurance by a hundred pounds or so."

CHAPTER 3

Dean, a large calm man, smiled at us, and settled back comfortably in his chair. "Whitebait!" he exclaimed. "I'd run a mile a day for a platterful, but I've got a mate who cheats fisher-boys out of nearly all they can net—makes a small fortune selling it to taverns for ten times what he pays for it—so there's never any left over for me. Yes, I'll stay with pleasure, Charles, and you ought to put your chopped pickle in sour cream if you want a proper sauce."

I shook hands with Captain Dean, and my father got up to look at Neal Butler, who made him the politest of bows and held out his poke of whitebait-filled sacking.

When my father fumbled in his pocket, Swede Butler stepped forward and touched his hat. "Sir," he said, "my boy and I ask you to accept it in place of a fee."

"This is Swede, Neal's father," I explained. "He asked me whether you'd trade him some advice in return for Neal's catch. He wants the advice for Neal. Neal's a good boy, and I told Swede you would."

"You did, did you?" my father asked. "That's the value you put on my advice, is it? A sack of minnows?"

"No," I said. "I thought you might earn two people's affection, and some entertainment as well—if Neal recites his Italian epilogue for you. That's fairly good pay, isn't it?"

My father put his hand on Neal's shoulder. "I'm mighty pleased with your whitebait," he said. "I'll ask you to take it to the kitchen and give it to Mrs. Buddage. She's our cook. She'll rinse your piece of sacking, so you can have it to use again. Oh, and could you remember to tell her that Captain Dean says to make the sauce out of chopped pickle and sour cream?"

"And just a little chopped onion," Captain Dean said.

"Sour cream, chopped pickle, chopped onion," Neal repeated, and somehow he enunciated the words in such a way as to make my mouth water.

He marched obediently toward the kitchen, and even his manner of walking, though unaffected, was a pleasure to the eye.

"Quite a boy," my father said to Swede.

"Yes, sir," Swede said. "I don't know where he gets it. Maybe from his mother. She'd have been a player herself, and a good one, too, if a gallery hadn't fallen on her when we were playing the Angel Inn–Duke of Norfolk's servants, sir. I couldn't bring up a baby, Mr. Whitworth, so I left Neal with his grampa and granma outside of Norwich and took to the Army. Then I tried the Navy and got to be captain of the foretop on the *Minerva* till a French musket ball caught me in the shoulder and put me in the hospital yonder." He nodded in the general direction of the palaces on the waterfront.

"What's your problem, Mr. Butler?" my father asked.

"Well, sir, here it is," Swede said. "This boy has something I've never put to proper use. I've taught him to read and write: he's the quickest study I ever saw, and I've seen some good ones. If I could be in the theatre with him, I wouldn't mind so much; but I'm too banged up to be any good to a young man like Penkethman. So Neal's going it alone in the theatre, paid about half the time if he's lucky, and nothing much ahead of him but getting to be a beggar, depending on benefit performances, which is charity, no matter how you look at it. I know the end of it–work a fifth of the year, and never save a penny: get spoiled by the women and the men, too, and wind up in rags or drudging for some rat like Langman."

Captain Dean leaned forward. "What's that? What about Langman?"

"Oh," Swede said, "he's a mate on one of these merchant vessels. She's laid up for repairs. He weaves nets for boys to catch whitebait with: then he collects 'em and sells 'em and makes a good thing out of it."

"Why, that's my mate," Captain Dean said. "That's Christopher Langman!" To my father he explained, "He beats anything I ever saw! Every minute of the day he's figuring how to make money, and he doesn't care how he does it."

"Sounds caddish to me," my father said carelessly. "Why don't you get rid of him?"

"The truth is," Captain Dean said hesitantly, "I can't."

"Since when," my father asked, "has a captain been unable to get rid of a mate when his vessel's in port? I can see how it might be a little difficult if you're halfway across the Atlantic, but you aren't. You're seizing spars, or fishing ropes or sheets—whatever it is you nautical people fish and seize—and you'll be lucky to get to sea inside of another two months."

"I know," Captain Dean said, "but it's a long story."

"Well, give me a hint," my father said. "I'm interested in this Langman and his whitebait ventures. First thing we know, he'll be making it into one of these stock companies —selling shares on 'Change Alley and ruining thousands just like the stock jobbers. How does it happen you can't get rid of Langman, John?"

"Well," Dean said, "he sailed on one of Woodes Rogers' ships two years ago."

"Woodes Rogers! Why, he's a buccaneer," my father said quickly.

"No, no," Dean said. "Not a buccaneer, Charles! He's a privateer. Privateers carry government commissions, and a tenth of their takings go to the state."

"Oh, don't try to tell me the law," my father said. "I know what the law is, and most of these privateers are nothing but buccaneers, no matter what the law says."

"Well, I don't know about that," Captain Dean said, "but I do know that Langman says he sailed with Woodes Rogers; and around the Gulf of Guayaquil, when Rogers was busy capturing some footling town or other, Langman went off in a small boat with a few of his seamen, came across a smart-looking galley and captured her. Then somehow he was separated from Rogers, couldn't find him again, and decided the safest thing he could do was sail home. He had no money, and his men hadn't been paid, so he hunted up my brother Jasper and offered to sell him the galley at a bargain, provided he was retained as first mate."

He stirred uneasily beneath my father's scrutiny.

"Sounds fishy to me," my father said. "What happened to the crew that was in the galley when she was taken?"

Captain Dean looked more uncomfortable. "I asked him that, and he said they just went ashore, all but two men that he persuaded Jasper to hire."

Neal Butler came back from the kitchen to stand beside his father.

My father snorted, raised incredulous eyes to the sky; then spoke to Neal. "What did Mrs. Buddage say, young man?"

"She said Captain Dean came here just in the nick of time," Neal said. "She said she'd just been thinking of making some cheese out of her sour cream." He sounded exactly like Mrs. Buddage.

"Good," my father said, "good. Now, Neal, this Langman you're working for: did you undertake to work for him for a certain length of time?"

"Yes, sir," Neal said, "I promised, when he gave me the trap, to fish for him every day when I had nothing else to do. He pays me threepence a quart."

"You know that's not a fair price?" my father asked.

"Yes, sir," Neal said. "If I had time to peddle 'em around, I could get more; but if I took out time to peddle them, I wouldn't be able to catch enough."

"Yes," my father said, "there's something in what you say, but I'm a magistrate and I herewith declare your contract with Mr. Langman to be null and void. I have friends who'll be glad to pay a shilling a quart for them, and that's what I'll pay you—a shilling a quart and guarantee to dispose of all you catch. Understand? As for Langman, I'll give him a talking-to. He sounds to me like a slippery customer."

My father turned to Swede. "Now, Swede," he said, "does it make you easier in your mind to know your boy's having no further dealings with Langman?"

"Yes, sir," Swede said, "that'll help, but I'd like to get him out of the theatre. When Penkethman finishes with Greenwich, he'll take his players back to London; and if Neal goes with them—well, Mr. Whitworth, he's too young to be around a theatre. I know what it means. He'll buy a periwig and become a fop—learn to drawl and take snuff: strut and cock his cravat strings. Ten to one he'll go to the Groom Porter's and run into debt over the turn of a dirty deuce."

"How do you feel about it, Neal?" my father asked.

"Don't ask him," Swede said hastily. "He thinks these actors are angels right out of heaven. He can already walk like 'em and talk like 'em, and the only thing he doesn't yet do, thank God, is *think* like 'em. He thinks like a human being, and I don't want him spoiled."

"It's understandable," I told my father. "There's something about the theatre that's mighty exciting."

"It can be mighty destructive, too," my father said. "What are the plays all about? Whoring, drinking, gaming! What are the manners of the fine ladies you see represented? Those of the tavern and the brothel, without relation to life or art!"

He turned to Neal. "See here, my boy: Miles tells me you recited one of Mr. Cibber's epilogues. Will you do it for us now?"

Neal said quickly that he would, but that he'd like a costume. My father went into the house and I heard him calling to Mrs. Buddage to bring him a shawl and a soiled tablecloth. How Neal wrapped those two pieces of cloth so deftly about him, I couldn't see, but he turned in a moment from a young boy to a girl, wide-eyed, pleading, provocative, looking at us over his shoulder as he spoke, and smoothing the tablecloth over his narrow hips.

I can't remember Cibber's lines; but the verses told how, eventually, English actors would be forced to imitate Italians, and it's impossible to reproduce the strange quarter English, quarter Latin and half imitation Italian that followed the line, "I give you raptures while I squall despair." There was something overwhelmingly ludicrous about this meaningless twaddle, so earnestly delivered, and with such coy and fetching gestures. My father snorted and Captain Dean said, "Haw!" but Neal seemed not to hear them.

" 'If this won't do,' " he quoted, coquettishly touching his finger tips to his lips, " 'I'll try another touch—half French, some English, and a spice of Dutch' " . . . and immediately he broke into another utterly meaningless song that made no sense although it seemed constantly on the verge of doing so.

When it came to an end, all too soon, my father slapped his leg delightedly, Captain Dean's face was red from repressed laughter. Swede was the only one who didn't laugh.

"I think I see what you mean," my father said to Swede, as I helped Neal fold the shawl and the tablecloth. "I see what you mean. It isn't easy to divert a talent like that. It isn't even safe. If I were you—if Neal were a few years older—I'd advise you not to try to do it, but as I say, I think I know exactly how you feel."

He seemed to think aloud. "It's London you're afraid of. Now suppose Neal had a profession to support him. We've had some good professional men in the theatre and they've done well. Take Sir John Vanbrugh. He was an architect. When Miles goes up to Oxford, I might be able to use Neal. He'd be a help to me writing briefs—writing insurance. What would you say to that, Swede?"

"I'd be forever in your debt, Mr. Whitworth," Swede said.

"Yes," my father said. "Well, that's one way of looking at it, so if you've been uneasy in your mind, you'll probably feel better. All of us can keep an eye on Neal till it's time for him to go to work for me in the autumn—and the work he's doing now is training of a sort: teaches him how to hold a tea-cup—how to seem to be at ease when he isn't."

When Swede looked dubious, my father seized his hand and shook it, tapped Neal lightly on the shoulder, and said, "See them to the door, Miles."

To Neal he added, "I'll remember to speak to Langman, so don't forget to bring us whitebait whenever you can."

Captain Dean got to his feet. "Just a moment," he said. "I've been thinking about that mate of mine, and about Swede's experience on the *Minerva*. How do you spend your days in the Naval Hospital, Swede?"

Swede laughed. "I spend 'em in the hardest kind of work, Captain. Doing nothing. Describing my aches and pains to others who have worse aches and pains."

"*Do* you have aches and pains?" Captain Dean asked.

"Everybody who does nothing has aches and pains."

"You don't look to me as if you had as many aches and pains as any one of my crew has. How'd you like to ship with me on the *Nottingham* Galley? I'd be glad to have you along, just to have the benefit of your advice. I'd sign you on as first lieutenant. We've got ten guns and a gunner who contrived to blow his eyes full of powder."

Swede looked from Captain Dean to Neal and back again. "Why," he said slowly, "I think that might be a good thing if my boy's going to help Mr. Whitworth. I felt like being a pensioner before my shoulder healed, but I don't feel like it any more. I think it would be a good thing all around if Neal had a first lieutenant as a father instead of a pensioner."

I thought, as I led Neal and his father to the street, how

odd it was that, because the tide had thrust my dinghy against Deptford Steps, the lives of two people had been altered–and greatly for the better, I earnestly hoped. How many people's lives that tide had altered, I couldn't dream. We never know: we never know!

Chapter 4

That was the beginning for my father, as well as for Captain Dean and me, of a course in the most popular of London's plays. Penkethman's playhouse was next door to the Hospital Tavern, and I'm bound to say Penkethman did well as a manager, for he went out of his way to add to his Drury Lane and Haymarket regulars, bringing in promising drifters from strolling companies like those in Dublin, Bath and Bristol. The plays he presented were held to be the best, and certainly Penkethman knew how to read his lines in such a way as to make words of no consequence seem irresistibly droll.

The curtain rose at five or six o'clock three times a week, and for a guinea apiece, the three of us had tickets that entitled us to see twenty-one plays. We by no means saw twenty-one, for our playgoing came to a sudden and unexpected end with the production of *The Walking Statue* on the last Saturday in July, the twenty-ninth; but until that day we talked theatre as though we ourselves were actors: of Penkethman as Daniel in *Oroonoko*, of Penkethman as Calico in *Sir Courtly Nice*, with Powell playing Sir Courtly: of Penkethman as Squib in *Tunbridge Walks*, of Penkethman as the painfully comical shepherd in *The Libertine Destroyed:* of Mrs. Kent's artistry as Caliban in *The Tempest* and of Mrs. Baker's beauty as Miranda: of the vast promise of Lacy Ryan in *The Fair Quaker of Deal:* of Penkethman as Fribble in *Epsom Wells*, and Spiller in *The Emperor of the Moon* and *The Recruiting Officer*.

If I were an artist, I could have drawn pictures by the score of those play nights in Greenwich: of wherries, barges and galleys unloading their tumultuous, half-drunken pleasure-seekers at King's Head Stairs while the hot July sun was still high enough to make the massed vessels in the river stand out sharply in black and white, and while the fishermen along the quays were still turbulent and noisy: of Londoners, both men and women, outside the doors of the innumerable Greenwich taverns, some standing, some sitting at little tables because the taverns were so crowded, each with a dish of whitebait and a tankard of ale before him, and each one tossing crisp morsels into himself with a great show of daintiness and refinement.

Even the sounds and odors of Greenwich on those play nights were fascinating—over everything the savory fragrance of the whitebait: and in the foreground the peculiar mangled gabbling of Londoners, who think of everyone beyond the sound of Bow Bells as being half witless and speaking a language incomprehensible to gentlefolk: the penetrating perfumes of the silk-clad playgoers: the squealing of orange and apple women who pushed through the crowds, crying their wares and reminding all hearers that there was nothing like an orange for throwing at actors:

the common sailors in blue and white striped trousers and coats always too big or too small, and caps made from pieces of stocking: the naval officers with tangled golden swabs on their shoulders, and half-moon hats the size and shape of the shallops that are forever running errands between barges and docks.

To me the most memorable of play-night pictures were those of the playhouse itself—the shouting, catcalling, orange-throwing roisterers in the gallery, the subdued and honorable citizens of Greenwich in the pit, the affected ladies in the boxes above the stage, and the incredible fops grouped on either side of the stage itself, and frequently all across the front of the stage, so that occupants of the pit had difficulty in seeing the movements of the actors. Some nights those wretched fops formed a background entirely around the rear of the stage, if the play was one that had made a reputation for itself at Drury Lane.

Some of these fops became as well known to us, by sight, as Penkethman, Powell, Spiller or Neal. All of them affected little mannerisms and great ones, too, for that matter. Their wigs without exception were enormous, sometimes tinted in strange blues and reds. Their speech seemed to be marked with peculiar sibilances and lisps; their gestures, as when they tossed back the lace from their wrists, or took snuff with a flourish such as a dancer makes when she poises herself for a pirouette, were airy and womanly. They were forever making play with perfumed handkerchiefs, touching them to their lips, or whisking imaginary nothings from their sleeves or weskits.

Sometimes they traveled in pairs, and sometimes singly, but even in the latter case they made a pretense of being disdainfully amused by those about them, bowing here: bowing there: staring out at those of us in the pit through quizzing glasses, as at animals in cages.

We had names for them—Sugar-leg for one who was constantly admiring his not too slender ankle: Jackdaw for one who was constantly bursting into cackles of laughter: Tintoretto for a little man with painted cheeks and lips who stood motionless for long periods of time, staring, so far as we could see, at nothing, his face a mask that never moved.

Only twice in all the nights we watched Mr. Penkethman's players at their antics did we see Neal on the stage, and on both occasions he recited that epilogue of Cibber's about the Italian opera singers, reading his lines in a way that brought smiles to the faces of those who listened, and downright guffaws when he lapsed from his lines into that queer running outburst of imitation Italian. On each occasion he was got up in the same costume: a blue gown, voluminous around the hips, with a pointed stomacher, a high collar that rose almost to the top of his head in back, and on his wig of auburn curls a little cap that looked as though made of pearls.

Mr. Penkethman, he told us, had begged the cap from some lady of title, for the especial purpose of being worn by the person who recited this epilogue. His youth and the soft brown of his face gave him the look of an Italian beauty; and when, at the close of the epilogue, he gathered up those full skirts and curtsied deep to the audience, he was as pretty a picture as a Rembrandt portrait of a young girl, glowing with reflected light—as pretty, surely, as Anne Bracegirdle was supposed to be. I found it difficult to believe that he was the same boy who had pulled whitebait from the Thames with his little four-cornered trap and had shied away from my outstretched hand on the afternoon when I had first seen him.

Sometimes, after the play, we waited for Neal and he walked home with us to tell us some of the many things concerning which my father, both as a magistrate and as an interested human being, was profoundly curious. He probed into Neal's mind to discover how some of the plays we had seen had impressed him, and we soon learned that allusions which seemed offensive to my father had appeared to Neal to be simply amusing, or just so many words written by an author and recited by an actor in order to further the action of the play.

"I suppose it's amusing in *Venice Preserv'd,*" my father asked politely, "when an actor says, 'In what whore's lap have you been lolling? Give but an Englishman his whore and ease, beef and a sea coal fire, he's yours for ever.' "

"Sir," Neal said, "that was a Frenchman said that. The answer was 'Frenchman, you are saucy!' " He seemed puzzled that my father should have questioned the speech.

We discovered how Penkethman's players had built up their wardrobes by begging discarded gowns and gentlemen's silks from such people of high station as were fascinated by theatrical matters—as so many of them were.

We learned how benefits were arranged to increase the pay of various actors—benefits to which the actors themselves sold tickets, running after the carriages of rich folk, begging them to subscribe, or calling at houses to sell tickets as a fishmonger might solicit patronage.

Such a benefit, Neal said, might bring as much as one hundred guineas to an actor, and make all the difference between a season without profit, or one that would let him live in comfort for two months or more if he were so unfortunate as to be unable to obtain work.

On one subject he was silent. He recognized, from our descriptions, the fops who had caught our attention by their posturings and grimacings as they stood in the stage entrances. He nodded understandingly at our imitations of Sugar-leg and Jackdaw; but when my father described the mask-like face of the little man we called Tintoretto, Neal's face and eyes were expressionless. He seemed almost to have stopped breathing.

We found out nothing at all from Neal when we first mentioned Tintoretto to him; but we learned a little more —not much, but more than enough—about him on the twenty-ninth of July, when Penkethman's company performed *The Gamester* and, as "a cup of tea," threw in a second play, *The Walking Statue*, with the gibberish-interlarded epilogue which Neal recited to appreciative laughter. *The Walking Statue* had been a great favorite at Drury Lane and was equally so in Greenwich. The words "a cup of tea," we knew from Neal, had come to be actors' slang for anything likable. Tintoretto, obviously, was not Neal's "cup of tea."

Probably my father and Captain Dean and I would have waited for Neal, the night of July 29th, and walked him home with us if it hadn't been for that epilogue, which made it necessary for Neal to get out of his costume and make-up. Unfortunately the night was warm and all three of us were eager for a bottle of chilled claret; so home we went.

When we got there, we did something we seldom did—opened our downstairs windows. This was a dangerous practice in Greenwich, as it was in any naval town, because of the almost unbelievable number of thieves, streetwalkers, wandering Jews, irresponsible sailors and light-fingered dockyard workers who roamed the streets at all hours of the night, alert to snatch anything from an unguarded room, provided only that the anything was small enough to be lifted through an open window.

We sat there in the semi-dark, listening to Captain Dean's comments on his *Nottingham* and his forthcoming voyage to America. Every sea captain considers his own vessel somehow superior to every other vessel, no matter how much larger; and I could sense how Captain Dean felt because of knowing how much finer my own dinghy was, in sailing qualities and clean lines, than larger shallops and even some yachts.

Since the *Nottingham* was a galley, Captain Dean explained, she was fitted with oars for rowing when necessary, and with guns so that she could fight if forced to do so, and she was faster than a running vessel, which is fast enough to sail without convoy. That meant she was designed to make quick voyages with small cargoes.

Behind Captain Dean's talk I was conscious of all the night-sounds of Greenwich—the bells from the vessels in the river; the distant shouting from taverns; the clatter of hoofs: the rattling of wheels of after-theatre carriages on the cobbles of the river front—when suddenly I heard something I didn't like at all. Captain Dean and my father heard it too, and liked it as little as I; for their heads turned slowly and questioningly toward each other.

What we heard was halfway between a gasp and a gurgle, as though someone had started to shout, and had been prevented by a gush of liquid in his throat.

CHAPTER 4

But if that sound was repeated, it was lost in all the other noises that made Greenwich, in summer, so difficult a place in which to sleep.

I pulled the curtain to one side, leaning from the window to listen. I thought I saw a blob of darkness on our front steps. When I stared at it half sideways, to see it more clearly, I decided it was nothing—there was no movement from it—and then, suddenly, I heard a long-drawn, quivering inhalation, such as one might make after holding his breath until his lungs are on the verge of bursting.

I ran to the front door and drew it open.

Neal Butler fell into the hallway as if he had been leaning against the door.

I pulled him to his feet. His appearance horrified me.

"What's the matter with you? You look sick!"

I took him by the arm and turned him toward the front room. My father and Captain Dean were on their feet, staring at us, and Neal's appearance led my father to hurry to the windows, draw them down and close the shutters.

He struck a light, and helped me put Neal in a chair.

We saw it was no ordinary sickness that troubled Neal, but some sort of mental disturbance that had left him half conscious. He seemed unwilling to look at either of us. His breathing was quick and shallow, with a deep shuddering breath at unexpected intervals.

"What happened to you, Neal?" my father asked. "Speak up! We're your friends."

When Neal didn't answer, my father reached for a claret bottle and filled a glass. "Here," he said, "drink this and tell us what happened to you."

When Neal continued to stare into space, my father

grasped his chin, and put the glass to his lips. Neal choked; then drew two of those long, shuddering sighs.

"He was waiting for me after the play," he said flatly.

"Who was?" my father asked.

"The one with the white face," Neal said. "The painted one."

"You mean the one we call Tintoretto?" my father asked.

Neal nodded. "He pulled at me—pulled at my clothes. I tried to walk around him so to get to you and Miles."

"This man—this Tintoretto. He'd pulled at you before?" my father asked.

"I had that knife," Neal said. "That one I'd sharpened. When we were almost at your house, I ran. He ran after me. When he caught up with me, I showed him the knife. He pushed it away. He—he laughed! That white face! That painted fish mouth! I never thought the knife would go into him so quick—so smooth!"

For the first time he looked directly at me and at my father. "When he fell over against me, I was glad I did it. I had to do it. You'd have done it if you'd been me! Then I was afraid."

My father put his hand on Neal's shoulder. "Had Tintoretto ever done this before?" Neal seemed to have run out of words. My father shook him. "I asked you whether he'd ever done this to you before tonight."

Neal gulped. "No, sir. The first time I recited Mr. Cibber's epilogue I could hardly get past him in the wings. He squeezed me, and my hand smelled of perfume. I couldn't get around him."

"Listen carefully," my father said. "Do you think others saw him squeeze you, as you put it?"

Neal nodded and swallowed hard.

CHAPTER 4

Captain Dean got to his feet. "Let's see about this," he said. "Charles, you sit here with Neal while Miles and I go out on the street for a few minutes. Neal, you're not to move! Understand?"

Neal nodded.

Captain Dean and I went out onto the street and turned toward the river. We found Tintoretto near London Street, between our house and the park. He was huddled against a hedge, a crumpled shadow of a man.

"The man's drunk," Captain Dean said loudly. "This is no place for him! We'll put him where he can sleep it off. You take him under one arm, Miles, and I'll take him by the other. We'll walk him toward the park."

When we pulled him to his feet, his head hung slack on his shoulders, and even in the dim light his painted face had the blank look of a clown's. The handle of Neal's knife still protruded from the black silk front of his coat. His garments had an abominably musky odor.

"Take out that knife, Miles," Captain Dean whispered. "We can't leave that in him. Toss it into your yard. We'll pick it up in the morning—if we can't find it tonight."

We supported Tintoretto draggingly toward the park, and it seemed to me that we did it so successfully that anyone who saw us would think we were merely doing a Christian act for a gentleman who had been oversedulous with the port.

At least, that's what I thought until two men came toward us from the direction of the park. Then I knew that Tintoretto's body was limper than any mere drunken man could be or could look.

As they drew nearer to us, Captain Dean muttered, "Better do some acting!"

He took Tintoretto around the waist and hung him, doubled up, over his arm; then bent over him solicitously. I bent over too and made retching sounds.

The two men halted beside us. One said, "Want any help?" I thought I recognized the voice of Lacy Ryan, one of Penkethman's young players.

"No, indeed," Captain Dean said heartily. To Tintoretto's body he said cheerfully, "Try hard! Better out than in." Again I uttered retching sounds and made play with my handkerchief.

The two men went slowly on, laughing; and when they were dim in the darkness, we carried Tintoretto to a wooded spot and left him there.

I was sweating, and with good reason, because I had no way of knowing how much the eyes of a keen young man like Lacy Ryan might have seen.

"Well," my father said, when we told him that Tintoretto was dead with a knife wound under his ribs, and that Lacy Ryan and another man had spoken to us when we were getting rid of the body, "there's nothing like an occurrence of this nature to help a man make up his mind. And there's one sure thing about it: we've got to get Miles and Neal Butler out of here before somebody starts asking too many questions."

He looked at Captain Dean. "How long before you'll be ready to sail, John?"

"Two weeks, maybe," Captain Dean said. "Our cordage is at Gravesend, ready to go aboard, but I've done nothing about the butter and cheese. I'm only taking on a little: just enough for a quick turnover in Portsmouth or Boston—Portsmouth probably."

CHAPTER 4

"Get 'em in Donegal," my father said promptly. "Go north-about around Scotland and Ireland: come down to the island of Aran, and just beyond it you'll see the red cliffs of Donegal. The best butter and cheese in the world come from those fields around Donegal Bay. They're the greenest fields you'll ever find. I'll tell you what to do, John: drop down to Gravesend on the early tide tomorrow morning, and pick up your butter and cheese when you get to Ireland."

When Captain Dean started to protest, my father jumped up to wag a magisterial finger before his nose. "Now listen, John! I can't have Miles mixed up in anything like this, and if Lacy Ryan recognized him, he certainly *will* be mixed up in it. So now I've told you what to do, I'll tell you what *I'll* do: I'll provide enough money to double your purchases, the profit from my part to be divided between us.

"I make this stipulation, though: Miles must go along as supercargo, and you'll make Neal your apprentice. He's a good boy, John. We can't let him start off in life with a murder charge against him—and that's what it'll look like to most London magistrates, no matter how it looks to us."

"It seems to me," Captain Dean said, "that this killing was justifiable."

"Bah!" my father cried. "Justifiable homicide: most dangerous thing in the world! What *is* justifiable homicide of a private nature? It's the defense against force of a man's person, house or goods. Ah! But how do you interpret the word 'justifiable'? Put all the judges in Britain in one room, and ask 'em to interpret a homicide you consider justifiable, and they'd argue for years! Take it to court, and

Lord Itchpate, C.J., would press a bunch of flowers to his nose and mumble that we are certainly not prepared to suggest that necessity should in every case be a justification. And what, to the mind of a learned judge with his nose in a bouquet, is necessity, for God's sake? Not the same thing that it would be to Neal Butler, harried, horrified and frightened half out of his wits by the insane maulings of a—a creature so frenzied that he impales himself upon a knife. No, no! I can hear Itchpate now!

" 'It is therefore our duty to declare that the prisoner's act in this case was willful murder, that the facts as stated are no legal justification of the homicide'—and the honorable Court, in a hurry to down two dozen oysters and a bottle of port, would briskly proceed to pass sentence of death upon the prisoner! No, John: you do as I tell you! Get the *Nottingham* to sea with Swede and Neal and Miles aboard, and with no loss of time!"

Captain Dean nodded thoughtfully. "Why not? With Neal aboard, Swede will work twice as hard. It'll let me have decent company aft, in place of Langman. It gives me an excuse to send Langman forward with the men. Your idea's a good one, Charles. You won't make a fortune on the venture, but we ought to clear enough to take on a good load of salt codfish in America. It smells, but it's a sure seller in England or France."

"Well, now, look," my father said. "There's a lot to be done tonight." He laughed ruefully. "Doesn't it beat hell how much inconvenience and downright misery just one misguided brute—one betwattled male doxy—who deserves nothing but to be officially and legally removed from this world, can cause by getting himself unofficially killed!

CHAPTER 4

"Anyway, go on back to the *Nottingham*, John. Go to-night—now! Take Neal with you. Stow him away in your own quarters where nobody'll see him. Keep him out of Langman's way until you're clear of the land. I hunted out Langman, hard at work at his fishmongering, and gave him a talking-to he'll never forget. I doubt that he knows which way is up, as the saying goes, but we can't take chances. He's Malice personified."

He put his hand on Neal's shoulder. "Are you hearing all this, Neal? We're doing this for your own good. Your father will agree."

Neal just stared at him.

"You go along with Captain Dean," my father said, "and try to forget everything that happened to you to-night, as well as everything we've said. Under Captain Dean you'll learn to be a mariner—a credit to your father and to all of us."

Captain Dean emptied his glass of claret and got to his feet.

"There's one more thing," my father said. "Swede hasn't boarded the *Nottingham* yet."

"He's signed on," Captain Dean said.

"I know," my father said, "but the hospital authorities don't know about it. I can notify 'em and make everything all legal sometime tomorrow afternoon; but we'll avoid any chance of delay by having Miles go to the hospital first thing in the morning."

To me he said, "The doors open at five o'clock. Find Swede and bring him to me. Tell him I'll arrange things with the hospital authorities after the ship has sailed. There'll be clothes for him here, and we should have him aboard the *Nottingham* by six o'clock."

To Captain Dean he added, "I'll send the money for the cheese and the butter by Miles."

I followed my father's instructions to the letter. Swede, when I told him the *Nottingham* must sail that day, and the reason why, looked almost relieved. "This is the way I've always wanted it," he said: "A way for us to be together. Ever since I signed on with Captain Dean, I've been like a fish out of water in this damned hospital, with all the political pensioners that don't know a futtock shroud from a wallpiece. If Neal killed a man, he did it for a good reason. I'd have done it for him if I could—but he wouldn't talk about such things. They made him freeze up inside. I suppose it was my fault for giving him the knife, but I'm glad I did it all the same."

He felt his shoulder and seemed pleased. "Damp mornings like this, my shoulder used to feel sore, but since I signed on with Captain Dean, it's been all right! Yes, sir, I can pull my weight!"

My father had two seamen's bags ready for us. "Get to the quay as fast as you can—and don't look so glum, Miles. Remember what I told you: a smile is the best ticket to Heaven that any man can carry."

He pushed us toward the door. "Get out of here before somebody finds that piece of carrion and comes running to me to do something about it."

He put my bag on my shoulder, kissed me lightly and coughed as if to show me he wasn't overly concerned at my departure. "Every young man ought to travel, and any kind of travel is uncomfortable; so you'll be no worse off aboard the *Nottingham* than all the other young Englishmen who run off to France and Italy every summer."

CHAPTER 4

I knew how my father felt. I was always low in my mind when I left him to go up to Oxford; but now I was even more unhappy, because he showed so clearly that he *was* concerned, and deeply. For the life of me I couldn't say a word: could only hope that someday I could show my feelings in a proper manner.

As we went down the steps and turned toward the oily, misty river, my father called after us, "Watch over him, Swede, as though he were your own boy." I always remembered his words, and Swede never forgot them either.

Chapter 5

An argument was in progress between Langman and Captain Dean, when we came over the *Nottingham's* bulwarks that morning of July 30th. Langman was protesting because Captain Dean had ordered him to remove his dunnage from the after cabin so that there might be room for other passengers—the others being his younger brother Henry, Neal Butler, Swede and me.

Probably for those of us who don't have villainy in our hearts—and villainy, of course, includes jealousy, which is responsible for most of the ills that beset this world—stupidity is our besetting sin. I have never been jealous of any man, but I have been stupid far too often. I was stupid not to see why Langman was so determined to retain a foothold in the after cabin.

"You made an agreement with me," he told Captain Dean. "I was to have a cabin, same as yours. I was captain of my own ship under Woodes Rogers, and captain of this vessel, too, before I sold her to your brother, and you've got no right——"

"Now just a minute," Captain Dean said. "My brother

Jasper made a gentleman's agreement with you. He bought your ship and paid three hundred pounds for it, and no questions asked. He made just one concession to you, and that was that you were to sail on her as first mate under me as captain, and could ship Mellen and White along with you."

"All those other things are in the contract," Langman said. "He promised me——"

"Come now, Langman," Captain Dean said moderately, "my brother has no secrets from me. He told me exactly the arrangements he made with you, and I've followed them precisely. You're first mate of this ship, and you'll continue to be so, no matter how many lies you tell me. Nicholas Mellen and George White were signed on as sailors on this ship at your insistence. First you said I'd promised you a berth in the after cabin. I didn't. Then you said my brother guaranteed you the same. He didn't, any more than he guaranteed Mellen and White any specific quarters. Through no fault of my own, there's no room for you in the after cabin, so you're to get forward and bunk with the men. If you find this too uncomfortable or too inconvenient, you can feel free to leave the ship at any moment."

"Now you're not only breaking your brother's solemn covenant, but you're trying to deprive me of a chance to make a living," Langman said.

"Stow it," Captain Dean said. "Stow all that guff about solemn covenants. I'm breaking nothing and I'm depriving you of nothing. I'd be within my rights if I discharged you for insubordination; but even if I did, you'd get along anywhere on the Thames Estuary as long as you could scrape up little boys to catch whitebait for you. Go forward,

Mr. Langman, and light a dozen sulfur candles in the foc's'l—a matter you should have attended to long ago, by the way. The place has enough bugs to stock half a dozen of those Woodes Rogers ships you're always talking about."

Langman stared at Captain Dean with that characteristic little one-sided smile of his—one that I soon came to recognize as a sneer: not a smile at all. "First thing I know," Langman said, "these passengers of yours will rank me. And if they do, I won't be first mate any more. Then you'll have broken your brother's solemn covenant again."

"Don't worry, Mr. Langman," Captain Dean said. "You're still first mate, but you'll be subordinate to these two gentlemen. Mr. Whitworth is supercargo and Swede here is first lieutenant, having served as captain of the foretop on one of Her Majesty's ships. As soon as I've got Mr. Whitworth settled in the cabin, I'll thank you to give him whatever help he needs to get our cordage aboard and stowed away. We've got to be out of this river in two days."

"She's not fit to sail," Langman said, "and you know it."

"I know nothing of the sort," Captain Dean said. "She's fit to sail as far as Ireland; and whatever needs doing, we'll have done when we get there."

"Four of our guns are worthless," Langman said. "You can't protect yourself if you get chased by a privateer."

Captain Dean looked surprised. "That's news to me," he said. "You fired all ten of 'em?"

"Well, not exactly," Langman said, "but I can tell."

"If they're guns and hold together," Swede said, "you only need to scale 'em and prick out their touch-holes. I'll make 'em worth something to you."

"We've got no water," Langman protested.

"We've got enough water to take us to Donegal," Captain Dean said, "and the best mineral spring in Great Britain is at Killybegs. Do as I tell you and do it quick."

Captain Dean pushed us into the after cabin. "Thank God you're aboard," he said. "That damned Langman! I'll bet your father was right when he suspected Langman of being a buccaneer! Remember how he said 'most of these privateers are buccaneers, no matter what the law says'? That would account for the way Langman fights me at every turn. That's a buccaneer to the life. A privateersman has order aboard his ship, but buccaneers live without government, spend all the money they capture, make no distinction between captain and crew, and are forever changing officers and fighting among themselves like tomcats."

He introduced us to his brother Henry, contenting himself with saying that Henry was the gambler of the family, and traveling for his health: wishful, too, of studying the methods of American merchants. Henry was a smaller silent copy of the captain, done in weaker colors, and he was an epileptic.

"Where's my boy?" Swede asked.

"I've got him copying something," Captain Dean said. "I'll keep him at it until we're safe away. He laid awake all last night, gritting his teeth. I probably gritted mine, too, because I had a lot of thinking to do–some about Neal and Miles, but more about this Langman."

We stowed our dunnage as instructed. Captain Dean put me with Henry Dean in one of the three small rooms, Neal Butler in a second room with Swede. The captain bunked by himself in the third and smallest room. There was a fourth room answering as a head for those occupying the great cabin—though the term "great" could only be applied to it out of courtesy. Neal was hard at work copying *The Seaman's Secrets* onto sheets of paper stitched together, but Captain Dean took me by the arm and urged me toward the deck when I stopped to look at Neal's writing.

"Don't waste a minute," the captain said. "This Langman is a troublemaker. He hates your father for giving him a dressing down, and somehow—probably by keeping his ears open at the Riverside Tavern—he found out that I insured this vessel and our cargo with your father. He's been gabbing about it all over the ship. Insured for vast sums, he's telling the men. Vast sums, for God's sake! You probably know how much insurance I took out—two hundred and fifty pounds!"

He halted me at the top of the companion ladder. "That's why I'm so anxious to stow that cordage, and get to sea before Langman has a chance to go ashore and talk. If he ever hears about that dead man, he'll put two and two together, and he'd be bound to figure ten as the answer."

For a time I feared that Langman might inflict some of his contrariness on Neal, but apparently he had been made wary by my father's protest against his employment of boys at small wages. He walked widely around Neal, but I often caught him looking at the boy out of the corners of his eyes, as one watches a thunderhead that may become dangerous.

Of course I couldn't be sure, but I felt that Langman didn't know that Neal had ever been in any way connected with Penkethman's players. Even so, I was apprehensive, and Captain Dean was equally fearful; so the two of us worked the men hard at loading the cordage, and I had my first look at the company with whom I was to spend the most important days of my life.

Sailors to me are a mystery, always, and I shall forever be at a loss as to why men of their own free will take to the sea. To my way of thinking a ship is no better than a prison, and those who sail upon her, barring the captain, do so out of desperation or out of their inability to make a living on the land.

Our ship's cook, for example, Cooky Sipper, could never have been a cook anywhere except on a merchant vessel, where there's little to eat save salt pork, salt beef and ship's biscuit. As a seaman and a stower of cordage he was useless; and being a fat man, he succeeded at only two things: perspiring easily and getting in everyone's way. He was of so little use to us that I asked Langman to send him back to his galley.

The *Nottingham* accidentally—and because of Langman's insistence when he sold the *Nottingham* to the Deans—carried two bos'ns, George White and Nicholas Mellen, both former shipmates of Langman. A bos'n, because he has charge of all sails, rigging, canvas, colors, anchors, cables and cordage, must of necessity be an able seaman, and White and Mellen certainly were able, even though they were thick as thieves with Langman. White had a depression at the end of his nose, like the stem-end of a peach, and Mellen was so cross-eyed that I didn't see how he could steer a boat.

The carpenter, Chips Bullock, looked a little like his name, for he would stand with head lowered, staring at a task to be done, then rush at it like a bull, pushing and heaving and grunting.

The other men in the crew—William Saver, Christopher Gray, Charles Graystock and Harry Hallion—were about the same sort of sailors that every resident of Greenwich was accustomed to see in taverns, or wandering aimlessly along the streets: people who seemed to have come from nowhere and to be bound for nowhere.

Saver had enormous ears and never smiled except when he heard of trouble occurring to someone. He wasn't particular. Anyone would do.

Christopher Gray was a gunner who had lost two fingers and had his eyelids blown full of powder grains. I doubted that he could lay a gun effectively, but I never found out, fortunately.

Graystock was a small man with a drooping lower lip. Whatever he was set to do, he always left it half done in order to talk to and interfere with someone who was doing well enough without assistance.

Hallion was a reckless sort, forever getting hurt because he did things in ways they shouldn't be done. He had a positive genius for doing things wrong, poor wretch.

Their faces were wrinkled and drab, as if they'd been salted in a beef barrel, instead of exposed to the sun. Yet all of them worked to the best of their ability, perhaps because that pale gambler Henry Dean worked with them, as did Swede and even the captain, except when the latter was ashore, getting the cordage into barges and making sure that it reached us with a minimum of delay. Only Neal Butler remained in the cabin, copying and copying *The Seaman's Secrets* onto his stitched sheets.

"We'll take no chances," Captain Dean said, "and I won't feel safe if anyone—anyone at all—catches a glimpse of that boy while we're still at this anchorage."

CHAPTER 5

So every one of the five of us in the *Nottingham's* cabin heaved a sigh of relief when, on the morning of August 2nd, the last bargeload of cordage came aboard. Even before it was lowered into the hold, our anchors were aweigh, and we were headed downstream for the Nore, that sandy islet at the mouth of the Thames where outbound merchantmen assemble to wait for warships assigned to convoy them out of England's privateer-infested narrow waters and in the general direction of their desired havens.

As we came down among the sixty-odd vessels anchored at the Nore, Captain Dean eyed them disparagingly. "Look at their hulls," he told me. "Hardly a galley among 'em: bluff bows, like tubs. If we get many like that in our convoy, we'll have to strike out on our own."

"If you strike out on your own," Langman warned, "this ship'll have another owner in a week's time."

"Is that a threat, Mr. Langman?" Captain Dean asked mildly.

Langman's face was a dusky red. "No!" he shouted. "But I took this ship myself when I was with Woodes Rogers, and I know how easy she is to take! You let a French privateer lay her aboard and where'll *you* be?"

"I'll be awake, Mr. Langman," Captain Dean said. "I think perhaps her crew was asleep when *you* took her."

Langman went forward, seething.

That passage between Langman and Captain Dean was characteristic of their attitudes. Captain Dean's idol, whom he quoted and to whom he referred more frequently than did Langman to Woodes Rogers, was Sir Isaac Newton. Dean had corresponded with Newton regarding an improved method of finding the longitude of a ship at sea;

and he admired Newton immeasurably for his invention of the reflecting telescope.

But at any mention of either of these additions to human knowledge, Langman became not only outrageous, but almost incoherent with fury.

"Longitude!" he'd sputter. "What do you want of more longitude! All you need is latitude! If this Newton finds out what you're hoping he'll learn about longitude, he'll take the bread right out of the mouths of sailors. Any damn fool will be able to navigate. I say let well enough alone! Why foul your own nest?"

His attitude toward Newton's reflecting telescope was even worse, and he went so far as to insist that such a telescope was impossible. Nonsense, he called it.

Captain Dean listened to his tirades against Newton and his reflecting telescope with a placid face. "Mr. Langman," he said, "I've looked through Sir Isaac Newton's reflecting telescope. By using prisms, he makes it possible to see things that you couldn't see at all through an ordinary telescope."

"Prisms!" Langman snorted. "There's no such thing! Even if there was, you couldn't clog a telescope with one of 'em and still use it!"

"Seeing is believing," the captain said.

"Like hell it is," Langman said. "I've seen ships sailing upside down! I've seen sun dogs, with four suns around a central sun! That doesn't mean ships sail upside down, does it, or that there's five suns? Prisms, for God's sake! You'd never get me to look through a telescope full of prisms! This Newton must be crazy!" His look implied that Captain Dean as well was more than touched with insanity. He stalked away, his neck swollen with suppressed anger.

CHAPTER 5

"What makes him like that?" I asked Captain Dean.

He shrugged his shoulders. "Who knows? The world is full of Langmans, believing in all sorts of worthless tarradiddle, but condemning things that might help mankind. Newton's a case in point. He's shown the world something new and valuable, so the ignorant attack him. Like all ignorant people, they're stubborn about it, and angry for fear they may have to eat their words. The Langmans always refuse to look through the telescope."

"Maybe so," I said, "but if I were captain of this ship, I'd make Langman keep a civil tongue in his head."

"Well, you *aren't* captain, Miles," Captain Dean said, "and to be frank about it, I wish *I* weren't. I'm captain to please my brother Jasper. I'd rather be of some service to my country in foreign parts—in America: Holland: Sweden, where I wouldn't be dealing day and night with sailors, who're forever seeing sea-serpents or the Flying Dutchman or privateers, and condemning everything decent like Isaac Newton or the reading of books."

He eyed me quizzically. "How would *you* make Langman keep a civil tongue in his head, Miles?"

"With a belaying pin, if I had to."

Captain Dean shook his head. "No, Miles. That wouldn't do. There's two ways of running a ship. One's by violence. The other's by letting the men think they're being consulted. I can't use violence, Miles, because I don't like violence. I'm afraid of it. I'm strong, and if I hit any man on this ship, I'd put my heart in it and wouldn't be able to keep my mind on my work for fear he'd be hurt—killed, maybe. Besides, Miles, we're shorthanded. A galley, by rights, should have a crew of twenty-five. We have fourteen, including you and me. I can't leave the quarter-deck to hand sails, and I can't risk losing a man for any reason. Don't expect heroics out of me, Miles. I'm just an ordinary individual, who has to go to the head like everyone else, makes mistakes like all the rest of the world, and is mighty glad he doesn't have to be burdened with listening to as many damned fools as surrounded Oliver Cromwell or Charles II."

On the seventh of August two sloops of war made signals indicating that they would convoy all merchant vessels wishing to proceed to northern Scotland or northern Ireland, and we soon learned that Captain Dean was right about the sailing qualities of the twelve vessels that moved off to the eastward to cluster around the sloops of war like fat goslings between two proud parent geese. They were slow, and by the time we had rounded the bulge of Norfolk and borne up into the North Sea, Captain Dean was in as much of a frenzy as a man so placid could be. His irritation was understandable, because in order to sail as slowly as the other tubs in the convoy, we carried nothing except topsails and headsails.

By the time we had reached the latitude of the north riding of York, with Whitby off our larboard beam, he sniffed the warm west breeze and could stand it no longer. "Get the rest of the sails on her, Mr. Langman," he shouted. "We've been five days coming this far, and alone we could have done it in two. Crowd on the canvas. We'll have this convoy hull-down by midafternoon, and be off the Orkneys tomorrow, sure as shooting."

Langman seemed horrified. "What do you want to do," he demanded, "throw this vessel away? What'll you do if you run into a privateer?"

"Do?" Captain Dean asked. "Why, I'll do what any sailor'd do. I'll run from her. Before I ran, though, I'd want to make sure she *was* a privateer. One thing I learned long ago, Mr. Langman, is that nearly every time a sailor-man thinks he sees a Black Flag, it turns out to be the captain's overcoat hung up to dry. Get those sails on her."

"The men won't like it," Langman protested.

"You mean Mellen and White won't like it," the captain said. "They won't if you tell them not to, so don't tell 'em. A few days ago you were howling we shouldn't sail because of not having enough water: now you're screaming we oughtn't to make a run for Killybegs, where there's plenty of fine water to be had. Get on with those sails."

That was the beginning of an oft-renewed argument between Langman and Captain Dean—an argument that came to one of its many heads when we did in fact round the northern tip of Scotland, slip through the narrow waters between the mainland and the Hebrides, swiftly skirt the north of Ireland and start down toward the Isle of Aran and Donegal Bay.

We were still short of Aran by a few miles when the lookout sighted two vessels in a bay near the tip of Aran. As soon as Langman heard the word, he went halfway up the mizzen ratlins to see for himself: then called down to Mellen and White.

"Privateers," he bawled. He came down the ratlins like a squirrel and ran to the quarter-deck. "Those are privateers," he told the captain. "All the men say so."

"What do the men know about it?" Captain Dean asked. "I know, and they probably don't, that Donegal Bay is full of British naval vessels and fishermen. This is no place for French privateers."

"I say they're privateers," Langman said. "I can tell by the cut of their jibs."

A voice reached us from the waist. "He wants us to be captured."

"Hear that?" Langman demanded. "That's what they're all saying: you want to be captured by a privateer."

"That's the silliest thing I ever heard," Captain Dean said. "Why in God's name would I want to be captured by a Frenchman?"

"You wouldn't act the way you're acting—you wouldn't run towards two privateers—unless you wanted to be taken."

"Look here," Captain Dean said. "This ship cost money, as you well know. So did the cordage we're carrying. We're within a few hours of a port where we'll take on another expensive cargo. I'd be the last one to run risks with this ship."

Langman was supercilious. "You insured the cordage, didn't you?"

"Of course I did," Captain Dean said. "Only a fool would fail to insure his cargo."

"Well," Langman persisted, "if you turned the ship over to a privateer, your brother Jasper'd get the insurance money, wouldn't he?"

"Certainly he would," Captain Dean said. "Also, all of us, including me and my brother Henry, would land in a French prison. If I thought I was in danger of being captured, I'd run the ship ashore."

Langman wouldn't stop worrying the subject. "If you *did* run her ashore, both you and your brother would get the money."

Captain Dean turned away from him and took the wheel

from Harry Hallion. "Harry," he said, "go forward and tell the men we're running between Aran and the main, and that we'll neither abandon this ship nor let any Frenchman have her."

Hallion went forward and spoke to White and Mellen, the two bos'ns. At his words both Mellen and White burst into derisive laughter.

"This has gone far enough," Captain Dean said. "Take the wheel, Miles! Keep her steady as she goes."

He ran from the quarter-deck to the waist, stepping in front of Mellen and White, who stared sullenly at the deck.

"What are you damned fools preaching to these men?" Captain Dean demanded.

Mellen gave him a sullen answer. "We're not preaching anything. We just don't propose to be turned over to the damned French."

"Do you know what you're saying?" Captain Dean said. "You're implying I'm a traitor."

When neither Mellen nor White answered, Captain Dean's two big hands shot out, seized them by the collars of their jackets and banged their heads together so that the sound came clearly to us on the quarter-deck. "I'll have common sense on this ship, and not a lot of buccaneery blathering about things you don't understand! Such as privateers! Such as insurance!" He threw them to the deck between two of the guns.

He didn't like violence, he had told me, and he had meant it. Both White and Mellen were able to get to their feet. The cracking together of their heads had been no more violent than the caning a schoolmaster gives a boy for writing verses on the wall of a privy. If the captain had treated them with the violence their conduct deserved, their skulls would have cracked like plover eggs.

It was easy to see that Langman, Mellen and White had conspired together. They used the same words: the same impossible false arguments, and I, like a fool, still couldn't understand why. I thought they behaved as they did because they were wrong-headed. God only knows why so many humans are afflicted with that terrible disease, or failing, or whatever it is; but I did know that wrong-headed men are responsible for nearly all the world's troubles; and so I thought Langman, Mellen and White were wrong-headed because they couldn't help themselves.

The captain had been right all the time, for the two ships paid no more attention to us than as though we'd been a fishing schooner. We ran safely through the strait that separates Aran from the main, and next day, August 13th, we rounded the red cliffs at the northern entrance of Donegal Bay. By nightfall we were anchored in the snug harbor of Killybegs, surrounded by the greenest hills I ever hope to see. On the slopes of all the hills were black and white cattle on whose milk and cream and butter, which even Cooky Sipper couldn't spoil, we lived in luxury.

We lay in the harbor of Killybegs for six weeks, not from choice, but because Captain Dean said we had to wait for cool weather before loading a thousand firkins of butter and the three hundred cheeses which he proposed to sell to the citizens of Portsmouth, New Hampshire. Otherwise both cheese and butter might spoil.

CHAPTER 5

Portsmouth people, Captain Dean claimed, were the best people in the world—the kindest, the most hospitable, the most generous, the most appreciative, the most civilized of any people anywhere in America and he'd run no risk of offering them rancid butter.

England, he said, except for its Langmans and gipsies, its beggars and whores, its thieves, snobs, toadies, fops, rakes, gambling schemes, press gangs, wasn't half bad; but if it weren't for his brother Jasper and his obligation to sail ships in accordance with Jasper's plans, he would get himself a home in Portsmouth.

"Sometimes," he said in his solid, mild way, "I think Englishmen are all a pack of bastards; but Portsmouth people aren't. They don't think the way we do. It's something about the climate, probably. Those who can stand it have something happen to them. Even the lobsters grow two big claws."

For the first time since that terrible twenty-ninth of July, Neal Butler's smile came back to him in Killybegs. When he finished his copying of *The Seaman's Secrets*, Captain Dean set him to drawing the coast line of America from a worn Mercator's Projection, starting with Cape Sable in Nova Scotia and working as far south as New York.

Perhaps the prospect of America helped Neal to forget the happenings of July 29th: perhaps the scents and the sights and the sounds—the calmness and remoteness—of that placid pretty harbor of Killybegs started him talking to the captain about fish. But talk he did, and soon, with the captain's permission, he and Swede were thick as porridge with a dozen fishermen, so that they knew where to go to fish, and kept the galley well supplied.

Soon, too, except for one thing, he was himself again. When he wasn't running errands for Captain Dean and cleaning our cabins, or carefully laying off the American coast in his notebook, he was helping Swede scale the guns, or learning the care and the use of a plane and an adze from Chips Bullock, giving him a hand at knocking together the water casks; or he was in the galley, peering at the messes Cooky Sipper concocted.

Yes, he was himself again except for just one thing. He wouldn't talk about the theatre or anything that had happened to him during his life in Greenwich. Swede and Captain Dean and I knew why this was, and were careful to make no reference to matters that Neal with good reason found painful. But not Langman. I'll never forget the glittering September morning when Neal was stowing fishing tackle in the *Nottingham's* small tender, and Langman stood at the top of the ladder, looking down at him with that derisive half-smile of his. Just what Langman said, we on the quarter-deck couldn't distinguish; but we heard him mockingly call Neal "Whitebait."

Captain Dean and I simultaneously started for Langman; but though we were quick, we were too slow. Swede, darting from the after-cabin, swung his long right arm scythe-like at Langman. Langman rose a little to fall across the top of the bulwarks, his arms flailing, hung there a moment; then rolled over and into the harbor with a gratifying splash.

Neal, ironically enough, gaffed him and pulled him out; and as Langman mounted the ladder to stand dripping on the ladder grating, Captain Dean eyed him impassively and told him to be more careful of his footing.

For once Langman, as his glance went from Captain

Dean's face to Swede's and mine, looked apprehensive, and he set off for the fo'cs'l without his usual disdainful reply. Neal, I was sure, would be free of Langman's attentions for some time to come.

The last of sixty thousand pounds of the best Donegal butter, all packed in firkins, and three hundred Donegal cheeses had come aboard when we set sail on September 25th on a voyage that for devilishness was enough to make me wonder again and again why any man went to sea of his own free will.

During all the time the *Nottingham* sailed the great circle, we saw nothing but mountainous waves—ran into winds so contrary that we spent more time blundering backward than we did wallowing forward. The men, forever shortening sail, making sail, battening everything down to ride out storms that seemed to have no ending, manning the pumps, were constantly complaining, and like all men everywhere, they blamed their misfortunes on Captain Dean until I marveled at his patience.

Our water casks sprung leaks so that we had to go on short rations: our beef turned sour.

October was a villainous cold month: November was worse; and in December the sun apparently disappeared for good in a gurry of fog and dirty gray clouds.

Early in December we sighted a ship—the only sail we sighted in all that time—and spoke her, at which Langman set up his now familiar squealing that she was a French privateer.

She proved to be the ship *Pompey*, London bound, and her captain told us only two things: that we were off the Banks of Newfoundland, and that the weather where he'd come from was worse than what we'd had, no matter how bad that had been.

On Monday, December 4th, we caught a glimpse of Cape Sable in Nova Scotia. Then the weather turned dirtier than ever.

"We could make Portsmouth in a day," Captain Dean told us, "but I've got to see the sun just once before I take any chances."

So we stood off and on, and a week passed before we saw the sun.

The wind was frigid and bitter, and in the northeast, and the seas kicked up by that northeast gale seemed to run at us from every direction, instead of from the northeast. The waves, too, were dirty and gray, as if they'd gone down deep and dredged up all the sand and seaweed from the bottom.

I well remember that Monday morning when we finally caught sight of the sun. Usually a glimpse of it after a northeast blow, Captain Dean said, meant that we'd have a little decent weather. Instead of that, the sun stayed out just long enough for us to stand in toward the land and sight the long, low coast line of New England, with tree-covered points thrust out toward us, and all the ledges and hills covered with snow.

Captain Dean was elated. "That's Cape Porpoise," he said. "Now I know exactly where we are. We'll head due south, and we'll be in Portsmouth tomorrow morning."

He'd no sooner spoken than the sun disappeared again behind a driving wall of snow.

December 11th, Monday

I remember that day for other things. Our food, bad to begin with, had become steadily worse; and on that morning of December 11th there was none at all. Cooky Sipper, Langman told the captain, was sick, with a throat so full of phlegm that he could hardly swallow, and none of the other men knew how to cook.

So Swede volunteered to do the cooking until we reached Portsmouth; and when he went to the galley, Neal went along with him to help, not only to carry food to the after cabin, but to dish out to the men forward when they came to the galley with their mess kids.

We wallowed creakingly south, with those dirty gray seas and stinging snow squalls hissing all around us, until nightfall, when the captain turned over the deck to Mr. Langman, and Neal brought us boiled beef, boiled potatoes and ship's bread; then disappeared. We ate our supper as well as we could in that heaving, lurching cabin beneath the dim lights swinging in their gimbals.

The cabin felt empty without Swede and Neal, and as

time went on I worried about them and so climbed on deck to go forward to the cookhouse. The quarter-deck, except for the helmsman, was empty; and when I half slid, half skated forward to the galley, I found Langman braced in the doorway of that narrow cubicle. Inside it the lamp cast a flickering light on Swede and Neal, both of whom were staring at Langman with eyes so shadowed that they seemed sunk in their heads.

When, to steady myself, I caught hold of the doorpost beside Langman, he opened his mouth as if to say something: then shut it again, turned, and worked his way back to the quarter-deck.

"Miles," Swede said, "something smells around here, and it's not the cheese. Langman's been in the hold after extra meat for White and Mellen."

"He's got no business tampering with the provisions," I said. "That's for the captain to do."

"Yes," Swede said, "and he also wants to head straight out to sea."

I couldn't believe my ears. "Straight out to sea! What for, for God's sake! We're running southwest before a northeaster. If we turn at right angles, we'll be in the trough and on our beam-ends before you can say Scat! Why would anyone want to take her straight out, anyway?"

"Tell him what you heard, Neal," Swede said.

"It was when he gave Mellen the meat," Neal said. "He said, 'If we can't wait for this blow to let up, we'll be in Portsmouth tomorrow.' Then he said, 'Tell 'em I'll get 'em more water too.' "

"That's what Neal heard," Swede said, "and as I see it, there's no two ways about it. Langman wants this ship for himself. He's waited till the last minute, all along, hoping for a fair wind and blue skies that would make it safe for him to take her over on one excuse or another. Well, he'll never get a fair wind or blue skies tomorrow, and he knows the only way to get 'em is to put straight out to sea and wait for the wind to turn. If he doesn't, we'll be in Portsmouth, and he'll have lost his chance."

I stared at him; and only now did I see clearly what I should have seen long ago. "Of course," I said. "And the extra meat and the extra water would be for bribes to get the others to side with him."

"What else?" Swede asked.

I told Swede to dowse the lantern, lock the galley and get back to the cabin with Neal as quickly as he could—and because I didn't like the way Langman had abandoned the quarter-deck to argue with Swede and Neal in the galley, I went behind them to make sure they got there.

When I reached the quarter-deck, I could just make out Langman in the snowy dark.

"I didn't see a lookout up forward," I told him.

"Lookout! What's the good of a lookout on a night like this?" I could sense the contempt on his swarthy thin face.

In the snug cabin Captain Dean had his coat off, readying himself for bed; but when I followed Neal and Swede through the door and started telling him what they had told me, he reached behind him for his coat.

Henry Dean, lying fully dressed on his bunk, climbed out heavily and pulled a knitted cap down over his ears.

They heard me out: then Captain Dean angrily pulled on his own hat, picked up the loggerhead from beside the cabin stove; and all of us went out again into the whirling snowflakes.

Langman wasn't on the quarter-deck. Captain Dean spoke to the helmsman, "Where's the mate?"

Gray, the helmsman, said, "He went forward, Captain."

"He went to the hold," Swede said. "That's where he went: to the hold for water."

The door to the hold swung open and Langman, carrying a lantern in one hand and a water jug in the other, stepped out on the snowy deck.

"You're supposed to be on watch, Mr. Langman," Captain Dean said. "Where's your lookout? You have no business in the hold. What are you doing with that water jug? You know everyone on this ship is on a strict water ration!"

"That ain't so," Langman said. "You have all the water you want, and the crew gets half enough! They're sick of you and your ways. They say you're aiming to run this ship ashore, now, tonight! They say you've got to alter your course and take her straight out to sea if you want to prove you're not aiming to wreck her."

"Wreck her?" Captain Dean shouted. "In a northeaster? Are you crazy, Langman? Do you think I want to commit suicide? I took my bearings from Cape Porpoise! There's no place to wreck her unless I steer due west. Wreck her at night? Wreck her in a northeaster? Wreck her in a snowstorm? Talk sense, Langman! And get a lookout forward!"

"By God," Langman said, "you'll take her out to sea or we'll know the reason why!"

Captain Dean raised his head and seemed to sniff the air. "Swede!" he shouted. "Go forward! Keep your eyes peeled!"

Swede left us, scrambling, his right arm hanging low,

ape-like, as if to keep himself from falling on the scum of slush amidships.

To Langman Captain Dean said, "I'll take no orders from you, Christopher Langman. You'll stop inciting this crew to rebellion! If you don't start acting like the mate of this ship, I'll take steps! What in God's name are you running without a lookout for?"

"How can a lookout keep his eyes open in gurry like this?" Langman demanded.

"He could hear, couldn't he?" the captain snapped.

Langman turned contemptuously away, and found himself squarely confronted by Henry Dean, who reached out and took the water jug, almost as though he took a child from its mother's arms. Langman resisted, shouting, "Mellen! White!"

On this Captain Dean stepped forward and brought the loggerhead down on Langman's skull. When Langman swayed but didn't fall, Captain Dean hit him again. Langman dropped to his knees, but, unfortunately for all of us, staggered to his feet again and reeled toward the cabin.

We heard Swede shouting something from the bow.

The captain ran forward, sliding precariously on the sloppy planks. Almost immediately he ran back past us to climb to the quarter-deck again and I was conscious of a hoarseness in the air about me, a sort of raucous wet humming that seemed to fill me with a deadening fright and turn my arms and legs to water.

"Starboard!" Captain Dean shouted to the helmsman. "Hard to starboard!"

The deck surged up beneath us. The whole ship lurched and seemed to cough, as a man, coughing, convulses himself.

The bow fell off to larboard, and the vessel sickeningly rolled and rose up and up on a monstrous wave.

"Get your helm to *starboard*! *Starboard!*" Captain Dean screamed.

The raucous wet humming all around us deepened to a menacing all-pervasive rumble, overwhelming, stomach-shaking—and the enormous comber on which the ship was riding seemed to hurl her forward.

She struck with a crash that threw me to the deck—a crash so loud that my brain crackled, and among the splinters was a faint hope that if any man lived within a mile of where we struck, he would be wakened by that dreadful sound and hurry to help us.

The rumbling, roaring thunder of which we seemed to be the center was the sound of breakers pounding at the unseen rocks on which the *Nottingham* shuddered and grated; and even in my despairing panic I had quick thoughts—if the disjointed fragments that flutter in a man's mind in an emergency can be called thoughts:

. . . that Langman's repeated insistence that Captain Dean had all along intended to run the *Nottingham* ashore now seemed to be true, but was in truth more untrue than ever:

. . . that never, in all our weeks of sailing against adverse winds, had we ever heard anything approaching the deafening tumult that now surrounded us:

. . . that nothing made by man could withstand the hammer blows that beat upon the *Nottingham's* weather side to pour torrents of icy water and slashing spray across her canted deck—and yet that this shore upon which we had struck had been here, unharmed, since the world began, in spite of innumerable storms—that among the crevices of those rocks were living things that would survive these pounding waves . . . and that perhaps we ourselves would similarly survive.

The *Nottingham's* stern was higher than the bow, as if bent on thrusting her stern more solidly against the shore, and the waist of the ship seemed filled with struggling figures, striving to reach the after cabin.

I found Neal pushing at Swede's buttocks: found a rope-end to which to cling: ran into Chips Bullock, with an axe and a hammer in one hand and his workbag in the other, making his way along the weather rail.

A breaker curled over the bulwarks, hit him squarely, and sent him sliding down the steep deck and into a gun carriage. My rope-end let me reach him, take his axe and hammer and pull him to his feet.

"My workbag!" he shouted. "Spikes! Nails!" He fell to his knees, scrabbling in the scuppers for his workbag. Another wash of icy foam struck us. By the grace of my rope-end we clawed free of the scuppers and pushed and pulled each other to the cabin companion.

The cabin was like a room insecurely poised on one of its corners, and something about a structure so tilted throws a man off balance, both physically and mentally. Every person in it is dizzy and, unless he holds to something, falls down: his mind, too, is so addled that he thinks he can stand, and so gets to his feet only to fall immediately, like a wounded pigeon.

The dark deck had been bad enough, what with waves, the icy torrents that drenched us, the crunching of the ship as she thumped upon the rocks; but the inside of the cabin was worse, and for the first time in my life I knew terror, as I think each of the fourteen of us knew it, even though some concealed it.

A single lamp still burned dimly, shuddering in its gimbals. Only Captain Dean was on his feet, supporting himself by the rudder case. The others were on the floor, some trying to rise, only to reel down again: the others just lying there. Cooky Sipper was moaning.

I found that if I closed my eyes the strange tilt of the room had next to no effect upon me. I could crawl to the cabin wall and pull myself erect by clinging to it. I made my discovery known to Neal and Swede and Chips.

Langman, when we crawled in, was striving to make himself heard by Captain Dean. "You were bound to do it from the very first!" he was shouting. "You've been looking for a chance to run her ashore since the day we left the convoy! You planned it!"

"Don't be a damn fool!" Captain Dean shouted back. "This is no time for such stuff as that! I want every man in this cabin to pray."

"Pray?" Langman demanded, and his voice was a squeal. "You think God's going to come down here and pull us off these rocks after you've put us on them?"

Captain Dean smashed his fist against the rudder case. "All right! All right! I put you here! All I know is there was no land on the course I plotted from Cape Porpoise, and there was no lookout forward when you had the deck. Now pray!"

"Pray?" Langman shouted again. "How's that going to help us? Nothing can help us, now you've gone and run us ashore!"

"Don't pray for help!" the captain told him. "Pray for the strength to help yourself! Strength!"

The whole ship sagged sickeningly to one side: reeled even more sickeningly to the other: a sea that must have been enormous struck her side with such force that my eardrums felt thrust against my throbbing brain. A splitting sound came from beneath us, and the cabin floor fluttered.

"Oh, God!" Captain Dean said, "give each man the strength to stand upon his feet and stretch out a helping hand to every other man. Say it, every last one of you, and mean it! God give me strength! Say it, Langman."

"God give me strength," Langman said.

"Again!" Captain Dean shouted. "Everyone! God give me strength!"

The men's voices quavered, thin and bird-like through the sounds of the smashing seas.

The whole after part of the ship straightened a little, then seemed to slide downhill.

"Get on deck," Captain Dean cried. "Get up and get out before she breaks in two or slides off." He reached out and pulled Chips to his feet. "Use your axe! Swede! Miles! Go with him! Cut the weather shrouds and ratlins! If the masts fall toward the land, we may have a chance! If they don't fall, chop the foremast!" He flung Chips toward the companionway. Swede and I followed him.

Behind us Captain Dean stormed among the men, kicking them and hauling them to their feet.

The task of cutting those shrouds and ratlins—of keeping a foothold on that steep and slippery deck—was difficult beyond belief. We couldn't trust ourselves on the chains because of the smashing of the waves against the side. For a time Chips insisted he could stand on the bulwarks and swing his axe. We hoisted him up to let him thrust a foot through the ratlins. He hooked his other leg around a stay, but when he swung his axe, one of those roaring towering breakers foamed against him and blinded us. When the foam subsided, Chips was in the scuppers once more, but still clinging to his axe.

We tried holding Chips pinned against the bulwarks with our shoulders; but the unending slash of icy foam and the driving snow numbed me: must have numbed Chips, too, for he couldn't seem to swing the axe.

"Give me that axe," Swede shouted. "We've got to get ashore somehow! Stand under me. When I fall, catch me if you can."

He pushed the axe handle inside his breeches, put an arm around Neal's shoulders, bellowed, "We'll be all right"; then went up the inside of the ratlins like a big spider. We lost him at once in the snow and the flying spray, but felt the jarring of his axe against the rigging—and then, suddenly, he came sprawling down among us. Almost in the same moment the foremast went over the side with a splintering crash. Then the mainmast went, and the ship rolled on her side to surge soggily as if agonized by the pounding of those roaring breakers.

"Look for the axe!" Swede said. "I threw it to leeward when I fell!"

"To hell with the axe," Chips said. "Get ashore! Wherever people live we can find another axe."

I agreed with him. We could have hunted forever for that axe or for Chips's workbag in the darkness and on that glacial deck.

"I'll go first," Swede said. "I want Neal close behind me. I want Miles behind Neal."

He left us, and we felt rather than saw him inching along the mast. We crawled out after him. Ratlins and shrouds were tangled around it. The foretop was like a fence to be climbed, but we climbed it.

The tip of the mast rested against something solid. That something was seaweed, and beneath the seaweed were rocks—solid, immovable rocks.

We were safe, I thought, secure from those bellowing breakers; and even as I write the words "safe" and "secure," I feel a sort of shame for those who, like myself, could let themselves think that there is ever any such thing as safety and security.

The seaweed was so slippery that if a person upon it was unable to see where to step, he staggered, he lurched, his feet went out from under him, pitching him upon his face or, even worse, wrenchingly upon his back.

Under the thick mop of seaweed that covered the rocks against which the foremast truck rested there were countless barnacles. When we put out our hands to break our falls, which were constant, the barnacles slashed our fingers, wrists and knees.

Eventually slipping and feeling our way up that treacherous shore, hopeful of removing ourselves from the unending roaring of the breakers, we came to naked ice-covered rocks on which no seaweed grew. To me that meant we were above high-water mark. Now we were truly safe—or so I idiotically thought again.

I caught at Swede's wet coat. "Swede," I said, "we'll have to find shelter from this snow and wind." Not only was the snow plastering itself against our faces with a force that numbed us, but the snow was mixed with spindrift, so that it seemed twice as cold as anything could be.

"Go to the left," I told Swede. "I'll go to the right. Chips can walk straight ahead. Let's leave Neal here to shout to us in case we're lost. Leave Chips's hammer with Neal, too, so Chips won't lose it when he falls. Hunt for trees or bushes–any kind of shelter. Anything–anything at all. Even an old shed, or a pigpen, or an overhanging ledge. Or a fence or a clump of thick grass. Or a hill. If you can find a hill, we can get in its lee. That would be better than nothing."

We blundered off into the thick, roaring dark. The tumultuous sea seemed to thunder from every direction. The footing, in that darkness, was nothing but rock–round boulders; sharp boulders; low irregular ledges, all slippery with a half-inch coat of ice.

Rocks turned beneath my feet; spilled me into pockets between them. The pockets had razor-like crushed sea-shells at their bottoms. The naked rocks were worse than the seaweed-covered ones on which we had landed, for when I fell I had the feeling that a leg or an arm must break.

These rocks, I thought, must lead to some sort of beach, or a marsh, or a field. Instead of that, my groping hands again felt seaweed. Either the coast had turned, or I had become confused and turned myself. I bore more sharply to the left, to escape that damnable seaweed that was even more slippery than ice, though more cushiony.

After all this exertion, this fever of activity, this terror of the pelting snow and flying foam–yes, and of the unending menacing crashing of the sea—my mouth and throat were like leather. In desperation I chipped ice from one of the boulders and sucked at it. It was almost fresh, with only the faintest trace of saltiness.

While I stood there, chipping more ice and crunching it to bits, I heard a thin piping ahead—a faint wailing or squeaking, dim amid all the uproar of the breakers. It might have been a sea bird: it might have been the screaking of one rock driven by a breaker against another.

I held my breath and listened—and heard it again: a faint call.

I crawled even more to my left, feeling for boulders, cutting my hands on barnacles, skirting ledges; easing myself head first to the tops of rocks: then lowering myself feet first on the far side.

On thus mounting a ledge I found myself looking down into a black cavity in which there was noise and movement and from which, as I balanced there, burst a desperate bellow, a prolonged "Hullooo!" from many voices.

"I'm Whitworth," I shouted into that black void.

I heard Langman's voice. "Whitworth makes nine. Where's Captain Dean? Where's Neal Butler? Where's Swede? Where's Chips? Where's Cooky Sipper?"

"I know where Neal is," I said. "I'll get him. I sent Swede to the left to hunt shelter when we got above high-water mark. I sent Chips straight out."

"Shout," Langman said. "One, two, three: Hulloooo!"

I joined in their shout with all my heart and strength, realizing horribly, as I did so, that the faint sound I had heard a few short minutes before had been the concerted bellowing of eight men, yet that outcry had carried only a matter of ten paces because of the wailing of the northeaster and the terrifying unending noise of that savage ocean.

There was a clatter and a cry of pain from the dark hollow. I heard Captain Dean's voice. "I've got Cooky Sipper! How many's here?"

"Nine," Langman said. "Eleven with you and Cooky." Swede's voice came to us throbbingly, half strangled by the snow and the wind. "I'm twelve. I've lost my bearings! Where's the boy?"

"Thank God," the captain said. "The boy's back there a rod and a half. He said Whitworth told him to stay. He wouldn't come along with me."

I shouted to Swede that I'd get him, and went lurching off into the teeth of the storm. The going seemed easier when I had a known goal. Maybe I'd learned how to handle myself more skillfully on those ice-covered rocks and ledges.

As I went I called Neal's name, and when at length I heard him answer, I had the first moment of mental peace I'd had since Captain Dean brought down the loggerhead on Christopher Langman's skull.

When I reached him he sank to his knees and huddled down into himself. "I haven't moved," he said. I could hardly understand his words, his voice was so shaken with cold. They came from him in shuddering gasps, most distressing.

"The captain found Cooky," he said. "The captain lost his coat. He cut his hands on the rocks. Where's my father?"

"He'll be all right," I said. I hoped to God I was telling

the truth. "Everybody's safe in a hole in the rocks. We'll go there now."

"Did anybody find a house?" Neal asked. Shudderingly he added, "Place to get warm?"

I didn't have the heart to answer. "You'll have to crawl, Neal," I said. "You'll fall if you don't. The rocks are icy. If you're thirsty you can eat the ice."

He still held Chips's hammer. I took it from him and with it pounded ice from a boulder. It came off in curved slabs about an inch thick. We bit into them as into slices of solid frosted bread. I could hear Neal crunch the ice. He would stop, overcome by a spasm of shivering: then go on crunching again.

When we got to the depression where Langman, Captain Dean and the other ten were huddled, I knocked more ice from a boulder and brought the slabs into the depression.

When I told them that the ice was nearly fresh, Langman protested that it couldn't be fresh: that it was nothing but frozen salt water and that those who ate it would lose their reason.

"How much have you eaten?" I asked.

"I haven't eaten *any*," Langman said. "I don't have to! It stands to reason it's got to be salt."

"I've eaten it," I said. "So has Neal. It's *not* salt. Didn't you hear me say it's fresh—almost?"

"Yes, I heard you," Langman said. "I heard another thing, too: heard Captain Dean say he didn't aim to run the ship ashore. Look at us now!"

Unseen hands fumbled at me and relieved me of my load of ice. Sounds of crunching came from all around.

"Has anybody got anything I can put on my head?" Captain Dean asked. "When I came to get off, the ship had slipped. To get ashore I laid off my coat and wig and had to jump. I can't see my hands, but I think I tore off some fingernails on the rock."

Nobody answered.

Swede called out, "Send Neal over here to me."

"I'll come too," I said.

The men were huddled together in an irregular oval between two outcroppings of ledge. The outcroppings were perhaps three feet high—no shelter at all until one rose to his feet and got the full force of the wind, snow and spray in his face.

No one stood up except from necessity, as when someone moved a boulder from beneath him and hoisted it to the top of the ledge.

To remove a boulder seemed to create more boulders. Underneath them was a hodgepodge of wet grit compounded of a million dead seashells.

"What did you find, Swede?" I asked.

"Same as Chips," Swede said. "Nothing. Just rocks and ledge. Then more seaweed."

"I think this is an island," Chips said. "When we get the spring tide——"

"Shut up!" Swede shouted. "Don't talk about things unless you're sure of 'em! Most of the hell in this world comes from loose talk!"

"Now look," Captain Dean said hoarsely. "We can't go on this way, or we'll freeze to death. My feet are numb already. I can't move or think as fast as I could before we went ashore. It took me quite a time to realize the mate was again implying that I ran the ship ashore on purpose."

Langman cursed him.

The captain's voice was as mild as it could be in such a tumult. "That's neither here nor there. I'm still captain, and I still give orders. Tomorrow you can elect a new captain if you think it's necessary. Right now I've got to do everything I can to see that there *is* a tomorrow for us. If we can last until daylight, and see where to put our feet, we'll find a better shelter. We can be warm. We'll be able to sleep. Maybe the ship will hold together. Maybe there'll be part of her left. What we've got to do is keep moving, two at a time, all night."

Langman spoke up at once. "I say No! If anybody moves around over those ice-covered rocks, he'll break a leg."

"Nobody's asking anyone to do so," Captain Dean said. "As near as I can tell from your voice, you're opposite me. All right: get to your feet. I'll get to *my* feet. All the rest start counting out loud. Count slow. Count to a hundred. While you count, the mate and I'll stamp up and down, standing in one place, and slap our arms across our chests. When the count is one hundred, the mate and I'll help those beside us to stand up. The rest of us'll count a hundred, while they stamp their feet and swing their arms, same as we did."

We had barely started when one of our number screamed horribly, and our rock hollow became a turmoil of flying arms and legs. "It's Henry," Captain Dean shouted. "Catch him and hold him!" Never before had I heard or felt a man in the throes of epilepsy, and when at last Henry Dean was pinioned and lay gurgling and groaning beneath us, I thought I had plumbed the depths of horror, and knew I couldn't endure another night like this.

All that night I rose, hunched my shoulders to the driving storm, stamped my feet, swung my arms; then pulled Neal to his feet and sank down to count to a hundred over and over again. It was like thunderous eternity, something beyond the power of a mere man to bear. If I'd been alone, I couldn't have borne it. I knew if I stopped that agony of struggling up, facing the driving snow that blistered my face—that added to the wet weight of my clammy clothes—Neal might stop.

The others might stop as well; so I couldn't stop. I could only hope and pray.

My prayers were as formless as my hopes—Oh God Oh God Oh God Oh God, over and over.

Deep within me, underneath the counting aloud and the praying, were other vagrant longings for warmth, for shelter, for an end to the deafening crashing of the waves: flashes of my father and his distress if he could know of our plight; of how he would blame himself for it; of how I, like a fool, had protested at being sent to Oxford; of how I would never again find fault with anything provided I could be warm and dry and have friends about me. . . .

December 12th, Tuesday

The time came, eventually, when, on stooping to pull Neal to his feet, I could see him dimly. Snow, mixed with rain, pelted us from the northeast, but the wet rocks on which we had ached and shivered through that long, long night were visible. All of us had ceased suddenly to be disembodied voices and were human beings once more—human but wild-eyed at the sights revealed to us by that pallid dawn.

We were on an island, as all of us had feared since Chips Bullock had dared hazard that awful suspicion after hunting for shelter the night before—an island, but *what* an island!

It lay low in the water, like the back of a whale. In a long-gone age it might have been a rounded mountaintop of solid rock, but one that a demonic force had smashed with giant hammers and made into a shattered travesty of flatness. On it there wasn't a handful of soil, or a bush, or any growing thing.

The sea was all around us, so close that from the hollow where we stood I could have thrown a rock into the raging breakers to north, south, east or west. Rimming the island was a border of blackness—the seaweed on which we had slithered and fallen the night before. Beyond the black weed the white breakers raced out of the north to spurt up in spray on the north side: then go galloping and bellowing down the west and east sides of the island; swinging around to pound the south side with a sort of ferocious maelstrom of foam.

Of the *Nottingham* there wasn't a trace—not that we could see.

Fourteen of us had spent the night in that rocky depression, and all but three of us were on our feet. Cooky Sipper lay on his face, shuddering and sobbing, great racking sobs that were frightening. Two seamen, William Saver and Charles Graystock, just lay there with eyes closed. Their faces were greenish.

"Please God," Captain Dean said. "We can't have this! You're frightened before you need to be! You're better off right now than if you were wrecked on a sand spit in the Indian Ocean. Here you've got good ice to keep you from getting thirsty. You can have it without stealing it, as you tried to do on shipboard. This is no time to be frightened."

Chips Bullock's hammer was fastened to his belt by a cord. Captain Dean took it from him. "I'm going to knock ice off the rocks so to have a path to the place where we struck. All those who can walk come with me. I'll need help with the things that have washed ashore. There must be something."

He was nearly wrong. No man would believe that a ship the size of the *Nottingham* could have vanished so completely and left so little behind, or that all that cheese and all that butter we had stowed so carefully, while we lay in the harbor of Killybegs, could have gone so completely to the bottom.

She must have struck at dead low water, around nine o'clock at night. Thus high tide would have been around four o'clock in the morning. Daylight probably broke about seven o'clock, so the tide should now be half out; and at the high-water mark there should have been heaps of material from the after cabin, from foc's'l and hold.

We found four lengths of deck plank, six timbers from the quarter-deck, a length of tarred rope, three pieces of canvas ripped from their fastenings, a bolt of Irish linen purchased by Captain Dean in Killybegs, a cutlass, the handle of a stewpan, a caulking mallet. Scattered among the shaggy masses of seaweed were fragments of cheese, small, like little sponges. And strangely—until I remembered Chips Bullock's workbag—there were as many spikes and nails in crevices beneath the seaweed as there were pieces of cheese.

Offshore, caught on something and held in one position, was a floating tangle of yards, sails and cordage that rose sluggishly to the top of each comber that rolled in to break on the fingers of black rock pointing out from every side of the island.

Captain Dean halted us just short of the seaweed and gave the hammer back to Chips. We could hardly hear him above the roar of the waves. "Langman, you and Mellen and Chips Bullock lay hold of the canvas, the planks and timbers and drag 'em back to the hole in the rocks. Take the tarred rope and set Cooky, Graystock and Saver to unraveling it. If they keep on being sick, drive 'em. We've got to get ourselves under shelter tonight."

He pulled at the waterlogged pieces of canvas, and with his pocket knife hacked off a small square.

"Yes," Langman said, "and while we're doing that, you'll eat the cheese."

"Mr. Langman," Captain Dean said, "I realize you're under something of a strain. Every scrap of cheese we find will be wrapped in this square of canvas and divided into equal portions. Make no mistake about that. On this island we'll all share alike."

Captain Dean motioned to us to come close to him. "Remember one thing above all else," he shouted. "It's better to crawl on hands and knees than to risk falling."

His hands had been concealed beneath his long vest. He held them out to us so that we could see them, front and back. Every finger had been cut almost to the bone by barnacles. Four of his fingernails were torn off. The finger ends were raw but, perhaps because of the cold, were not bloody.

"That's what a fall can do to you," the captain warned. "You can't afford to break an arm or a leg. Now spread out and hunt for those scraps of cheese."

He spoke heavily to Langman. "If you can't make Cooky and Saver and Graystock pick oakum, you and Mellen and White do it yourselves. There's just a chance that we can get fire out of it somehow—if it'll ever dry." For the benefit of the rest of us he said, "I've got a pistol and some wet powder. They're no good till the powder's dry."

We crawled over that slippery brown seaweed like animals nosing around a midden. We found fragments of cheese forced into and under the brown wet weed. Every piece of weed had to be lifted up to expose the rock hollows beneath. The coldness that went with handling that weed was unbearable. After two minutes of it, the pain in my hands forced me to hug myself until the sharp agony subsided. Tears ran down my cheeks, but there was nothing I could do about it.

Acting on the captain's orders, Neal went from one to another, with his square of canvas, collecting the fragments of cheese we pressed together in apple-sized pellets as boys make snowballs. After a search that seemed endless, we had picked up about as much as would have made three whole cheeses.

Neal, making a final round, passed us the captain's orders. "He says to go back to the hole and rest," he told us. "We'll hunt again at dead low tide."

On hands and knees we dragged ourselves back to the hollow in the rock. Perhaps something about the salt water in the wet seaweed had added to the pain in our feet, but so intense was that pain that our faces were contorted to the semblance of gargoyles—something not human.

At the hollow, we found that Langman, Mellen and Chips had fixed two short planks over the ledges on either side, folded the ragged piece of sail across them, and weighted both sail and planks with boulders.

There was room to lie flat beneath it, packed close together. Flimsy as it was, it partly screened us from the pelting snow and rain. It wasn't much of a shelter, but it *was* a shelter; and we crawled beneath it to lie inert. My brain, as numb as my hands, moved slowly.

Captain Dean's voice was calm and full. "We've got to find some way to reach the canvas that's afloat. We must have that cordage for making oakum." To Langman he said, "What did you do about oakum?"

"Nothing," Langman admitted. "By the time we rigged the shelter, we were so close to frozen we crawled under it."

"Now look," Captain Dean urged, "we've got to have oakum. We can lie on it. We can braid it into something to pull over our heads and faces. Maybe we can dry it so a flint and steel will work on it."

"Where's that cheese?" Langman asked.

"All right," the captain said. "We picked up twenty-six balls of it. I'll cut 'em in even parts. We'll eat half today and half tomorrow."

"Why should *you* cut 'em?" Langman asked. "Why should *you* say how much we can have? Since you ran us on this rock, I don't trust you to do anything right. Anyway, you promised we could take a vote today on who'd be captain. You shouldn't be captain, now there's no ship."

Captain Dean was long silent. When he did speak, his voice was placid. "How long do you think it'll take you to decide?"

"Not long," Langman said, "especially if you go outside. It won't be a fair vote if you don't."

Captain Dean seemed unruffled. "I suppose you'd like my brother Henry to go outside, too."

"Yes," Langman said, "if it's going to be really fair, your brother should go. So should Whitworth. They're all on your side." There seemed to be no end to his effrontery.

Swede spoke up. "That doesn't sound reasonable, Langman. Why don't *you* go out? You're voting for yourself, aren't you?"

"I haven't made up my mind yet," Langman said.

Swede laughed, but without humor. "I've heard that before! When anybody says that, it means he's made up his mind to vote for the wrong man."

"We're wasting time," Captain Dean said. "I'll go out, but my brother won't. Neither will Miles Whitworth. They're entitled to vote on who they'll obey. I'll stay out long enough to cut seaweed for us to eat with the cheese. Seaweed can't hurt us, and it'll make the cheese go further."

He backed out into the snow and the rain, leaving the canvas-wrapped balls of cheese in my hands.

"Now," Langman said, "we want to do this all fair and honest. I don't care who's made captain, but I know Cooky Sipper wants me to be. He said so just after we got the canvas up. So did Graystock and Saver. All three of 'em voted for me." His voice sounded painfully virtuous.

"Cooky hasn't said a word since the captain helped him into this hole," Swede said. "If you know what Cooky wants, you must have read his mind."

"I tell you I heard him," Langman cried. "Mellen heard him, too. Didn't you, Mellen?"

Mellen agreed promptly. "Yes, I certainly did. I heard him say, 'I want Mr. Langman.' "

"Well, I didn't," Chips Bullock said. "I didn't even see Langman talk to Cooky. When we were stretching the canvas, Langman said people as sick as Cooky and Graystock and Saver ought to have a separate hole in the rock, all to themselves. If I get sick, I don't want to be put off in a hole in a rock with somebody that can't talk to me. I vote for Captain Dean."

"You're an awful fool, Chips," Langman said. "You know as well as I do he's been trying to get us in trouble ever since we left the Nore. First it was privateers and then there was this insurance money he was bound to get."

"Well, Mr. Langman," Swede said, "you've seen the size of this island. We didn't pile up on it because of anything Captain Dean did. We had bad luck. If Captain Dean had been aiming for it, only a miracle would have brought us within a mile of it on a night like last night."

"Neal is youngest," I said. "He ought to have first say in this voting."

"I vote for Captain Dean," Neal answered quickly.

Langman sat up straight, bumped his head against one of the crosspieces that supported the canvas and fell back again between his fellow conspirators, Mellen and White. "Neal says that because he's the captain's favorite," he said in a shaking voice. "If a captain gets you into trouble, anybody ought to have sense enough to know he'll never get you out of it. Probably the captain threatened young Neal with punishment unless he voted for him. I say his vote ought to be disallowed."

"What's the matter with you, Langman?" Henry Dean asked. "Why are you so dead set on discrediting my brother? What do you hope to gain by it?"

"I don't expect to gain anything by it," Langman snapped. "I've got a great respect for the truth, that's all. If any British sea captain does the things your brother has done, he ought to be exposed so he can't make a nuisance of himself on the high seas."

"Langman," Swede said, "you're a hard man to argue with. Everything you say is wrong. You make a liar out of any person who tries to set you right. I vote for Captain Dean."

"I vote for Captain Dean," I said. "That's five. Why

doesn't somebody try to get a word out of Saver, or Graystock, or Cooky?"

"I'm ranking officer of this ship's company until this vote is settled," Langman said. "I refuse to let men as sick as Cooky and Graystock and Saver be interfered with! I told you they've settled on me. I know Mellen and White are for me, and so I'll vote for myself, and that makes six."

"Well," I said, "that accounts for all but Christopher Gray and Harry Hallion. Gray's a gunner and he scaled the guns with Swede. He must know Swede wouldn't be for Captain Dean if Mr. Langman's charges are true. I know they aren't true, and so does Swede.

"There's another thing to be considered. We have no way of knowing where this island is, but it can't be far from Portsmouth, and Captain Dean has friends in Portsmouth. If anybody's ever going to need friends, we are, when we get ashore. I can't imagine anything more unwise than cutting away from Captain Dean at a time like this.

"And bear this in mind, too. He was willing to leave this shelter so we could vote, but Mr. Langman wasn't. Doesn't that prove something to you? It does to me! It proves the captain plays fair, but Mr. Langman doesn't. I'm going to ask both Hallion and Gray to vote for Captain Dean."

Captain Dean's boots clattered on the rocks outside, and he came crawling back among us with an armful of dripping rockweed clutched to his chest. "The wind's dropping," he said. "Inside half an hour the tide will be as low as it'll go with this wind."

"You got no right coming in here like this," Langman shouted. "We haven't finished voting."

"I vote for Captain Dean," Gray said.

"Me too," Hallion said.

I told the captain that there had been seven for him and six against.

"I'm surprised," Captain Dean said. "I only expected three against me."

"Mr. Langman voted Cooky Sipper, Graystock and Saver against you," I said.

The captain stared contemplatively at Langman: then got his knife from his pocket and started cutting the rockweed into foot-long sections. The weed was brown and slippery, with little oval bulbs at intervals.

"Here," he said to Neal, "pass these around and I'll cut the cheese. Take a bite of the cheese and right away bite off a piece of rockweed and chew them up together."

"You got no right to tell these people what to eat," Langman said. "You never know what's poison and what isn't."

"You don't have to eat it if you don't want to," Captain Dean said. "It's just a way of making the cheese go further."

He pressed the balls of cheese together to form a single cake, halved it and rewrapped one half in the piece of canvas. The other half he carefully divided into fourteen cubes while all of us rose on our elbows to watch him. He passed a cube to each of us who could stretch out his hand. Cooky Sipper, Graystock and Saver didn't move.

"I'll keep their portions till they ask for 'em," Captain Dean said. Then he turned his head to look at Langman. "On second thought," he said, "I'll let Neal hold it for them."

The seaweed, slippery to the tongue, had something of the sea's freshness about it, and when chewed with cheese it wasn't bad. I could have eaten all the cheese that the captain had wrapped in his square of canvas. By itself, though, the weed wasn't good, and when my little square of cheese was gone, I ate no more weed.

On our second journey to the northern shore of the island, the captain, by the grace of God, found a coil of cordage wound around a boulder that could just be reached when a receding breaker went hissing and rattling back over the black seaweed. Twice the captain lowered himself toward that precious rope, only to come scrambling back among us as another breaker churned toward us.

We tried forming a living chain extending from the unseaweeded rocks down across the seaweed, but that was no good. While the captain tried to untangle the rope from the boulder, a wave surged in; and before we could pull him up over that damnable seaweed, he was soaked to his armpits.

He shivered, slapped himself and stamped his feet. "Think of something," the captain urged. "We've got to have that cordage and canvas! We've got to reach it somehow. The next high tide may rip it loose; it may go out on tomorrow's low tide, when it'll be too dark to see. If we wait twenty-four hours these breakers are sure to wash it away!"

Chips stepped forward to the captain's side. "If we could get a running bowline on the cordage beyond the rock," he said, "it might hold until we caught it."

"Running bowline!" the captain said. He turned to stare speculatively at the rock around which the cordage was twined. A wave roared in to cover it; then hissed away.

The boulder was set in a patch of crushed shells and

pebbles, on which there was no weed. The cordage was jammed between the gravelly stuff and the boulder's base.

The captain motioned for Swede to come and stand beside him. I knew what they discussed, though I couldn't hear a word they spoke because of the roaring of the breakers.

In the end Swede nodded his head, and the captain sent Langman hurrying off. In no time he was back with the piece of rope out of which the oakum was to have been made. Five minutes later Swede and the captain, with Neal between them, were showing Neal the working of a running bowline.

When Neal stood there on the edge of the rock, with that fearful background of foam and roaring waves beyond him, I couldn't bear to look at him: yet I couldn't bear not to. I knew we had to have that cordage: knew that somebody had to go for it, and I knew, too, that the captain was right in picking Neal. He was the lightest: in all likelihood he was the quickest.

At a signal from the captain he slid down the weed in the wake of the receding wave. He put me in mind of an otter. He threw the rope before him and over the boulder as a boy throws a skipping rope: fell on his stomach over the boulder-top; slipped the loose end of the rope under the cordage and through the noose. Just as a towering breaker curled before breaking, he darted back, the rope-end in his hand, no wetter than when he had jumped down.

Swede, stretched far forward, grasped one of his wrists, the captain the other, and the two of them snapped Neal up over the face of the ledge.

Whether that running bowline would grip the cordage

tightly enough to let us haul in the floating yards and sails to which it was attached, we couldn't know. The captain pulled it tight, then drew it gently toward him. The cordage rose up to the level of the top of the boulder around which it was snagged. Chips Bullock joined the captain in his pulling. When the bowline held, we all pulled, but still the cordage didn't come loose.

Twice more Neal went down into that foaming hole to move the bowline higher on the cordage—and at last we had our hands on the tangled wet rope.

The rest of that day was horrible beyond words. We hauled at that dripping cordage, fearful each moment that it would part from the floating timbers and sails to which it was attached. When we'd taken in all the slack we could, we strained and struggled to bring the tangled mass closer to shore.

The labor of hauling in that raft of junk seemed greater than mere men could undertake. The raft was attached to something—perhaps to a part of the sunken hull: perhaps to an anchor cable: perhaps to the stump of a mast, so that I had the feeling that we were trying to draw up a part of the ocean floor.

Worse than that, it was dripping wet, and the handling of wet cordage in a December northeaster becomes insupportable because of the violent aching in the hands. One can pull at it for a minute or two, but then he must stop and clutch his hands between his thighs in order to be free of that terrible aching.

Equally bad was our dubious footing on the surface of that rock. As we gained ground on the cordage, we staggered, slipped, fell on the icy ledges, and still contrived to move more and more of the cordage inshore: to find boulders around which to belay it, lest our gains be snatched from us by the voracious seas.

For the first time, that day, we saw the flood tide march up to the high-water mark, to leave our poor island shrunk to a mere nothing, barely rising above the tops of the combers that swept at us and past us—though in the sweeping it helped us in our efforts to draw the sails and spars closer.

In my pain and weariness and terror—and in that terror I was not alone—I had thoughts that helped and thoughts that hindered. If at flood tide the breakers crowded up so close to us, where would they be when December's full moon and spring tide were upon us—and every shore has its spring tide twice a month, at new moon and full moon—tides far higher than ordinary tides: so high that they seem bent on submerging land that cannot be submerged at any other time.

And how could my tutors and professors at Oxford have pretended to find truth and beauty in the adventures of Ulysses? Ulysses, confronted by such tribulations as those that surrounded us, couldn't have helped himself—could only have turned to and been succored by a god or a goddess in the shape of somebody or other—perhaps by Minerva in the form of an eagle. If he had been in our dire straits, ever-dependable Mercury would have built for him a stout ship from newly cut lumber—yes, and seasoned it for him, too. Mercury would even have done it for him on Boon Island, where no tree grew!

In a vision Minerva would have told him how to discover a great store of cheese. In the depths of his distress, Minerva would have appeared to comfort and encourage him—to restore to him the beauty of his youth; Jupiter would have thundered from heaven, ordering the seas to subside!

But the unhappy truth was that nothing like the *Odyssey* has ever been or ever will be. The troubles of Ulysses were brought upon him by his own stupidity and not, as Homer would have us believe, by the vindictiveness of Poseidon, that green-whiskered ruler of the vasty deep. The dreadful facts we faced on Boon Island taught me that Ulysses was a dilatory and philandering old fool; and if he had been with us on our rock, he'd have been exactly in our situation—despairing, helpless, hopeless, and perpetually on the verge of death.

December 13th, Wednesday

I hoped that when the northeaster blew itself out, the sea would grow calm, but it didn't. When the wind swung, it backed into the northwest and west, meaning that bad weather had only temporarily abated. We were free of driving snow and rain, but breakers still roared deafeningly on the north and west. They pounded less on the south and east, but still they pounded, throwing off manes of white foam. The wind seemed colder than on the night we were wrecked.

With the break of day I heard Captain Dean calling Neal to come outside. I went out, too, to find the captain staring off to the northwest.

"Neal," the captain said, "see if you can remember those maps you drew in the little book."

Neal said he remembered.

"Can you recall the chief places you lettered on the maps, starting with Cape Porpoise?" the captain asked.

"Cape Porpoise," Neal said, "Cape Arundel, Bald Head Cliff, Cape Neddick—"

"That's it," the captain cried. "Bald Head Cliff! That's

where the waves shoot up, yonder, and this is Boon Island! The last time I sailed east from Portsmouth, I sailed between Boon Island and Cape Neddick! Boon Island was to starboard and Bald Head Cliff to larboard!"

As the eastern sky grew brighter we could see the high dark red rock face of Bald Head Cliff. Spouts of spray rose high against it.

If we'd gone ashore on Bald Head Cliff in a northeaster, instead of on Boon Island, the ship and every last one of us would have been battered to a pulp in a minute's time.

Captain Dean, cheered by the sight of the mainland, lay flat to crawl beneath the shelter and shout the good news to those within.

"Listen," he said. "I know where we are! We're on Boon Island! Just south of us are the Isles of Shoals, where the Pepperrells and other Portsmouth people have fish stages. All winter there's fishing off the Isles of Shoals. There'll be fishing shallops passing us from every direction —Portsmouth, Kittery, York. If we set up something they can see, they'll find us. They'll take us off. But unless all of you get out and go to work, we won't be able to set up anything. Your blood won't circulate. You'll die. You've got to come out and drag cordage and junk."

Nobody said a word.

"Another thing," Captain Dean said. "There's seals off the south side of this island. I saw their heads in the water, following me and watching me, just after dawn, the way they always do. There's ducks, thousands of 'em, swimming in big flocks off the south shore.

"Seals have to rest somewhere. If I can catch one of 'em asleep around midnight, we'll have enough to eat for a month. He'll have fat that maybe we can set fire to."

"Where's the rest of that cheese?" Langman asked.

"Right here with Neal Butler," Captain Dean said. "Those who want it must come out and get it."

He backed out himself, and behind him crawled the remnants of our wretched company, with the exception of Cooky Sipper. Even Graystock and Saver came out, looking like corpses.

The captain took the canvas-wrapped cheese from Neal. "Go for seaweed to eat with it," he told Neal. "I'll cut and pass out the cheese myself."

He gave each of us a little cube of cheese. When he came to Graystock and Saver, he went upwind of them and eyed them contemptuously.

"You didn't eat your cheese yesterday," the captain said. "It's been saved for you, and I'm giving you yesterday's and today's too. You don't deserve either. You've been letting the rest of us work for you, and by rights your rations ought to go to those who've been doing the work."

"We were sick, and couldn't work," Graystock said.

"You're a liar," Captain Dean said. "Cooky Sipper's sick and can't stand up, but you're no sicker than the rest of us. You're scared, that's all! If you weren't, you'd get up and move off to do what has to be done, same as the rest of us. You've got to stay human, not be like helpless babies, or pigs that can be smelled a mile down-wind!" The captain was furious, no doubt about it, but he held himself under control, which isn't easy when dealing with people like Graystock and Saver—or Langman.

He gave them their little ration of cheese; then turned back to the rest of us. "Up to now," he told us harshly, "I haven't said anything about Saver and Graystock, but now I know where we are—now I'm able to see the things

God gives us, so we can help ourselves and help each other —I'm going to say something. Yes, and about anyone who thinks he can do like Saver and Graystock."

"It's your duty as captain," Langman said, "to encourage your men: not to discourage 'em."

Captain Dean rounded on him. "What do you think I *am* doing? You ought to be called Wrong-end Langman! I want Graystock and Saver to go to work and help save themselves, instead of refusing to work. They're doing nothing but setting the rest of us an example in discouragement and despair. Nobody ever accomplished anything in this world without working day and night; but most people are such damned fools that they don't want to work at all, not at anything, just like Saver and Graystock. Give 'em a free hand and they won't even work to save their lives! You know the most discouraging thing in the world, Langman? It's for a lot of hard-working people to have to look at and listen to those who'd like to keep on living without doing anything at all."

"I suppose," Langman said, "I was Wrong-end Langman when I said you wanted to run us ashore."

Captain Dean looked at him long and hard. "Mr. Langman," he said, "don't forget that you were No-lookout Langman before we struck. Just what is it that you'd do, right now, if you had the say?"

"I'd build a boat," Langman said promptly.

"With nothing but a hammer, a cutlass, a caulking mallet and our pocket knives?" Captain Dean asked.

Langman glowered at him.

"I'll tell you exactly what we must do first of all," Captain Dean said. "We have to locate the highest point on this rock able to hold a mast that won't blow down. A mast that people on shore may be able to see if they ever come to the water's edge to look for driftwood or seaweed, or if they ever put out for fish or lobsters. Then we have to build a tent around it.

"Even before we do that we need oakum to lie on: oakum to protect our faces and hands and feet: oakum for caps and mittens and bellybands: oakum to keep the wind from blowing the tent to pieces: oakum to keep the rain from driving through the canvas. What's more, we can't build a boat until we have oakum. The sort of boat we build will need all the oakum we can pick between dawn and dark for a year!

"So right now we'll start to separate all the junk we pulled ashore yesterday.

"While we do that, I want Chips Bullock and Swede Butler to pick the highest spot they can find—preferably a smooth piece of ledge that has a crack in it that will let us step a mast with a canvas flag on top—a big one, that can be seen six miles away.

"I'm putting Neal Butler in charge of making white oakum from the tangled cordage and black oakum from the tarred shrouds. He's to take Hallion with him and Saver and Graystock and George White.

"I want Mr. Langman with me—also Mr. Whitworth and Gray—Mellen and my brother Henry. We'll free the yards of whatever junk is fastened to them, and save all the cordage that can be used to lash down the tent.

"When the mast for the new tent is stepped, all usable things are to be brought close to the mast.

"In addition to all these things, we'll have to patrol this island at dawn each day, and at sundown, and again at high tide and low tide. I'll take the first patrol with George

White. Miles Whitworth will take the second patrol with Neal Butler. Mr. Langman'll take the third patrol with Nicholas Mellen. Swede Butler will take the fourth patrol with Henry Dean. Chips Bullock will take the fifth patrol with Christopher Gray."

For the first time Langman seemed to have no objection to Captain Dean's plans. "What about this shelter we've been living in for the past three nights?"

"You mean last night," Captain Dean said. "I'll tell you what about it. We'll floor it with oakum, and if any one of us falls so low that he can't relieve himself as he's supposed to do—by going to the place I select as a head and taking his breeches down and otherwise behaving in a civilized and Christian manner—he'll stay nights in this shelter until he's fit to live with other humans. For that matter, we may all have to stay here one more night, until the oakum's picked, the canvas separated from that pile of junk, and the cordage straightened so it can be used.

"Meanwhile the cutlass and Chips's hammer and the caulking mallet are to be used by those who do the separating. And I'll be responsible for them.

"Those who pick oakum will have to do it with their own pocket knives—and before the oakum-picking starts, I want Neal Butler to take Saver and Graystock to a pool of water on the south side of this island and see that they clean their breeches as well as they can be cleaned. Let it be a lesson to you—that I have to put a boy in charge of grown men to make sure they keep clean."

The ruin a furious ocean can wreak on a stout ship in an hour's time is beyond the comprehension of those who haven't seen it. It wrenches spikes from wet wood. It knots cordage into such intricacies as hangman's knots, six-strand Matthew Walkers, double cat's-paws, three-bight Turk's-heads. It smashes a main yard in the slings, strips a stern post from an inner post as readily as a child twists off a doll's foot.

The first thing we freed from the mass of junk was the foretopsail yard for Chips and Swede to use as the center post of the tent. It was lodged in a frozen hoorah's-nest of canvas, rigging and ratlins that defied our knives almost as though it had been made of iron.

Captain Dean constantly urged us to cut the tarred rope in eight-inch lengths. "If ever we're able to make a fire," he said, "we'll probably have the tarred rope to thank for it; and the lengths'll have to be short or they won't dry."

The foretopsail yard was only half freed when Neal came stumbling to us.

"Cooky's dead," he told the captain.

The captain snapped his pocket knife shut, stared hard at Neal: then straightened up to look at the breakers, dirty green-white in the watery morning sunlight.

"How do you know?" he asked heavily.

"I took him the first oakum we made," Neal said. "I thought it might make him easier. His mouth was filled with phlegm. I tried to get it out, but couldn't." He stared at his hands and added, "His face was black. He must have choked to death."

"I see," Captain Dean said. He examined his damaged fingers, stooped for a stone with which to pry open his knife again; peered at the blade as though he found it strange: then caught up a rope-end and haggled off a fifteen-foot length.

"Well," he said slowly, "go back to your oakum pickers.

Send White to the shelter. He and I'll take care of Cooky. We'll have to take him to the south shore and put him in the water. There's just a possibility he might float to York and start someone looking for us."

To me he said, "Keep right on as you are. See the others do, too."

He gave me the hammer.

"Couldn't you take his coat for yourself?" Neal asked.

"Why yes," Captain Dean said, "I think it would be all right to take his coat."

They stumbled off together across the icy rocks, and we went on freeing the foretopsail yard of its twisted accumulation of junk.

I was sorry to see them go, because there were a few things that I should have said to Captain Dean.

I wanted to speak about eating. This morning and yesterday morning each one of us had eaten as much seaweed as could be packed into a pint mug, and less than half that amount of cheese. Already my stomach felt gassy and abraded, as though I had been kicked there.

Now the cheese was gone. The captain had spoken about going out at midnight in the hope of finding a seal asleep on the rocks, but I knew a little something about seals from watching them come up the Thames after whitebait.

Neither Captain Dean nor anybody else was going to find a seal sleeping on ledges in this kind of weather, when a single wave could crush a seal against a rock as readily as it could crush a cheese. They slept while floating where waves only rocked them like a cradle.

There was a thought hidden in all this, but it eluded me. My brain, like all the rest of me, was numb from cold and wet clothes, which felt as though nothing, not even heat, could ever dry them.

Seals, I thought confusedly, ate anything. They'd certainly eat cheese, and I'd heard that somewhere on the lower Thames a seal had killed a woman and eaten her. If that was so, then a seal would be quick to bite at Cooky Sipper's body, whether it floated or sank—whether it was clothed or unclothed. Therefore there was no reason why Captain Dean shouldn't take Cooky's coat for himself, and the rest of his clothes for those who needed them—and there wasn't one of us who didn't need more clothes.

I looked over my shoulder toward the patch of canvas under which we'd sheltered. Captain Dean and George White were dragging Cooky's body over the icy rocks and ledges. The rope was fastened around Cooky's neck, and I was glad to see that the body was unclothed, so there apparently was no need for me to mention those confused thoughts of mine to the captain.

There were some other things, though, that I hadn't said, and it was hard for me to remember what they were. With our cheese gone, we would have nothing to eat, so if the captain wanted Cooky's body to float ashore, it seemed to me, he'd do better to leave the body on a rock, where it would freeze. If it were frozen, it would float, maybe, as a cake of ice floats.

I wondered whether I was right. Only a little of an iceberg shows above water.

"What happens to a frozen body?" I asked Langman.

"What do you mean?" Langman demanded.

"I mean, would Cooky Sipper float if he were frozen?"

"Of course he wouldn't," Langman said.

"How do you know?" I asked. "Did you ever see a frozen man in the water?"

"No," Langman said, "but he'd sink."

I felt fairly sure that Langman was wrong about this, as about everything else. An iceberg never sank, did it?

The captain and George White made hard work of getting Cooky to the seaweedy rock-fingers of the south shore. They would pull Cooky's body forward until his head was almost at their ankles, then they'd get themselves across another ten feet of ledges, flat on their stomachs like two frogs; then rise and cautiously pull Cooky to them again.

If I hurried, I told myself, I could reach them even now, before they put the body in the water.

I felt Langman looking at me, a mocking twist on his thin, sallow face. That was a bad habit of his—staring fixedly at those he disliked, apparently under the impression that the person at whom he stared wasn't conscious of his stare—which of course wasn't the case. That was like Langman. He was about as perceptive and sensitive as a pig.

"What you got on your mind?" Langman asked.

"Why, nothing," I said. "I've got nothing on my mind."

He looked over his shoulder at the captain and White pulling and hauling at Cooky's body.

"Well," I said, "this isn't clearing that foretopsail yard."

We had it cleared by midafternoon, soon after Swede and Chips came for it and for a square of canvas to use as a flag. They had, they said, found a ledge with a deep crack in it—one into which a spar could be pushed and shimmed into place with wedge-shaped rocks.

"Once we get that spar in place," Swede said to Langman, "it'll outlast you."

Langman looked scornful. "If we don't build a boat, it'll outlast all of us."

Chips swung his head from side to side. "I wish I had my axe," he said irrelevantly. "When we were cleaning that slot for the spar, we found slivers of rock. They're shaped like splitting wedges. We can use 'em for chisels if they don't splinter when pounded."

He and Swede carried away the foretopsail yard and the square of canvas; but dark came down on us before we were able to unsnarl the sails that were wrapped with rigging as a fly is wrapped in a spider web.

So we spent that night in the shelter in which Cooky had sobbed and moaned night after night.

Night after night?

Had we been three nights in that shelter? Why no! It was only *two* nights. I found it difficult to keep track. The first night we'd spent in a crevice, without covering. The next two nights we'd had a strip of canvas above us.

Things were different with Cooky gone. Not better, perhaps, but quieter. Cooky had always groaned and sobbed; and lying somewhere near him was another who moaned and groaned. It may have been Graystock. It may have been Saver. It could, God knows, have been almost any one of us. Now, with Cooky gone, there was a lot less sobbing.

December 14th, Thursday

I think our labors of the day before, and our depression because of the death of Cooky Sipper, would have kept us from even thinking of continuing our work on the tent on Thursday. The bitter northwest wind was more biting than that of the northeaster. I thought wryly of the winter chill of the Bodleian, often so penetrating that students insisted they couldn't read. This was a different cold, and its effect upon us forced us to do things we couldn't otherwise have done.

And that's another thing my sojourn on Boon Island did for me: it made me impatient of a person who, because of fancied ill-health or discomfort, fails to execute a task or complete an undertaking. No man is worth his salt if, by such a failure, he inconveniences others.

A man can't, I know, stay awake indefinitely, though I think he somehow contrives to sleep or to lose consciousness in spite of pain or mental trouble. Yet I'd have sworn I never slept on the night of the thirteenth. All night long my feet and legs either throbbed or burned or itched. Each one of those three ills seemed unendurable by itself, and certainly there was no respite from the constant movement of the men around me—an uneasy thrashing, as dogs thrash when wounded and in distress.

When daylight came I could see as well as feel the reason for my ailing legs and feet. My legs had swelled until they filled my sea boots, and a discoloring ridge of flesh puffed out above the boot tops.

Captain Dean, examining his own legs, said there was no help for it: the boots would have to go.

"It's the wet," he said, "and the cold that comes with this northwest wind. The only good thing about a northwest wind is that there's a calm after it stops blowing—if it ever does."

He raised his voice to make it heard above the rumble and smashing of the breakers.

"Sharpen your knives, everyone," he said. "You'll find whetstones under you. That'll remind you there's always something good to be said about anything or anyone. There'll never be any shortage of rocks on this island; none of ice, either.

"Here's what you'll have to do—and save the stitching. We'll need it to tie bandages." He severed the top stitch of the seam that runs down the inner part of the leg, then picked out the remaining thread as far down as the ankle. From the ankle he cut straight down through the leather to the edge of the sole. From that cut he slid his knife blade around the heel, pressing the blade against the sole. He did the same to the forward part; then folded the whole boot outward from his leg and foot.

When he rolled up his long underwear, both foot and leg were shocking sights. The leg, puffed and blistered, had open sores where his underwear and wet breeches had rubbed. The toes were pallid. Some of the toenails came away when the boot was folded over; but the toes didn't bleed: they just stayed that queer grayish white.

The captain drew a sharp breath. "You'll have to expect a little pain at first," he said, "but that's only the blood coming back into your legs."

The captain studied those nailless toes.

Then he said slowly, "Before any of the rest of you start cutting off your boots, you'd better go out for canvas. We'll have to make something to put on our feet so we can walk."

"Walk with feet like that one of yours!" Langman cried.

"I don't have to answer that, do I?" Captain Dean asked. "We've *got* to walk. More cheese might come ashore. We must have more oakum. We must move out from this wet shelter into a tent. We must have a place where we can pick oakum under cover. We can't make oakum or raise a tent unless we go outside. To do that we'll have to wash our legs in something warm that'll clean 'em."

Langman groaned. "Something warm! Where'll you find anything warm around here? Even if you found something, what would you put it in?"

"I've watched everyone urinating about ten times a day, haven't I?" Captain Dean asked. "I hated to see it wasted, but I couldn't give up my powder horn if there was a chance of getting a fire from the powder. Well, the powder's as wet today as it was when we were wrecked, and I've carried it next to my skin day and night. So now I'll put the powder in a canvas bag. We'll use the horn for the warm stuff you think we haven't got. Now take White and Miles with you and go for that oakum. And remember: don't urinate till I tell you to."

He sawed delicately with his knife-blade at the stitches in his other boot top, and picked out the thread as carefully as though his life depended upon it—and perhaps it did.

I was shocked and frightened by that glimpse of the captain's leg and foot, and by the stench that had come from it. I was sure my own feet and legs were no different; and while it seemed impossible to walk at all on feet so painful, I not only knew that I could do it, but I was filled with a frenzy to pick the oakum necessary to protect our legs and feet.

Those who have never picked oakum—and few people do it except sailors when there's nothing else to be done on shipboard, or those who live in prisons or poorhouses—find it tedious, hard on the hands and on the nerves, to separate those stiff strands of fiber that make up a rope: then, with finger-twistings and knife-points, to fluff out each strand so that it becomes again a flattened mat of hemp.

But when oakum is needed to keep legs and feet from rotting, almost anyone works hard and quickly learns the knack of reducing a cable or a hawser to its original state of untwisted strands.

At the captain's direction we practiced first on him, cutting two six-foot lengths of linen from the bolt, and a short length to use as a sponge. Each six-foot strip was a bandage, down one side of the leg, across the foot, and up the other side of the leg.

I don't know what we'd have done without that bolt of linen. For years I woke screaming from a dream of what would have happened to me if we'd had no linen to bind our legs.

Each side of the bandage lapped twice around the leg; but before the lapping was done, a poultice of oakum was set in place on the upper and lower part of the foot, from ankle to knee. Then the protruding linen was folded over the oakum, and narrow bands of linen held the whole in place. Over the outer linen was wrapped a square of canvas. Thus our feet and legs were cased in a quadruple bandage—a single layer of linen, a layer of oakum, a quadruple layer of linen, and a canvas leggin.

The captain had us slit the long legs of his underwear, and the legs of his breeches as well, and these were tied in place with the thread taken from his boots.

Since all these bandages were so bulky as to make the boots useless, he cut off the boot tops and made each top into a sort of knee boot, or knee pad, bound around his knee by strands of tarred rope.

We tried to economize on urine, but couldn't. The powder horn, its thick end removed and its stopper pounded tight, held about a pint, and we had to have one and a half hornfuls for each two legs and feet. In this we were fortunate, for the entire company, fearful of losing feet or legs, was consumed with the need to urinate, and calls for the powder horn were constant.

When we had finished with Captain Dean, he helped Neal and me to cut off our own boots and bandage our legs and feet. Before he turned back my first boot, he put his hand on my knee. "Don't look at them," he said. "They aren't as bad as they look, and you'll gain nothing by seeing them." There was no doubt in my mind that he was right, and I think that, by obeying him, both Neal and I saved ourselves from self-pity or despondency–states of mind that never bettered anyone.

With Neal and me to help him, Captain Dean sat the rest of the crew on the two ledges that had formed the wall of our shelter, and over their knees he laid the canvas beneath which we had slept. While we worked on them, they picked oakum, using the canvas as a table. Below the canvas the captain, Neal and I, on our padded knees, washed all those legs and feet with the warm contents of the powder horn. This washing was painful beyond belief, and the sailors howled and cursed as their legs and feet were sopped with urine. Nor could I blame them, for the toes of some of them broke off in our hands, and their blisters and abscesses, in some cases, were so deep that the bone showed through.

December 15th, Friday

Six of us were able—perhaps "willing" is a better word—to crawl from beneath the canvas on the morning after we had bandaged our legs. All thirteen of us should have come out, for the tide, high at daybreak, might have deposited something edible on shore, and our craving for something to put in our stomachs was almost overpowering.

Those beside myself who dragged themselves into that cold dawn were Captain Dean, Neal Butler, Swede Butler, Langman and White—and God knows I probably couldn't have done it if the captain hadn't crawled out first, with Neal close behind him, and Swede close on Neal's heels. What Neal could do, I told myself, I must do. Langman only came with us, I think, because of his overwhelming fear that one of us might find a scrap to eat and conceal it from him. White, I thought, came because he was a bos'n, and bos'ns regard themselves as being hardier than other seamen, and averse to being outdone by anyone.

As we made our painful patrol of the high-water mark, we saw two seals playfully nosing at a floating object, and simultaneously Captain Dean came across a slender stick of wood that might have been a broom handle.

The seals swam around and under the thing with which they played, and whisked at it with their hind flippers, until the water shoaled. Then they abandoned it, and lay offshore, rising high in the water, puffing out their whiskers and watching us from staring round eyes. I would have given anything I ever hoped to own if I could have got my hands on one of those seals, though I well knew I could never have held him.

When a breaker thrust their plaything against the rock, we found it to be two bones from salted beef, held together by the muscles of the joint. To add to this bit of good fortune, Captain Dean came across a lump of cheese the size of a child's head, and Langman found a mussel from which grew scores of long streamers of thin kelp, which Langman insisted were good to eat. The mussel he discarded with an expression of distaste, before the captain could stop him.

"A mussel is full of meat," the captain protested. "Well, one mussel wouldn't have gone far among thirteen men, but there's more where that one came from."

When we returned to the canvas shelter with this treasure trove, the others came out, dreadful haggard objects. Each was given a streamer of kelp; and all of them, as intent as an audience at a play, watched us smash those beef bones with rocks, and, with knife blades, extract a dab of marrow for each man.

"We'll eat all the cheese right now," Captain Dean said. "We'll lash that saucepan handle to the end of this broomstick with spun yarn. Maybe, when the tide is right, we'll find enough mussels to give us a real meal–and can pry 'em off the rocks without losing our hands.

"Then," he went on, "we'll all go to the flag mast and build the tent and pick more oakum for it. We can't spend another night in this rotten shelter."

The men, haggard, bearded, misshapen, just stared at him. I think they were only a quarter conscious, partly paralyzed by the biting cold of the night just past. Three of them–Saver, Graystock and Mellen–crawled silently back beneath the canvas.

Captain Dean stooped to peer after them. Then he gave up. After all, there's no use driving those who have passed the limit of endurance.

The size of the tent was determined by the area of the rounded ledge that held the center pole.

The ledge was shaped roughly like a humped-up triangle, sliced from the side of an enormous hogshead. This triangle rose from a welter of boulders. It was narrow: then widened as a wedge of orange peel widens, to descend, still widening, and vanish among more boulders. Thus the tent of necessity was three-sided, like a pyramid. Its height was regulated by the distance between the rock and the lowest lashing of the canvas flag.

Captain Dean helped us pick the corner posts for the tent. When they were set in place, Swede, Langman and Harry Hallion formed a living step ladder on which the captain mounted to lash the posts to the mast. The rest of us dragged pieces of sail across the rocks, arranging them so they could be fastened to the corner posts with spun yarn.

The canvas at the base of each of the three sides was anchored by broken pieces of deck-planking. The planks were held down by boulders.

The placing of the boulders was a source of great concern to Captain Dean. "If those timbers aren't properly secured," he said, "the canvas is sure to blow down on us. Such things always happen on the coldest night, when you won't be able to see your hand in front of your face."

So outside the single row of boulders atop each plank, he made us lay another row of boulders. Then he insisted we lay a third row on top of this double row—big boulders, too large to be handled by one man. How, with my half frozen hands, I could have been of any help in the handling of them, I cannot recall. All I remember is that in order to do so, I had to take a firm grip with my feet, and when I did, they felt as though I stood in nettles.

Langman worked as hard as anyone, but he never stopped talking about the boat. As in the matter of privateers, he couldn't drop a subject for a minute, once he was embarked on it.

"If the full-moon spring tide rises above the top of this rock," he said, "what good's a tent going to do us? Nothing will help us then but a boat."

"Look," Captain Dean said, "I've measured this rock. Right here where we're standing, as near as I can figure, it's fourteen feet above normal high-water mark. According to my reckoning, the tide rise here is seven feet. I don't believe any spring tide could be three times as high as a normal tide."

"It *can* be," Langman said. "There's some places only a little north of here where the tide rises and falls twenty-eight feet. I've heard Woodes Rogers say so when he was sailing to Newfoundland."

"I know those places," Captain Dean said, "but that's 'way north of here. The same thing's true in England. You get some terrible high tides in the Severn estuary, but you never get any such tides on the Isle of Wight, which isn't far away, as the crow flies. And I'll tell you another thing, Langman. This is the fifteenth of December, and according to my lights——"

"It's the sixteenth," Langman interrupted. "Tomorrow's Sunday."

"No," the captain said, "this is the fifteenth. Sunday isn't until day after tomorrow."

"I figured it out," Langman said. "Tomorrow's Sunday."

"We've got to get this tent finished," Captain Dean said, "and there's no sense arguing over which day's Sunday. The thing I want to impress on you is that my reckoning shows full moon to be due December 27th, a Wednesday. We must have had one spring tide already, because there should have been a new moon day before yesterday."

"The twenty-seventh would be a Thursday," Langman said.

"Well, whichever day of the week it is," Captain Dean said, "it's twelve days to spring tide, and if we don't get this shelter done, and the tide *does* rise that extra fourteen feet, and we *do* have another onshore blow, and we *do* have to have a boat to save our lives, we can't *have* a boat unless we shelter ourselves during those twelve days between now and spring tide. The tent has to come first."

☆ ☆ ☆

Those of us who worked on the tent were the captain,

Swede Butler, Langman, Neal, Harry Hallion and George White.

All the rest—Henry Dean, Christopher Gray, Nicholas Mellen, Saver, Graystock and Bullock—as soon as the sides were up took shelter within it, and three of them—Chips Bullock, Saver and Graystock—looked as though nothing on earth could ever induce them to come out again.

The others, under the urgings of Henry Dean, did their best to pick oakum; but when they wouldn't work, and just lay or sat there, their eyes opaque like those of a fish, holding their hands to the pits of their stomach and crouching over them as if to send a little warmth into those numb extremities, there seemed to be nothing to be done about it.

We could hear Henry beg them to get on with their picking. That was one of the advantages of the new shelter. We couldn't sit up in the old shelter, and so had to go outdoors to pick oakum.

In the tent we could stand up, if only three or four stood at a time. The rest could sit up.

The day we finished the tent Henry Dean and Nicholas Mellen, fumbling around a little pile of junk we hadn't yet untangled, came across the rawhide seizing of one of the yards. It was still fastened to a fragment of the yard, and when it was pried loose and unwound, it looked like a piece of soggy cowhide about eighteen inches wide and two feet long.

When Henry Dean brought it back to the tent, even the men who seemed half dead sat up to look at it, and there was an instant demand that it be distributed for food.

"Food!" Henry Dean exclaimed. "You can't . . ." Then he stopped and said, "I'll speak to my brother."

He came out to where we were rolling boulders against the bottom of the canvas. "The men inside," he told Captain Dean, "want this rawhide divided. They think they can eat it. I think it might hurt 'em instead of help 'em."

The captain felt it with speculative fingers. "No," he said slowly. "It wouldn't hurt 'em. Food is what you think it is. A lot of critters live on things that wouldn't be much help to other critters. So do a lot of men. Probably you wouldn't care much about eating a mouse, but Chinese do and think they're nice. They eat 'em, and like 'em. You divide this rawhide into thirteen pieces. Give one piece to each man, and make him chop his own into little pieces, just as fine as he can mince 'em."

Perhaps that rawhide did give everyone a little strength, for after each had eaten his share, those in the tent went back to picking oakum. When night came we not only had shelter over us, but we had a layer of oakum beneath us—a thin one, to be sure, but one that wasn't wet. It was damp, yes; but it wasn't wet, and up to now we had been wet every night—wet, and cold with a cold that beggars description. Those who live beneath roofs, or in dry caves, with dry clothes next to their skins, can't imagine what it's like to exist surrounded by a tumult of breakers, in wet clothes, on sharp wet rocks, and in cold so intense that every boulder in sight is covered with a thick armor of ice.

But we had a little more room than we'd heretofore had, though we still lay tight against each other, belly to buttocks so to take advantage of the slight warmth that each of us, by the grace of God, contrived to hold within himself.

December 16th, Saturday

The world, I've found, is full of people who cannot realize that *everything* is hard work– everything. People turn to sailing, or to fishing, or to acting, or to painting, or to play writing–to any one of the thousand different occupations –with some sort of a vague idea that it's easy work. Sometimes work can be enthralling if it's done as an avocation instead of out of dire necessity, but it's hard work just the same.

So I question that the building of our boat on Boon Island was harder work than writing a play, or sheepherding, or chopping wood; but I suspect that no work has ever been done under such adverse circumstances.

The place we selected to build the boat was on the south side of the island, where ledge-fingers ran slopingly out toward the south. The ledges were less abrupt there than on the other three sides, and the surf less violent.

It was on the south side, always, that the seals thrust their bullet heads from the water to watch us, and it was aggravating to see twenty or thirty of those round heads examining us from popeyes, and puffing out their whiskers at us, as if amazed by our presence on their island.

Sometimes, surprisingly, even though the wind blew from the north, a huge swell would roll in toward that south side and there'd be the watery shadows of ten or more seals floating in it, seemingly higher than we.

Just before the wave broke, the seals would rise shoulder-high for a clearer look at us, then slip away, down the far side, while the wave curled over with a roar. I couldn't imagine Boon Island without breakers hurrying toward its shores from every direction, as if to a boisterous and senseless rendezvous.

The day had started inauspiciously because Langman, having determined that the day was Sunday instead of Saturday, had whispered sulkily with Mellen and White, during the night, and come to the conclusion that to work on Sunday was wrong. All of us, he told the captain, should observe Sunday with him and Mellen and White. I knew, as well as I knew my own name, that he was just being contrary.

Captain Dean shook his head wearily. "Mr. Langman," he said, "I have no intention of attempting to speak for God, but you evidently have a personal God that differs in some respects from mine. My God accepts those who worship Him, regardless of whether they worship on Greenwich time or on Cape Porpoise time."

"That's blasphemy," Langman said quickly.

"What's blasphemous about it?" Swede asked.

"Let him call it anything he likes," Captain Dean said. "In good weather we've always observed the Sabbath on my ships in a fitting manner, provided the weather made it possible for us to do so.

"But if a storm happened to hit us on Sunday, we did anything necessary for the welfare of the ship.

"You've insisted for days that our lives may depend on this boat because the full-moon tide may force us off.

"Very well, Mr. Langman. I think I can speak for God. I think I can say you'll be forgiven for working on Sunday, just as God would forgive you for eating a seal on Friday, if you were a Catholic—and if we were so fortunate as to kill a seal.

"So you'll take your turn hauling plank, Mr. Langman, and so will Mellen and White, just as if it were Saturday, which it is."

"That's more blasphemy, and it's still Sunday," Langman insisted.

Swede looked at him as if he wanted to kill him, and I wish he had.

A smooth piece of ledge, sprinkled with boulders, lay just above the seaweed fringe. This ledge sloped easily toward the seaweed fringe and ended between two rock fingers.

That rock was our shipyard, our launching stage, our naval storehouse.

Our only tools were our pocket knives, Chips's hammer, the caulking mallet and the cutlass.

Our only shipbuilding materials were the remnants of the *Nottingham*. With Chips's hammer we had strained our muscles to draw nails and spikes from the few wet planks we had recovered, but we had failed so lamentably that our chief reliance for putting the boat together were the nails and spikes salvaged from Chips's workbag.

While those of us able to walk dragged timbers, planks, canvas and cordage to the launching stage, the captain and Swede undertook to make the cutlass into a saw—a task that would never, I thought, be accomplished except by the direct intervention of Mercury, Minerva and another half-dozen Greek divinities like those who were forever getting Ulysses out of his difficulties.

Neither Mercury nor Minerva, however, had a helping hand in the transformation of the cutlass. Chips thought of the way it could be done, but was too weak to do anything except advise us in our labors.

He had come down with the same sort of sickness that had finished Cooky Sipper. Being a heavy man, the blisters and ulcers on his feet and legs were worse than ours, and he couldn't stand upright. So he stayed in the tent, while Captain Dean and Swede worked beside him on the cutlass. His voice was weak and choked with phlegm, as Cooky's had been, and he found difficulty in making himself heard above the everlasting slashing and crashing of the breakers.

The captain and Swede brought sharp-edged rocks into the tent. While Swede held the blade of the cutlass at an angle against the sharp edge of a rock as a man holds the blade of a razor at an angle against his cheek, the captain would smash at the blade with a similar rock. Thus a V-shaped nick would be broken out of the cutlass blade.

They started with a nick at the hilt end, a nick at the point and a nick halfway between each of the three nicks. Then they subdivided each space between the nicks until the blade became a series of jagged saw teeth.

Then Swede took one of those chisel-like rocks and

Chips took another, and they rubbed and rubbed at each nick until both sides had beveled edges and the teeth were sharp.

When they started I didn't believe they could do it. Since Boon Island, I believe the right sort of man can do anything.

Even less than I believed a saw could be made from the cutlass did I believe that a seaworthy boat would emerge from the materials at hand, but we *did* build it, even though we had less with which to work than strolling players would need to build a stage in a barn.

In spite of all our handicaps, we had something to hearten us, for on this day mussels in quantity—though little different from the one Langman had thrown away—were discovered in the western pools and indentations.

Early in the afternoon, at low tide, Captain Dean and George White left the shipyard to patrol the island for scraps of wreckage and our daily repast of seaweed and ice. The captain carried his broomstick with the saucepan handle wrapped to the end by rope yarn and strips of linen.

In cutting seaweed, they uncovered a pool in which a mussel was attached to the hard-packed mixture of shell and rock fragments that lay at the bottom of all such depressions.

It was one of the big mottled sea mussels, unlike the clean blue ones that grow in beds on gravel spits near the mouths of rivers. This one was an old, old mussel, survivor of countless storms such as those through which we had passed—survivor, too, of the crashing blows of countless millions of breakers, exactly like those that had thundered in our ears for six long days and nights—or was it five—or was it seven, as Langman said?

☆ ☆ ☆

Even in the writing I am constantly uncertain of dates when I trust to memory.

The days seemed endless: the nights were a torment of aching cold, of fear, of trepidation—ah, those nights, with the breakers thundering at our very shoulders! Always, in the night, I had thoughts of eternity: of death, and of never ending punishment that might continue forever, forever, forever, forever . . . No wonder our companions cried aloud to God so frequently! No wonder Langman thought Saturday was Sunday! No wonder I must so often go back to the calendar I reconstructed with the help of Captain Dean and Neal Butler. Sometimes even the captain couldn't remember, and both of us had to rely on Neal's proficiency as a "quick study."

☆ ☆ ☆

Old as the mussel looked, however, it was unquestionably a mussel, and a mussel is food, no matter how overgrown and thickened it is with pink and gray encrustations, with sprigs of seaweed.

Captain Dean prodded at it with the stick to which the saucepan handle had been lashed, and when the shell was free of the trash in which it grew, White snatched it from the water. So Captain Dean and White, crawling to other pools, raked the weed back from the edges. In the end they uncovered thirty-nine. A few were young and blue: mostly they were ugly, encrusted, ancient.

The captain said he and White could have got more if

their hands could have stood it; but the pain that results from repeatedly immersing hands in icy water, even when the immersion is momentary, is such as to agonize the most hardened sailorman. It can't be borne.

When White and the captain returned, the captain held his hands behind his back, White doled the mussels into them one by one, and the captain passed them around, picking us at random, so that there was no way of telling who would get which mussel.

There were three apiece, repulsive-looking, lumpy, with hard, mottled fungus growths upon them, and with a sort of beard attached to one end. We opened them by forcing a knife-point between the tight shells, then sliding the blade around through the hinge. In spite of their looks, they seemed savory enough to us—once we had learned how to rid them of the infinitesimal pearls with which they were infested. The pearls could only be removed by squeezing them out; by rubbing the meat between the tongue and the roof of the mouth.

Certainly I have never wanted another mussel since those days, but they gave our seaweed a fishy juiciness wholly lacking when the seaweed was eaten alone.

Langman, protesting that in all likelihood they were poisonous, for a time refused to eat them; but when he saw Mellen and White swallowing them avidly, he ate them too, sneering at all of us.

I think they must have given us a little strength, for after I had choked them down I returned more hopefully to my labors on that hopeless boat.

For the bottom of the boat we stretched an oblong of canvas flat on the sloping rock, weighting each corner with a boulder so it couldn't blow. On the canvas we laid three planks side by side, fastened together, but fastened in a way that would have sickened a savage from the heart of Africa.

The ends of those planks were jagged. We had no way of rounding them off except by smashing them with a hammer, since the saw was too precious to waste on anything trivial; so all that day was spent in getting ready to build rather than in building, and–seemingly most important of all–in endless discussions as to who should go in the boat if ever it was finished.

December 17th, Sunday

Even Saver and Graystock, those lumps of men who wouldn't pick oakum unless they felt like it, and Chips Bullock, who was willing to work but couldn't, wanted to be in that boat when she was launched, if she ever *was* launched.

Probably this was because today, our first Sunday, the captain discovered, on the snow-covered fields of the mainland, moving specks that must have been people—churchgoers, in all likelihood.

I think by that time we were all of us half demented, for we shouted and waved our arms, hoping to catch the attention of those far-off specks—and surely there wasn't a one of us who didn't know that we, all brown and gray, with grizzled beards and wrappings of oakum, could be no more apparent to those on shore than a seal would have been.

But the sight of those moving specks upon that distant slope made each of us conscious of how near we were to bread and meat, to warmth and drink and other people, to houses and soft beds and dry clothes, to salves for our festering feet and the sores on our knees and hands; so even before the floor of the boat was completed, all but a few were urging that they be allowed to go ashore in her.

Two exceptions were Swede and Neal. Swede didn't say it openly, but he was determined Neal must be saved, if anyone was. And equally apparent was Neal's determination not to leave his father.

I sympathized with Swede.

If I had the say as to who should go in the boat, I'd have picked Captain Dean first and Neal second: the captain because he was strongest and would have influence on shore: Neal because he was youngest and with the greatest possibilities. But I never would have picked Swede. His feet were so crippled that I considered him useless—which eventually taught me never to underrate a determined man, no matter how helpless he may seem.

Even poor Chips Bullock argued his case to the captain in a faintly raucous voice, pleading that without his hammer and his nails and spikes, the boat would have been impossible.

The captain said, "Yes, Chips. We'll do the best we can."

Graystock and Saver, useless as they were, united in saying they deserved a place in the boat because of their physical condition, which was bad.

Strangest of all the arguments was that of Harry Hallion, who said he thought he ought to go because he spoke Indian.

"Indian?" Captain Dean asked. "What kind of Indian?"

"Nova Scotia Indian," Hallion said. "I lived with an Indian woman all one winter."

"Nova Scotia Indians are Micmacs," Captain Dean protested. "The Indians around here are a different breed. In the winter they live in the woods—and that's one place we're not going when we get ashore." He never said "if we get ashore." He always said "when we get ashore."

Becoming suddenly angry at all this pretense, the captain ordered all those not working on the boat to return to the tent and pick more oakum—more oakum—more oakum.

"There'll be *nobody* go in this boat," he shouted, "unless we can plug every hole with oakum. Right now she looks as though she'd have more holes in her than she'll have wood."

Repeatedly, that day, we stopped working on the boat and went to the tent to help in the picking of oakum—not only because of the intense cold, but to consult with Chips Bullock as to the best way to erect a stanchion at each corner of the floor boards.

The glimpse we'd had of those people on shore must have made each one of us, even the captain, worse than desperate; for he took out a piece of black oakum from next to his skin. He let us feel the oakum. "Is it dry?" he asked us. "Feel it!" He passed it around. Swede and Neal and I said that to us it still felt damp; but all the others, Langman included, pretended to find it dry. Langman was always wrong, and the captain knew it, but this time he wanted to take Langman's opinion.

So he took a pinch of gunpowder from the canvas pouch, produced his useless pistol and cocked it; then did what he'd already done a thousand times—put powder in the pan, wrapped the lock and the pan with the oakum, snapped the flint . . . snapped it: snapped it: snapped it, over and over.

We could see the spark inside the oakum: smell a delicious, tantalizing odor of tarry scorching. There was even a faint hint of smoke. He kept on pulling the hammer back and snapping it; pulling it back and snapping it.

Then he passed it to Langman, who did the same. Then Langman passed it to me, and I tried and tried.

All we got was a faint wisp of tarry-smelling smoke.

Another thing I learned to dislike on Boon Island were the wiseacres who are forever saying, "Where there's smoke there's fire." At Oxford I often heard Latin-speaking dons—the worst kind—throw that remark at each other. *Flamma fumo est proxima.* Where there's smoke there's fire.

It's not so; but there's no more use arguing with people who quote that saying than there would be in wrangling with the old Roman who is credited with first uttering it. The old Roman is dead: the others nearly so. "Where there's smoke, there's fire," indeed! I'd have liked to hear them talk like that on Boon Island!

Since this was Sunday, we held services in the tent. Captain Dean led us in a prayer that thanked God for His mercy in letting us stay alive; that thanked Him for granting us ice to chew and mussels to eat; that implored God to let us be seen from the mainland; that begged Him to send a ship near this dreadful rock.

All of us repeated his words in a hoarse and shivering chorus—all except Langman and White and Mellen, who, having decided the day wasn't Sunday, refused to pray with us.

I think, though, Langman was somehow helped by those Sunday services, in spite of being so certain that our Sunday was the wrong one; because when Neal and I made our last patrol of the day at dead low tide, around three o'clock in the afternoon, Langman came with us, and so did George White. They helped us in our daily search for mussels, so that we were able to bring back eight for each man.

December 18th, Monday

I know how a condemned man must feel when he is about to die for no sin of his own: then is half promised a reprieve that never arrives.

Seven oars for seven men we'd planned for the boat, and a longer steering oar. In order to make them we had to saw planks to the proper length: then split the planks with the sharpened rocks Chips Bullock had discovered.

That was a labor undertaken by Neal and Swede and me while the captain and Langman planned the fastening of the boat's sides.

The cutlass-saw was the instrument we used to saw those planks; and for incarnate devilishness that saw was perfectly designed to plague persons already plagued to the limit of endurance.

The handle was too small to allow the use of both hands; and the starting of a cut with those jagged teeth was a trial. All the wood was wet, and there seemed to be no way of holding the planks firm. We succeeded at last, after a fashion, by wedging one end of the plank beneath a boulder and forcing the opposite end upward.

Then the wielder of the saw, stretching himself under the plank, would haggle at it, always drawing the saw toward himself, until enough wood had been gnawed away to allow the plank to be broken.

We called the different days of the week by the names of occurrences, and I thought for a time that this day would be called Oar Day—the day before having been our first Sunday, and the day before that Boat Day, and the day before that Tent Day, and the day before that The Day We Cut Off Our Boots, and the day before that Cooky Sipper's Day.

But our labors on the oars were dwarfed by a discovery made by the captain.

At dead high tide, around ten o'clock, the captain raised a hoarse shout and pointed off to the south with his oakum-wrapped hand.

Beyond the breakers, beyond the round seal heads that watched us and watched us, were the sails of three vessels.

They might have been fishermen or coasting schooners, but at least they were vessels—the first sign of a sail we had seen; and to me, who had felt sure that no fishermen would venture out of port at this season of the year, they were a sight that sent through me a choking surge of hope.

They were moving straight out from shore, to the eastward, probably out of Portsmouth, the captain said: taking provisions to the Isles of Shoals, perhaps, or going for cargoes of salt cod.

Again everyone crawled from the tent to see those three wonderful sails, and to wave their arms and halloo hoarsely. The three vessels looked to us to be about nine miles from us, but still we hallooed. No shout can be heard at a distance of nine miles. All of us knew that. Perhaps our shouts were a form of prayer.

When the sails, sliding gradually to the eastward, became dim specks on the horizon, the oakum pickers crawled back to the tent. They looked like sick bears, and felt, if I could judge by my own feelings, even sicker than they looked.

Neal and Swede and I went back to making oars. The task before us seemed insurmountable—as impossible, almost, as drilling a hole through a block of granite with a needle.

December 19th, Tuesday

Those oars, I thought, were the most troublesome thing about the boat—though I suppose that each part of every enterprise always seems most difficult and most important to the one to whom it's entrusted.

Nonetheless, the oars seemed vital, for unless the wind was in the east, we couldn't depend on our sail to carry us to the nearest land, which, if Captain Dean's reckoning was correct, was six miles away. Even under favorable circumstances—better circumstances than the bitter ones we had so far encountered—we would be three hours, at least, rowing that clumsy boat to shore.

And row we must, not only to get the boat across that turbulent stretch of water, but to keep ourselves moving so we wouldn't freeze.

Yet the oars, split with rock-wedges from boards, were the same width from end to end. They had to be narrowed at one end, and smoothed, so that men could use them effectively. The saw was useless to smooth those sharp edges. Our knives made no impression upon them, for the wet boards only roughened when we tried to bevel the corners.

The best we could do, in the end, was to knock the ice from a ledge and rub each oar against the rock, working the oar around and around, rasping at it until we brought it to some faint semblance of smoothness. I couldn't let myself think what such oars would do to the hands of those who paddled with them, even when the hands were padded with oakum.

Tide was high at eleven; so at daybreak, before we went to work on those devilish oars, Neal and I patrolled the island.

The wind, for a change, was in the south and the seals had moved around to the north side.

For a change, too, there were four gulls at high-water mark, wailing dolorously. One was eyeing something, first from one side, then from the other, as gulls do; and as we made our way toward it, the gull picked up the something, flew straight up with it: then dropped it on the rocks, so that we knew it was a mussel.

When we shouted and waved our arms, the gulls flew away, mewing. Neal picked up the mussel, broken by its fall, and divided it with me.

As he chewed at that orange-colored meat, spitting out seed pearls as he did so, he moved from me to stare off to the westward, where low, shelving ledges made an easy descent to the rising waves.

I followed the direction of his gaze, and my eyes caught what his had caught—a short stick, a trifle bent, standing up straight from those shelving ledges.

There was something about the curve of that stick that

filled me with an almost insupportable excitement. I knew it couldn't be what it vaguely resembled! It couldn't be! Such things happen only in the *Odyssey*, and through the direct intervention of Minerva.

The surf swirled around the stick as we hurried toward it as rapidly as our bandaged and aching feet would let us.

Neal crawled out on the seaweed. I held his arm while he reached for the stick.

It was exactly what it had looked like the moment we saw it. It was an axe helve, and on the end of it, yellowed with salt-water rust, was the axe head, with the hone-marks still showing on the still sharp blade!

It's amazing how small a thing can make such a difference to so many people! Without that axe we were almost helpless, though I think we were never wholly hopeless.

With the axe, our spirits rose, our work no longer stood like an impenetrable wall before us.

We shouted the news of the axe to Captain Dean and Langman: showed it to those in the tent, to raise their spirits. They passed it from hand to hand.

"That's mine," Chips said. "The nails are mine, too. I ought to be allowed to go in the boat."

Nobody answered him. He was the only one who didn't know how sick he was.

"We'll need that oakum tomorrow," I reminded them. "If we have the right wind but shouldn't have enough oakum, we wouldn't dare to put her in the water."

Everyone, even Saver and Graystock, struggled to soften pieces of cordage, to separate the strands, to pick the hemp apart.

We went back to the oars.

DECEMBER 19TH, TUESDAY

With Neal holding each board upright, wedged between rocks, the axe chipped smooth slivers from the corners of the planks. The portions to be gripped by the hands of the rowers became round. Neal and I exchanged places at intervals, for the sake of warmth; but I think the thing that kept us warmest was the feeling of miraculous accomplishment.

December 20th, Wednesday

The boat was shaped like a punt, with square ends and square sides, and we spent all day putting the final touches on her—if anything about that boat could be called final. She was a marvel of incompleteness.

We had no way of judging how high she'd ride in the water when seven men were in her; nor was there any way of knowing how our caulking would hold.

All day long we drove oakum between the stern board and the sides: the bow boards and the sides.

The floor boards had been laid on canvas; and when they had been caulked as well as we could do it, the canvas was drawn up around the sides and ends like a shroud.

We stretched canvas over her bow and stern, binding the canvas with cordage. "It might be," Captain Dean said, "that if waves start slapping us, that canvas may help to keep out some of the spray."

Her height was a little increased by running a long strip of canvas around her, fastened to the stanchions; but it was too low. It had to be, so that the men who knelt in the boat could use the oars as paddles.

Remembering now how that boat looked, I can't believe that so many of us were eager to trust ourselves to her. Today I wouldn't trust such a travesty of a craft to get me across the Isis at Oxford, but it's easy to forget what a man will do when he's faced on the one hand with certain death, and on the other hand with a chance to live.

The easiest thing to say is that we were insane because of the things we'd endured. Surely I was insane, because I was eager to go. I was even sorry for Swede and Chips, who weren't strong enough to do so, and for all the others who couldn't for lack of space.

Yet we weren't wholly demented, because we made half a dozen bailing scoops—a simple matter now that we had the axe, though without the axe it would have been beyond our powers.

And we spent the last hours, right up to dark, in clearing seaweed-covered boulders from the narrow passageway down which the boat would have to be pushed in order to reach the sea. So we were sane enough to know that if a wave let this strange boat down on such a boulder, we'd have small chance of saving ourselves.

We spent those hours, too, in cutting seaweed to floor the ledge on which the boat rested, and to cover all the interval down to the growing seaweed. Without that protection, the canvas shroud on which the floor boards had been laid would have been cut to ribbons on barnacles by the time we got her to the water.

As we cut the seaweed, we ate as much of it as we could stomach; for the tide, high at noon, had shut us off from the mussel pools that were reachable only at low water.

In the tent, that night, I may have slept a little, but only a little, because of the excited discussions as to when the boat should be launched. Sometimes my hearing blurred, and there seemed to be breaks in the talk. This, I suppose, was sleep, for when my ears snapped open, someone, always, was talking.

The tide was low at seven in the morning, high an hour after noon, and low again at two hours after dark.

What, then, was it best to do?

To start at dawn, when the ocean might be stillest?

No: there was the great stretch of seaweed to be crossed at low tide, and the danger of falling!

Yes, but over against that was the hazard of arriving at our destination when the tide was high, concealing perilous ledges and possibly covering beaches that might, at low tide, be reached even though the boat were swamped.

To start at flood tide, then? That would mean that the tide would be falling when we reached our destination, and that offshore currents might push us away.

Ah yes, but beaches would be exposed–more safely approached. Offshore ledges would be revealed–more readily skirted.

Some argued for starting on the half-risen tide in the morning.

Langman in the beginning argued against all starting times that were proposed, and in the end argued for all of them. I think he wanted to take credit for anything good that happened, and dodge the responsibility for anything bad. The world is full of people like that, but most of them haven't Langman's malice.

December 21st, Thursday

The day, to the amazement and delight of all, was better for our purpose than any we had so far seen, though bitter cold. The sun rose red but unclouded, and there was a glassy sheen to the sea. On the north shore there were breakers, though not bad ones. On the south shore the swells came in from both directions, to gurgle, hiss and sigh along the brown seaweed-covered fingers of ledge, but for the most part they surged in without breaking to spend themselves in foam.

The captain urged everyone from the tent at daybreak. "Tide's dead low," he shouted. "We've got a lot to do today, so try to get enough mussels to last you through tomorrow."

I knew what he had in mind. He hadn't liked the looks of that red sky in the east.

When we were back in the tent, hacking with our knives at those miserable mussels and chewing our hated seaweed, the captain said, almost diffidently, that he had been thinking about the boat and her launching.

"I know we made seven oars," he said, "but I've come

to the conclusion that seven is too many to pack into a boat that size and shape, even when she's well built. It seems to me that two would be better than seven."

When he would have continued, his words were drowned by a roar of protest. The loudest roar came from Swede Butler, but Langman's was almost as loud.

"If only two go," Swede cried, "you wouldn't take Neal, and it was Neal found the axe! Without the axe you'd still be working on that boat! If anybody deserves to go, Neal does."

"It was my axe to begin with," Chips rasped. "I need medical help."

"It wasn't yours any more after you'd lost it," Swede said. "It belonged to all of us, same as a seagull would belong to all of us if we could catch one."

Langman shouted, "You needn't think I'm going to sit here like a bump on a log while the captain goes ashore all alone to spread the news about how he didn't wreck us on Boon Island on purpose! No, sir! I'm going in that boat if anyone does!"

Captain Dean looked sick. "I still think seven is too many. Would you be willing to try it with just me alone?"

"Oh no!" Langman said. "I haven't forgotten how you hit me with the loggerhead the night we went ashore! I wouldn't want anything like that to happen again."

The captain looked at him intently. "I hit you because you'd stolen supplies that rightly belonged to all of us. You were mutinous! You planned to take the ship for yourself and White and Mellen."

Langman's eye was sardonic. "Who'd believe such drivel! Just to make sure you don't slander innocent men without giving 'em a chance to answer, I insist on taking

White and Mellen. They'll have fair play or I'll know the reason why."

"In that case, Captain," Swede said, "you'll have to take my boy, and you'll have to go yourself, because you're captain. You might as well take two more. You'll have to do a lot of rowing, and the best men we've got are none too strong."

"It's too many," the captain repeated. "But if that's the way you want it, Mr. Langman, I'll fill the boat. I'll take my brother because he *is* my brother, and I'll take Mr. Whitworth because I promised his father I'd share and share alike with him."

A chorus of complaint went up from Saver and Graystock, that wholly worthless pair, from Chips Bullock, who was so weak from his lung trouble that he could hardly get to his feet, from Christopher Gray the gunner and Harry Hallion. We crawled from the tent as fast as we could, and for once were grateful for the ear-filling rumble of the breakers, which kept us from hearing the brainless clacking of those we left behind.

It was decided that when we slid the boat into the water at dead high tide, the captain and Neal Butler should be in her, while the rest of us waded in to hold her firm until she was free and clear. Then the captain was to pull in Langman, whereupon the two of them would hoist in the other four, with Neal steadying the boat with the steering oar.

Those we were leaving, barring Chips, who couldn't stand, came to the launching-ledge and crouched there, five unkempt specimens of humanity, all haggard and hairy. I suppose none of us, with the exception of Neal, looked better; but we could use our hands and feet, whereas those we were leaving either couldn't or pretended they couldn't. Thus we felt sorry for them, and those for whom one feels sorry seem sadly woeful.

"Well," the captain said, and his eyes wandered from man to man of those sorry five, "pray for courage, and don't stop moving. If we can reach shore, you'll have help and warmth and food and decent clothing."

He seemed to search his mind for something more to say, couldn't find it and so laid hold of the bow of the boat and started her down the seaweed-strewn ledge toward the water.

I imagined I knew how he felt—empty inside, wrung dry by cold, hunger and the prospect of that long row to the mainland in this cranky contraption of driftwood and old canvas.

"Where's the axe?" Langman asked. "Where's the hammer?"

Swede shook a fist at him. "You don't need the axe and the hammer!" he cried. "You've got to leave us something!"

White stumbled up with both tools and gave Langman the axe.

"Captain Dean," Swede shouted. "Don't let 'em take those tools!"

The captain spoke mildly to Langman. "You might as well leave them."

There was something snake-like about Langman's face, in spite of his black beard. He lowered his head and faced Dean defiantly. "They couldn't use 'em, even if we left 'em," he said. "Even if there was anything to use 'em on, their hands won't hold 'em. They've got the saw. When we reach land we may need those tools to build a better boat."

Nobody answered. We were too intent on the long swells rolling toward us—on waiting for the large one, the third wave, after which we might expect two rollers that would be less troublesome.

The captain raised his hand and shouted, "Now!"

"Push her in," Langman cried. He dropped the axe in the stern, bawled at the captain to get aboard, and signaled Neal to climb in as well. White tossed the hammer after the axe.

She slipped easily enough over the thick layer of seaweed we had spread beneath her. Her bow floated and rose up. With the canvas strip we had stretched above her sides, she had only eighteen inches freeboard.

We waded in with her, up to our knees, up to our middles. The shock of the water on my feet and legs was indescribable, because pain cannot be described.

Captain Dean, looking seaward, waved his arms wildly. "Hold her!" he screamed. "Back her!"

Ahead of the boat I saw a long swell moving in from the south. On its crest were the heads of a dozen seals, all staring down at me.

"Pull her back!" Captain Dean cried. "Pull!"

The boat was sluggish and immovable in my hands, and the icy water around my middle drove the wind from me. I had no strength to pull.

I felt her rising and rising. I caught her gunnel to rise with her. She turned sideways and loomed, tilted, like a slanted roof, before my face. I saw Captain Dean and Neal slide down against the gunnel, with oars tumbling all around them. I made a despairing, fruitless clutch at the axe, caught among the oars.

Then the wave broke, the boat turned over and above me, and I was buried in a choking smother of foam through which I struggled while icy thoughts darted like needles in my brain.

This was the end of it! Our precious axe was lost again; the hammer as well; all the oakum we had picked so endlessly; all the oars that had tortured us; all the planks and boards so painfully and hopefully pieced together; the stanchions, the canvas, the nails and spikes so arduously assembled! Everything was gone—everything but life itself.

December 22nd, Friday

Our clothes froze that night, though we lay close together.

Probably we had thoughts, in spite of the shudderings that racked all of us when we crawled back to the tent after getting ourselves from the water. If I *did* have thoughts, I can't recall them, though I remember cursing Langman for putting the axe in the boat.

Nor can I remember what I thought when Swede came in alone, after we were bedded in our nest of dank oakum.

"She's gone," Swede said. "Lock, stock and barrel. I tried to hold her, but the tide pulled her out and the waves broke her into a tangle. She floated off to the south."

He hunted for Neal and wedged himself down beside him.

"It's started to snow," Swede said. "Thick: from the south. You couldn't have made it!"

He said no more. In that frigid tent there was silence that was almost tangible, like a fog. Even Captain Dean lay there, staring up at the peak of the tent, above which hung the canvas flag that had failed us as utterly as had all our puny but excruciating efforts.

With the coming of daylight Swede pulled himself to the tent flap. "The snow's stopped," he said. "The whole world's plastered with it."

He looked helplessly from the tent, made an effort to get to his feet, fell to his hands and knees.

"It's got to be scraped off the tent," he said.

"Why has it?" Langman asked. "Don't Eskimos make houses out of snow? I say leave the snow on the tent. It'll protect us from wind."

Swede rolled over clumsily to look at Langman. "Langman," he said, "you're a whoreson, beetle-headed, flap-ear'd knave! You're against everyone and everything, and you keep right on telling lies to try to prove you're right. If we leave the snow on the tent and get more snow, the canvas will split, or it'll fall down on us. Snow's heavy! And you talk about Eskimos!"

"Eskimos *do* live under snow," Langman said defensively.

"Why don't you tell the truth?" Swede snapped. "They live in ice huts, and they have fur clothes and fire—yes, and tools. We've got none! It's thanks to you that we're without tools."

Captain Dean got heavily to his feet. "Now, now!" he said. "We've got to live together. And Swede's right. We'll have to scrape the snow off the tent. If we do, maybe those on shore will see the tent and the flag against the snow."

"I don't believe it," Swede said bitterly. "If those ashore had their eyes open, they'd have seen this tent and flagpole long before now. They're probably like most of the farmers where I come from–spend half their lives walking around with their heads hanging and their mouths open. Well, I'm going to *make* 'em see us!"

"I say with all this snow, we ought to stay in the tent," Langman said. "We're all half frozen. We'll slip in the snow and break our legs."

"No," Captain Dean said. "That's exactly why we can't stay in the tent. We're more than half frozen, and unless we keep moving, we *will* freeze."

"If they want to freeze," Swede said, "let 'em! They'd probably be more help to us dead than alive!" He crawled out into the snow, glittering white on the boulders and ledges, and bright blue in the shadows.

Neal went to the tent-flap to join his father. We heard them scratching at the snow to dislodge it from the sagging tent sides. Then they set off slowly toward the ledge where we had built the boat.

Since the tide was low at eight in the morning, the captain and George White and Langman and Christopher Gray went to the north side for mussels. We had nine apiece that day, with seaweed in place of bread and sauce and dessert.

I think the loss of the boat had shocked all of us: first into a state of horrified resignation, then into desperate activity–though Swede's openly contemptuous attack on Langman may have had something to do with waking us from our lethargy. Certainly there was rancor in the mind of everyone able to think–even in the minds of Langman's cronies, White and Mellen. In all their faces I saw sullen fury at Langman's folly in putting the axe and the hammer in the boat, and at his insolent insistence that he did so to let us build a better boat when we got to land.

We knew that wasn't so: knew that his seizure of the tools was unreasoning hoggishness on Langman's part, and there was hot resentment against Langman, and an irritation against everything. I think that was why there was a general outcry against the mussels on the ground that they were too cold, too tough, too bitter, impossible to swallow, too hard on the bowels.

There was even more unrest when Swede and Neal crawled back. Swede had found the tattered remains of two hammocks. Neal dragged in one. Swede dragged in the other and went to Captain Dean for his mussels.

"Look at these hammocks," Swede said proudly. "Just what we need for a raft!"

Captain Dean peered from Swede to Neal and back again. "Just eat your mussels, Swede," he said. "You worked hard to save that boat. There's plenty of time to discuss a raft."

"Oh no, there isn't," Swede said. "I've already lost the use of my feet, but I can still use my hands. I may lose them any minute. We'll have to build the raft before I lose my hands too."

A groan went up from the circle of scarecrows huddled in the tent.

"We'd work ourselves to death," White protested, "and have the same thing happen that happened to the boat."

"No," Swede said. "It wouldn't be anything like the boat, because it wouldn't be overloaded, and I wouldn't launch it till I had the wind with me."

"Swede," Captain Dean said, "let's talk this over some other time."

"Some other time—when my boy and all the rest of you are dead?" Swede said politely. "No! I'm building a raft while I've got my hands. If nobody else helps me, Neal will."

Harry Hallion spoke up. "He won't help you much when it comes to spiking her together. We used all our spikes on the boat. If there's any left in the junk, he'll never draw spikes without a hammer! What'll he use? His teeth?"

"We'll build it without spikes if we have to," Swede said. "We'll lace it together with cordage."

"On a raft," Captain Dean said, "a part of you would be in water most of the time—*all* the time, maybe. The nearest land is six miles away. How long would you last in water like this?"

"I don't know," Swede said, "but I prayed to God yesterday while I was trying to hold the boat. I prayed again this morning. I prayed to Langman's God, whose Sunday is Saturday, and to our God, whose Sunday is Sunday—to Langman's God, who wants us to observe Christmas the day before Christmas, and to our God, who doesn't care when we observe it, so long as we celebrate it with an understanding of what Christmas means. Both Gods told me what to do. They told me to build a raft."

I realized suddenly what Swede was saying. He was saying that God gave his only beloved son to save the world from itself. Now Swede, having communed with that God, was willing to give himself in order to save *his* only beloved son from a cruel and lingering death. He was not only willing to give himself: he had, in his mind, already done so.

December 23rd, Saturday

This was the day of the seagull—a Langman Sunday, the day before Langman's Christmas, and the day we started the raft.

In making the boat we had deliberately ignored the foremast yard, not only because of its awkward length—twenty-four feet, a veritable tree—but also because it was so tangled and cluttered with the innumerable confusing attachments of such a spar that by general agreement it had been spurned by all—passed over after one look at the tattered shreds of canvas still clinging to it, and its wrappings of frayed and frozen preventer stays, lanyards, bowlines, bridles, sheets, lifts, yard tackles.

Just that yard alone was enough to turn me against ships, and I wondered why three-masted square-rigged vessels were ever made in the first place.

I asked Captain Dean, as we dragged it to the spot chosen by Swede; but he didn't know.

"Probably," he said, "we build square-riggers because nations like France and England have to fight wars every few years. To fight wars you have to have warships; and warships have to carry a lot of men. If you put a lot of men aboard a big schooner or a big brig, both easy to sail, there wouldn't be anything for sailors to do between fights, so they'd make trouble like Langman–mutiny, probably, or die of boredom. To keep 'em busy you've got to have a hundred sails for 'em to set or take in every half hour, and five or ten thousand sheets and lifts and tackles for 'em to haul on at five-minute intervals."

He cogitated: then added, "Maybe shipbuilders are like Langman. Maybe they get a foolish idea in their heads, and can't recognize a better one when it's presented to 'em."

Swede and Neal had been at that spar since dawn, pounding the ice and snow from it and its attached junk.

"I've got it all figured out," Swede told Captain Dean. "First we'll sharpen up our knives and cut through each piece of cordage on the top side. Then we'll roll the spar over, knock the ice off the other side, and pull the cordage free. All that cordage is slushed with tar, so the short pieces can be burned later, when you get fire."

When we got fire! Ah, would that day ever come!

Captain Dean nodded. "If we start at the center when we strip the junk, two of us can start knifing a groove around the middle. We'll hammer our knife-blades with rocks. Maybe we can cut an inch-deep groove all the way around. That'll leave only a ten-inch cut to be made with the saw."

I suspected irony and glanced at him quickly, but he was serious enough.

A ten-inch cut through that tree trunk of a spar! And with a saw made by pounding a cutlass into jaggedness against the sharp edge of a ledge! I tried to figure the amount of sawing we'd have to do in order to make that yard into a pair of logs.

If Langman hadn't lost the axe, two men whose hands weren't frost-nipped might, by spelling each other, do the cutting in half an hour.

But without the axe—with the saw alone: that miserable saw which would only cut when pulled backward—that was different!

Would two men make half an inch an hour?

Not through the thick part of the yard, they wouldn't.

Perhaps when they were nearly finished, and the yard could be balanced on a boulder, so the blade wouldn't bind in the cut, they might make half an inch in an hour. *Perhaps* they might.

In any event, half an inch an hour was the best we could expect—and with ten inches to go, we'd be twenty hours making the cut. But there were only nine hours of daylight in each day, provided there was no snow or rain: provided the wind wasn't so piercing that working in it was impossible.

And how many of us, afflicted with gurry sores and partly frozen hands and feet, were capable of using that saw at all?

"Clear away the junk in the center," Swede told Captain Dean, and his voice was jubilant. "Then I'll start the groove. Neal can hold the knife. I'll do the hammering."

In the face of Swede's excitement, I banished my doubts about our ability to sever that detested spar. If Swede's faith was so unconquerable, I could have faith too.

I went to work on the twisted cordage. It resisted my knife-blade like strands of metal.

"Take it a strand at a time," the captain said. "Wriggle

your knife-blade under a single strand: then drag the blade toward your stomach."

There were eight of us working at that spar, and we must have looked like hairy bears, nosing at a log in hungry curiosity.

Langman came from the tent to watch us. In his hand he held the saucepan handle we had salvaged in the distant past.

"Get your knife and go to work," Captain Dean said.

"It's Sunday," Langman said. "Remember the Sabbath day to keep it holy."

"It's Saturday," Captain Dean said. "What excuse will you have tomorrow for not working?"

"Tomorrow's Christmas," Langman said, almost indulgently.

He seemed disappointed when the men on both sides of the spar made no reply. He had to have attention, Langman did; and he didn't care how he got it.

He left us, slipping and sliding across the wet seaweed toward the mussel pools on the south shore.

The tide was low. I hoped Langman's respect for his private Sunday wouldn't prevent him from hunting food for the rest of us—though the mere thought of mussels almost made me retch.

Gradually we gained on the cordage and junk, half numbed by the clack, clack, clack of Swede's rock as he rapped it against the back of the knife-blade that Neal clutched.

Into that monotonous clacking, suddenly, intruded an uproar as startling as it was unexpected. Shrill through the noise of the breakers came a raucous screaming that brought us up all standing. Against the dark background of the seaweed-covered ledges we saw a preposterous mixture of man and wings that gyrated and flapped and rolled about.

"It's Langman," Captain Dean said. "He's caught a seagull!"

He had indeed, or the seagull had caught him, for the big bird was screaming, squalling, flapping its wings, beating Langman's head with giant pinions. I thought for a moment that the gull had lifted him from the rock. But the gull fell at last and Langman leaped upon it, and we saw he was beating it with the saucepan handle. At last the gull ceased to flap and flop, and lay still.

The air above the man and the struggling bird had been alive with gulls, wheeling, squealing and wailing; but when the bird was quiet, every last one of those gulls fell silent and winged off toward the mainland as if terror-stricken. Not one remained behind. There was something oppressive about the sudden departure of all those noisy creatures whose screams had shrilled through the roaring of breakers from dawn to dark each day.

Langman came slowly back to us, dragging that huge bird across the icy ledges, and threw it down beside the spar.

"There!" Langman said. "There's some food that's better than mussels!" He was proud of himself, and with good reason.

We crowded around that enormous gull, fondling it, burying our fingers in its beautiful warm white breast, and sniffing its dusty clean smell. It was a black-back–snowy white on belly, head, neck and tail, but with black wings and a black saddle: largest of all gulls; almost twice the size of ordinary large gulls with pale blue backs: nearly three times that of young gray ones.

"I'll skin him," Langman said importantly, "and we'll eat him. I wish you could have seen how I got him. I cut enough seaweed to cover me, and then I raked up a mussel and put it on a flat place, right near the hole I'd picked to squat in. Then I hung the seaweed all over me, so I looked like a boulder. When that old gull came overhead, twisting his neck and squinting at that mussel from all sides, he looked as big as a goose! Yes, sir! Then he stuck out his feet and came down all sprawling, a regular ostrich, and I just put out my hand and grabbed him. That was the surprisedest gull that ever landed on *this* island!"

For a moment I almost liked Langman—almost forgot his effort to oust Captain Dean; his almost certain plot to seize the *Nottingham;* his insistence that Captain Dean had purposely wrecked the ship; his stubborn refusal to admit the well-established fact of Sir Isaac Newton's reflecting telescope; his willingness—eagerness, even—to blacken Captain Dean's reputation and by implication to damage the reputation of all who sided with the captain; his persistence in observing the wrong Sunday. Yes, for a moment, but only for a moment, I forgot that persistence in wrong-headedness is the most dangerous of all human failings.

Langman skinned that gull with loving care, making an incision at the top of the head and running the cut all the way down the center of the back to the tail.

"We can make ear muffs with this," he said as he worked. "We can fasten feather pads inside spun-yarn caps, so that those who go out on patrol can have better protection for their ears and noses. We can make a pair of feather-lined gauntlets and take turns wearing 'em."

I was amazed to hear such helpful thoughts from Langman. Sometimes it's hard to remember that the leopard never changes his spots: that the most hardened criminal has endeared himself to someone, but is no less dangerous.

Langman peeled the wings back to the first joint, leaving all the wing-feathers attached to the skin. When the skinning was finished, he had a rude square of feathers almost three feet long and three feet wide.

"How'll we dry it?" he asked Captain Dean.

"Tie it around Neal before it freezes," Captain Dean said. "His skin's smoother, and chances are he isn't as lousy as the rest of us."

So that was what was done. Swede took the big black and white skin and went with Neal to the tent, to be out of the wind.

The division of that bird's body among thirteen men wasn't easy, and I was glad Langman turned over the task to Captain Dean.

First the captain gutted it, finding two six-inch tommy cod in its gullet. The intestines and the small fish he placed on a board to freeze, along with the thigh joints, the wing joints, the thick neck, the feet, and the skull.

"We can chew 'em later," he said.

Then he laid off the breasts, still warm, and cut them into thirteen lengthwise strips, taking a little from the long, thick center strips to add to the thin side strips.

The men watched the division with jealous eyes, each one certain, after the manner of hungry men, that his was the smallest portion.

Chips Bullock wouldn't come from the tent, even for meat, so the captain called for Neal to take Chips's portion to him.

"Make him eat it," the captain told Neal.

Langman was derisive. "I suppose," he said, "you don't trust any of the rest of us to take that to Chips."

"I don't even trust myself," the captain said.

When a man's hungry, he doesn't waste time thinking how meat tastes. There's blood in it, and a little hope and a little strength. He just chews at it until it dissolves and trickles down his throat. Then he's angry and desperate because there isn't more.

December 24th, Sunday

Langman, inflamed by his success in capturing the seagull, was at us all Sunday to celebrate that day as Christmas.

Swede, equally determined to keep on with the raft while the weather was endurable, spoke to him sharply.

"What is it you want to celebrate, Langman?" he demanded. "Don't you remember what Christmas was like in London? Remember how all the sluts and beggars and cripples gathered in front of church doors, all mealy-mouthed and pious, and their eyes rolled up, hoping they looked as if they were talking to God? Remember, Langman?"

Langman, his lip curled, eyed him sideways.

"Well, I remember," Swede said. "When the church doors were opened and the alms and doles were handed out, all their piety disappeared and they fought each other like cats and dogs, each trying to get the others' alms away from 'em. They'd go off down the street, cursing and fighting, and push their way into public houses and get roaring drunk on gin!"

"You're against Christmas!" Langman said angrily.

"There you go," Swede said, "twisting things around! I'm not going to have any first mate telling me how to celebrate the birth of Christ, or when to do it. You say today is Christmas, but you're wrong. When the proper time arrives, I'll celebrate Christmas in my own way."

Captain Dean turned to me. "Miles, you were in Christ Church. You must have heard talk about the celebrating of Christmas."

"Yes, sir, and my father and I often talked about it. He said it should be a festival for children and for the poor—not a time for people to cripple themselves financially by exchanging expensive gifts that most givers can't afford and most recipients don't want. He said Christ would be the first one to pity those who can't decide which day to celebrate, and to laugh at those who, because of politics, say how it shall be celebrated."

"That's blasphemy again!" Langman cried.

"No, it's not," I said. "Every don in Christ Church knows that the Puritans by act of Parliament forbade merriment or religious services on Christmas. They said it was a heathen festival. Charles II revived feasting on Christmas. That's politics."

"Anyway, the date has always been the same," Langman insisted.

"That's not so," I told him. "I've heard professors lecture on it. Some of the ancients said Christ's birthday was May 20th: others said April 19th: still others put it on the seventeenth of November. One man held out for the twenty-eighth of March. Then January 6th was celebrated as his birthday for hundreds of years."

"I say this is Christmas," Langman persisted, "and the rest of my seagull should be divided for a feast."

"All right," Captain Dean agreed. "Go ahead and divide it up. You'd better give Swede at least half of the neck. He seems to be doing most of the work on the raft."

The junk was completely stripped from the spar that Sunday noon, and we took turns using the cutlass-saw. The saw didn't really cut the wood: it abraded it: chewed it: wore it away.

By noontime Langman had divided the body of the gull and summoned us to the tent for what he persisted in calling our Christmas dinner.

"We can't distribute this by lot," he explained, "because some are better able to eat than others, and if I passed it out by lot, the wrong man might get the wrong thing and not be able to eat it. So I've taken Captain Dean at his word: I've gone ahead and divided it up.

"Now take Chips Bullock. He can't eat much, and he can't hardly chew at all, so I've given him the heart and the liver. Then there's Graystock and Saver. They claim they can't work or walk or do anything to help us, so I've given each of them one of the fish we found in the craw. The captain gets the two wings. There's not much meat on the wings, but there's some, especially when they're pounded on rocks. The same thing is true of the feet. You might not think there was much in seagulls' feet, but there is, especially when they're pounded to a pulp; and they last longer than plain meat when you suck at them, so I'm giving Christopher Gray the feet.

"I figure there's about as much in one of the thighs as there is in two wings, so I'm giving Henry Dean one of the thighs and Harry Hallion the other.

"Then there's the back: that hasn't got much on it, but the bone is thin and can easily be pounded; so I've divided it into two parts and White gets one part and Mellen gets the other.

"There's a good deal of nourishment in the skull and in the neck, so I've split the skull in two and cut the neck into three parts, one of them a little larger than the other two. I'm giving Swede half the skull and one of the small pieces of the neck.

"Whitworth gets the other half of the skull and the other small piece of neck. Neal gets the large piece of neck."

As he talked, he passed around these fragments of bone and gristle.

"That seems fair," Captain Dean admitted. "What's left for you?"

"Well," Langman said, "I may seem to have a little more than some of you, but I really haven't. I'm taking the windpipe and the intestines. They're frozen; and when they're pounded up together, they'll probably be about the same thing, in the long run, as a piece of neck—especially when they're mixed with seaweed."

By the grace of God, when that cutlass-saw had chewed its way half through the spar, we lifted it and banged it against the edge of a ledge.

To our triumphant amazement it cracked and split; so that when four of us took one end and four took the other, and we put our weight on it, it broke all the way across—jaggedly, it's true; but it broke.

So when we crawled into the tent for the last time on

that false Christmas, the two pieces of spar lay side by side on the flat ledge, ready to be joined together in a raft—though my half-frozen brain was incapable of knowing how it could ever be done.

December 25th, Monday

Christmas on Boon Island!

I write the words reluctantly because they deny each other. They're unreal and don't belong together. Christmas belongs with warmth, with love, with good cheer, with feasting, with happiness, with gratitude for years past and years to come, with an understanding of the meaning of Christmas. . . .

There were spittings of snow and a northwest wind that drove snow-dust beneath the tent and through every crevice, no matter how solidly we packed oakum along the tent-bottom.

Swede, when he went out at dawn to work on the raft, crawled back in again, baffled.

"The wind's so cold the whole sea's smoking," he said. "That wind cuts like a knife. Let's see that seagull's breast."

He fumbled at the oakum wrappings that Neal, like all the rest of us, wore inside his coat; and when he pulled out the beautiful black and white skin, it had lost its stickiness. It wasn't dry, but it was flexible, like parchment.

"If we could cut this apart," Swede told Captain Dean, "we might make protectors for our ears and noses. Then some of us could stand this wind."

The captain took the skin from him, stretched it over his knees and stroked it.

"It's a shame to cut that breast," Swede said. "We could make a whole helmet out of it."

"Only a helmet for one man," the captain reminded him.

"What would do us the most good," Swede said, "is to cut it into pieces to fasten inside our oakum mittens so our hands won't get numb. Of course, we ought to have some for our ears and noses."

Taking the skin from the captain, Neal pressed it tight over his head. He was the only one among us who didn't have a grizzled beard; and his face, beneath that soft, white gull breast, with the black wings hanging down on either side, reminded me poignantly of how he had looked on the stage at Greenwich, reciting Colley Cibber's epilogue to *The Walking Statue*.

He lifted the gull breast from his head and studied it. "If you take off the large parts of each wing," he said, "you could run spun yarn through them and tie one over each ear. They'd be big enough to protect your ears and your cheeks, too."

Langman took the skin from him and examined the wings. "What about the ends of the wings?" he asked.

"Well," Neal said, "you could cut off the stiff quills and weave the feathers in and out of our oakum ear muffs. You could weave 'em in on a slant. They'd cover your ears a little, and stick out over your eyes and nose and mouth."

In the end we used the black back-strips to thicken the

backs of mittens. The beautiful white breast, after long discussion and the drawing of diagrams on the skin with the points of knives, we cut into strips long enough to pass from ear to ear across the nose.

At the base of the breast were the tail feathers. Captain Dean looked up at Langman. "This tail doesn't fit much of anywhere," he said. "How about giving it to Neal for a Christmas present?"

Langman sneered, but nodded his head in acquiescence.

All that Christmas morning we wove and patched our oakum headgear and mittens with those strips of seagull skin. There were enough to make five feather-lined helmets that would let five men work at one time in the teeth of that northwest wind.

The captain took the first helmet we finished. When he had clumsily tied it on with spun yarn, he said abruptly, "Low tide's about now. We've got to eat something! That something's going to be seaweed, and we can't stay alive unless we eat it."

He went out after the seaweed, and when he returned, four more helmets were finished.

We choked down the seaweed. Then Swede crawled on his hands and knees to the captain, to Langman, to George White, to me. All he did was take us by the shoulders and look into our faces; but that was enough to shame the four of us into following him out into that searing wind.

We had no hammer: no spikes: no nails. We had to build that raft out of four lengths of plank that Swede and Neal had somehow worried from the junk the day before.

All we had to fasten the planks to the spars was rope that

could be cut into desired lengths and slapped against ledges until, freed of ice, they were flexible.

We must, the captain explained, do everything with cordage, so he showed us how to haul cordage into place, thread it beneath the two pieces of spar in such a way that the pieces were four feet apart; then bring the ends of each piece of cordage together and splice them. Thus the spars were joined loosely by a series of rope loops.

Into these loops we thrust the four lengths of planks. Spun yarn was knotted from side to side of the loop and between the planks to prevent the planks from folding against each other. Then each loop was tightened as is a tourniquet. With one man on each end of a loop, a stick was thrust through the slack and twisted and twisted, until the loop was as tight as it could be made.

When any one of us reached the limit of his endurance, which was often, he told Swede, who went back to the tent with him, helped him relinquish his feathered headgear to another, who crawled reluctantly into that whistling, spume-laden blast. Swede was the only one who had faith in what we were doing. The rest of us were helping him rather than ourselves.

By dark of that Christmas Day the planks were laced in place: the tourniquets that held the lacing were fastened so they couldn't slip or come loose. When even Swede was willing to stop, and went from one of us to the other, patting our backs and thanking us for the work we'd done, I had a momentary thought that Christmas was truly Christmas, even on Boon Island.

December 26th, Tuesday

Our lives depended on the weather, and if that northwest wind had blown another day, if for another twenty-four hours the combers, each one whitecapped, had raced at us and all around us, steaming and smoking, as the sea always does in frigid spells, I think our work would have been wasted and our hopes dashed.

But on the day after our true Christmas, the weather moderated.

I may seem to speak overmuch about the weather—about the hours of high tides and low tides; about the spring tides that threatened our lives and the neap tides that let us go farther out on the seaweed-covered rock fingers in our search for mussels; about the snow or sleet that might crush our tent; about the offshore winds that bit into our bones, and the south winds that could, if Providence so ordained, float evidences of our existence to the distant beaches that we sometimes saw, always fogged by mist from breakers.

Yet weather *was* our life, and so must be explained to those who see weather with different eyes; and to one who has been exposed to the ocean and its winter furies, the words "the weather moderated" bring inexpressible relief —a surcease from agony, from despair, from dark depression. . . .

Londoners—city dwellers—who despise sailors and countrymen, can never in their ignorance know the beauty of those words, just as they can never know, in their restricted world, the marvels that exist in the worlds of others, or appreciate the magic qualities of all the things they look upon as commonplace: the wonders of fire, of sweet water, of shelter.

In Greenwich we listened in amazement to those Londoners who longed for and acclaimed cloudless skies at times when countrymen were praying for rain and losing their crops and even their farms from drought; who were perpetually being caught in thunderstorms because they turned resolutely from the west and put their faith in a narrow strip of blue sky in the east; to whom a tree was merely a tree, and they unable to distinguish between a pine, a fir, a spruce or a larch; to whom a bird smaller than a pheasant was merely a bird, without a name, without a song. . . .

Ah! Fortunate, fortunate city dwellers: fortunate that so many countrymen and seamen are inarticulate, unable to express their thoughts concerning those who dwell in cities and are so profoundly lacking in knowledge!

And so, to our joy, the weather moderated!

The wind, what there was of it, couldn't make up its mind what to do. It blew gently from the east: then came fitfully from the west.

Swede, working at the pile of junk for materials to strengthen his raft, nosed at those breezes like a weathervane. He was afraid, and so were the rest of us, that the wind would back up—move to the west and south without first going to the eastward and the southeast. When, after a storm or a blow, the wind backs up, unpleasant weather will soon return, just as some sort of evil follows the appearance of a ring around the sun or around the moon.

We stepped a fence post of a mast on the raft and hung the two hammocks on it, to serve as a sort of double lugsail. We fastened three pieces of wood—oars, we called them, and were too weak to laugh at ourselves—to the spars. Then, because Swede insisted we must, we lashed bridles to both ends of the spars, with long rope-ends trailing from them.

At noon the tide was lower than ever before, because of the full moon, and we brought in a treasure trove of mussels. We left half of them unopened. There was something about that raft that sickened those who worked on it.

Only Swede grew constantly more cheerful.

"There's got to be two little pulpits built up at each end," he told Captain Dean. "We can lay two piles of cordage, bow and stern: then lace the piles in position. That'll keep us out of the water. They ought to be big enough so we can kneel on them."

"Who's we?" Captain Dean asked. "You and who else?"

"I don't know," Swede said. "The Lord will provide."

The captain shook his head and let his eyes wander around the horizon as if in hopes of finding the something that the Lord would provide. He studied the tall rusty face of Bald Head Cliff, the long sands of York and so on to the open sea beyond. Then he straightened, as if incredulous.

"Why," he said, "there's a sail! There's *two* of 'em!"

He raised his voice shouting, "Sail! Sail!"

We dropped our armfuls of cordage. We got ourselves to the highest part of the rock and stared longingly at those two far-off sails. They seemed to be sloops, but they were so distant, we couldn't be sure which way they were heading: whether they were inbound or outbound. We could hardly see their hulls, but our unreasoning longing to be rescued was so strong within us that we shouted and waved, waved and shouted—all of us but Swede.

When we stopped our waving and our shouting and just followed the progress of those small pink sails, Swede laughed at us.

"You think I haven't got a chance to reach shore on this raft," he said, "yet you go shouting and waving at two sloops that are fifteen miles away if they're an inch. You'd never have seen 'em at all if the wind hadn't blown from the northwest all day yesterday. There isn't one of you that can see a man when he's over six miles away. There isn't one of you whose voice could be heard a mile away. If that's the way you feel, every last one of you ought to be fighting for the chance to go on this raft with me."

I had to admit that he was right, and that our behavior in shouting and waving at those two far-off sail showed we were close to panic. Yet the sight of those sail, and our shouting and our waving, had done something to our spirits so that when we had finished Swede's cordage pulpits, and went to the tent to eat our seaweed and ice, we were more hopeful about Swede's venture than we had hitherto been.

When he stayed behind us, brooding over his raft and talking endlessly to Neal, he put me in mind of a bridegroom, garrulous over the inescapable fate awaiting him on the morrow.

December 27th, Wednesday

Love, true love, is, I suppose, always intemperate, whether it's the love of a man for a woman, a woman for a child, or a father for a son. Certainly Swede's love for Neal was a consuming passion, and equally certainly Neal's comprehension of that love was unusual and beautiful.

Even before sunup Swede had left the tent, and Neal with him. I couldn't hear what Swede said to Neal, but there was a buoyant quality to his voice. When I went outside, I found the wind, wambling and uncertain the day before, had dropped to a dead calm—and when I say calm, I'm speaking only of the wind. The canvas on the tent pole hung flat against it; but the sea—ah, that damnable sea! There may be such a thing as a dead calm around Boon Island, but it must be in the summer. When we were on the island, the sea was perpetually heaving, surging, on every side, as if afflicted with waves of nausea.

If the breakers came at us from the west, the island seemed to catch them and pull them around, billowing, on either side, as a woman, battered by wind, draws a cape around herself.

But the air, at least, was still and frost-laden. There was frost on the seaweed: ice on the naked boulders–spume-ice left by the northwest wind.

I went over to the raft on which Swede and Neal were sitting, lashing two oars to the sides with spun yarn.

"I know the signs," Swede said cheerfully. "That wind's coming around. When the tide's low at one o'clock, she'll move in from the south. No doubt about it."

"How're your feet?" I asked.

"Gone," Swede said lightly.

"Wouldn't you feel better if we cleaned them?" I asked.

Swede shook his head. "I don't want to see 'em," he said. "I don't want anybody else to see 'em. They don't hurt, and if you did something to 'em, they might start hurting again."

The captain and George White crawled from the tent just as the sun came up. Against its rising disk the rollers on the horizon were like the teeth of our cutlass-saw.

"Well, Captain," Swede said triumphantly, "this is the day! Full moon! Onshore wind!"

The captain shook his head and with his oakum-swathed hands dragged at the spar that formed one side of this spider-web of a raft, laced together with cordage. The spar pulled free of the ice beneath it. It was too frail a support for my taste. The two hammocks, rigged as sails on its stump of a mast, hung limp and ineffective, like the folded wings of a sleeping bat.

"I've made up my mind to one thing," Captain Dean said. "If this raft sets off, I won't be on it."

"That's your privilege," Swede said.

"I won't be on it," Captain Dean said, "because I've

weighed the chances, and the chances of getting ashore alive with this raft aren't as good as staying alive on this rock. I ought to forbid you to go. Yesterday we saw two sail heading east. They must have come out of the Piscataqua River, making toward the Isles of Shoals. I'd say they're probably running out of salt fish in Portsmouth. Either that, or they need fresh fish. If they run out of fish in Portsmouth, they're bound to run out in York, too, or Cape Porpoise, or some such place. Boats'll put out of those ports, just as they put out of Portsmouth."

Swede put his arm around Neal's shoulders and spoke to Captain Dean. "Captain, I'm leaving here at low tide. You'll help me put her in over yonder, where those ledges point out to the west, won't you?"

I was watching Neal. His eyes seemed to be examining the lashings of that strange raft. They lifted suddenly, met mine and instantly dropped again. They looked hurt, like the eyes of a dog whose master is deserting him.

"Help me get seaweed, Neal," I said.

He climbed obediently from the raft, and as he went, his father's fist rapped him affectionately on the shoulder.

We skirted the tent and started that hated circuit of the island, hunting for any useful thing that might have been sent to us by the sea's grace.

"Neal," I asked, "has your father ever told you he'd like you to go with him on the raft?"

Neal shook his head. "He wouldn't let me. I said I'd go, but he almost snapped my ears off."

"He'll never make it," I said. "Have you asked him not to go?"

"No," Neal admitted. "He *wants* to go. He's *determined* to go."

"Yes," I said, "I can see that."

"He *might* make it," Neal said, "if he had an onshore wind and a strong man to use the paddle. Anyway, nothing can stop him." He hesitated; then added, "I don't want to stop him."

When I was silent, Neal added, "When he was in the Naval Hospital, he thought he was as good as dead. He said he wasn't pulling his weight, and he was ashamed to be seen in the hospital uniform. On the *Nottingham* he pulled his weight. He was happy again. He was even happy on this island–until his feet froze. Then he couldn't pull his weight any more. He thinks this raft'll let him pull his weight."

"Not if he doesn't get ashore," I reminded him.

"He doesn't look at it that way," Neal said. "He says everything's in his favor. He says somebody may see him if he gets halfway to land. He says if he gets almost to land, somebody's *sure* to see him. He says if he doesn't get to land and the raft does, they'll find the raft–and then they'll find us."

"You wouldn't stop him if you could, would you?" I asked.

"No, I wouldn't," Neal said. "If he let me or anybody or anything stop him, he'd never forgive himself. He knows he's going to die, and so do I. I don't want him to die unhappy. Once he's on that raft, headed for shore, his mind will be at ease, no matter what happens."

There wasn't anything I could say to that. Neal, when I'd first encountered him in Greenwich, was a fine boy–the sort of boy anyone would be proud to have as a son or a brother; but the things that had happened to him in five months had changed him from a boy into a man—a man who would be a credit to any society, to any country, no matter along what lines his life might be cast.

Swede was right about the wind. At noon it moved in faintly, a little east of south, and the captain gave the word to drag the raft to the spot Swede had chosen. The dragging wasn't easy, and we did it by inches. Swede counted for us as he probably once had counted in the St. George's Light Dragoons—"One, two, three, hup,"—and at the "hup" we'd all lift together. By "all" I mean the captain and Neal on one side with Langman and me; on the other side Gray, Hallion, Mellen and White.

The others couldn't lift, they said, but they had crawled from the tent to watch, all but poor Chips Bullock.

Between every few lifts we crawled forward to move rocks from our path, and came back to lift again, sliding the raft forward three inches, five inches. The hardest part was finding footholds sufficiently secure to make lifting possible.

At the water's edge the captain stepped back from the raft.

"Put her in," Swede shouted. "She's headed right for shore!"

"Yes, put her in," George White said. "I'm going with him. With this breeze I think we can make it."

Langman, I thought, as well as could be seen on a face so covered with whiskers, had a smug look. If one of his own men hadn't been going with Swede, I was sure he would have protested bitterly. He never would have gone himself, and he would have done everything possible to prevent Swede from going alone.

"If you're determined to go," the captain said, "I won't try to stop you, now that you've gone this far—"

"Push her in," Swede said.

"But I want to urge you to wait one more day, or two days."

"What for?" Swede demanded. "Get her in the water!"

There were murmurs from the oakum-draped figures sprawled on the rocks around us, their limbs at odd angles, like those of dead men.

The captain fumbled in his clothes and with difficulty produced coins, which he gave to Swede. "These are all I saved," he told Swede. "They may help you, one way or another. And there's just one thing, Swede. When you get to shore, have somebody light a fire on the beach. Have 'em light two fires. Have 'em do that before they do anything else."

"Two fires," Swede said. He crawled aboard the raft and swept us with a glance that made my heart contract. "I know you wish us well," he said. "I wish all of you well." He steadied himself by grasping the spar on either side, and we ran the raft into the water. George White climbed over the stern, and we pushed as hard as we could.

The raft moved heavily between two ledge-fingers, and her hammock-sail flapped. She almost stopped, settled down as a wave receded, then picked up way again. She moved out until she was parallel with the tips of the ledge-fingers: then sluggishly swung broadside to the distant coast line. A slow surge moved her forward. The bow rose a little. The surge slid back and left the side of the raft caught on an unseen ledge.

White struggled with the lashings of his oar. The free side of the raft slipped under water. The surge returned and the raft tilted sharply. Then another surge moved down from the north side of the island, pressed against the submerged side, and the raft rolled over. A crying rose around us like the squalling of seagulls above a school of fish.

The raft had spilled in deep water. I found myself on a ledge-finger near the wallowing contraption. Swede came to the surface, gasping, and swam easily to shore, holding a rope-end in his hand. Neal and Langman dragged him up on the seaweed.

I saw the captain, at the end of another rock finger, reaching and clutching for a piece of wood—White's rude oar. He caught it and pulled. White's head emerged from the water. I thought he was dead. The captain dragged him up on the ledge, hoisted him to his feet and held him by the waist, doubled over. I saw he couldn't be dead, because he still clung to the oar.

Swede, clutching his rope-end, seemed able to say nothing but "Help me! Help me!" in a voice that quavered so the words were hardly distinguishable.

Incapable of using his feet, he straddled a seaweed-covered boulder, pulling at the rope-end until others came to help.

Between us we got the overturned raft into the cove and ashore at the spot from which we had launched her.

"Help turn her over," Swede gasped. "Turn her right side up!"

"You can't make it, Swede," the captain said. "White's finished. He's full of sea water. He's sick!"

"I'll go alone," Swede said wildly. "Turn her over, Captain. I've got to go!"

"You can't go, you fool," Langman said. "It'll be dark

before you get ashore. You'll freeze in those wet clothes. It's too late."

"It's not too late," Swede cried. "We'll never get a brighter night than tonight—full moon, no clouds, onshore breeze, high tide at seven! Make 'em turn it over, Captain!"

"Not if you're going alone," Captain Dean said.

Swede, on his knees, caught the captain's hand. "Don't do it for *me!*" he implored. "Do it for these others!" He swung an oakum-swathed hand in a semicircle to include all those stooped, bearded, wild-looking creatures. I was afraid to look among them for Neal.

Harry Hallion shuffled across the slippery seaweed to stand beside Swede and the captain. "I'll go with him," he told the captain. "I can swim. White couldn't. If Swede feels the way he does, I think we can make it."

The captain eyed him dubiously.

"Anything's better than this," Hallion said. "You're wasting time. Get her turned over for us."

Captain Dean motioned to us to help him drag the raft from the water and turn her right side up. Swede, half sobbing and half laughing, scuttled among our legs like a shaggy dog, wanting to help, trying to help, but only succeeding in getting in our way.

She slid up easily on the seaweed, and we turned her gently for fear of smashing her. The mast and the hammock-sails were gone, but the pulpits hadn't been dislodged.

"Push her in!" Swede shouted, and there was a terrible urgency in his voice. "We don't need a sail! Get her in before the tide turns!"

He rolled himself onto the raft, rose to his knees, unknotted the lashings of the oar still fastened to her side, and shook the oar at us like a spear.

We slid her into the water, and as she left the ledge Hallion crawled in with White's oar.

A swell from the south raised her. Miraculously she slipped down it, toward the mouth of the little cove. A cross-swell from the north pushed her to the west and she cleared the mouth of the cove, Swede and Hallion thrashing the water with their makeshift oars.

Behind me someone prayed, the same incoherent prayer that had risen so often to my own lips—Oh God Oh God Oh God Oh God . . .

I felt sick all over at the smallness of that miserable raft, the cold immensity of that heaving ocean, the far far frosty distance over which the raft must float, the seeming pitifulness of those two human specks—yet who was to feel sick when those two specks were in truth, and unknown to themselves, great in spirit, and therefore happy!

There was distance and haziness between the raft and Boon Island when Swede turned, raised his oar and waved it. I looked for Neal. He wasn't among those who knelt on ledges or clung to boulders, following the slow movement of the raft with straining eyes, urging it on, urging it on. Neal would, I knew, have felt that same empty sickness I had felt.

I got myself back to the tent. Neal was sitting beside Chips Bullock, holding one of Chips's hands in both of his.

"He was alive when I came in," Neal said. "He held out his hand to me and I took it. He didn't say anything, but his eyes asked. I told him about the raft. I think it made him feel better."

Chips's eyes were closed. His face was peaceful, and I was glad he was gone. He hadn't died alone in a hole on the rock, with someone who couldn't speak to him, as he had feared he might if Langman, on Election Day, had become our captain.

There was coming and going in the tent. At dusk, the captain said, the raft seemed to be halfway to land. Sometimes it would go from sight: then rise again on a wave. Nobody talked about it. We were exhausted. Also around high tide time, the wind rose and howled around the tent and through its many chinks, and the surf made speech next to impossible for exhausted men.

December 28th, Thursday

God only knows why so many of us are unable to tell the truth about occurrences. A man is said to blench at a distressing sight, when in reality his color changes not at all. A lady, supposedly, swoons or blushes at a word she has heard her father and her brothers use a thousand times, whereas the swoon or the blush occurs only in the imagination of the lady herself, or in that of the narrator of the incident. If a writer dislikes wine, all drinkers are drunkards, staggering and revolting. Those of whom we approve have smiling countenances and warm hearts: those of whom we disapprove are hyenas in appearance and behavior. If two nations are engaged in a war, the one we dislike is a land of beasts, brutes and matricides; whereas we, to them, are bullies, murderers and patricides. Each nation is fighting a righteous war, brought about by the intolerable knavery of the other. Too many of us write of men and affairs as we think readers would have us write. Perhaps most of us are not only incapable of seeing things truly, but never do.

I think that when Captain Dean called me from the tent

at dawn on the day after Swede and Harry Hallion had gone floating off on the raft, and Chips Bullock had died, he knew what that day would bring forth, and I think he was struggling desperately to find the inner strength to face it.

Captain Dean was what is known as civilized. He recognized and detested the bad days that selfish and greedy men, civil war, French influences, gambling, bad laws and worse law enforcement had brought upon England. On Boon Island he had willingly done physical things that those beneath him hadn't the moral strength to do. He had endured without anger the cowardice of Saver and Graystock: the helplessness of his own brother; the malicious opposition of Langman, White and Mellen. He had ventured out into the black cold of midnight in the hope of catching a seal unaware. He had washed our ulcerated legs and feet with urine: persuaded his unwilling crew to pick oakum for their own protection: almost paralyzed his hands to dredge up mussels for us; and now I think he foresaw that a worse trial was upon him—one that would require him to ignore standards that civilization builds up within a decent man.

As I crawled from the tent, Captain Dean stopped to speak to the men. "We'll make the full circuit of the island," he said. "Tide's high at eight. When it starts to fall, I want Chips's body on the ledge nearest the tent. White, that salt water you swallowed yesterday hasn't hurt you. You're still the strongest—you and Langman. Drag out Chips's body. Put it on the ledge. When Mr. Whitworth and I come back, we'll say a prayer over it and roll it in the water."

He followed me out. The tide was higher than we had

ever seen it. The breakers, pounding and bellowing, were close and enormous.

"There's no doubt about it," Captain Dean said. "There *have* been spring tides that washed right over this island. There *must* have been."

He looked back at the tent. There was no sign of movement within its sagging sides.

We made our slow circuit of the island, watching for floating objects or anything usable cast up by the sea. There was nothing in sight—nothing except the seals that reared head and shoulders from waves to follow our every movement with insatiable curiosity: little black and white sea-swallows, skittering from wave to wave with limp feet trailing, and everywhere an infinity of sea ducks, swimming in vast shoals; chunky round black ones with white cheeks: little slender brown ones with bristly combs, diligently raising pointed beaks to heaven and genuflecting to each other—and all complacently ignoring us.

Our rounds completed, the captain peered intently toward the distant mainland, then glanced disconsolately toward the tent.

"They haven't done as I told 'em," he said. "They haven't taken him out."

When I didn't answer, he said, "Go in yourself, Miles. I can't allow them to disobey orders like this."

I went to the tent and pulled aside the flap. Earlier, when I had crawled out, they were lying down, huddled together, as motionless as Chips Bullock.

Now only Chips lay there. The others, even Saver and Graystock, were sitting up. I sensed a feverish excitement.

"Why didn't you take Chips out?" I asked. "The captain said to put him on the ledge."

"We haven't the strength," Langman said. "We're weak from lack of food."

I looked from one to another. Neal crawled out from among them and stood beside me. "They want to eat him," he said. "They're afraid to ask the captain. They want you to do it."

"I never said any such thing!" Langman said. "I'd never eat a fellow creature."

"We'll get mussels for you at low tide," I reminded them.

"Mussels!" Henry Dean exclaimed. "I gag whenever I try to swallow one!"

"Look, Whitworth," Graystock said, "those mussels make every last one of us sick! The captain'll do whatever you ask him to do. Ask him to let us have Chips. There's no use wasting him, the way we wasted Cooky!"

Well, there was no use lying to myself. When the captain rolled Cooky into the sea, I'd almost protested—almost, but I hadn't quite dared. I hadn't let myself formulate clearly in my mind that there was no good reason why we shouldn't have eaten him.

I stood looking from them to the body of Chips Bullock. I had no feeling at all except pity for Captain Dean.

When he came in among us I said, "Captain, these people want to eat Chips Bullock."

"Not me!" Langman said.

"Captain," I said, "we ate a seagull last week. Mr. Langman killed it, and Mr. Langman ate a mouthful of it, like the rest of us. He was glad to get it and so were we."

"What's that got to do with it?" Langman asked sharply.

"It's got this to do with it," I said. "Gulls are scavengers. They eat anything dead. The one we ate might have eaten part of Cooky Sipper."

"Everyone in England eats eels," Christopher Gray said. "Eels eat anything that's dead."

"You'll never catch me eating the body of a fellow human," Langman said. "My conscience would never let me rest."

"You've already got more on your conscience than any one man should be called on to endure," Captain Dean said.

"Eating a man would be a sin," Langman protested. "If I agreed to it, I'd be forever damned."

"It's a terrible thing," Captain Dean agreed, "but in my opinion it's not as much of a sin as swearing to a lie that robs a man of his good name. You've lied about the insurance my brother and I carried on the *Nottingham*. You lied when you said I purposely ran the *Nottingham* ashore. I think you're damned already."

Langman eyed the captain sourly.

"Captain," Christopher Gray said, "Hallion lived with Indians in Nova Scotia, and Hallion said that when one Indian killed another in battle, he ate the dead Indian's heart. Hallion said Indians thought it gave 'em courage."

"We could use a few Indians' hearts on Boon Island," Captain Dean said. "I think all of us could! We've lost the only one who didn't need to eat an Indian's heart . . . Swede Butler."

"Are you accusing us of cowardice?" Langman asked.

"Mr. Langman," the captain said, "I ordered you and George White to drag Chips Bullock's body to the ledge nearest the sea. Why didn't you do it?"

"I told Mr. Whitworth," Langman said. "We're too weak."

"If you're too weak to do that, you're weak from hunger. And if you're hungry enough, you'll eat anything. I know. Yesterday I tried, like a dog, to eat my own frozen excrement. I think you didn't move Chips because you secretly wanted to eat him but lacked the courage to say so."

"I'll never eat a fellow human," Langman repeated.

"We'll vote," Captain Dean said. "We'll vote whether or not we'll eat this body. Neal, you're youngest, but you won't vote until after all the others."

"I want to vote," Neal said. "My father would have voted Yes, and that's how I vote."

"Mr. Langman?" asked the captain.

"Never shall it be——"

"All right," the captain said. "You vote No. Christopher Gray?"

"I vote Yes," Gray said. "Captain, we're almost dead from lack of meat."

"Henry Dean?" the captain asked.

"Yes," his brother said.

"Charles Graystock?" the captain asked. "I'm in no doubt about you or Saver."

"Yes!" Graystock shouted.

"And Saver?"

Saver said Yes in strong, firm tones. Nobody could have guessed, from the quality of their voices, that from the moment we dropped from the *Nottingham's* foremast onto the seaweed of Boon Island, those two had been the malingerers, resented by all, perpetual thorns in the captain's flesh, refusing to work; sullen, even, when fed with mussels gathered by others.

"Now let's see," the captain said, "that's five in favor of eating. That only leaves three to vote—Whitworth, George White, Nicholas Mellen. So there's no need to vote further. We'll eat him."

"What about *you?*" Langman asked.

The captain ignored him, and I knew why. The captain didn't want to vote Yes; but if he had, Langman, at the first opportunity, would have taken oath that the eating of Chips Bullock had been done at the captain's suggestion. He might even have implied that the captain killed Chips in order to eat him. That was the sort of person Langman was. Unfortunately there'll always be Langmans in this world, to set people and nations against each other—to condemn the good and extol the bad—to spread sly rumors and spit on the truth.

There was something horrible about the open excitement of Saver and Graystock when the captain agreed to the eating of Chips, but ironically I was not horrified by the inner relief I felt myself.

I was even puzzled by the steadfast refusal, on the part of those who had most feverishly urged the eating, to help carry the body from the tent.

When Neal and I offered to help the captain, he waved us sharply aside. He wanted the others, the responsible ones, to do it; but when he gave the necessary orders, they lay in their places like dogs that, even though whipped, refuse to carry out their masters' orders. Their eyes rolled up at him, exactly like those of cowering dogs, and it was plain that no orders, no prayers, no punishment, would persuade them to take part in the act they'd begged the captain to permit.

In the end, Neal and I helped him drag out the body.

He had tried to do it alone, but it was too much for him. Even with our help it was almost too much for all three of us, so that when the body lay on the cold ledge, we were numb mentally and physically, and the captain took us back to the tent, where he lay with eyes closed, until the men again wailingly asked for meat.

At half tide he roused himself, and instantly the men were silent, watching him, their eyes stubborn. They wouldn't help. They just wouldn't help.

We had the saw, made so laboriously from the cutlass, and we had our knives. We had nothing else except spun yarn, taken from the tent, and two squares of canvas, cut from the boulder-weighted slack we had left when the tent was built.

"First," the captain said, "I'll make a bag of the clothes and put 'em in that rock crevice yonder. Then I'll wrap the head in the clothes, and the feet and the hands and the skin—and the other things. And the bones. We'll have to bone out the meat, so we can wrap it and cut it into equal pieces. We'll put the clothes in a crevice with boulders piled over it. We'll make a cross out of two pieces of wood and wedge it in the boulders."

His mention of the cross made us feel better.

He hefted the cutlass-saw.

"Now," he said, "I want the two of you to go to the north side of the island. See whether anything's come ashore. Look at the mainland for signs of boats. I've got things to do, and I'm reconciled to doing them. To me, this is meat."

He touched Chips's body with the tip of the saw; then

continued, "Eventually it will be meat to both of you: something over which to say grace. Nothing more. Until then I'll do what has to be done, but I'll do it alone. You aren't reconciled yet; and what I'm doing, I'm doing for your fathers' sake as well as for your own."

When Neal and I hesitated, he impatiently waved us away. "I'll need help in skinning and boning out," he said. "When I'm ready, I'll wave and you can come back."

The labor of skinning a human body is beyond belief. Perhaps a surgeon would make nothing of it. It might seem simple to a butcher. To us, with our scarred and half-frozen fingers and hands, it was next to impossible.

When in exasperation I cursed my helplessness, Captain Dean urged me on. "We can't stop," he said. "If we stop now and wait till tomorrow to finish, it may freeze so solid we can't do anything with it."

The skin wasn't like a rabbit pelt or a deerskin, that can be raised a little at the neck and then pulled off cleanly from the whole body. This skin had adhesions, so that when it was raised at the neck, it had to be pared away from the flesh beneath by continuous slicing and slashing. Also, unlike an animal's skin, it was tender in spots, so that it was forever ripping or being pierced by our knives.

I thanked God we were no longer hampered by the gulls. If they had been about us, as they had been before Langman killed that progenitor of all gulls, they would have swooped upon us to snatch the flesh from our very hands and soar away, yelling in triumph.

The tide was on the make before the meat had been

stripped from the leg bones and arm bones, and laid off from the ribs and back. All these were rolled by Neal in tight cylinders and tied with rope yarn.

We wedged the bones into the crevice in such a way that no seal or gull could dislodge the boulders above them.

Even then we weren't finished, for the rolls, the slabs of meat from belly and buttocks, the liver, the heart and the fat-encased kidneys had to be sunk in an even deeper crevice nearer the tent, covered with three feet of seaweed to guard against freezing, and the seaweed in turn topped by a double layer of boulders.

We worked in silence, except when Neal brought the kidneys back to the captain, after washing them in salt water.

"Keep those on top of everything," the captain said. "That fat is just as good as mutton tallow. Maybe we can use it for poultices."

When we returned exhausted and depressed to the tent to feed those comrades who had lain there, sunk in helplessness because of some frightened quirk of their disgusting brains, Langman, White and Mellen, as able-bodied as any of us, refused to eat.

"An insult," Langman mumbled, "to the spirit of a friend."

"Langman," Captain Dean said, "my duty by you is done. Eat or don't eat, as you please. But my duty to the rest of us is *not* done, and if I hear any more talk out of you about this meat being anybody's spirit, you'll rue the day!"

"Are you threatening me?" Langman asked.

"Yes, I'm threatening you," Captain Dean said. "If you pour out your spleen on these others, I'll protect them by stopping your mouth. This meat I'm offering is nobody's spirit. It's beef. It was animated once by a soul and a spirit, but the soul and the spirit have gone from this island, leaving only beef behind."

He threw up his hands in disgust at Langman's mutterings, drew his knife and carefully divided the rolled meat into slices.

"Listen carefully," he said, before he handed out the slices. "We have enough beef for a week, if we're careful. If Langman, White and Mellen don't eat, we'll have enough for a longer time. But this you must do: you must scrape the beef to a pulp, and with each piece of pulp you must chew seaweed. You mustn't gulp it down. You must *not* gulp it down."

He handed around the meat, and the tent was filled with the soft sound of scraping and chewing, audible above the angry roaring of the breakers.

I tried to remember what Captain Dean had said about being reconciled. I expected to be revolted by the meat and the seaweed, but I wasn't. It wasn't offensive. It wasn't nauseating. It had no more taste than raw beef or raw venison.

All I could think of was Langman, meatless, staring out from the darkness with hard and hating eyes, and once I thought I felt Chips Bullock behind me, a little stooped, his head lowered, laughing that silent, belly-shaking laugh of his at Langman, Mellen and White.

December 29th, Friday

Boon Island taught me the danger of trusting those who at any time have lied about their reasons for doing things. It taught me, too, that no man should ever say, "I'll never do this," or "I'll never do that," or should ever affirm, "Nothing could persuade me to do this; nothing could make me do that."

Never, Langman had sworn, would he eat human flesh. It was sinful, it was unlawful, it was repugnant to all the dictates of his conscience. He had implied that the eating of *any* human flesh was heinous, but that to eat the flesh of a friend was worse: was obscene, infamous, abominable—and somehow he had persuaded White and Mellen that such a specious argument was worthy of consideration.

The wind had threatened us by backing up on Thursday. On Friday that threat materialized. Shortly after midnight a mixture of snow and rain from the southwest slatted against the tent; driblets of water trickled down upon us, first from one spot and then from another.

Even before daybreak the men, restless, were demanding meat. The snow and the rain, they said, might damage it, freeze it, ruin it. It should be brought out and distributed.

"You'll get your meat," Captain Dean assured them, "but I made up my mind to something yesterday, when able-bodied men lay here and wouldn't lift a hand to do the necessary work to provide the meat because they pretended to be too weak: then ate with the strength of wolves. This is what I decided. If they've got the strength to eat meat, they had the strength, yesterday, to help me cut it up. They wouldn't do it! I'm sick of people who won't help themselves."

Nobody said anything.

"So," Captain Dean said, "let's see where we stand. Swede is gone and Harry Hallion with him. Cooky Sipper is gone. Chips Bullock is gone. Mr. Langman's conscience won't let him eat human flesh. Neither will White's nor Mellen's.

"That leaves seven of us. All seven will draw a reasonable ration of meat this morning, but each one of us must do something in return, and that's pick enough oakum to thatch this tent.

"That means Saver and Graystock will pick oakum or get no meat. It means my brother will pick oakum, even though he *does* have epileptic fits once in a while. It means I'll pick oakum, Mr. Whitworth will pick oakum. So will Neal Butler and Christopher Gray. Is that understood?"

"Just give us the meat," Graystock said.

"That's not enough," Captain Dean said. "I want your promises, made in the hearing of all in this tent. Each one of you must swear that if he eats meat, he'll pick oakum as long as he can move his hands. Saver, do you solemnly swear you'll pick oakum with the rest of us?"

Saver said he did, as did Graystock and the other four of us.

"All right," Captain Dean said. "I expect every one of you to live up to your promises. If you don't, I'll take steps."

He went to the tent-flap, hit it with his fist to clear it of snow and ice and peered out into the storm.

Langman got to his feet and moved close to the captain. "Captain," he said, "we've changed our minds about the beef."

The captain looked at him incredulously. "You mean to say you and White and Mellen changed your minds? It's not a sin to eat this beef?"

"No," Langman said. "It's not a sin to eat beef. When we understood it was beef, we saw we'd made a mistake."

Captain Dean shook his head. "But only last night your consciences were bothering you! How did you persuade your consciences to accept this as beef?"

"Why," Langman said, "we just told our consciences it was beef. For a while our consciences wouldn't listen, but in the end they did. I almost woke you up in the middle of the night to tell you our consciences had stopped bothering us."

"Well, I'm glad to hear it," Captain Dean said, "but there are two or three other little things that your consciences will have to consider before we admit you to our society. In the first place, you have to give us your word that you'll pick oakum for thatching the tent."

"You have my word," Langman said.

"Now I'll have to have White's word," the captain said, "and Mellen's."

Both White and Mellen spoke up quickly. They'd pick oakum.

Captain Dean seemed pleased. "There are two other things," he said. "One is the matter of Sunday. It's of small moment to me what day of the week a man worships his God, but if he arbitrarily picks a Sunday that differs from the one we celebrate, he creates unrest, and we have all the unrest we need without creating more. Your Sunday, Langman, is an irritation. If you eat meat with the rest of us in spite of your yesterday's conscience, you can persuade your conscience to accept our Sunday, too."

"All right," Langman said. "But tomorrow's Sunday just the same."

"Then you won't want any meat," Captain Dean said.

"Just a minute," Langman said. "I didn't say I wouldn't worship on the day you do."

"For God's sake," Saver said. "Stop talking. Give us our meat!"

The captain looked as genial as a dirty, tired, whiskered man could look. "Now you know how we felt, Saver," he said, "when you and Graystock just lay there and let the rest of us do your work for you."

He turned back to Langman. "You had your chance yesterday. You were offered a fair share of all we had, and with no strings attached. But you made a show of yourself by refusing to take what we offered. You weren't honest about it. So if we give you meat now, you'll have to pay a penalty for past dishonesty: you'll have to be honest with us—if you can regard that as a penalty, which I don't."

Langman was indignant. "I've always been honest! Didn't I divide that seagull with you?"

"That's physical honesty," Captain Dean said. "Almost everyone is physically honest. I'm talking about mental honesty. Most of the men in this tent are both physically and mentally honest. I think even Mellen and White are mentally honest. They're just indebted to you, and so they accept the things you tell 'em as being true, which they aren't."

"I don't know what you're talking about," Langman said.

"If you don't, you're weak-minded," Captain Dean said, "and that's the last thing I'd accuse you of. You said repeatedly I ran the ship ashore purposely, and that's the stupidest, silliest piece of mental dishonesty I ever heard."

Langman widened his eyes at the captain. "If that's all that's bothering you," he said, "I'll trade my opinion for the same amount of meat that everyone else gets."

"That is to say," Captain Dean said, "you give me your word you won't repeat that outrageous lie, ever again."

"Why, of course," Langman said, all mealy-mouthed.

The captain pulled aside the tent-flap and went out into the snow.

Langman looked around at the rest of us with his lip lifted in that sardonic smile of his. I thought I knew the meaning of that offensive smile.

Unless I misjudged Langman, no promise of his was worth anything at all. No matter what he promised, he'd make a mental reservation that would free his twisted mind of the need to carry out his promise.

Even if he were somehow prevented from making a mental reservation, that devious brain would invent a loophole that would release him from his obligation.

Statesmen, often, are like that, and so are men of business—which may explain why the English guard themselves so carefully against men of business as well as against some statesmen—usually the wrong ones.

I think the captain, having brought Langman around to his way of thinking by a sort of justified blackmail, tried to make sure of his conquest by being kinder to him and Mellen and White than to the rest of us. He gave them slivers of liver, whereas the rest of us got along with slices of muscle, full of tendons from which the meat separated reluctantly. The best I could say for it was that it was better than the rawhide we had chopped and swallowed so avidly.

Tough as the meat was, there wasn't one of us who couldn't have eaten three times our allotment, and Langman even demanded more as a reward for picking oakum all day.

"Look here, Langman," Captain Dean said. "You undertook to pick oakum for the same amount of meat that the rest of us have. If I give you more, I'll have to give more to everyone else. Then, before we know it, there won't be any for anyone."

Langman argued senselessly that he and Mellen and White were entitled to more because they had refused to eat the day before, when all the rest of us had eaten.

"Whose fault was that?" Captain Dean asked.

"It was yours," Langman said, "because you didn't tell us the meat was beef until we'd made up our minds it was something else."

The captain, however, was adamant. "All right," he said, "but you're asking for too much, and it's bad for you to eat too much. Not wicked: not sinful. No more sinful than eating seaweed. But you refused your ration yesterday and you've had your ration for today. Now you can keep right on working."

He only left the tent to drag in more cordage for us to pick apart and make into oakum; and while we made it, he wove it. By dark that Friday he had woven a thatch of oakum that covered the top of the tent and extended two-thirds down the southeastern side.

So thanks to Chips Bullock and to Langman's slippery conscience, we were not only fed, but were free, all night long, of the rivulets of icy water that had trickled down upon us all through that snowy, rainy day.

December 30th, Saturday

"Have somebody light a fire—two fires—on the beach," Captain Dean had told Swede before he set off on the raft; and for days our minds, if they could indeed have been called minds, were centered on hunting for smoke on the mainland.

Because of Friday's rain and snow, we couldn't see Cape Neddick or the beaches; but on Saturday the snow and rain stopped, and land was once more visible—a land of dark pines, long sands, forbidding cliffs, with no trace of smoke discernible anywhere.

Neal was out of the tent at dawn, studying that shore line.

We did what we could to buoy up his hopes—and ours, too.

"Yesterday was so rainy," Captain Dean said, "that there wouldn't have been dry wood on the beach."

Neal glanced at him, and the captain looked away.

"They might have had to go far before they found a house," I said. "Two or three days might pass before fires could be lit."

Neal didn't reply. He just crept back into the tent and went to picking oakum.

I don't know what happens to the minds of prisoners or of men in circumstances such as ours; but I suspect they move more slowly, always—more and more slowly, until they scarcely move at all. If that weren't so—if their minds worked actively on their situations, their lives would be unendurable and they'd die.

While there was a possibility of seeing smoke, we seemed content to sit and pick oakum: to wait until the captain had finished carving more beef for us: to wait until the next time someone went to the tent-flap to scan the land for a wisp of smoke.

We were like sleepers half awake, who mutter disjointed sentences, utter words that seem to a dreamer to be intelligible. Like those aroused from dreams, we resented attempts to make sense from our mumblings.

Altercations broke out unexpectedly. When Langman gabbled something about "This day our daily bread," Christopher Gray, the gunner, flew at him.

"What you want to talk that way for?" Gray demanded.

"What way?" Langman asked.

"You said 'This day,' " Gray said. "That means that this day's Sunday, but you know it ain't. It's Saturday. You promised the captain you'd have the same Sunday as us."

"I never said today was Sunday," Langman said.

"You said, 'This day,' " Gray repeated, "and 'This day' means Sunday."

"I never did," Langman said, "and if I did, 'This day' doesn't mean anything except *this* day. This day can be *any* day."

Gray, enraged, lunged at him, and they thrashed ineffectually around our odoriferous oakum floor.

We caught Gray and set him upright. Forgetting Langman, he picked numbly at the hemp before him.

The captain came in among us and gave us our slices of beef.

"Any smoke?" Henry Dean asked.

"None that I could see," the captain said. He looked apologetically at Neal.

Langman sneered. "You wouldn't have seen it, even if you had one of Newton's reflecting telescopes. Any fool would know they never got ashore."

"Keep your mouth shut," Captain Dean said.

"That's not part of our bargain," Langman said. "First thing I know, you'll tell me I can't have meat unless I stop hearing and seeing and smelling."

The captain groaned in disgust and collapsed heavily beside his coil of cordage, only to rise again when Mellen and White, without warning, belabored each other.

The captain pulled them apart and sat between them. "What's all this?" he said. "Why waste your strength on each other?"

"Nobody can call me a liar," Mellen said, "just because I recall one or two things that happened when I was with Woodes Rogers."

"I was there," White protested. "He talked about how a beautiful woman cooked for him when we stopped in Brazil to give the ship a pair of boot tops."

"Well, she was!" Mellen insisted. "Shaped like a fairy queen."

"Fairy queen hell," White said. "I saw 'em. They looked like cows and smelled like pigs, all of 'em!"

White and Mellen cursed each other.

The thought came to me that their dispositions had changed, and their voices, too. Their voices were breathless, squealing, like pigs struggling at a trough. I wondered whether the meat had done it, or the salty ice we chewed to quench our thirst, or the unending cold, or our inner fears of the eternity that had drawn so close.

I pulled at Neal's sleeve, and we went out on the rock. We looked all along the coast for smoke. Like the captain, we saw nothing.

"Neal," I said, "it might help these men if you recited parts of plays to them."

Neal shook his head.

"Why not?" I said. "It might keep them quiet."

"No, it wouldn't," Neal said. "Nothing would keep them quiet. They'd laugh at any part of any play, because plays aren't worth believing. Nothing's true except this." He swept his arm from the tent toward the ocean and the mainland.

There wasn't much I could say.

"Anyway," Neal said, "I've forgotten everything. I don't want to remember, and I never will. I'll only remember that my father hated the stage and wanted to keep me from it. I want to forget my name, even. I want it to be what it should be—Moses. That's what my father and my mother named me.

"If I'd never gone near the theatre—if I hadn't done what my father didn't want me to do—the *Nottingham* wouldn't have sailed when she did. She wouldn't have gone to Killybegs to take on butter and cheese. She'd never have struck this island. It's all my fault."

"Look, Neal," I said, "If you want to start thinking that

way, you can trace every bad thing in the world back to some little incident that nobody was to blame for. Instead of blaming yourself, blame the circumstances that brought that nasty little fop to Greenwich. Blame the thing that made him a fop in the first place."

Neal's eyes had a hunted look. I think if there'd been a hole on that barren rock into which he could have crawled, he'd have crept there to get away from me, from Captain Dean, from his memories, from the eternal thundering of the breakers all around us.

"I know how you feel," I said, "and I'm glad you do. My father was right, too, and I wish I could tell him so. I can hear him now—'pint-sized clowns in tatters and tarnished gold lace, making faces and laughing like hyenas at their damned dull witlessness.' "

Singularly, I thought of Sir Isaac Newton and his discovery of the reflecting telescope: of Langman, who said there could be no such thing—who laughed at the truth. And ironically it came to me that there would be people like Langman who would say that there was no truth to this island or to the tribulations we'd endured upon it: that our labors were nonsense. It came to me suddenly that when I left this island, if I ever did leave it, I wanted nothing to do with the Langmans of this world—nothing to do with those who derided the truth, and defiled it.

We went back to the tent. The captain, carving pieces of fat from Chips Bullock's kidneys, looked up at us sharply. "Any smoke?"

When we shook our heads, he sliced off a piece of the fat, laid it on a board and pounded it with the handle of his knife, spreading it into a thin sheet.

"There," he said. "That's pretty near the same as the mutton tallow my grandmother used to make. Each one of you can have an equal amount. You'll have to make it go as far as possible.

"We'll flatten it out, flatten it out, and when it's as thin as we can make it, we'll take off these oakum bindings and wash our feet and legs again, same as we did before. The fat ought to be good for deep sores. It's bound to help those who've lost toes."

December 31st, Sunday

If a man, on the last day of any year, chooses honestly to consider his shortcomings, he must always be depressed; and if any people anywhere ever had occasion to be downcast on the last day of that year, it was we on Boon Island.

The sight of our legs and feet on the day before, when we applied the poultices of kidney fat to them, had frightened us. They were worse—much worse—than they had been in the dim and dreadful past, when we cut off our boots and first swathed ourselves in oakum. The sores were deeper: the toes broke off more easily, though without pain.

Then Henry Dean screamed that horrible epileptic's scream of his in the deep dark, and flung himself around the tent as though he had eight legs and eight arms, all made of steel. When we finally pinned him down, he twisted and turned in our hands with almost unbelievable violence, and on top of that he groaned horribly, and there's something catching—something poisonous—about groans.

The whole night was a bad one and after Henry Dean

had stopped thrashing and writhing, and had fallen into an epileptic's heavy sleep, I lay staring upward, afraid of the dark, afraid of what must happen to my feet and legs if this cold continued—if we went on and on, being drenched daily by the salty spit from the breakers—if I lost the use of my hands and could no longer occupy myself in the brain-deadening task of picking oakum.

In my thinking I groaned, realized too late what I was doing, tried to turn it into a cough, and produced a sort of squawk, like a crow with a beakful of food.

I felt a hand fumbling at my shoulder and heard Neal say, "Are you all right, Miles?"

"Of course," I said. "Of course I'm all right. Are you all right?"

"We're *all* all right," Captain Dean said. "Even my brother's all right—or will be when he wakes. All of you felt how much strength he has. Just remember you're all as strong as Henry if only you make up your minds to be."

He hesitated: then added, "I've been thinking. I don't believe we've been praying right. We've been praying as if we didn't know God at all—as if he was some sort of distant image, away up above the stars somewhere—an image with whiskers, like ours.

"Well, he isn't an image. He's real. And since we expect him to answer our prayers, he can't be far away. We believe he'll help us if we deserve to be helped, but we don't ask him for that help in the same way we'd ask our own fathers for help."

He hesitated again. "Would anyone like to speak to God? If you can't find the words, I'll speak for you, but I think you might feel better if you did your own speaking."

"I'd like to speak to God," Neal said. "I'd like to speak about my father. God, I'd like to have my father told that I know what he did for us. You must know what he did, God, and I hope you won't let it be wasted."

"What do you mean by that, Neal?" the captain asked.

"God knows," Neal said.

After a time the captain spoke again, conversationally, as if God were in the tent with us. "God," he said, "you've been kind to us, though some might think you haven't been. By giving us ice to eat, you've saved us from the most horrible of all deaths: you've given us work to do, so that we've preserved our sanity: you saved us from disaster when you overturned the boat: you let the sea wash up the cordage from which we made clothing and shelter: you gave us seaweed to eat: you gave us Swede Butler to strengthen our courage . . ."

Langman spoke up. "Don't forget the seagull."

"Yes, God; the seagull," Captain Dean said. "The seagull helped us. All things considered, God, we've done as well with these blessings as any equal number of men could be expected to do, and all we ask, God, is that you don't withdraw your favor from us."

"Aren't you going to ask for a ship to take us off?" Langman demanded. "Why don't you ask him to send the seagulls back? There hasn't been one sighted since I killed mine!"

"Ask for fire!" White demanded.

The captain shook his head. "Ask for them yourselves if you think it'll do any good," he said. "If God feels we should be helped, I think he ought to be allowed to work it out in his own way. I don't feel qualified to tell God what to do or how to do it. I wouldn't feel justified in asking him for more seagulls. He probably had a good reason for sending 'em away from the island."

I couldn't improve on what the captain had said, and the others were silent as well; but I think we all felt better because of Neal's and the captain's talks with God.

For the first time I felt about God as I'd so often felt about my father: felt that he'd do anything reasonable I asked him to do, and that if he should refuse, he'd only do so for my own good.

There were lines of light showing around the edges of the tent-flap, so I went out with the captain to help him with the meat.

Neal followed me. He didn't even look toward Cape Neddick or York.

"Neal," the captain said, "I want you to find another hole in the rock where we can store part of this meat. I want you to attend to moving half of it, and I don't want to know where you put it. I don't want anyone to know: not even Miles."

Neal nodded and moved away.

Captain Dean watched him go, then turned to me. "Was it three days ago, Miles," he asked, "or four days ago that Swede and Hallion put off? I forget. Every day seems a year long."

"It was Wednesday," I said.

"Miles," he said slowly, "I think Neal knows his father's gone."

"I know he does," I said. "I know it, too, and so do you."

"Yes," Captain Dean said, "but he knows more than we do."

"Yes," I said, "I know that he *thinks* he knows, but that doesn't necessarily mean he's right. I hope he isn't."

When the captain didn't answer, I asked him what he meant by asking Neal to find another hole in the rock.

"I don't quite know," the captain said. "I think this meat has made some of the men a little crazy. Have you noticed Saver's and Graystock's eyes when I pass around the meat?"

I said I hadn't.

"Well," Captain Dean said, "I had a ferret when I was a boy. I'd turn him loose in the stables, and he'd kill rats. When he jumped on a rat, his eyes looked red. I don't think they *were* red, but that's how they looked. That's how Saver's and Graystock's eyes look when they get their meat. If that's how they feel about it, they might crawl out of the tent any night. Being the sort of people they are, they wouldn't hesitate to steal what rightly belongs to all the rest of us, and they haven't enough brains between them to exercise restraint or common sense in their eating. They'd eat until they dropped dead."

He watched Neal coming slowly back to us, picking his way over the icy ledges.

The captain drew four large bundles of meat from beneath the seaweed and piled them in Neal's arms. "Be sure they're covered with three feet of seaweed," he told Neal.

When Neal was out of hearing, the captain asked, with seeming carelessness, "What is it Neal thinks happened to his father?"

"Well," I said, "you know how I feel about Neal. From the moment I saw him, I've thought of him as a brother—a younger brother. I wouldn't want you to think that there's anything odd about him—that he has hallucinations, or anything of that sort."

The captain sniffed. "I know hallucinations when I see 'em, Miles. The night the *Nottingham* was wrecked, I was sure none of us would last until morning. Then when morning came, I had a feeling. Not an hallucination. I don't know how you get feelings, or where they come from; but I had the feeling we were going to come safely out of this. I still have it, and I still think I'm right. That's no hallucination. Now what is it that Neal feels about his father?"

"Well," I said, "he thinks he saw his father in a dream, or something like that. His father told him the raft hadn't a chance of getting to shore with two men on it. He told Neal that since he was a good swimmer, he was going to get into the water and swim and push. He thought that if he did that, the raft might get to shore, so he was going to try it."

The captain nodded. "I see."

"Well, that's what Neal thinks, Captain. He thinks his father swam as long as he could, and then just slipped off."

"I can think of worse ways to go," the captain said.

January 1st, Monday

This was the day we saw the smoke.

Neal saw it first and was less affected by it than the rest of us. He left the tent early, no doubt to make sure that nothing or nobody had disturbed the place where he'd hidden the beef.

When he came back he said, almost idly, "There's smoke on the mainland. It's blowing to the eastward."

We jostled each other to crawl from the tent to see this sign—the first hopeful one we'd seen in three long weeks. There it was—a plume of smoke from a fire that must have been newly kindled, for the plume, a mere smudge to begin with, grew constantly longer and longer, drifting ever farther to the eastward as we watched. What it meant, we couldn't know, but Captain Dean insisted that it must be a signal—a signal to let us know our plight had been discovered.

As near as we could tell, the smoke was rising to the south of west, probably, the captain thought, from somewhere between York and Portsmouth.

Langman insisted it couldn't be a signal, because the

fire was so far south of the direction in which the raft had been heading when it put out from Boon Island; but the captain said this didn't necessarily follow.

"Why would anyone bother with a signal?" Langman asked. "There's an offshore breeze, and only six or eight miles to go. Any sloop or schooner could sail that distance in less time than it took somebody to start that fire."

"I don't know," Captain Dean admitted, "but I know that raft got ashore. If it got ashore, somebody saw it. Anybody who saw it would recognize it as the work of seamen who had next to nothing to work with. That raft was laced and knotted with everything from bos'n's knots to granny knots. Where else but on Boon Island would a lot of wrecked seamen have nothing to work with?"

All day long we argued the matter. Only Neal refused to discuss it; but the arguments of the rest of us rose and fell like waves. At one moment we were elated in a firm belief that the smoke was a signal: in the next moment we decided it couldn't be a signal: that it must be an accident; a hay barn afire; a farmer clearing land.

One thing was apparent. Before we saw the smoke, my companions were images of Death itself: horrible, haggard, slow-moving creatures, tangled of hair and beard, stooped with hunger, swathed about the head and hands and legs with clumsy bands of oakum.

After they'd seen the smoke, they stood straighter: their voices were stronger: their eyes less wild and staring.

What was worse, they were hungrier than ever, and quick to demand more meat from the captain.

"If you're so sure that smoke's a signal," Langman said, "you must be equally sure that they'll send a ship for us. Why shouldn't we divide half of the meat that's left?"

The captain shook his head. "When they say they want more," he said, "they want three times what they've been getting. That's too much for half-starved men to have.

"There's another thing: we've none of us ever had meat like this. There's no telling what it may do to us. You must know what happens to half-starved men when they eat too much. They get sick. Sometimes they die."

He lifted the seaweed covering from the store of meat, drew out a generous chunk and sliced it quickly into ten parts, each part almost twice the size of those we'd hitherto received. With each slice went a handful of seaweed from the pile that had covered our little stock.

They crawled off in two groups: Langman, Mellen and White in one group: Graystock, Saver and Gray in another. All of them scraped diligently at their meat, and chewed at their seaweed; and from time to time they turned their heads to gaze covertly at the captain, Neal, Henry Dean and me.

There was no doubt about it: each group was plotting something.

Captain Dean shuffled his feet on the icy rock. "I don't like it," he said. "We'll have to put a guard over this meat. I said I was sure the smoke was a signal, but I'm not sure at all. I'm not sure of anything but this: if they steal this meat and eat it all, they won't hesitate to kill someone in order to have more."

The rest of that day was a nightmare. The wind cut cruelly, but all day long we were in and out of the tent, not only to scan the far-off coast line in the hope of seeing a sail outlined against it, but to keep watch on the spot where our beef was stored.

By midafternoon, while the smoke continued to drift

from west to east, the tide was half out and it was apparent to all of us that no vessel would venture out in the short time remaining.

That night the captain lay across the tent-flap. Neal lay between the two of us, and in the early dark I could feel Neal shaking, feel him swallow, as people do when their minds are not at rest. His shaking may have come from the cold, but I somehow knew he was thinking about his father. Remembering how Neal had shrunk from me when, on that long-gone summer day in Greenwich, I had inadvertently touched him, I did nothing; but the captain said, "Neal, roll over on top of me and keep me warm. And Miles: come closer, Miles."

We huddled together.

I could feel rather than hear the soft patting of the captain's hand against Neal's shoulder. Neal's shudderings and swallowings lessened. I suppose we slept.

January 2nd, Tuesday

When, because of bad weather, there was little or nothing to do on Boon Island except pick at that loathsome oakum, or stumble around the island on our eternal patrols, the days sometimes seemed endless because of their monotony and the biting cold.

Probably the very monotony was so deadening that the time passed more rapidly than we thought.

There was no monotony, God knows, to that second day of January; and the endlessness of that one day, by comparison with other memorable days of my life, went on and on until, at nightfall, I felt as though I had lived years.

The captain, as usual, was first out of the tent, and the tent-flap had no sooner fallen behind him than sounds came from him, a sort of hiccuping and gasping, broken by quavering hootings, such as come from a loon.

Thinking he might have caught epilepsy from his brother, I crawled out to help him. He was on all fours, pawing feebly at the rocks, as if trying to return to the tent.

I thought of broken bones: of a captain made helpless at the hour of our greatest need, and my heart sank.

"What's the matter?" I asked, frightened sick by his apparent weakness.

I got him by the arm and tried to help him up.

He caught me by the shoulders and leaned against me. I couldn't tell whether in falling he had knocked the breath from himself, or was in such excruciating agony that his face was contorted by it into a twisted travesty of a grin.

"Sail," he gasped. "Boat!" Tears ran down his cheeks: snuffling like a child, he swung an arm to the westward, turning me in that direction.

There, halfway between us and the shore, a scant three miles away, was a little sloop, bobbing and bowing, curtsying and rocking over the heavy lead-colored swells, heading straight for the center of the island's western shore on a cold and sharp northwest wind.

I couldn't believe my eyes. I rubbed them, looked all around the horizon: then looked back at the sloop. I wasn't dreaming! I wasn't imagining things! She yawed a little as she slipped down the face of a following sea. A man holding to her mast flapped an arm at his helmsman. She was a real vessel with a patch at the foot of her jib. She had people aboard—living human beings. My throat constricted: my breath caught convulsively at my chest. I couldn't speak: I couldn't draw air into my lungs.

I pulled at the tent-flap and croaked, "Neal!"

He crawled out, white-faced, saw the sloop and made a whimpering sound. The others came out, too. They just stood there, staring at the beautiful little vessel, while tears of which they were unconscious trickled from their eyes and clung in silvery drops to their matted beards.

We spread out along the western side of the island, trying to convey by gestures, to that man who stood before the sloop's mast, a part of our joy, our gratitude. . . .

Captain Dean waved and waved, pointing to the southeast, where the sloop could run close to the island–close enough down-wind to hear our voices; but the sloop brought to at the north end of the island, came into the wind, and dropped her anchor and jib. She was as far offshore as the island was long.

"Wave her off," Captain Dean told us. "She'll drag her anchor–pile up on a ledge!"

There were three men aboard her–smoothly shaved men with rosy faces, warm clothes, fur hats. Well-fed men, quick-moving, firm on their feet, unlike us: strong men, pillars of strength: symbols of life and salvation.

Captain Dean pointed out to sea, flapped his hands to warn them off. With his arms he made slow circles. To us his meaning was apparent. He wanted them to pull off shore: to sail in circles until high tide. He pointed again and again to the southeast, where they could safely come into the wind and speak us.

Certainly their anchor was dragging, or their roding too short, for she was constantly drawing nearer, pushed by those damnable swells out of the north.

We groaned with relief when she hoisted her jib and fell off a mile to the eastward, headed north, tacked into the west, and then stood off and on, lively as a duck, waiting for flood tide.

Under the best of circumstances, waiting can be one of the worst curses that man is called upon to endure–waiting for a loved one, while the mind conjures up visions of injury, disaster, death: waiting tensely, despairingly, for a reply to a letter: waiting fearfully for a battle to begin: waiting for a ship to sail: waiting for a guest to arrive or to go: waiting sleeplessly through the watches of the night for the day that seems determined not to come: waiting, all a-sweat, for the cessation of pain, or for the doctor who may relieve it: waiting apprehensively for a storm to strike or, when it has struck, to abate. Never, I thought, as I waited for that sloop to return—as all of us waited, torn by our fears, our nerves a-jangle—would I wittingly add to man's burdens by keeping anyone waiting.

With that sloop in the offing, waiting became a poison, so that voices all around us broke, arms and legs jerked uncontrollably, minds and thinking were disarranged. Some laughed like women: fell into black depressions, trembled, cursed, groaned, stammered, yawned cavernously.

Captain Dean, once more calm and composed, carved our meat and passed around the seaweed—and after an eternity the little sloop slipped in to coast back and forth across the southern tip of the island. With each pass she drew closer. We could see she carried no boat; only a bark canoe lashed alongside her cabin.

The behavior of the three men who sailed her filled me with anxiety. They eyed us warily: glanced at each other, as if in doubt. They didn't like what they saw, and I couldn't blame them.

"You've got six feet at flood tide," Captain Dean shouted. "Fifteen feet offshore you've got six feet."

The sloop's master waved his hand, brought the sloop into the wind, dropped his jib and spilled the anchor over the bow. The three men ducked under the sloop's boom and studied us again. They looked worried.

"Ship *Nottingham*," the captain shouted. A wave curled over and fell noisily. He waited for the roaring to subside: then tried again. "Ship *Nottingham*. London to Portsmouth."

We couldn't tell whether or not the three men could hear.

Captain Dean turned to the rest of us and spoke sharply. "I don't dare tell 'em how much we need food. They might not come ashore."

To the sloop he shouted again, "Fire! We need fire! Cold! Frozen!" He held his ears: bent over, he hugged himself.

The three men conferred.

Captain Dean knelt and went through the motions of using a tinderbox. He pretended to blow on a fire and then to warm his hands before it.

Two of the men unlashed the canoe, lowered it over the side and held it while the third man stepped down into it, knelt in the middle, and took two paddles that were handed to him. One he stowed beneath the thwarts. With the other he pushed off from the sloop and, still kneeling, headed for the cleft in the rock where we were gathered.

"Remember," Captain Dean warned us, "don't say a word about our meat."

The man in the canoe held his paddle steady, looked behind him, waited for a swell to come near his stern: then dug in his paddle and came rushing toward us on the slope of a roller. Captain Dean and George White braced themselves at the head of the cleft, caught the canoe by the bow and held it where it was while the wave slipped back. The canoeman, still clutching his paddle, climbed out over the bow and helped White and Captain Dean carry the canoe up higher, out of harm's way.

"We knew somebody had been cast away, and probably here," he said. He spoke slowly, and with assurance, a little like those who came up to Oxford from Warwick or Hereford–from places like Stratford-on-Avon or Broadway, where people have had the benefit of schooling.

"I'm John Dean," the captain said, "master of the *Nottingham* Galley. We went ashore——"

He broke off, looked from the canoeman to Langman and back again: then asked, "What day is this–sir?"

"This is January 2nd, a Tuesday," the man said. "I'm Nason. Richard Nason. Kittery. Part owner of the sloop *Head of Tide*."

"It can't be Tuesday," Langman said. "It must be Wednesday."

Nason looked at him oddly. "Why must it?"

"Because I kept count," Langman said.

Nason turned back to Captain Dean. "Yesterday was Monday–New Year's Day."

Captain Dean nodded. "We went ashore Monday, December 11th. There was a northeaster blowing."

"You've been on this pile of rocks since the eleventh of December?" Nason asked incredulously. His eyes swept over us, examining us from head to foot–from our oakum hats, with bits of seagull feathers and seagull skin woven into them, the oakum mittens on our hands, the oakum wrappings fastened to our shoulders, chests and legs, the clumsy oakum sheathings of our feet. He shook his head as if he found us incredible.

"Kittery?" Captain Dean asked. "Isn't that across the river from Portsmouth?"

"Yes," Nason said, "and I better not waste time. We'll have to take word to Portsmouth about you. You need help as much as anyone *I* ever saw!"

"Yes," Captain Dean said. "We need help. When you send word to Portsmouth, see that Captain Long and Captain Furber are told. They're old friends. You tell 'em I'm John Dean of Twickenham, Jasper Dean's brother."

"Wait a minute," Nason said. "I'll write it down." He fished in his clothes and produced a small account book: then stared at Captain Dean again: at me: at Neal Butler.

"No fire all that time?" he asked. "How could you live!"

Christopher Gray broke into a sort of snuffling, such as a dog makes when he whuffles for the scent of an animal behind the wainscoting.

"It seemed like a long time," Captain Dean said apologetically. "We built a boat and lost it. Then we built a raft. This boy's father built it." He put his hand on Neal's shoulder.

Nason cleared his throat. "Oh, yes," he said. "The raft! We figured there'd been two men on it. We figured a lot of men worked to make it, on account of the knots. We found it at high-water mark. Under a tree beyond high-water mark there was a man. One man. With a piece of wood tied to his wrist. He'd used it for a paddle. His hands were all raw, with the bones showing. He got as far as the tree and then I guess he lay down and froze to death."

He shook his head, put his account book back in his pocket, and became suddenly busy. "I'll start a fire for you. Got any wood?"

"One or two pieces," Captain Dean said.

"You've probably got knives," Nason said. "Slice up wood slivers for kindling." He moved toward the tent.

"What color was the man's hair—the one under the tree?" Captain Dean asked.

"Black," Nason said, "with white streaks."

He looked at Neal. "Was this boy's father—the one who built the raft—was he on the raft too?"

"Yes," Captain Dean said, "but he had yellow hair."

"That's too bad," Nason said. "That's a shame."

He took a tinderbox from his shirt—a tin one, with a candle ring on the top—then went into the tent ahead of the rest of us, being more active and quicker on his feet; but he came out more quickly than he went in. His cheeks had lost their rosy, clean-shaven look, and were gray and mottled. He held to the canvas of the tent.

"The men are pretty weak," Captain Dean explained. "When it snows or the wind's bad, they don't make the effort to go outside. I've stopped trying to make 'em. You get used to it."

Nason swallowed. "You go in and make a fire hole," he said. "Clear away the oakum in the center. Lay up a circle of rocks. Cut your shavings and put 'em in the circle; then I'll light the tinder and a candle. I'll leave the tinderbox with you."

When Neal and I came past him with rocks to make the circle, Nason put out his hand and took Neal's rock from him.

"I'm sorry about your father," he said.

Neal just nodded, his shoulders back and held high—a fine-looking boy, in spite of his oakum helmet and his outlandish swathings.

"That was quite a thing," Nason said. "Paddling a raft ashore in the dead of winter."

"He wanted to do it," Neal said.

Nason examined him attentively. "We hunted everywhere," he said, "up and down the beaches."

"I saw him in a dream," Neal said. "He got off the raft so it would be sure to get to shore."

Nason turned to look at the sloop: then at the sky in the southeast. Some of the color came back to his cheeks. "Yes," he said slowly. "That would explain it."

"Could I find the place where the raft came ashore?" Neal asked. "I've got to go there."

"I'll take you there myself," Nason said heartily. "You can stay with us. I've got five brothers and four sisters. There's so many Nasons in Kittery that we've worn grooves in the river, sailing up and down it. You come and stay with us: you'll fit right in between Benjamin and William."

Neal looked at him, then at me. For the first time since I had known him, he was on the verge of tears.

Nason seemed embarrassed. He gave the rock back to Neal, took a deep breath and entered the tent again.

The circle of rocks was almost finished. The slivers of wood were stacked in the center.

Nason fell to his knees, pried the cover from his tinderbox, took out the flint and steel and placed a small piece of charred linen on the slivers. He struck the flint with the steel rod; the spark ignited the linen; but when he gently held the point of a sliver to the flame, it wavered and died.

"Here," he said to the silent, kneeling figures around him, "slice the ends of those slivers so they're shredded." He pulled a sheath knife from his belt and feathered the end of one of the slivers. Captain Dean, Langman, George White, Neal and I did the same.

"Now I'll do what I should have done first," Nason said. "The sight of you people started me off on the wrong foot. I'll try to light the candle."

He stood the stub of a candle in the candle ring on the top of the tinderbox, rested a piece of tinder against the wick, and again struck sparks from the flint. The tinder ignited: flickered; went out.

"Damn it," Nason said, suddenly exasperated, "don't crowd up so close to me! If you can't move back, stop breathing! How can I start a fire with you blowing your breaths all over me!"

He looked at Neal and was suddenly contrite. "Hear me talk," he said disgustedly, "and you without fire for more than three weeks!"

He produced another piece of tinder, placed it on the candle wick, struck the flint with the steel–and the tinder caught: the wick smoked–and a yellow flame stood up from it!

Nason turned his head away and whooshed with relief. He stacked up the feathered bits of wood like a little tent, lit one of them from the candle. The flame spread from one stick to another.

Captain Dean leaned down and caught one of Nason's hands in his.

The odor of smoke must have affected my eyes, because I couldn't see for the wetness in them.

Fire! Warmth! Cooked food! Who knows what it's like to be without them?

Only animals! I had the thought that some of us had truly become animals.

For the second time Nason took out his little account book and a stub of a pencil, and in the book he wrote down the facts that Captain Dean had given him.

"I'll go to Portsmouth tonight if I can," he said. "If I can't, I'll go first thing in the morning. I'll see Governor Wentworth. I know Captain Furber and Captain Long. They'll send proper-sized vessels for you, and proper boats to take you off–and food."

He looked at the emaciated, bearded faces, accentuated by the flickering light of the fire. "What have you lived on? What have you had to eat?"

"We saved some things from the ship," Captain Dean said. "Some cheese and meat. Then we had mussels and a seagull and seaweed."

"My God!" Nason said. "Seaweed!" He made another note in his account book, thrust it in his pocket and scrambled from the tent.

"The wind's moving into the southeast," he said. "I don't like it."

The tide was half out, and the breakers were pounding on the uncovered ledges.

"I can't run the risk of launching that canoe where I ran in," Nason said.

Captain Dean agreed. "I think the safest place is around to the northwest. There's a deep cove we can show you."

Nason studied that rim of surf. It was pounding the island from every side, but certainly the waves were less frequent, the sudsy area larger to the north, showing that the drift was toward the mainland. Everywhere else the drift was onshore.

"All right," Nason said, "I'll send the sloop around to

the north." He looked at us uncertainly. "Can any of you people help me get my canoe across the island?"

"We'll all help you," Captain Dean said. "Four men'll have to stay here and tend that fire. Miles, you stay. And Langman. Keep Graystock and Saver here, too. Watch that fire! Whatever you do, don't choke it! Nurse it! And put the tinderbox and candle out of harm's way."

He went into the tent and looked at the brisk little fire while Nason set off in the direction of the sloop, gesticulating to his shipmates–sweeping his arm around to the north: pointing insistently to the northwest.

The others followed along behind him, the captain and Neal, Christopher Gray, George White and Charles Mellen–all but Henry Dean, who lay near the fire, twitching dangerously. If Henry should have an attack of epilepsy now, there was no telling what might happen to the fire.

The sloop's jib rose: her anchor came up and was catted, and she went dipping off to the north, over the long surges; then bore around to the westward, so that we knew Nason had been understood.

The little fire burned brightly, and we stood damp pieces of wood around the circle of rocks, hoping that the burning shavings would dry them out. While we cut more shavings, Graystock and Saver pleaded for meat–for just one slice of meat. "We're wasting this fire," Saver said. "We could be roasting meat over it."

"Keep on cutting shavings," I told them. "Under the circumstances, I think the captain'll let us have more tonight, when there's no danger of losing the fire."

To watch the progress of that bark canoe across the island was harrowing. Nason and the captain carried the front end: White and Mellen the stern, while Neal stumbled alongside Nason showing him where to put his feet, and Christopher Gray did the same for Captain Dean.

They had overturned it on the two paddles, using the paddles as carrying poles, and because the four men slipped constantly, the canoe's progress was erratic and fumbling, like that of a beetle on a rough field.

The little cove for which they were headed was one we all knew well, because into it, after the wreck, we had pulled all the cordage and most of the junk from which we'd built the boat and raft. It had a smooth gravelly bottom; and when the four men righted the canoe and lowered it at the head of that little cove, I drew a deep breath of relief. That, I thought, was all there was to it: news of our whereabouts, of our hunger and our miserable condition, was already as good as in Portsmouth.

Langman, evidently angry because Nason had disagreed with him as to the day of the week, watched the proceedings with a jaundiced eye.

"What's going on down there?" he suddenly demanded. "By God, that fool Nason is going to run the captain out to that sloop! He can't do that! He can't let the captain get to Portsmouth ahead of the rest of us!"

He shouted, "Here! Here! No! No!" and ran from the tent.

Nason slid the canoe into the water. Captain Dean, holding a paddle, knelt in the bow.

Before Langman reached them, Nason stepped into the stern, and pushed hard with his paddle. Both men took a few quick strokes. The canoe veered sideways, as if twisted by a current. Her starboard side dipped sharply. When Captain Dean abruptly leaned to larboard to preserve her balance, she dipped even more sharply beneath him. A cataract of green water poured over her gunnel, the canoe slid out from under them, and both Nason and the captain went overboard in a surge of foam. Everybody, it seemed to me, was shouting, running and falling down.

Nason came up gasping, caught the canoe and pushed it ashore. The captain staggered to a seaweed-covered ledge, looking half drowned.

Hands grasped the canoe, emptied water from it, and swung it gently to the water again to let Nason hoist himself aboard. This time Nason, kneeling alone in the middle, stroked his little craft out of the cove, surmounted the green surges, and went safely aboard the sloop.

The western sky was a dingy gray, and the little sloop, weewawing toward that grayness, was too small and fragile for my peace of mind.

"I thought I was gone," the captain told us when he dragged himself to the tent. "I must have swallowed a tubful. The sloop looked so close to shore, I thought maybe we could all get away this afternoon, but the currents suck around that north side like a millrace! There's something dirty blowing up from the southeast."

He stopped outside the tent to hang over a boulder and rid himself of the salt water he had swallowed. I went on in to see Langman draw from beneath the edges of the tent an armful of tarry rope-ends, hidden away for just this purpose.

"Now that we've got the fire to cook it," Langman said, "there'll be an extra meat ration tonight."

He ignited the end of one of those pieces of tarred rope,

laid it carefully on the flickering shavings: then criss-crossed a dozen other rope-ends above it.

The rope burned with a sound of sizzling. Up from it came a cloud of yellowish-green smoke that on the instant thickened the air within the tent to a sort of dry, strangling soup.

All in a moment's time our eyes, our chests, our stomachs were choked. We couldn't breathe: we couldn't think: we could hardly make the effort to get ourselves past the tent-flap and into the open air.

When we had clean air in our lungs again, we hoisted Neal on our shoulders until, clinging to the flagpole, he could cut away the cap of oakum around the apex of the tent and slash holes in the canvas. Through them a spurt of discolored smoke went drifting out to sea.

That night, when we had recovered from our sickness and the fire was burning with a clear flame, the captain was generous with the store of beef; and we, taking turns in charring it over the bright fire, found it delicious . . . heartening . . . and gave no thought to its origin.

January 3rd, Wednesday

If we hadn't been racked by disappointment, exhausted from overexertion, befuddled from hunger and dazed by the smoke within that tent, I doubt that Graystock and Saver would ever have been put on watch that night. They had been spared most of the labors that had drugged the rest of us and so they were assigned to stand fire-watch —the last watch before daybreak.

Perhaps this had come about because of their constant malingering—because of their repeated insistence that they were too weak to work; because of the filth in which they lay in spite of our freely expressed disgust. Perhaps, because of all this, we had come to feel that they were too weak to be harmful, too helpless to be dangerous. I know now, of course, that those who seem weakest and most harmless are the greatest threat to any society, and the most to be feared.

Richard Nason and Captain Dean had been right in looking askance at that southeast wind, for its gusts grew stronger and stronger: then snow came whirling in at the top of the tent. Sometimes the wind pulled the smoke up with it and set the fire to glowing. At other times it beat at the blaze with icy fingers, flattening the smoke around us.

God only knows how Saver and Graystock had discovered where Neal had hidden our reserves of meat entrusted to him by Captain Dean. Perhaps they had loosened the foot of the tent and watched him when he first hid it, or when he went back to thicken the protecting seaweed above it. But discovered it had been.

Thanks to the warmth of that ineffable fire, I had truly slept that night, instead of shivering in a sort of intermittent nightmare; but before dawn on that tempestuous Wednesday morning, I came to my senses to find Neal prodding me. The captain, too, was awake, because I saw the glimmer of his eyes in the light of the fire.

Beside the fire sat Graystock, feeding it with bits of tarred rope, and inching forward the end of a board, drying it above the flame. I could see the surface of the board boiling and sizzling in the heat before it reluctantly caught fire.

Neal put his lips close to my ear, so that I could hear his whisper. He could have shouted without being heard by Graystock, because of the pounding of the breakers.

"Saver went out," Neal said. "I heard him talking to Graystock. He went to get meat."

"He couldn't do it," I whispered back. "He couldn't find his way. His feet wouldn't let him."

"He knew where it was," Neal said, "and he couldn't wait."

So we lay motionless; and out of the snowy darkness came Saver, that complaining, querulous, inert, filth-smeared lout: that weak-willed laggard, incapable—according to his own whining protests—of standing on his feet. For three long weeks he had battened on our sympathies—and now, coated with snow, he stood on those supposedly useless feet, grinning as he readjusted the tent-flap, and drew from beneath the oakum coat that others had woven for him a roll of the meat from the carcass we had dragged from the tent for him—and skinned for him, and dismembered for him, and boned out for him, and rolled and tied for him—because he was too weak to do any of those things himself.

Too weak, indeed! His determination to live on others was as the strength of ten!

They were delighted with themselves, Graystock and Saver were! They grinned and tittered as they crouched over the fire, carving little chunks from that roll of meat, impaling them on the points of their knives, and placing them carefully on the glowing coals.

The odor of the roasting meat filled the tent, piercing and mouth-watering.

Captain Dean got carefully to his knees. When Saver and Graystock speared the roasted chunks with their knife points and popped them into their mouths, he reached out with those long arms of his, seized each one by a shoulder and pulled both of them flat on their backs.

"Get up, all!" Captain Dean shouted to the rest of us. "Wake up! Look at these two, caught red-handed, their mouths crammed with the meat they should have defended with their lives. Animals steal food that belong to others —unless they're trained. Then they can't be made to steal their master's food! Look well at these two! Not men! Untrained animals!"

He picked up the roll of meat and gave it to Neal to hold.

"You, Saver! You, Graystock! What do you have to say for yourselves?"

"I heard a seagull," Saver quavered. "I was afraid the seagulls might get it. I was going to divide it as soon as daylight came."

Langman snorted. "There hasn't been a seagull near this island since I killed the one we ate."

"There's nothing on this earth worse than an ingrate," Captain Dean said slowly. "You're an ingrate, Saver! Graystock, you're an ingrate! Ingrates never change, no matter how much they're coddled and babied! They want more and more! If they don't get more, they steal the belongings or the good name of those that coddle 'em!"

Graystock pointed at Saver. "He was the one! He knew where it was! I didn't do anything."

The captain laughed. "You've both bitten the hands that fed you. How do you say, those of you who've been bitten? How should these ingrates be punished?"

"I've wanted 'em out of the tent," Langman said, "ever since they started fouling themselves. I say put 'em out! Let 'em get along the best they can!"

"Make 'em wash their clothes in salt water," Henry Dean said. "Make 'em strip to the skin and wash, starting now."

"Why waste time on 'em?" White said. "Let's kill 'em! Let's kill 'em quick!"

"We'd be justified in doing so," Captain Dean said, "but Nason, yesterday, saw how many of us there were. He was a careful, good man. He won't forget anything he saw here—ever!"

Contemplatively he added, "But White's suggestion has merit. This would be a much better world if it were rid of its ingrates."

"Most ingrates don't recognize themselves as ingrates," I reminded the captain. "They'd put up a strong argument as to why they shouldn't be killed."

"I suppose so," the captain said, "and most of 'em, probably, would think they'd made out quite a case for themselves. Anyway, we can't kill Graystock and Saver, much as they deserve killing."

"You could send them out to bring in all the meat that's left," Neal suggested. "They know where it is. If all the meat were divided now, we wouldn't have to stand watch to make sure they didn't steal the rest."

"That's a good idea," the captain said. "Graystock and Saver, hand over your knives. Then go out and clean yourselves. After that, bring back what's left of the meat. There are three pieces. Bring back the seaweed it's covered with, too. And don't eat any part of those three pieces of meat! If you do, I swear to God we'll throw both of you in the surf."

Protesting, Saver and Graystock stumbled out into the snow. There was a pallid gray light in the east, so that they could see where to put their feet. How Saver had made that journey in the pitch-dark is something Saver himself couldn't have answered. Perhaps if a man has an animal's craving for something, a mysterious inner sense guides him safely to it.

What with the snow and the high seas and the thick slabs of meat that Captain Dean gave us, we hardly moved from the tent all day. We took turns roasting slivers of meat, stoking the fire, and dozing in its faint glow—a mere breath of nothing to anyone who has known a real fire in a real fireplace; colder, far colder than the Bodleian at its coldest; but a bit of heavenly radiance to us who had lived so long in a frigid hell.

We looked, of course, toward shore, but not in hopefulness. No vessel could have approached Boon Island in that abominable storm, and we were afraid, even, to speculate as to when Nason might reach Portsmouth. We knew in our hearts that he and his little sloop, with that unexpected wind to harry them, might never have reached Portsmouth at all.

January 4th, Thursday

The snow stopped, the wind dropped, the tent was warm, and we must have slept like logs; for when I woke, we were sitting up, all ten of us, wild-eyed, hair on end. I was vaguely conscious, in the recesses of my mind, that a gun had been fired: that I was still hearing its echo.

The tide was almost dead low: the sea had fallen: the wind was a light breeze, offshore, so that the tops of the swells had a slick look—and rising and falling on those rollers was a craft so sturdy, so smart, so daring in the way she slipped around those brown ledge-fingers, almost touching them, that I couldn't shout, or even speak. All I could do was stand there, empty of thought, devoid of sensation, barely alive.

The little vessel was odd-looking. She had a high sharp bow and an even higher sharp stern, and under her boom rested a broad, high-sided skiff with a narrow, flat bottom. There were five men on her deck, one lying out on the short bowsprit watching for ledges, one at her tiller, one reloading the musket that had aroused us, and two wrestling the skiff over the side.

"That's a pink," Captain Dean said in a strangled voice. "Nothing like 'em to nose in and out of a rocky coast."

Captain Dean lowered himself halfway down the seaweed.

The man on the pink's bowsprit jumped up and let go an anchor: then joined those at work on the skiff. The man at the tiller left it, took two coils of rope and tossed them into the skiff: then four men slid her into the water and jumped in.

One made fast a rope to the bow: another did the same in the stern, tossing the unattached end of the rope to the man who had held the tiller.

The man in the bow stood up, cupped his hands around his mouth and shouted to Captain Dean. His voice carried strongly to us on that gentle but frost-laden land breeze. "The dory's made fast astern. We'll pay out easy. When we're close enough, we'll throw the bow rope ashore. Get some men down there with you and lay onto that bow rope. Hold it taut so we can't be swamped."

Two of the men in the dory stood up, pushing at oars. They faced in the direction they were rowing, which seemed strange and awkward. It wasn't right, I thought numbly, for a rower to be able to see where he was going, instead of turning his back to his objective and seeing nothing, as do rowers in England.

I wondered why these Americans had to be so different, sailing something called a pink, sharp at both ends: recklessly approaching ledges in a flat-bottomed dory instead of a skiff: standing up to row so to face forward.

I looked around for someone to help the captain. Only Neal, Langman and White had come from the tent. The others must be helpless, sick, probably, from too much meat, too much smoke, the unaccustomed warmth.

The four of us joined the captain. When the man in the dory's bow tossed us the rope, we fumbled for it, caught it and clumsily took it high up onto solid rock, above the seaweed.

The dory, held bow and stern, jerked at the ropes like a fractious horse.

The newcomers picked their way over the seaweed and stood looking at us as we laboriously made the rope fast around a boulder. I never saw such incredulity as was written on their faces.

Captain Dean, testing the hitch, looked up at the foremost of those sturdy heaven-sent figures.

"You probably don't remember me," he said. "We'd pretty near lost hope—" His voice broke.

All four men stared at us, their brows wrinkled, their mouths half open.

The man Captain Dean had addressed seemed both horrified and puzzled.

"Nason said I'd find John Dean here," he said. "I'd like to—"

"I'm John Dean," the captain said. "You're Furber." He turned to another. "You're Captain Long. I–I–I—"

He sat down suddenly on a boulder, clasped his hands around his middle and rocked himself back and forth.

Long and Furber jumped forward and hoisted him to his feet. Long patted his back. Furber held his upper arm with both hands.

"We caught the outgoing tide as soon as we heard," Furber said. "Nason said to hurry, so we hurried. You'll be all right, John!" He hesitated and asked uncertainly, "You're John Dean of Twickenham?"

"Jasper's brother," Captain Dean said. "I'll be all right

when I get away from these damned breakers! Can't seem to hear a thing! Where's Nason?"

"He's in Portsmouth," Furber said. "He ran into a southeast squall and piled up on Kittery Point. Too much of a hurry to get back, I guess. He lost his sloop, but he got word to Colonel Pepperrell, and Colonel Pepperrell got word to us. We sail Pepperrell's ships, John."

"We got gruel aboard the pink, John," Captain Long said. "You'll feel different when you get some gruel into you."

He spoke to the two silent sailors, who were examining us as if we were dangerous animals in cages. "Put the captain in the dory."

"You're William Long," Captain Dean said in a shaking voice. "And Jethro Furber! I never thought I'd see the day!"

"Now, John," Captain Long said. "We'll have you out of here in a jiffy." He took Captain Dean's arm and steered him toward the dory.

"Take the others first," Captain Dean said. "They're in the tent. Had our first fire last night—breathed a lot of smoke. Tent smells pretty bad. Things weren't easy. I had to stop trying to drive 'em."

"You can't drive 'em if you're human," Captain Furber said.

Captain Dean's voice was suddenly shrill. "Hurry up and help those others. We can't tend this rope all day."

Captain Long, Captain Furber and the two seamen scuttled off toward the tent as rapidly as anyone could move across those snowy, icy rocks.

Captain Dean rubbed his face with both hands, and examined them as if surprised. "I'd know Furber anywhere.

Name of Jethro. Only Jethro I ever saw. Used to keep running into him—Antigua, Halifax. Where was I? Oh yes, he sailed under John Frost. John married Mary Pepperrell. Pepperrells marry all over. Is John Frost here with Furber? Or is it Long? I met John's wife once."

I saw his mind was wandering. When I went to help him, he half turned, put out his hands gropingly and fell heavily.

Neal tried to lift him up.

"Let him alone," I said. "Let him rest. He's been through a lot. A rest won't hurt him."

Long, Furber and their two sailors came cautiously to us, each one carrying a man on his back.

"The captain had a fall," I told Captain Long. "The fire smoked last night—tarred rope—no wood. I think he's a little tired."

"I wouldn't wonder," Captain Long said. "Now look: I'm in command here! Put Dean in the dory right now." He pointed at Neal. "Put him in, too. That's two passengers and two to row."

He signaled to the man on the pink, who tightened the dory's stern rope.

"All right," Captain Long said to Captain Furber. "Slack away on that bow cable. Hold it tight till she's halfway out."

We stowed the captain in the dory: Neal got in by himself.

The two rowers faced the pink, and when a roller lifted the dory, they dug in their oars and pushed hard. Aboard the pink the man pulled at the stern rope. The dory went stern-first as readily as bow-first.

"How many left in the tent?" I asked Captain Long.

"We couldn't see," he said. "We brought out four. Who are they?"

I looked at them, sprawled just above the seaweed. They all seemed to be exactly alike. They might have been quadruplets—bearded, foul, horrible-looking.

"One's the captain's brother," I said. "I think the others are Graystock and Saver and Gray. Gray was a gunner."

I couldn't remember what it was that Captain Long had asked me, and so shook my head.

Captain Long, seeing that I was confused, reached out and slapped my cheek, so to jolt me back to reality. "No offense meant," he said. "Who else is there? Have we got 'em all?"

"Let's see," I said, "Neal and Langman and the captain and I hauled in on the bow rope. That's four. Yes, and White. That's five. You took out four. That's nine. There must be another in the tent. Mellen. He can walk. It must have been that damned smoke. That's ten. There were fourteen to begin with."

Captain Furber nudged Captain Long. "The dory's coming back," he said.

They went as close to the water's edge as they could, watching the dory lift with the surges, rock toward us, pushed by the two sailors. When one of them tossed the bow rope ashore, the two captains belayed it around the same boulder we'd used.

The rowers climbed out and hurried back to the tent.

Captain Long came to stand beside me. "Nason told us there were twelve: that two were lost on the raft, though only one was found."

"No," I said, "there were fourteen. The cook died of lung complaint. We set him adrift. Then the carpenter died. The men wanted to eat him. We finished him up last night."

Captain Long took me by the shoulder. I saw he once more thought my mind was troubled, and was about to slap me to sensibility again. "I'm all right," I said, pushing his hand away. "You'd have done the same in our place."

Langman crowded up to Captain Long. "I was against it," he shouted. "I said it was barbarous, unchristian and a sin!"

Captain Long dropped his eyes from mine: then looked hard at Langman. "So you didn't eat him?" he asked.

"I didn't eat him as Chips Bullock," Langman explained earnestly. "I didn't eat him the day he was skinned. I only ate him the next day, when he was beef."

"That's a nice distinction," Captain Long said.

He became suddenly irascible, impatiently lifted Henry Dean, and shouted at Saver, Graystock and Gray. "Get on your feet! Stow yourself in that dory!"

He pointed a stubby finger at Langman. "Help 'em if they *need* help; then get in yourself! Don't stand around! All we need is a capful of wind to be stuck on this damned island ourselves! God knows how you stood it! I couldn't have stood it a week without losing all my anchors!"

His two seamen came back, pushing and pulling at Mellen.

"Get him in! Get him in!" Captain Long shouted. He tapped me on the shoulder and pointed to the southwest. There, coming up fast, were two schooners and a brigantine, all three of them running before the wind.

"Word's got around," Captain Long said. "And that wind has shifted! Pack 'em in! Pack 'em in!"

Five minutes later I was hauled over the side of the pink,

her anchor was up, and we were moving to the westward. Between us and that miserable island there was the mist of breaking seas and the haze of cold air above salt water. That island had visited upon us every conceivable form of misery, disappointment and torture, but it hadn't been able to destroy us, and in spite of my aches and my discomfort, I felt a great peace—a blissful quiet.

Around me men spoke quietly and I heard them—heard small sounds: the sighing of the breeze in the rigging: the screaking of the boom against the mast: the faint rustle of the seas along the hull. The world, after an eternity, was blessedly silent once more. Gone forever, thank God, was the deafening tumult of breakers, bellowing and roaring like furious beasts determined to destroy our minds as well as our bodies.

The brigantine and the two schooners hove to and waited for the pink to come within hailing distance: then cruised along on either side and spoke us.

"Get 'em all?" they shouted. "Anything we can do?"

Long used his speaking trumpet. "We got 'em all. Ten of 'em. If you beat us in, see there's canoes at Pepperrell's Wharf in Portsmouth. Take word to Dr. Packer. Get barbers. Find Nason and see what he's arranged."

The skippers of the three vessels nodded vigorously: held their hands clasped high in air and shook them.

Captain Long resumed his shouting. "Plenty of warm water! They're lousy, all of 'em! Plenty of bandages! All kinds of ointments!"

One of the skippers, perched in the ratlins, bawled, "How many days on the island?"

"Twenty-four," Captain Long shouted.

The skipper slid down from the ratlins, and I could see the crews talking and gesticulating. I knew they didn't believe it.

The three vessels sheered away from the pink and drew ahead, as if racing for Portsmouth.

A sailor brought me a tot of rum and a slice of bread. "Captain's orders," he said. The rum burned my gullet and went heatedly around in my stomach. My first bite of bread had a flat taste, but the second was better: the last better still.

The same sailor came back with a cup of gruel and stood before me while I drank it. Then he quickly took the mug from me and moved to a distance. "I'll stand here so you won't fall overboard," he said.

I didn't know what he meant until the pink skittered on the top of a wave, then sank sideways down it. On that my ears roared, my insides were contorted, and everything in me churned up and out. I hung over the pink's bulwarks while the sailor held my knees. This, I thought, was death.

Dimly I heard the sailor say soothingly, "This'll clean you out. Everyone was sick after the gruel, even the captain."

Just at that moment I didn't care what had happened to the captain. I didn't even care what happened to me. I was seasick.

Pepperrell's Wharf was crowded when the pink slid alongside it at dusk. It was a mystery to me why so many hundreds had gathered on that wharf to see a few scarecrows, but in spite of the bitter January cold there *were* hundreds of them, women and men, too. Almost all had lanterns made of pierced tin. They were somehow different from any such throng that might collect in Greenwich. In Greenwich there would have been beggars among them and hangdog-looking folk, and deformed, dwarfed people, slyly seeking pockets to pick. Those of substance would have been smaller and would have seemed contemptuous. Almost certainly there would have been some who jeered, or laughed raucously at our hairiness and raggedness and queer oakum garments.

But those hundreds on Pepperrell's Wharf stood straight, had solidity, and all of them, without exception, were concerned about us. They were compassionate people, deeply interested in our welfare. When I was helped over the bulwarks and saw all those solicitous eyes, glittering in the light from their upheld lanterns, I couldn't help gulping to think that strangers should be so kind.

Nason came from the crowd to lower me into a canoe with Neal. "You're going to Captain Furber's," he said. "Captain Dean's going there, too. He's already gone." He put his hand on Neal's shoulder. "I'll see you tomorrow," he said. "We're all your friends. You needn't worry about a thing."

The canoeman took us a short distance downstream, helped us ashore, pulled his canoe half up the bank, and motioned us to follow him.

"Tell us where it is," I said, "and we'll go there. You don't need to leave your canoe."

"Why not?" he asked.

"Someone might steal it."

He looked baffled: then urged us forward, between two warehouses and across a street to a two-and-a-half-story wooden house. The door of the house was open and before it stood two women and three children, all peering in through the doorway.

Our canoeman touched one of the women on the shoulder. She stifled a cry and whirled to face him.

At the sight of us, she pressed her hand to her lips and shrank back, drawing the children against her skirts. They were pretty little plump things, and I had the thought that has come to me, against my will, a thousand thousand times since then, whenever I see a sturdy child or a woman with a large arm or heavy buttocks—the thought that, if the need arose, that child or that woman would make good eating. No wonder the women were afraid of us!

"What's the matter, ma'am?" the canoeman asked. "I was told by Captain Nason to bring these people here, orders of Captain Furber, and Captain Dean's already been brought here."

"Oh," the woman said, "he frightened us to death, just the look of him. When he stood here and started to speak to us, we screamed and ran out. He went in. I think he's in the kitchen."

"Well, go on in," the canoeman said, "and take these two with you. Treat 'em the same way you'd want Captain Furber to be treated if he'd been cast away on Boon Island for a month."

"Only for twenty-four days," Neal said.

Mrs. Furber looked at Neal: looked away, then studied him carefully. "Only!" she said. "*Only* twenty-four days! You come in the house, right this minute!"

Captain Dean was in the kitchen, as Mrs. Furber had suspected. On the fire he had found an iron kettle filled with beef stew, and had forked out pieces of beef and turnips and potatoes, and had covered the top of the kitchen table with them to let them cool.

"I'm sorry, ma'am," he said to Mrs. Furber. "When you screamed and ran out, I figured the wise thing to do was to stay here instead of running after you and maybe frightening you and the children even more."

He looked at the children in what he doubtless thought was a genial manner; but I knew too well that he was entertaining the same understandable thought that had passed through my head—that they would be tenderer to eat than Chips Bullock had been.

Mrs. Furber's initial horror was passing. "You can't have all that beef and vegetables you've put out on the table," she said sternly. "And just because you're starved is no reason you shouldn't eat like human beings." She brought a bowl and three plates, forked a moderate amount from the table top to each plate; then put the remainder in the bowl.

"Now," she said, "that's all you can have!"

"Ma'am," Neal said. "I'll ask you to put us in the room where we'll stay. We'd better eat there."

"Well I never!" Mrs. Furber exclaimed.

Neal scratched himself deliberately, first his head: then his arm.

"Well," Mrs. Furber said, "we'll put you in the barn. There's three stalls and a summer oven, and lots of hay and blankets. When you're cleaned up, we'll move you to the house."

There was a knock on the door. Mrs. Furber opened it to admit three men—Dr. Packer and two barbers.

The doctor took one look at us, then beckoned us to

pick up our plates and follow him. To Mrs. Furber he said, "Bring us hot water as often as you can. And get tubs. If you've only got one, borrow two from the neighbors."

I can hear Dr. Packer's voice, after all these years, exclaiming over our sores and over our feet. "It's a miracle," he said over and over. "I've got to send word to Boston! Urine and oakum? Seaweed? God knows! But it's a miracle, all the same!"

Warmth, blankets, soft hay on which to lie, clean bodies, shorn heads, shaved faces, white bandages, soothing ointments! I felt as the sailors of Ulysses must have felt, when freed of Circe's spell.

The Last Chapter

I waked, the next morning, to the sound of jingling, faint and far off, couldn't remember where I was, and sat up straight on my hay-stuffed mattress, half frightened by not hearing the unending roaring of those Boon Island breakers: bewildered by my flannel nightgown, smelling of lavender. Lavender, of all things, instead of the stenches of our Boon Island tent! The jingling sound went on and on.

Captain Dean spoke up from the adjoining stall. "Sleigh bells! People moving around! Probably there'll be a few of 'em come to see us today. Probably they'll want to know all about us. We'd better decide on what we'll tell 'em about Neal."

"That's simple enough, isn't it?" I asked. "He learned to read and write while working for my father. And my father got to know him because Neal's father was in the Naval Hospital."

"Yes," Captain Dean said. "That's close enough. Are you listening, Neal?"

From a third stall Neal politely said he was.

"Probably," the captain went on cheerfully, "we won't have occasion to say much. Shipwrecked sailors aren't a novelty nowadays, considering how our good countrymen in Devon and Cornwall make a business of getting them wrecked. These New Hampshire people aren't much different, probably."

Probably! Probably!

How little Captain Dean knew about America, in spite of the high opinion he'd expressed to us in the harbor of Killybegs concerning the people of Portsmouth.

How little anyone, anywhere, knows about America! About its insatiable curiosity concerning the welfare of others! About its generous eagerness to help strangers achieve the same health and happiness that its own citizens enjoy! About its limitless resources: its enormous latent strength! And above all, about its friendliness to those who deserve its friendship: its implacable detestation of false men and evil measures!

Captain Furber came banging at the door that led from the barn to the woodshed, which in turn opened into the kitchen. With him he carried a kettle of fish chowder, three bowls, a ladle and three spoons.

"Haddock!" Captain Furber said portentously. "The Woman"—and I took The Woman to be Mrs. Furber—"cooks the heads and bones in one kettle, and the onions and potatoes and fish in another. Then she makes a mess of pork scraps, and breaks up some ship's bread, and mixes 'em all up with the liquor from the bones. Every sea captain in Portsmouth claims his wife makes the best fish chowder in the world, but I'll put The Woman's up against any of 'em. It's the liquor from the heads and the backbones that grows hair on your chest!"

He ladled the stew into the bowls; then discoursed while we rolled that hot and fragrant chowder over our tongues, crunching the pork scraps through the soft and savory ship's bread, the tender haddock and the melting potatoes. My toes, what there were left of them, would have curled, if that had been possible, at the life-giving sweetness that trickled down my throat.

"The Woman," Captain Furber said, "makes fried pies that would stand a dead Indian right up on his feet. Doc Packer's in there now, eating fried pies. The Woman wanted me to take in a few for you, but Doc Packer said No. There's a couple of nurses coming over—Governor Wentworth authorized 'em—and Doc Packer says maybe you can have one fried pie apiece along about four bells."

As a seeming afterthought he said, "There's been people coming around with stuff already, but Doc Packer says they can't come in till after he's looked at you. He says maybe some of 'em can come in after you have your dinner."

"What sort of stuff?" Captain Dean asked.

"Oh, knitted small clothes," Captain Furber said. "Linen shirts. Woolen stockings. Big parcel from Mrs. John Brewster—the one that was scalped. Good woman. Got a silver plate in her head to close up a hatchet hole. Hair never grew back, so she wears a wig. Kind of starchy-looking woman, but she softens up considerably toward those who've been in trouble. I'll have a table brought in so you can spread things out on it."

Dr. Packer came in, followed by two women in gray dresses. One, the Widow Hubbard, was short and stout and had a luxuriant mustache. The other, Widow Macklin, was tall and cheerful-looking with a cast in one eye that made her seem to be examining a distant object when in reality she was looking straight ahead.

"Now then," Dr. Packer said to Captain Dean, "we'll have off these bandages. Colonel Pepperrell sent word he wants to see you as soon as you're fit to be seen. There's some others too. They want to hear all about it. How do they think I'll get around to seeing all my other patients if I yap, yap, yap all day about you!"

The nurses brought buckets and rags, stoked the fire, swept the barn floor and set up a table for the gifts Captain Furber had mentioned.

As the doctor sopped at our legs and feet with rags dipped in the concoction in one of the buckets, he rumbled fretfully about our condition. "Hurt much?" he asked. When we said No: no more than an aching tooth, he demanded further details about the treatment our feet had received after the cutting off of our boots.

"There's something here I ought to get to the bottom of," he mumbled again and again. "You'd lost toenails when you cut off your boots, and some toes came off when you washed 'em in urine. Then you put on pieces of linen and some layers of oakum. Then you went out on the rock and kept getting your feet wet, and had no fire."

We said that was correct.

"Hurt much?" he asked again.

Captain Dean said—and Neal and I agreed—that the most painful of all was when we put our hands in water to loosen mussels. We tried to explain to him the excruciating agony that almost paralyzed us after the fifth or sixth immersion; but pain, of course, can't be described.

"Mussels, now," the doctor said. "Could mussels have anything to do with it?"

We didn't know.

"And you ate seaweed every day," he ruminated. "Could seaweed be a remedy against frostbite?"

"I don't know *why* I made 'em eat seaweed," the captain said. "I knew we *had* to eat it. There wasn't much of anything else till Chips Bullock died. The fat from Chips's kidneys helped us a little. You'd better not forget to mention kidney fat if you make a report to those Boston doctors. It certainly eased the pain in our feet and legs."

"It's annoying," Dr. Packer said. "We can't go out to Boon Island and carry on experiments under the conditions you encountered, because in the first place nobody'd be such an idiot as to go there under those conditions; and in the second place, everybody that went would die before we found out anything. Exasperating!"

"How long before we'll be able to walk?" Captain Dean asked.

"Well," Dr. Packer said, "we could move you to an upstairs room today, if you felt you'd like to get out of this barn and into a comfortable bed."

"I don't want to," Captain Dean said. "I'd feel choked in a comfortable bed. I'd rather stay here, where we can practice walking again with only about half our feet."

Dr. Packer looked relieved. "That's the best thing to do—stay where you'll be out from under foot, and handy to the privy."

"How's my brother?" Captain Dean asked. "How's the rest of 'em?"

"Your brother's all right," Dr. Packer said. "He's just

the same as you. He lost toes, the same as you did; but when they fell off, they sort of healed themselves, just like those lizards down in Antigua, that shed their tails if you so much as look at 'em."

He pronounced it Antigga, so I knew he'd sailed there—probably in one of Pepperrell's vessels.

"When can I see my brother?" Captain Dean asked.

"Since you'll stay here in the barn," Dr. Packer said, "I think I'll move him over here later today. I don't think much of the sailors he's with. If I tell 'em they can have a certain amount to eat, they eat three times as much."

"Saver and Graystock," the captain said. "I'll be glad to have Henry here where I can keep an eye on him."

The doctor eyed Captain Dean peculiarly. "You've got some others that'll bear watching," he said.

"I know," Captain Dean said. "Langman and Mellen and White."

"If I was you, I wouldn't trust 'em," Dr. Packer said.

The captain snorted. "I don't trust 'em as far as I could throw a whale by the tail."

From my earliest days I had seen, wherever I'd gone in England, beggars of all sorts pleading, imploring, praying for alms, for food, for cast-off clothing; but never had I seen generosity freely offered. Now, in Portsmouth, where beggars were unknown, I saw what I would never have believed, unless I had seen it with my own eyes—an outpouring of all the good things of this earth to people, strangers, who had suffered adversity during the same storms which had howled around the sheltered homes of their benefactors.

Captain Furber complained and fulminated at the surplus offerings of money, piles of clothing, fur hats, flowered weskits, boots and shoes that accumulated in his best room—the room unused, except for funerals and weddings, in the front left corner of every large Portsmouth house. No matter how rapidly Widow Hubbard and Widow Macklin sorted them into piles of three—one pile for ourselves, one for Langman, White and Mellen in the Motley house, and the third for Graystock, Saver and Gray in the Swaine house—they continued to accumulate, so that Captain Furber, at Neal's suggestion, tacked to his front door a card reading, "*The Grateful Survivors of Boon Island Have More Than Enough.*"

Another thing for which Neal was responsible was the writing of letters of thanks to those who had left their names with their offerings. "People like to be thanked," Neal said, "but my father said most people forget to teach their children to say 'thank you.' So if Captain Furber will buy us some paper, I'll write the letters."

More people came to see us or call on us than I would have believed lived in Portsmouth. Merchants, sea captains, tavern keepers, King's Councillors, Lieutenant Governor John Wentworth, John Plaisted, Theodore Atkinson, Colonel William Pepperrell, Richard Nason, Robert Almory, Roger Swaine, Edward Toogood—fine men: the finest, barring my father and Captain Dean and Swede Butler, I ever met.

Every one of the men who called upon us without being turned away by Dr. Packer was solicitous about our welfare, and in a few weeks' time I had more offers of positions than I would have had in England in half a century.

As for Neal, word had gone around concerning the manner of his father's death, and everyone who saw him was instantly seized with the idea of planning his future.

Colonel William Pepperrell and his partner Governor Wentworth came to call on our second day in Portsmouth. Everything, Governor Wentworth said, would be done for us, and at the expense of the Province of New Hampshire. We were entranced by his elegance, his affability, and the attentiveness with which he listened to our answers to his questions. His companion, Colonel Pepperrell, seemed more remote—more interested in scrutinizing the ceiling than in listening to us.

Then Colonel Pepperrell came again alone. Neal, when the colonel walked in, was sitting at our gift-table. The gifts had been pushed away from the end at which he sat, and his pen was scratching diligently at one of his many letters of thanks.

The colonel went to the table, picked up one of the letters and read it aloud:

"Hugh Gunnison, Esqre.

The officers and the crew of the Nottingham Galley wish to express to you their profound gratitude for your sympathy and your kindness to them after their rescue by the citizens of Kittery and Portsmouth from their bitter days on Boon Island.

"John Dean, Master"

Colonel Pepperrell was a broad, powerful man with a bulldog face, and he waved the letter exultantly. "Look at that! I read every word of it, easier than print! Takes two men to translate *my* writing." He narrowed his eyes at Neal. "Where'd you learn to write?"

Neal stood up. "In Greenwich, sir."

"He's to work for my father," I said, "in law and insurance."

"Law!" Colonel Pepperrell cried. "Quibble, quibble, quibble! That's no life for you, my boy! Here, sit down! Sit down! Dr. Packer said he had to trim off half your foot."

"I don't know how much he took off, sir. It feels no worse than it did before he trimmed it."

"Yes," Colonel Pepperrell said. "I see!" He looked carelessly at Neal, glanced at Captain Dean and me: then seemed to come to a decision.

He spoke thoughtfully and jerkily, almost as if meditating aloud. "I talked to John Wentworth about you. Twice. Slow man, I am, like folks in Devonshire. Think slowly but make up my mind quick. Always wanted to go to America, but couldn't make up my mind to go till I was sixteen. Then I went quick."

"My brother Jasper speaks of you often, Colonel," Captain Dean said. "He heard all about you from David Waterhouse."

Colonel Pepperrell looked mellow. "Yes. Handles my accounts in England." His eyes strayed back to Neal.

"Mustn't wander from subject," he grumbled. "My boy William Junior! He's fourteen. I can write, but what I write I can't read. William Junior can't write at all, and of course he can't read my writing either. He's got to learn to write, because my other son Andrew's at sea, learning the things a shipowner needs to know. Andrew's delicate. He couldn't have come through Boon Island the way you people did."

He tilted back in his chair and ran his eyes over us, a shrewd, farseeing old man, wondering, I suspected, whether he could have endured Boon Island.

"I know a little about England," he said. "I ought to. I was born in Revelstoke, near Plymouth. I didn't like it. It's no place for a man without money. Upper classes everywhere protecting themselves from lower classes, and with good reason!" He snorted. "Been thinking some of going back to Revelstoke: buying a few hundred acres in the country: being upper classes myself."

He glanced at us sharply, as if to get our reactions. I, for one, had none.

"The thing that stops me is William Junior. I've built a big business. William Junior's got to write letters to me about the business, so I can buy books and learn to chase foxes at Revelstoke! Chase foxes! Those fools that chase foxes never kept hens. If they ever had, they'd kill all the foxes before they had a chance to grow up!"

He clucked disparagingly at himself. "Wander, wander from the subject! Now here: we got no schools. Imagine that! John Wentworth says he's going to build a school with his own money, but he hasn't done it, and William Junior still can't write. Time's getting short! Nine vessels I've got—one of 'em picked you up—the pink *Joanna*." He named them, ticking them off on thick fisherman's fingers: "Ship *Frenchie*, brigantine *William and Andrew*, brigantine *Dolphin*, sloop *Miriam*, sloop *Fellowship*, sloop *Nonesuch*, sloop *Olive*, sloop *Merrimac*."

He looked proud, and he had reason. The poor boy from Revelstoke had truly prospered.

"You know what that means," Colonel Pepperrell went on. "It means having our accounts handled in half a dozen ports–invoices–letters of instruction to captains, enough letters to drive anyone crazy." He pounded the table. "William Junior has *got* to learn to write, and you, young Butler, have got to learn him."

Neal quickly wrote the word "teach" on a scrap of paper, and showed it to the colonel.

"Yes, yes!" the colonel said. "That's what I meant, but don't start me wandering! The point is, William Junior is a problem. He gets into bad habits. He goes over to Bray's and gets into the pigpens and rides the pigs. Then he comes home and hides his boots where his mother can smell 'em but not find 'em. Now then!"

He leaned forward and fixed Neal with a steely eye.

"Well," Neal said, "I half promised——"

"I know what you half promised!" Colonel Pepperrell said. "You half promised Richard Nason you'd go with him to see where your father was lost! Well, I've had a talk with Richard Nason. He lost his sloop coming back from Boon Island–no fault of his. I've made him captain of one of mine. We'll both of us take you to where we think your father was lost."

At the look on Neal's face he turned suddenly toward Captain Dean and me. "Well, what about it?"

"If I had such an offer," Captain Dean said, "I'd say Boon Island was worth it."

"What about you, Whitworth?" the colonel demanded.

"His father would have been–probably is–mighty grateful," I said.

"Then that's all right," Colonel Pepperrell said comfortably. "We'll see a lot of each other before the two of you are healed up and ready to take one of my ships to Barbados."

Captain Dean drew a deep breath. "I'd feared something like this," he said.

"Feared!" Colonel Pepperrell protested.

"Yes, feared," Captain Dean said. "Feared that I might not be able to take advantage of such an offer. There's something you don't know—"

"You probably mean Langman," the colonel said. "Well, John Wentworth and I know all about Langman. He's jealous because you're getting all the attention—because everybody's stopped going to see him and his two cronies. As soon as he began telling everyone that you purposely ran the *Nottingham* ashore on Boon Island, Portsmouth had a bellyful of Langman. My God, Dean, this is a seafaring town! Do you think *anybody* over the age of three and a half would believe that anyone—anyone at all—would, for the sake of *any* amount of insurance, run a vessel on Boon Island in a northeaster? And in the dead of winter? Pish! Portsmouth doesn't want people like Langman and his fellow conspirators around. They've been in the Motley house, but the Motleys have ordered them out."

"Colonel," I said, "we know people like yourselves and these wonderful friends we've made in Portsmouth wouldn't believe Langman; but people in England aren't like that. Those around the docks believe anything they hear about people of property or position. They're too ignorant to investigate—to find out the truth. They have no judgment. From the first Langman has hated Captain Dean, and we've never known why. Perhaps it's because bad men always hate good men, and rejoice in their downfall.

"At all events, if Langman has started telling his lies—

though he gave the captain his word of honor that he wouldn't—then he'll keep right on. He'll tell them in England, unless he's bought off. He might even have them printed. Then there's no escaping the fact that the captain will have to tell his own story, with two witnesses. Even then there'll be so many to believe Langman's lies that Jasper Dean's home and even his life may be in danger from mobs. In all likelihood Langman will drag my father into it, for my father handled Captain Dean's insurance. We're mighty grateful to you, Colonel, but I'm afraid this means that Captain Dean and Henry Dean and I must go back to England."

Colonel Pepperrell glowered at us, his eyes belying the thin line of his lips. "I never go back on my word," he said. "There'll always be room for the Deans and Miles Whitworth in the Pepperrell fleet—and when your feet are healed, we want all of you at Kittery Point, so you can see Neal Butler in the surroundings I hope he'll always call his home."

Our worst fears were justified when, a month later, Colonel Pepperrell notified us that Langman, Mellen and White were to appear before his friend Samuel Penhallow, a justice of the peace, to take oath that Captain Dean had deliberately run the *Nottingham* ashore and that Captain Dean had in addition treated Langman in a barbarous and inhumane manner.

The colonel went with us to Justice Penhallow's residence on the following day to hear Langman, Mellen and White swear to the truth of a tale that put anything in the fairy tales of Edmund Spenser to shame. Justice Penhallow looked up at Langman before writing his signature. He didn't say a word: he didn't need to. He just looked. Then he raised his eyebrows at Colonel Pepperrell. "Any comments, Colonel Pepperrell?"

The colonel asked politely, "Would I make any comments if you swore that the moon was a netful of sardines?"

Justice Penhallow signed the paper, pushed it across his desk, and without a word stood up and opened the door for Langman, White and Mellen to go out.

He came back and shook hands with all of us. "There's nothing to be done in a case like that," he said. "If you could spare the time and the money, you might prosecute him for perjury, but you'd do yourself more harm than good. That man would feel honored to be noticed, but he'd never be noticed by anyone worthy of the name of mariner."

We took our departure from Pepperrell's Cove on a soft April morning, with the southeast breeze bringing us the sweet Maine odors of young willows, damp beaches and newly turned earth. A shipowner couldn't want a pleasanter cove than Pepperrell's. It was shielded from the sea by the spruces of Odiorne's Point and Champernowne's Island, and from the north by the hills behind Braveboat Harbor. It was a safe anchorage, always, and I hated to leave it; but our testy good friend Colonel Pepperrell had arranged for Captain Dean, Henry Dean and myself to sail from it on one of his brigantines. Langman he avoided as he would the pestilence.

"If it hadn't been for Langman and his lies," the colonel told me disgustedly, "you and Captain Dean would be working for me today, instead of wasting the best time of year doing nothing! John Wentworth wanted me to provide Langman and his cronies with passage on this same brigantine, and at government expense. I'd see 'em in hell first! Let the British Navy take charge of Langman and his two dogfish, I told John. All three of 'em need a taste of the cat every day or two, just to remind 'em to be human! Drat such dod-ratted truth-twisters, and drat the fools who always believe 'em!"

The colonel eyed his son William, the problem child, with disfavor. He and Neal Butler stood beside me on the colonel's wharf. I'd always thought of Neal as a younger brother, but he suddenly seemed grown up, and to me his new friend William didn't look like a problem: he looked like a young man who'd be handy in an emergency.

On the shore behind the colonel and Neal and William stood half the population of Kittery Point, studiously scanning the cloudless sky, as if they had found themselves near the wharf purely by accident. By now I had come to know these Maine people a little, and I suspected why they were there. They wanted us to know they were resentful of any person who expected them to believe that Captain Dean would have wrecked a ship on Boon Island in a December northeaster. Under most conditions they were patient; but when aroused, they took steps.

"Seems to me," the colonel said severely to his son, "you'd be better off up at the house, learning to write."

"Yes, sir," Neal said, "but we figured you wouldn't mind if we said a final word to Miles about coming back. Also I wanted to tell him something."

"Well, go ahead and tell him," the colonel said.

"I wanted to tell him that someday I'd try to be worthy of what's been done for me—for us—here."

The colonel looked from Neal and William to Captain Dean and me. He cleared his throat. "Why," he said, "that's all right. Under the circumstances, both of you can have the day off."

"Yes, sir," William said, "and I'd like to say that if Miles will come back, there's quite a few things we'd like to show him when summer's here. It's pretty country—a lot different from Boon Island."

The colonel blew his nose loudly. "Oh my, yes," he said. "I talk about going back to Revelstoke, but I'll never do it!"

I tried to speak, but couldn't. They had us by the arms, urging and helping us into the long boat. There was a fluttering of hands and a babel of cries. The oars rattled in the thole pins; the gulls squalled and squealed overhead; the shore seemed misty and the Braveboat hills wavered a little.

Well, who could tell? God, if we're fortunate, is good to us. How many of us have our Boon Islands? And how many have our Langmans? But doesn't each one of us have an inner America on which in youth his heart is set; and if—because of age, or greed, or weakness of will, or circumstances beyond his poor control—it escapes him, his life, to my way of thinking, has been wasted.

THE END

POSTSCRIPT

In 1745 Captain Moses Butler of Kittery served under Lieutenant General William Pepperrell in the attack on the French fortress of Louisburg on Cape Breton. He led the 7th Company, and fought with distinction at the taking of the Royal Battery, the Island Battery, and in scouting attacks on the French and Indians in the wilderness to the westward. The fortress surrendered on June 17th, 1745, and there was great rejoicing in Kittery, York, Berwick, Wells, Arundel, Biddeford, Falmouth and places farther to the eastward. General William Pepperrell was knighted. Captain Butler married Mercy Wentworth. His daughter Sarah married Joshua Nason of Arundel.

Captain John Dean so successfully defended himself against Langman's attacks that he was made His Majesty's Consul for the Ports of Flanders, residing at Ostend, and held his post for many years.

In the writing of *Boon Island* the author had generous assistance from

Marjorie Mosser, *Kennebunkport, Maine*
Major A. Hamilton Gibbs, *Middleboro, Massachusetts*
Clara Claasen, *New York City*
David Leggatt, *Librarian, Central Library, London*
Professor J. G. Bullocke, *Royal Naval College, Greenwich*
Sybil Rosenfeld, *Society for Theatre Research, London*
Dr. Vilhjalmur Stefansson, *Hanover, New Hampshire*
Robert C. Gooch, *Library of Congress*
Henry J. Dubester, *Library of Congress*
Legare H. B. Obear, *Library of Congress*
Margaret Franklin, *London*
John J. Connolly, *Boston Public Library*
Dorothy M. Vaughan, *Portsmouth (New Hampshire) Public Library*
Dr. Dean Fisher, *State House, Augusta, Maine*
Dr. Angus M. Griffin, *George Washington School of Medicine*
Harold B. Scales, *Portland (Maine) Water District*
W. A. R. Collins, *London*
Walter M. Whitehill, *Boston Athenaeum*
Herbert Davis, *St. John's College, Oxford*
George A. McKenney, *Kennebunkport, Maine*
And the Editorial Staff of Doubleday & Company—Ken McCormick, LeBaron R. Barker, Jr., George Shively.

University Press of New England
publishes books under its own imprint and is the publisher for Brandeis University Press, Dartmouth College, Middlebury College Press, University of New Hampshire, University of Rhode Island, Tufts University, University of Vermont, Wesleyan University Press, and Salzburg Seminar.

Library of Congress Cataloging-in-Publication Data
Roberts, Kenneth Lewis, 1885–1957.
Boon Island : including contemporary accounts of the wreck of the Nottingham Galley / Kenneth Roberts ; edited by Jack Bales and Richard Warner.
p. cm.
Includes bibliographical references.
ISBN 0-87451-744-3 (pa : alk. paper)
1. Shipwrecks—Maine—Boon Island—History—18th century—Fiction. 2. Survival after airplane accidents, shipwrecks, etc.—Fiction. 3. Nottingham (Galley)—Fiction. 4. Boon Island (Me.)—Fiction. I. Bales, Jack. II. Warner, Richard H. (Richard Hyde), 1936– . III. Title.
PS3535.O176B66 1996
813′.52—dc20 95-43292